Pam,

Thanks for all your support.

Love ya, girlfriend

GIRL CODE

An anthology by

Debbie

Cait Jarrod
D.C. Stone
Jessica Jayne
Lea Bronsen

~Table of Contents~

~Copyrights~

~Introduction~

The late, great Maya Angelou said it best. "I love to see a girl go out and grab the world by the lapels. Life's a bitch. You've got to out and kick ass."

When I was approached to write the forward for this charity anthology about a group of strong women who were struggling, changing, growing, and opening themselves up to the possibility—and the *vulnerability*—of love, all while supporting and being supported by each other, I couldn't sign on fast enough. Having been raised in a house full of women (I have three sisters) and working in an industry full of women (I write romance novels) I've had a lifetime of living, laughing and toiling alongside brave and brilliant women. So anything that shines a light on the challenges women face, the hurdles they must overcome, and the unbreakable bond that is "the sisterhood" is something I'm thrilled to be a part of.

We all have women in our lives, sisters, mothers, aunts, cousins, friends who are positive influences, who are women of meaning and substance. Strong women. Confident women. And, yes, flawed women. (Aren't we all?) Women who make our lives richer, fuller, and *better*. Women we can look up to. Women we can depend on. Women who personify the phrase "strong female character". So it is with great pleasure that I present to you Girl Code, an empowering book written by women, about women, for women and those who love women. A book filled with strong female characters. A book guaranteed to have you shooting a fist in the air and yelling, "Go, go, girl power!"

Now let's all grab the world by the lapels and kick some ass!

~Julie Ann Walker

~HOPE~

By

Jessica Jayne

~Dedication~

There are times in life when you agree to a project without knowing exactly how big it will be or exactly what it will entail. *Girl Code* was that project for me. It happened quickly—four author friends discussing a potential anthology of sorts—BOOM! We set deadlines and off we go! There had been some laughter, some bickering, perhaps even some tears, but in the end I've never been more proud of a project. And as with any project, there are so many people responsible for its success.

D.C., Lea & Cait—thank you so much for your patience, your expertise in certain areas, your support and most importantly—your friendship. This has been an awesome journey and I'm so lucky to have shared it with you.

To my husband—thank you for not killing me for the weeks of 5 a.m. wake-ups so I could write or edit or revise HOPE and thank you for forcing me out of bed during that time despite my begging of needing more sleep. You knew how much this project meant to me and you helped me make sure I got it done. Love you.

To my children—thank you for letting me go for a few hours here and there to get HOPE done and thank you for your enthusiasm of mommy being an author. I love the look of pride in your eyes when you ask "Mommy, did you write this?" Love you tons.

To Mallory—Girl, your feedback and edits on this story changed it from a good story to something rather amazing. HOPE is stronger because of you. Thank you!

To my dear friend Natalie—thank you! Aside from being a great friend, you are an amazing first set of eyes on my stories. Your insight into what a reader really wants has helped me craft better stories and I trust your judgment and oh-so-honest feedback. Thank you! Love you, girlie!

To Julie Ann Walker—thank you for being one of the coolest girls in the world. Thank you for doing the introduction to *Girl Code* and thank you for all your support, advice and guidance—especially on places to see in Ireland. You rock!

To Jay Aheer—thank you so much for the awesome *Girl Code* cover! Your talent is amazing and you are a pleasure to work with!

To Chris from Book Blog Emporium—thank you for taking some time to beta read HOPE. I truly appreciate your feedback—as always!

To all the people that have grown up with alcoholics, love alcoholics or are an alcoholic—it's a tough road. I've seen the effects it can have and it's hard on everyone involved. Remember, there is always hope! Hold on to it!

~Jessica

Chapter One

Girl Code #3: Fainting is allowed, but only if someone is there to catch you.

Josephine Lockhart pressed on the black shutter release button in constant intervals on her Nikon D7100. The reception servers, dressed in black slacks and white button-down shirts, delivered dinner plates to the bride and groom first, then their attendees and fifty-some guests. People *oohed* and *ahhed* at the beautiful display of grilled chicken, blackened grouper or pork tenderloin over garlic smashed potatoes and green beans, garnished with an edible day lily. Glasses of wine were poured, beer bottles twisted open, and water was refilled.

Soft music and murmuring drifted through the reception venue, an old horse barn gutted, except for the loft, on the rural property. The perfect place for a rustic wedding. Typical country charm—horseshoes, boots, wooden wheelbarrows, and rusted stars—shrouded the barn walls. Strands of twinkling lights draped from the thick wooden beams overhead and casted a soft glow over the crowd. The parquet dance floor at the front of the building remained empty, for now, while the guests sat at tables cloaked in white linens and ate their meals.

Joey captured it for her friends—the new Mr. and Mrs. Snyder. She'd met Jade and Michael recently through her blossoming friendship with Talon Manness. Talon and she had been bumming around together on their free time for a few months, and slowly, he introduced her to his world—rural Florida—and his friends.

Having moved to Florida several years ago from Pearl, Ohio, Joey had always believed Florida to be sun, sand, and the ocean, all things Ohio didn't have in abundance or at all. The west coast of Florida had some of the best beaches in the country, but, because of Talon, she came to learn it also had some of the things she missed most about her small town in Ohio—large trees and wooded areas, open fields filled with cattle or horses, and small town people with big hearts. Some of her favorite work had been photographed in Rye.

Photography was her life. For her tenth birthday, her grandmother gave her an old SLR film camera and Joey never looked back. It was an escape from the craziness of her home life with a drunken father, who was either absent or in a rage. And an enabling mother, who always had an excuse for his behavior. Joey used her camera as a means of expressing herself and helping others to see themselves, including her three best friends—Laydi, Juls, and Selena, who had their own struggles and were more like sisters than anything. Now, photography was her career.

At some point, she dreamed of owning her own photography company and taking on whatever projects she desired. For now, she worked for Elegance Photography's owner, Carol Stancer, one of the best-known photographers in the Tampa Bay/Sarasota area. Elegance had been Carol's baby, but Joey wanted to make a name for herself and Carol enjoyed her fresh approach and ideas. That didn't mean Carol was an easy boss. She had high expectations for the company and Joey. She challenged Joey, who appreciated someone taking a chance on her. All her hard work had finally paid off. People requested her for shoots and events because they loved the sincerity in her photographs.

She had a niche, priding herself in being the best at candid shots. People had always been her favorite subject. Not landscapes. Not portraits. Or posed pictures. She did those, too, but she liked to catch people when they least expected it—at times when their facial expressions weren't guarded and their true thoughts and emotions were readable. It was easy for people to put on the face they believed everyone wanted to see while posing for a picture, but it was in those moments when people didn't think anyone watched that she could see the true essence, the true beauty of a person—the vulnerability, the insecurity, and the happiness, or, in some cases, the sadness.

A few more photos of dinnertime and then she'd wander outside to catch the exterior of the barn in the sunset while everyone finished eating. After, she'd need to be ready for the best man and maid of honor speeches, the cake cutting, the father/daughter and mother/son dance, and so on. Weddings were a lot of work.

Peering through the viewfinder of her camera, she scanned the room and snapped several photos of the crowd chatting and laughing at their tables. Her breath stopped when her gaze fell where the green-eyed boy who wreaked havoc on her heart without knowing it, sat with several of his friends.

She pressed the shutter release button and captured him mid-laugh, his eyes dancing with golden flecks and his smile wide. The hints of red in his sandy brown hair flickered in the soft light. Her heart pitter-pattered in her chest. She'd been crushing on Talon for weeks—really since she met him—but his friendship meant too much for her to pursue anything. They had fun together, confided in each other.

He, too, had been raised by an alcoholic father. That commonality opened their lines of communication and understanding rather quickly. More than anything, she could be the Josephine Lockhart that wasn't influenced by fear or judgment around him. He allowed her to be herself—quirky, stubborn, and, at times, carefree—and that meant more than getting her rocks off with him. The thought of ruining their friendship left a hole in her heart. She snapped several more unsuspecting photos of him.

No one would describe Joey as a girl with a lot of experience with men. *Ha.* She'd dated—and slept with—two guys in her twenty-five years. Neither caused her heart to race when around them, nor had they brought her close to anything resembling an orgasm. She'd begun to think it was her. That she was incapable of all those things romance novels talked about—the rush, the longing, the lust.

Then she met Talon.

Walking into Manness Auto Shoppe three months ago to drop off her beat up 2004 Toyota Corolla for repairs, she experienced her first real male-causing rush. Seeing the back of him bent over the engine of some vehicle kicked her libido into gear. It had caught her off guard.

His black t-shirt pulled tight across the muscular planes of his back and rose enough to show a hint of his tanned skin above his jean's waistline. A tattoo sleeved one arm. She couldn't quite make it out, but it was the sexiest tattoo she'd ever seen.

She'd thought the back of him stunning. Then he turned around. Her breathing ceased. Her heart pounded. His eyebrow, dissected by a small scar, shot up in surprise at finding her standing there. He was, by far, the most attractive man she'd seen.

Lost in thought, she stood there with her camera focused, snapping pictures of Talon, who stared at her with that same scarred eyebrow raised, giving him just enough of a bad boy look to make her crazy. He'd caught her staring. Heat flooded her cheeks and her heart accelerated for the umpteenth time. His lips turned up at the corners, revealing a small dimple in his cheek, and she snapped another picture. He teased her with a wink. Lowering the camera, she grinned at him in a playful manner and waved, trying to disguise her embarrassment.

She spun on her heels and captured a few other photos of the bride and groom feeding each other at the head table, before ducking out the side door of the barn. The warm, moist air hit her, instantly causing her skin to glisten. Even after seven years of living in the Sunshine State, she had her limits with the oppressiveness of the humidity. Yes, it was autumn by date, the second week of October to be exact, but this was Florida and autumn wasn't a recognized season.

She strolled around the edge of the barn, taking in the beauty of the property. Hundred-year-old oak trees surrounded it, filled in by thousands of slash pines that shaded the various shrubs from the autumn sun. She clicked several shots of the colorful sky and turned the camera on the big red barn, nicked and faded from years of enduring the Florida sun and heat, capturing it from various angles.

She squatted for a shot. Her cell buzzed in the back pocket of her jeans, indicating an incoming text. Instantly, her pulse kicked in her throat. Perspiration misted her brow. Letting the camera dangle around her neck by the strap, she rubbed her clammy hands on the front of her jeans.

Should she look at it? It could be one of her "sisters" from back home trying to catch up with her. She hadn't spoken to any of the girls in over a week. She missed them like crazy.

It could also be her boss, making sure the wedding photography was going off without a hitch.

Of course, it could be her mother informing her of the results of Daddy's latest test. After all these years of drinking to the bottom of every whiskey or bourbon bottle he could put his hands on, his liver had finally waved the white flag. He'd been in and out of the hospital for testing the last several weeks. None of the results were positive and she dreaded getting the message of more bad news.

There had been a time when she was daddy's little girl. He'd let her curl in his lap to watch *Sesame Street* or the evening news or take her for piggyback rides in their backyard. He'd drank during that time. She remembered the pungent smell of whiskey on his breath, but he'd still desired to be home with them and he hadn't been so angry. She'd come to learn that's what people called a functioning alcoholic. Around the time she turned five or six, something happened. She didn't quite know what it was, but he lost interest in her and her mother entirely, and his moods shifted. It had broken her heart—it still did. Now he was sick and the doctors weren't certain his liver would recover.

She exhaled long and slowly, trying to regain her composure. Even though she'd never classify her relationship with her father as close or strong, tears welled at the thought of him sick or suffering.

On the other hand and as big of a reason not to check her phone, it could be the anonymous creep that had been texting her for the past seven days. Always a number she didn't recognize. Always a comment on what she wore, her location, or activities. Someone had their eyes on her. She'd felt it for days—a prickly sensation down the spine that came with the awareness when someone was watching her. The constant urge to look over her shoulder. The texts just confirmed it.

Regardless of who it was, she had to check it. *What if it was about Daddy?* Even with her anger at him for the years of emotional abuse and absenteeism, he was still her father. A part of her longed to be daddy's little girl again. She stood, tugged her phone out of her pocket, and tapped her password. An unrecognizable number floated on the screen, and Joey squeezed her eyes shut briefly.

I see u!

Sucking in a breath, she jerked her head up and scanned her surroundings. A good seventy-five yards of grass separated her from the edge of the wooded area, but even at that distance, the hair on her neck stood.

Her stomach roiled with nerves and her skin itched like it had for the last week whenever she'd received the prior texts. Keeping her focus on the wooded area, she scooted backward toward the barn until the rough wood scraped against her skin exposed by her sleeveless shirt.

She glanced around the perimeter of the property again. Why her? Why was someone bothering her? She kept to herself. Some might even call her a loner. She had a handful of friends. Her presence in Florida these last seven years had been under the radar. She didn't go clubbing or barhopping or socialize much at all, except for Talon and one or two acquaintances she'd kept from school. She hadn't been involved with a man since college and she graduated three years ago. Her main contact with the world around her was on assignment for work. She couldn't recall anyone in the last several weeks that had struck her as strange, creepy, or worrisome. Whoever this was had turned her simple existence into a rollercoaster ride.

Something moved beyond the brush. Her breath hitched. The crack of a branch under the weight of something heavy splintered over the soft sound of dinner music. Her heart raced. Her grip on her phone tightened. Panic seeped into her veins.

"Joey," a rough voice barked next to her, and if she could have jumped from her skin, she would have left it like the molting black racer snake did on her patio earlier in the week. Her vision blurred. Her chest vibrated with the fierce beat of her heart. Fear of coming face-to-face with the unknown overtook and everything faded to black.

* * * *

Her body felt heavy, like she'd sloshed through a swamp, weighed down by all the muck. Her back ached on a hard surface, a grogginess clouded her head, and something scratched the skin of her arms. Voices whispered around her, but she couldn't make out the words. What the heck was going on? Where was she?

She remembered her world turning black as if someone had switched the lights off. As the fog lifted from her mind, the words of the text filtered back and her heart beat faster.

Had he knocked her over the head? It didn't hurt. Had he covered her mouth with chloroform or whatever that stuff was criminals put on a handkerchief to render their prey unconscious?

For the love of God, she'd watched way too many *Criminal Minds* episodes. She lolled her head to the side and tried to open her eyes, but was unable to do so because her eyelids weighed a hundred pounds each. She didn't feel restrained or in pain, just panicked.

Then, a familiar woodsy scent mixed with grease and Irish Spring soap floated over her. She'd know the aroma anywhere. Ahhh, Talon Manness. His masculine pheromones caused her heart to pound and her breath to evanesce.

Her heavy eyelids fluttered a few times until she could hold them open. The soft light of dusk and a known face greeted her. Green eyes flecked with gold narrowed with concern. His brows drew down, scrunching the scar above his eye. A smile pulled at her lips.

"Holy shit, Joey. Are you okay?" Talon's rough voice washed over her like a blanket, warming her from head to toe. She blinked several times before reality hit her like a ton of bricks. Yes, Talon leaned over her, but this was no private moment between the two of them. Several people circled, staring at her with concern. The sky spread out before her like a canvas brushed in oranges, pinks, and purples. She rocked her head to the side, bringing the barn into view.

"What's going on?" Her voice croaked and it caught her off guard. She cleared her throat with a small cough.

"You passed out, Sweetness." Concern deepened Talon's voice, but the endearment pulled at her heartstrings. His calloused fingers brushed a few stray strands of hair out of her face, and she tingled from head to toe, like always when he touched her. His hands were rough from working on cars all day, taking apart engines, changing the oil, and flushing systems. She never imagined the coarseness of his fingers would stir her the way they did.

But they did.

She never thought she'd be stirred at all. This whole thing with Talon threw her for a loop. She'd had serious conversations over the years with one of her besties, Laydi Michaels, about the possibility she might be frigid. Two relationships with different men and neither had brought her to any memorable level of desire. *Ha!* Laydi had broken into hysterics when she'd called to tell her about meeting Talon.

"He's going to be your first orgasmanator." Laydi teased.

If only there were a way for that to be true without ruining their friendship.

Shaking her head in an attempt to bring her back to the present, Joey lifted on her elbows. The grit of the sandy earth under the sparse grass dug into her skin. "Passed out?" She couldn't remember ever passing out in her life.

"Yes. I walked out of the barn and you were whiter than the sands of Siesta Key. I caught you before you hit the ground, thank God. Otherwise, you would have cracked your head on the barn, the ground, or both." Worry lines etched his forehead and tenderness softened his voice. His gaze scanned her closely for several seconds for any signs of injury.

"Okay, everyone." He twisted toward the crowd and waved his hand, convinced she was all right. "Show's over. Go back to the party." His deep voice and large presence had a way of commanding a situation. After he fended off several inquiries of her well-being, people dispersed back to the party. His brow still furrowed as his gaze found her again. "You okay?"

"Yes. I think so." She pushed into a seated position and fidgeted with her shirt that had ridden up her waist. "Oh God! Oh frak! Carol will kill me. I passed out on the job. What sort of recommendation or review will Michael and Jade make of Elegance Photography now?"

The unsettled feeling gnawed at her stomach. After two years of working as Carol's apprentice of sorts, her boss finally allowed her to take on her own projects. Disappointing Carol didn't settle right with her, and her chest tightened.

"This was my opportunity to prove I could handle a client, a big session on my own." Her camera. Where was it? It had hung around her neck by a strap. She swore it. "Did I break the camera? Oh God! Carol will kill me for sure."

She patted her jeans in frantic movements. "My phone! Where's my phone?" Panic rushed again. Her chest squeezed and heaved. The sky swirled in a mix of purples and pinks, making her dizzy even seated on the ground. She'd gotten another one of those texts.

"Joey. Relax." Talon grabbed her hands. "The blood is draining from your face again. Once I laid you on the grass, I removed the camera from around your neck. It's over there on the bench by the door." She followed his pointed finger to her Nikon camera, unharmed and on an old park bench refurbished for the property.

The camera was fine. Phew. One disaster averted.

"Where's my phone?" The words from the text flashed in her mind. *I see u.* What. The. Fuck? God, she hated using that word, even if only in her mind. It reminded her of all the f-bomb tirades her father spewed when on a bender. But sometimes *fuck* was the only appropriate word.

"You dropped it on the ground when you collapsed. I picked it up." He stood and pulled her cell from the pocket of his jeans. A small circle of dirt clung to his pants from where he knelt over her. "Here you go."

She reached for it, her hand shaking with hesitation. He pulled it out of her grasp and stashed it back in his pocket.

"What is going on, Josephine? You're shaking like someone who's come upon a hungry alligator on the river bank." The use of her full name startled her. He only used it when he was irritated or upset with her, which was rare.

"Give me my phone, Tal." Pushing to her feet, she brushed her clammy hands, rubbing off the dirt.

"Tell me what's going on." He took a step toward her, and she instinctively stepped back.

Any sort of aggression reminded her of her father—intimidated her. In those rare opportunities where she hadn't escaped her father's drunken fit, he cornered her. He may not have ever struck her, but his harsh words yelled in her face with the stench of whatever culprit pushed him over the edge, shrunk her every time.

Talon's gaze softened and held hers. He continued to walk in her direction until her back pressed to the side of the barn. His hands rested against the wall on either side of her head, caging her in. Her head fell forward and her gaze plummeted to the ground.

"Listen. The look on your face is the same look I saw when I walked out here just before you fainted. Fear." The protectiveness in his voice was evident. His forefinger slipped under her chin and lifted her head until she could see those golden-flecked eyes. His mouth pulled tight. "I don't like it on your face. Serious as shit, I want to know what's made you put your tail between your legs."

His breath hit her face, leaving the scent of club soda with a twist of lime between them. He didn't indulge in alcohol. He forbade himself to go anywhere near it because of his father's alcoholism. He feared it would turn him into his father.

"Someone's watching me." There! She'd said it aloud. Now it was real. At first she'd thought it had been a wrong number. Someone had to have transposed a number or something because there was no reason to send those sort of texts to her. Once she recognized it wasn't a mistake, she prayed ignoring it would make whomever lose interest—much like dealing with a disobedient toddler. If they were given attention for their bad behavior, it would just continue. But ignoring had apparently failed.

Telling her sisters would have resulted in their worrying until one of them—or all of them—flew down to handle the situation. She loved those girls to death, but sometimes they coddled her. Knowing Talon had taken on a protective role, he wouldn't let something like this go.

"Come again?" He cocked his head and his eyes widened as if he hadn't heard her correctly. His gaze roamed over her face, waiting for the punchline to the joke. When he didn't see it, his body tensed, the muscles in his arms and shoulders bunched around her.

His torso inched closer, shielding her from prying eyes. Heat flared over his skin, turning his cheeks red and permeating through her at their proximity. His protective nature was instinctual. He glanced over his shoulder and surveyed their surroundings. The sun had lowered behind the trees and the sky turned darker.

"Someone has been spying on me. Stalking me. For days," she said, tapering off the end and dropping her chin.

"What?" His voice escalated to a level that caused her to tense. She fisted her hands and pushed into the barn wall, hoping it would swallow her. She hated yelling. When Daddy used to come home in a fit, if she couldn't get out of the house in time, she'd curl in a corner of her closet with her headphones blaring. Anything to avoid the yelling.

Reaching around his torso, she pulled her phone from his pocket. She swiped across the screen and tapped out her password before turning the phone to show him the text messages.

He grabbed the phone and scrolled through the messages. "'I see you.' 'Leave your hair down.' 'Leave town.' 'Nice ass.' 'Get out of here. You are not wanted.' What the fuck is this shit?" With each text, his voice intensified to an almost roar. She gnawed on her thumbnail and squeezed her eyes shut.

Breathe in. Breathe out. He's not yelling at you.

"How long have you been getting these?" She opened her eyes to find him pacing in front of her.

"A week."

"A week? Someone has been following you and sending you these creepy ass messages and I'm just hearing about this now?" He held her phone in one hand as if he might chuck it. His flushed neck and face had her heart pounding against her ribs.

His initial reaction to this situation was anger, which was why she hadn't told him. He'd lived so much of his life buried in his anger—at his father, his brother, and sometimes at his mother—she hadn't wanted to be the reason to bring him back to it—not after he'd been happier over the last weeks.

"I thought it was a wrong number at first." This whole situation pained her. She nibbled on her thumbnail again. After this week between this texter and her father's health, she may be without any nails for a while.

He ran a hand through his disheveled hair and pinned her with his gaze. His eyes softened, but worry still drew his brows. He inhaled, expanding his chest and stretching his black button-down tight across his pectoral muscles. Another breath. Then another.

She recognized his efforts of trying to calm, get a handle on the anger before it turned into rage. In the past, they'd done breathing exercises together and he put them to good use. He cracked his knuckles on both hands like he always did before he'd hit the punching bag in his garage.

He wanted to hit something, someone.

Another breath. A roll of his head from side to side, trying to ease the tension in his neck. A small smile. Then, he walked over to her.

"I'm sorry I yelled." He pinched her chin between his thumb and forefinger. "I know you don't like it. I'm sorry. But these are threats, Sweetness. Someone is clearly following you around. It's dangerous and I don't like it. Not. At. All."

She nodded. "I really did think the texts were coming from a wrong number until a few days ago. I was sitting in my car at the Riverwalk, waiting for clients for a family photo shoot. I'd pulled my hair out of my ponytail to brush it and put it back up. I got that text saying 'Leave your hair down' after pulling it back again. That's when I knew it was meant for me."

A chill scampered down her spine like it had when she received the text. She'd frantically glanced around the parking lot, which had been full, searching for anyone who appeared to be looking at her, but most of the cars sat empty and the people she could see were preoccupied. She hadn't stepped out of her car until the family she was photographing appeared.

"Why didn't you call me right away? I can't protect you if I don't know you need it." His voice cracked and it broke her heart. He was a protector.

"I'm sorry. I guess I thought if I ignored them, if I just pretended like they weren't bothering me, then the creep would leave me alone. Then I got the one today. He was here. Watching me while I worked. It freaked me out. I thought I saw something move in the woods over there and I panicked. That must have been when you came out."

"I'm not letting you out of my sight." He pressed his lips to her forehead and heat flooded her. His strong arms wrapped around her and pulled her tight against him. Despite being raised by an abusive father, Talon exhibited affectionate behavior. He always hugged her or put an arm around her, making his presence and support known. It was one of the most attractive things about him.

The scent of Irish Spring soap engulfed her as her face pressed into his chest. She inhaled deeply, letting it calm her. She hugged his waist and rested her cheek against his chest. His heart pounded and she knew his calm exterior only masked the anger. "I want you to go back in and finish up Jade and Michael's wedding. You've only missed the end of dinner. Everything sort of stopped when people realized you fainted."

"Oh, God! I'm so embarrassed."

"Don't be. You didn't do anything wrong. I'll grab my buddy Trevor and we'll case the perimeter with security. It's getting dark, so I doubt we'll find anything. But I'm going home with you tonight."

"Talon," she interjected. Though she only lived about twenty miles from him, traffic could make the drive last forty-five minutes, particularly during the tourist season, which began earlier and earlier every year because of the bad winters up north. It started in October.

He'd once told her he didn't like staying too far from home. He worried about his drunk brother, Jarrod, causing his mother more heartache. In the few short months she'd known Talon, Jarrod had been arrested for a DUI, wrecked his four-wheeler, and disappeared for three days without telling anyone where he went. Talon's mother had been beside herself with disappointment and worry. He didn't show for work at the auto repair shop for several days, and when he did, he had thrown back a few drinks. Talon took it upon himself to deal with all of Jarrod's issues, much to his own frustration.

"Don't even start with me, Josephine. Either I'm coming home with you or you're staying at my place. I'm not going to argue with you about it." He nudged her in the direction of her camera and the door to the barn. She turned her head to look at him, and he smiled, but it was strained. His teeth clenched and his jaw ticked. He shoved his hands into the pockets of his jeans and lifted his chin in the direction of the doorway, indicating he wanted her to get inside.

Despite the fact she didn't enjoy Talon being angry, having someone concerned about her well-being warmed her. Being an only child meant she had no siblings to fend off problems or bad people, and her parents were always too busy dealing with their own issues to be her support. Thank God for Laydi, Juls, Selena, and now, Talon.

* * * *

22

Holy Mother of God! Jesus Christ! Mother fucker. Talon Manness punched the unforgiving exterior wall of the red barn. He hated the idea of bringing anger or negativity to his friend's wedding, but he had to hit something. The itch had been there the moment Joey muttered the words someone was following her. The force of his punch reverberated through his arm and into his shoulder.

Ouch! Fuck. That hurt. He shook his hand, hoping to take some of the sting out of his foolishness. His father used to tell him not to hit anything harder than his hand. Clearly, the barn qualified. He'd have to ice his hand after the wedding or it'd be swollen and tender by morning.

Adrenaline coursed as he danced around on boxer feet for a few seconds to shake off the want to pummel something. His heart pumped hard and fast, and his breath burst out of his lungs. Fight mode—he knew it best. He was most comfortable in it, mainly because he'd spent so much time in it. If his drunk father hadn't been whooping his ass, his older brother Jarrod had. Dukes up. All. The. Time.

He'd love to punch the face of the guy texting Joey. Smash it in, and his phone, for that matter. This guy was following her, threatening her, scaring her. That shit didn't fly with him. He didn't become angry for no reason. No one threatened people he cared about without answering to him.

Who the hell could it be? Someone they knew? Someone attending the wedding? He wracked his brain combing through all their friends and town folks. None of them seemed like the type to terrorize a person. Even some of the people he hadn't always seen eye-to-eye with weren't the type to stalk someone or scare them. Could it be someone she'd run into from work? She met people at various locations to take their photographs. It wasn't like they ran background checks on people they photographed. *Christ!* It could be anyone.

What if he hadn't followed her outside? What if he hadn't wanted to catch a moment with her alone? He'd watched her slip out the side door and thought it'd be the perfect opportunity to steal a few minutes with her. He couldn't help it. Even though she just wanted to be friends, he wanted to spend all of his free moments with her—get to know her, listen to her laugh, and laugh with her.

Thank God he'd done it. She might have passed out and that guy—whoever he was—could have grabbed her and done who knew what else. Protecting her had now become his priority.

Several months ago, he'd never thought he'd care so much for anyone, especially a woman. Women came and went in his life. He mostly distanced himself, because dealing with feelings and emotions wasn't his strong suit. If he didn't have feelings for a girl, then he couldn't get his feelings hurt. But Joey was different—in so many ways. He'd let his guard down. Now, he couldn't imagine his life without her.

The heat of his fury washed over him. *Breathe! In. Out.* He allowed the mantra Joey taught him to play over and over in his head, taking deep breaths to keep his frustrations at bay.

He'd do anything for Joey. Anything. For the rest of his life he'd remember the day they met. Her long mahogany hair tied at her neck. Her milk chocolate eyes scanning his auto repair shop.

"Can I help you?" He had croaked out with what remained of his breath. She'd stood at least six inches shorter than him, in skin-tight jeans hugging the muscular curves of her legs, and thin-strapped flip flops that showed her pink toe nails. A loose tank top revealed toned arms, hung to her hips, and fluttered with each breath she took.

"My-my Toyota Corolla keeps mak-making this weird sound. *Sceel-Sceel-Sceel.* Every time I step on the brake. My friend Jennifer recommended your shop. She said you do great work for a reasonable price." Her nose scrunched when she imitated the noise of her car, and it was the most adorable thing he had ever seen.

"Sounds like the brake pads. I'll take a look. How soon do you need it?" He had three cars dropped off that morning, and one tractor for Mr. Howard down the road. With Jarrod showing when it suited him, Talon's plate was full for the next few days. He could hire another mechanic, but that would cut into profits and those profits kept his mother afloat. She'd suffered enough.

"This afternoon?" Joey's head tilted and she looked at him under her lashes. Her voice was hopeful. So hopeful, in fact, he couldn't tell her no. She had hung around the garage for the next couple of hours while he worked on her car. He'd been covered in grease. Sweaty as all hell, probably stinking like a greasy hog, but it had been a turning point for him.

The three hours in the garage felt like a date. Two people getting to know each other. It took her a while to warm up, but once she started talking, she seemed unable to stop. They'd discussed sports, the snowbird season, her passion with photography, his passion for cars. They'd laughed, and laughed, and laughed. By the time he finished with her car, he knew he couldn't just let her walk out.

"Can we hang out some time?" His voice cracked with nervousness. He'd never asked a girl out. Never needed to. He didn't know if he could handle the rejection, but he had to ask. The thought of never seeing her again had scared him more than being rejected.

"You mean as friends?" She spoke softly and her eyelids dipped in a shy manner. Pink rose in her cheeks, making her the most adorable woman he'd ever seen.

He wanted to say no, not as friends. He wanted to ask her out on a date, but he hadn't been sure how to go about doing it, and he didn't want to come on too strongly. So instead, he simply said, "Yes, as friends." He'd never forget the drop-dead smile stretched across her face or the way her eyes danced with joy.

He may not have been laid in three months since meeting her, quitting his trolling of the bars, clubs, and beach, looking for willing one-night-stand participants. He hadn't been this celibate, and his right hand hadn't received this much action since he was fourteen. But he was happy. He hadn't looked forward to each day as much as he did now. He owed that, in part, to Joey. So, yeah, he'd do anything for her.

"Hey, Claws!" Talon's friend, Trevor, walked around the corner and shouted. One of the very few allowed to call him by that nickname—sort of a play on his real name—and not get his ass kicked.

"Trev. Hey, man." He fist-bumped his friend and then wrapped an arm around him, patting him on the back.

"Can you believe Michael's tied the ol' knot?" Trevor shook his head as if in disbelief, which made Talon chuckle. For crying out loud, they were twenty-eight years old. Getting married wasn't so far-fetched, was it?

"I think it's great. I love Jade. She's good for him. Balances him." If Joey hadn't walked into his life, he'd probably share the same view as Trevor. Another one bit the dust. Trevor crossed his arms over his chest and glared at his friend.

"Awe, shit. Are you losing your balls, Claws? I think Joey is making you soft. When you gonna claim that ass as yours anyway? I know you're dying to."

Talon took a playful swing at his friend. They began the usual duck and jab until Talon wrapped his arm around Trevor's neck, putting him in a headlock and giving him a nuggie until they both laughed.

"I called you out here for some serious shit. Not to talk about my sex life." Talon released his friend. Trevor straightened his dark red button-up, tucking the areas that had come out of his black jeans.

"You mean your lack of a sex life, right?" Trevor ran a hand through his hair, which stood on end from Talon's nuggie. Talon chuckled. "What's got you all riled like a rattlesnake tonight?"

After taming his hair, Trevor placed his hands on his hips. They'd been friends since kindergarten. Trevor's house often offered reprieve from Talon's father's abuse, at least until he'd realized the abuse redirected at his mother. Trevor was more like a brother to him than Jarrod had been.

"T-bird," Jarrod said, wandering out of the barn and kicking up dust under his cowboy boots. The sound of his brother's voice grated on his nerves. Not to mention, he hated that nickname. No one called him that but Jarrod, and it chided rolling off his tongue.

Looking at his brother sparked all sorts of emotions. His pulse kicked in gear and his hands clenched and unclenched at his sides. *One slow breath at a time.* No matter how illogical the reaction, it happened every time. Jarrod resembled their father almost to a tee with his darker brown hair, low brows, and sharp nose and jaw. A younger version of Justin Manness in looks and sometimes attitude.

Jarrod followed in their father's footsteps with his love of alcohol and the use of his fists to get his way. Talon took beatings from Jarrod when he was younger. The five-year age difference gave Jarrod the advantage as teenagers. However, that didn't last long once Talon learned to hold his own.

"What's going on out here? What're you two assholes up to?" Jarrod's words slurred a bit. Figured. Before the end of the evening, he'd either cause a scene or pass out somewhere.

"Great to see you, too, Jarrod," Trevor said, not doing a thing to hide his sarcastic tone. Trevor and Jarrod had their rounds of arguments and fights, often started because he stood up to Jarrod. It bothered Jarrod when others took Talon's side. Jarrod often expressed his jealousy of Talon's close relationships through a fight of some sort. Given the state of Jarrod's sobriety—or lack thereof—he feared he'd start a fight at Michael's wedding.

"Are you drunk?" Talon asked, shaking his head. His entire life involved dealing with some drunk ass from his family. It was getting old. First, he'd cleaned up the messes of both his father and his brother. Now with his father gone, he was still in charge of cleaning up after Jarrod. If it weren't for his love for Mom, he'd have been long gone by now, escaping somewhere—anywhere.

"I threw back a few. It's a fucking wedding for Christ's sake." Jarrod laughed. He stood with his back against the barn, arms folded over his chest and his legs crossed at the ankles. His typical "you gonna make something of it" stance.

"No shit it's a wedding. Michael used to be your best friend. You'd think you'd show a little restraint and respect." Talon ran his fingers through his hair. Saying that would tick his brother off, but it pissed him off he couldn't keep his shit together.

Michael and Jarrod had been inseparable as kids—the best of friends—playing cops and robbers on their bikes or rounding up friends for a game of kickball in the field. When they hit their teenage years and Jarrod turned to the bottle for his escape, he ruined just about every friendship he'd had with his belligerence and violent streak.

"*Used to* being the correct words, little brother. You steal a bit of everything from me." Jarrod narrowed his brows and glared at Talon, who rolled his eyes. Jarrod hadn't got over their mother turning the auto repair business over to him. He'd thought since their father died leaving Jarrod as the oldest male, he should be the one to run the shop, but their mother didn't think it'd be good for business. Being an alcoholic made Jarrod unreliable. If he didn't show to the shop drunk, he was hung over and late, or a no-show at all, leaving Talon to not only manage the business, but do all the work on the vehicles.

"You're thirty-three years old. Grow up." Talon dismissed him with a wave of his hand. "I need to talk to Trevor. Why don't you head back in?"

"Anything you have to say to Trev, you can say to me. We're brothers, no?" Jarrod pushed off the wall and walked toward them. "Are you going to tell him you finally banged that Joey chick? I mean, for fuck's sake, T-bird, this is the longest I've seen you hold out. What's the delay?" Jarrod laughed and the sound grated on Talon. Jarrod lacked a filter when he had one too many drinks. Between Talon's mixed up feelings for Joey and her receiving these creepy text messages, his head was all over the place. He wasn't in the mood for dealing with Jarrod.

"Fuck off." Talon tensed. He crossed his arms over his chest, hoping his scowl looked menacing.

"Are you a little sensitive about that piece of ass?" Jarrod laughed again.

Heat rose over Talon's neck and face. Grabbing his brother by the shirt collar, he brought him closer. "She's not a piece of ass, and I don't like it when you talk about her like that." Talon's breath came out in hard, fast pants. Every muscle tautened with agitation. Out of the corner of his eye, he noticed Trevor rolling up the sleeves to his shirt, preparing to help subdue Jarrod, if necessary.

"Have I found your weakness?" Jarrod slurred.

"Go near her and I'll break you in two, big brother. I promise you."

"Relax," Jarrod said. "I'm not the slightest bit interested in her. She's too girl-next-door for me." He pushed away from Talon and stumbled before regaining his ground. "Boy, you two need a drink to lighten up a bit." He turned and faltered back into the barn.

"After all these years, you'd think he'd become less of an asshole," Trevor said, relief in his voice.

"You'd think." Talon paced, trying to calm the surge of adrenaline. First, the texting stalker. Then, his fucking brother. His heart pumped with such ferocity he thought it might punch out of his ribs.

"Fuck him, Claws. He just likes to get under your skin. Don't let him. Tell me why you called me out here in the first place." The change of subject worked as the energy coursing through him, making him fidgety over his brother, shifted to the person stalking Joey. His need to do whatever necessary to protect her took over.

Talon explained the situation. After peeking inside the barn to see Joey taking pictures of the Maid of Honor's speech, the two men conversed with the security guards on duty and grabbed flashlights out of their trucks. The group scanned the perimeter, as well as the back seats of all vehicles looking for any sign of something being out of place. Finding everything secure, they rejoined the wedding celebration. But Talon never settled—tight with anticipation—or lost sight of Joey. He knew where she was every second for the next two hours. No one would get to her now that he was aware. They'd have to get past him, and that wouldn't happen.

* * * *

"You done?" Talon approached Joey as she unsnapped her lens from her camera and tucked it into its protective case. She raised her head, her long hair pulled into its usual ponytail. Her lips stretched into a beautiful smile that made his knees weak.

"Yes. I believe I am." She lifted the camera strap over her head and placed it in its own case, zipping the case up along its three sides. "What a great wedding. I've never been to a barn wedding before. It's so gorgeous here." Her gaze lingered around the massive barn, and Talon looked with her.

"It used to be an active barn housing some horses for the Reddingtons up until about fifteen years ago. Old Mr. Reddington struggled to maintain the horses and cattle. Rumor is none of his children were interested in working the farm, so he sold most of the acres to some neighboring farmers and let his two daughters keep a few acres and the barn. They've done an amazing job with it."

Growing up in Rye, he knew more than he needed to know about the residents, and he was positive they felt the same way about him and his family. He knew who'd cheated on their wives, who'd lost their job at the local phosphate plant, and who'd sold their property to a large developer to make a quick buck. And they'd all known his father beat the shit out of his mother until Talon lost control and gave it back to him, beating him to within an inch of his life. Right before his father slammed his car into a tree.

"If you're all set, I'll help you carry the equipment out to your car, and follow you home." He flung one of the bags over his shoulder and bent to pick up the tripod.

"Tal, I can't let you stay at my place. You've told me more than once you worry about your mom being alone. I don't want to be the reason you're away. But I will accept your help getting this stuff to my car." She waved her hand at the few bags left containing flashes and other lenses.

"Josephine, there is someone stalking you. Terrorizing you with text messages are an obvious reflections of his close proximity. I'm not letting you out of my sight until we know who it is and stop him."

"Talon." Her voice pitched.

"Don't *Talon* me. Either I stay at your place or you stay at mine. Any way you look at it, we're spending the night together. I'd never be able to live with myself if something happened to you." His fingers brushed a few stray strands of hair behind her ear. The softness of her skin against the callousness of his own always surprised him.

He may not deserve her, with his past and overabundance of anger and self-loathing, but he wanted her. More than anything. And he'd stop at nothing to protect her.

Blowing out a resigned breath, she picked up the last two bags. Her soft eyes opened wide, searching for something in him, perhaps his intent? "I'll stay at your place."

He pursed his lips and bit the insides of his cheeks to stop a smile, but to no avail. God, he loved hearing those words from her.

Her eyelids lowered at his reaction. "I'll need to borrow something to sleep in. I didn't expect to be anywhere other than home, so I don't have anything."

"I have plenty of T-shirts you can borrow." He threw an arm over her shoulder, bumping the bags he carried with the ones strapped to her as they walked out. "We can stop at the sheriff's office on the way to my place. I think we need to file a report."

"I don't want to involve the police." Her voice was adamant.

"We don't know who this guy is. What if he escalates? Don't you think it would be best if we get the police involved before it gets to that point?"

"I don't want to go to the police tonight. I'm exhausted." Her shoulders sagged against him, so he didn't want to push the issue—at least not now.

"Tomorrow then?"

"Perhaps."

Chapter Two

Girl Code #10: Your friends should always have your back and you theirs. Always.

Jiminy Cricket! Joey followed Talon's black Chevy Silverado through the winding roads to his property a few miles away. During daylight, it was a breeze to whip around the bends of the country roads. But at night, it turned downright frightful. There were no street lights. Acres and acres of land where anything, including wild boars, could dart out in front of the car and cause a person to swerve into the nearest ditch. Her heart raced a little faster than normal.

Because of the drive? Or did it have more to do with the events of the evening? She couldn't say her first big solo photography event went off without a hitch, because she'd passed out in the midst of dinner. Having scanned through some of the photos on her camera, she'd done a good job. The Snyders would be happy despite the fainting spell.

But she'd received another text. A chill rolled through her. Should she go to the police? This guy obviously wanted to scare her, but why? And who was it? Maybe Talon was right. Maybe she needed to go to the police.

His blinker flickered to turn right into a long dirt road driveway that would take them past his auto repair shop first. She'd been to his house a few times. A little two-bedroom ranch-style house that screamed bachelor. Little to no landscaping. One white plastic chair sat on the cement porch. No artwork on the interior walls. Basic blinds on the windows. But a sixty-inch television mounted the wall in his family room. *Ha.* Men and their toys.

His house sat a half mile from the auto shop in one direction, and a half mile from his mother's in the other. When they pulled up, he parked to the right of the garage. Jumping out of his truck, he left his headlights on, and lifted the garage door, waving her in.

She lowered her window and shouted, "What're you doing?"

"Park in here." He flipped the overhead light before he walked over to where her car idled. "What's the problem?"

"You're already letting me stay here. I won't let you leave Betsy out in the elements overnight." He was a grease monkey. Working on engines wasn't just his livelihood, but more his passion. He loved it and he loved his jacked-up truck more than any other possession. It had more personal touches than his house. He parked the truck under cover as often as possible to avoid scrapes, dents, or dings.

His eyes narrowed, and for a second he looked angry, but his chuckle gave him away. "Pull the car in the garage, Joey. So, we don't have to lug all your equipment in the house, too. Besides, Betsy will survive." He winked.

"You're a pain in the ass." She thought about calling him a stubborn fool, but felt it would likely get turned around, given her own obstinacy.

"Takes one to know one." He laughed. She glided her car into his three-car garage stocked with car equipment, a four-wheeler, a weight bench, and a punching bag. She parked in the large spot reserved for his truck, her Corolla barely taking half the space. Climbing out, she grabbed her jean satchel, secured it over her shoulder, and locked the door before closing it. Even parked inside his garage, she had thousands of dollars' worth of photography equipment stashed inside. She wasn't taking any chances.

Talon killed the engine and locked Betsy, causing the glare of the truck lights to vanish. He rattled the garage door closed and secured it with a lock. He clomped behind her in his thick work boots he never seemed to take off. She stared at his feet. Come to think of it, she'd never seen him without his boots on.

"Why the weird look on your face?" He cupped her shoulder and ushered her inside the door leading to his small kitchen. The smell of bacon assaulted her. He'd put bacon on anything. The memory of him sprinkling bacon bits on his vanilla ice cream a few days ago made her smile.

He hung his keys on the hook by the door and walked to the fridge. Popping open the door and settling it against his hip, he grabbed the milk jug and guzzled it back.

Eww! Why did guys think it was okay to drink right out of the bottle or carton?

She asked, "Do you have some sort of foot fungus or something?"

Milk spewed everywhere. His eyes widened to saucers. "What the hell are you talking about? Foot fungus?" He screwed the cap back on the jug and slid it in the fridge. He tore a few paper towels off the roll on the counter, dabbing at his shirt, the cupboard next to him, and the countertop.

"I've never seen you barefoot. You're always wearing those boots—even to the beach." She pointed to his feet. His shoulders quaked before laughter burst out of his mouth.

"Oh God! Serious as shit, Joey, you kill me." He barreled over.

"Well, do you?" Her own voice cracked with laughter. When she'd met him, he hadn't seemed like a person who spent a lot of time laughing. He took his responsibilities seriously, having to run the family business, not just to keep afloat, but also his mother and brother. Quite frankly, he took life seriously, so she loved seeing him laugh—a real, hearty laugh. One of her sisters, Selena Bodine, told her laughter was good for the soul. Few truer words had ever been spoken. Just looking at the sparkle in Talon's eyes made her own soul full.

Bending to his knee, he lifted his pant leg and started untying and unlacing his boot. Once the laces were loose enough, he tugged the boot off his foot, and yanked his sock off, throwing it at her. She dodged the white blur. "Does it look like I have foot fungus?" He laughed again, and wiggled his toes. For the love of God, even his feet were sexy. A little smattering of light brown hair on the top of his foot, a high arch, and toes that looked like they did their own push-ups daily.

"I can't see the other one." She set her satchel on the small kitchen table in the corner. Her smile stretched from ear to ear. He untied his other boot in the same fashion as the first.

"Do you want a closer look?" He hoisted his bottom on the counter and wrapped his legs around her waist, pulling her into him. Her hips pressed into the apex of his legs, heat from him seeping into her.

She blew her breath out in a whoosh. Perhaps from the force of his pull, but more likely from being this close to him—her body between his legs, flush against parts of him she not only wondered about, but also desired.

"They might smell a bit from being in those socks all night, but I'm pretty sure there isn't any fungus."

She stared at him and laughter ceased between them. The golden flecks in his eyes sparkled, and his breath burst out in hot pants against her cheeks. He looked ravenous. Starved. Was that desire in his eyes? The muscles in his jaw ticked, alluding to some sort of internal struggle. She melted into goo from the heat and gripped the edge of the countertop to keep from falling further into him.

His rough hands grasped her bare arms, moving over her shoulders until he cupped the base of her head where her ponytail hung loosely. His thumbs grazed over her jaw. The coarseness of his calloused skin sent sparks of lust through her, straight to her core, unlike anything she'd ever experienced. This was what Laydi, Juls, and Selena talked about—desire, lust, longing.

His gaze roamed over her face, devouring her, until resting on her lips. His pupils dilated, leaving only flecks of the greenish-gold irises. The masculine scent of Talon Manness conquered and made her woozy. If it weren't for the grasp of his legs, she'd be a pile of mush on the vinyl floor.

Pulling her lower lip between her teeth, she bit off the sigh slithering up her throat.

But her body had a mind of its own. Her lip slipped from the hold of her teeth, and she did it—she sighed. A great, big, satisfied sound.

A growl rumbled through his chest, reverberating against her, and his gaze shot up to meet hers.

For the love of God, would he kiss her? Her heart thudded against her ribs so hard her body pulsed with its beat. She wanted it. She wanted to feel his lips on hers. He lowered his head, inching closer to her, his gaze never leaving hers, and parted his lips. Oh, God, this could ruin everything.

She pulled her head back just as a loud pulsation from the kitchen table broke the silence. Her phone shuddered again from inside her satchel, signifying a new text. Talon tensed, his legs constricting her in place. Her muscles tightened at the dreaded sound and interruption. His forehead fell to hers and he huffed a breath, closing his eyes as if trying to gain control.

"We better check your phone," he breathed. "Do you want me to check it?" Without waiting for an answer, he released her and hopped off the counter, crossing to the table.

"What if it's him?" The faintness in her voice bothered her. She wasn't a little girl anymore, having to hide from the things that scared her or didn't want to face. Yet, receiving the texts had brought her back to the childlike, insecure feeling, as if she were incapable of handling things. Yes, it was frightening to know someone watched her.

Could he be watching now? She glanced to the small window over the sink. Could he have followed her here and be watching through the window? She couldn't let this man scare her into weakness. She may have been afraid of her shadow growing up, knowing Daddy would come home drunk and go into his rage, but Daddy wasn't here, and she wasn't ten years old anymore.

She reached for her bag and Talon grabbed her wrist. "Nothing and no one is going to hurt you, Joey. I promise you." His voice was hard and filled with determination, but his eyes softened.

His thumb traced over her Zibu Angelic symbol tattoo on the inside of her left wrist. The one she'd gotten with her sisters to solidify their friendship permanently. The symbol represented hope, and she'd intentionally picked it. Laydi, Juls, and Selena had given her so much hope. Her sisters. All the encouraging talks a child should receive from her parents had come from her friends.

It had been Juls, not her mother, who had helped her buy tampons and explained how to use them when she had gotten her period at thirteen.

Laydi had helped her pick up the pieces of her heart when her first boyfriend broke up with her shortly after she had finally conceded to sleep with him.

Selena had been the one to find the Ringling College in Sarasota, and encouraged her to apply to their photography program.

They'd always been her support, her encouragement—her family. Now Talon filled those gaps left by physical distance between her and her sisters. She found herself confiding in him more and more, turning to him for advice and companionship. Though she'd always have her sisters, her friendship with Talon had become a huge part of her world.

"I've got your back, Sweetness. Anyone trying to get to you will have to go through me first." He lifted her hand to his mouth and pressed his lips to it before releasing her. Her skin tingled from the warmth. Stretching open her satchel, she pulled out her cell.

"It's Carol." The relief in her voice was evident as the breath she released. "She wants to know how the wedding went." She tapped out a quick text to her boss and slipped the phone back. Then she turned to Talon, who watched her closely.

"What did you want to do? Watch Saturday Night Live? A movie?" He crossed his arms, causing his biceps to bulge under his shirt. His muscles weren't bulky, but rather defined and intimidating.

Looking over his shoulder at the clock on his microwave, she stretched her arms overhead, lengthening her torso. Being on her feet all night and crouching into awkward positions to get a shot took a toll on her back. She was spent. "Wow! It's almost midnight." His gaze wandered over her stretched body and heat followed, as if his hands had trailed the same path. Part of her wanted him to look at her—the part of her that wanted to open herself to him, not just physically, but with her heart. The other part blanched when his heated gaze drank her in, because she feared crossing the physical line with him would not only change their friendship, but destroy it, like it had when she'd had sex with her friend Marcus. Everything turned awkward afterward and eventually, they stopped talking.

Her cheeks flushed. "Let's do a movie, but I can't promise I'll be able to keep my eyes open. These weddings take a lot out of me."

"So does passing out." Concern formed on his face. His brows drew down, and his lips pulled tight.

"I'm okay." She hoped she sounded convincing, though she wasn't so convinced herself. Despite all the internal pep talks, the texts bothered her and the feelings they initiated concerned her more. "Do you think I could shower first? I feel sweaty and yucky from working all night."

She needed to change the subject. Talon worried about her. If he knew she was upset and stressed more than she admitted, he wouldn't let her out of his sight.

Early in their friendship, his protective nature demonstrated itself. He went out of his way to make sure she was comfortable. He sat or stood next to her the entire night he introduced her to some of his friends. He even stood outside the restroom every time she used it that night, not wanting her to be nervous about not knowing anyone.

"Sure. Follow me." He cocked his head in the direction of the hallway, before turning on his heels and strutting through the kitchen doorway, his bare feet slapping along the floor. A smile stretched her lips at the fact he was barefoot. She grabbed her satchel and followed.

Despite the craziness of the day, she couldn't help but admire the way his jeans hung low on his hips and hugged his behind and thighs like a second skin. A masterpiece she'd never tire of looking at him. He walked past the guest bedroom and bathroom, heading toward his bedroom.

"Hey. Tal, I can shower here." She stopped in front of the guest bathroom, hearing the panic in her voice. In all the times she'd visited his house, she'd never been in his bedroom. Entering now intimidated the heck out of her. Crossing the threshold could give her some insight into a side of him she didn't think she was ready for or ever would be.

"No way. You're my guest tonight. You'll shower and sleep in *my* room." She tensed at his words. No way could she share a bed with him. *Shizzle stick!* Being around him in the daylight hours kicked her hormones in gear and sent her pulse to what was surely an unhealthy level. Lying next to him in nothing more than a pair of underwear and T-shirt—his T-shirt—would kill her.

"I'm fine in this shower and the guest room. It's called a guest room for a reason." She added some playfulness to her voice. He rotated and set his hands on his hips.

"I'm not going to take advantage of you." The sincerity in his eyes made her feel bad for conjuring up all sorts of dirty thoughts of him doing exactly that, and her liking it. "I'll sleep in the guest room. My bed is much more comfortable than the one in there. I'd rather you take my room." He turned again and opened his door. "I'll pull out a T-shirt and a pair of boxers for you to borrow and leave them on the bed. An extra towel will be on the counter in the bathroom."

She sighed. Clearly, he wasn't going to let it go, so she followed him into his bedroom. When he set his mind to something, it wasn't easy to change it, and she had little energy to continue arguing. Her feet and back ached, and the tension in her shoulders crept to her neck, the familiar twinge of a headache forming. This

36

past week had been a bit much—the texts, her father's health, her first solo wedding job, and her mixed feelings for Talon. A few minutes to herself in a hot shower would do her good, clear her head.

* * * *

Scalding water sluiced over her shoulders, chest, and back—the hotter the better—and washed away the dirt and the grime of any day, particularly a bad day. Shutting the faucet off, she wrung her sopping hair and reached through the steam for the dark blue towel folded on the counter.

She dried off and stepped onto the soft cream rug. His bathroom had clearly been remodeled. A large walk-in porcelain tiled shower with two showerheads. More than enough room for two.

A sunken tub that didn't look like it got much use sat next to the shower. She giggled at the image of Talon soaking in a bubble bath. She could see herself there, but Talon didn't seem like a person who took advantage of such luxury without a woman present. Did he bring women here? The thought soured her belly. Even though she forced herself to keep their friendship intact, the idea of him being intimate with other women bruised her.

Opening drawers by the dark brown marble sink, she discovered a hairbrush and pulled it through her tangled locks. Using Talon's shampoo-conditioner combination would work a number on her hair. After several minutes of wrestling with the brush, she placed it back in the drawer, and opened the door from the ensuite bathroom to his bedroom.

The room was not large. Chocolate walls, espresso dresser, and a queen-sized platform bed with a tan comforter presented a masculine feel. No throw pillows. *Ha!* Men didn't think of throw pillows or accents, for that matter. Or at least none she'd met.

One small picture frame sat on his nightstand. A black and white photo of a little boy—resembling a very young Talon—and a young woman, who had to be his mother. She'd had the opportunity to meet her a couple of times. Sweet lady. Quiet. Timid. Much like Joey's own mother. Perhaps those were traits of spouses married to alcoholics. But this picture portrayed a different woman than the one she'd met, and it seemed as if Talon held on to her with this picture. She held the little boy on her knee, her head tilted to him, extreme love in her eyes, while he smiled brightly for the camera. The innocence and happiness in his expression melted her heart. That expression seldom appeared on his face these days. She'd taken so many candid photos of him while he worked on cars or talked with his friends. Years of abuse by his father and brother and the need to protect his mother made his face hard, his body rigid. But this picture—it broke her to see him so happy, so innocent. She wanted to see that look on his face. She wanted to be the reason for it. Emotions shifted inside of her. She wanted to be the reason, at least in part, for his happiness.

Setting the frame on the nightstand, she let the towel drop, and grabbed the black boxer shorts Talon had laid out. She pulled them up around her hips. A little big, but they'd have to do. She rolled the waistband over a few times to make them stay.

"Joey." The door swung open and she yelped. Standing before him in nothing but his boxers, she covered her breasts and turned her back to the door. Embarrassment surged through her.

"Oh shit, I'm sorry! You've been in here forever. I was getting a little worried." He rattled on and she recognized embarrassment in his voice, but something else lingered too, something made his voice rough and strained.

Flipping her wet hair over her shoulder, she turned her head. His gaze burned her skin, fixated on her bare skin. His lips parted and his breath blew out in quick pants. He gripped the door handle so tight his knuckles turned white.

"Can you give me a minute?" she asked.

His gaze shot to her face and his eyes smoldered in the same way they had in the kitchen. *Like he wanted her.* Her skin flushed at the heat. It was overwhelming. Then redness spread over his cheeks and his eyelids lowered. "I'm sorry." He backed out of the room and pulled the door shut.

She pushed out the breath she hadn't realized she'd been holding. Her heart beat in her throat and her hands shook as she seized the T-shirt on the bed. He'd chosen his Kenny Chesney concert T-shirt, the one he'd bought last month when he brought her to the concert. Her first concert ever. Leaving that particular shirt was sweet. Even in small ways, he did things with her in mind.

Pulling the shirt on, his scent flooded her. A woodsy, outdoor clean scent mixed with Irish Spring soap that was all Talon wrapped around her, and made her lightheaded. How would she make it through this night with her sanity?

Grabbing her satchel off the floor, she pulled her phone out and tapped a text to Laydi and Selena. Juls was still without a phone. God, she missed the heck out of her sisters.

Joey: *Miss you guys!*

Selena: *Aw! Miss you too!*

Laydi: *What's going on, girlie? Miss you too!*

Laydi could always tell, even via text, when Joey wasn't quite herself. Of the three girls, Joey knew Laydi the longest. Joey had been eight years old when they'd met. Her father had come home in a particularly foul mood and she couldn't take another second of the yelling, so she slipped out the back door and wandered into the woods behind her house. Her parents always forbade her from going into the woods, saying it was dangerous—anything could happen there, but it wasn't like they knew—or cared—what she did.

She'd drifted through the trees and thick brush, following an overgrown path. Birds chirped. Butterflies fluttered about from one aster bush to another. Squirrels rushed up trees and chipmunks sunk into their holes at the sound of her shuffling through the foliage. She didn't know how much time had passed when she'd realized she had no idea where she was. Her little heart had raced. Her parents had been right—it was dangerous in the woods.

Then she heard the soft voice of a girl drifting through the air and she followed the sound to a clearing in the woods. There sat a beautiful lake wrapped by trees on all sides and a little blonde haired girl playing in the mud near the shore.

"Hi!" The girl had said, appearing only slightly startled by Joey's appearance.

"Hi," Joey squeaked. Her arms crossed over her chest, shielding herself from the unknown.

"My name's Laydi. You wanna play? I'm making mud pies for my dad." The girl studied her a moment before going back to patting some mud into a tiny Easy Bake oven-type round aluminum pan.

Thinking she had two options—head into the woods to try and find her way home to Daddy's tirade, or plop down in the dirt and make some mud pies—she chose to make the mud pies and never regretted the decision.

Joey: *Nothing. Just a long day.*

Laydi: *Josephine!* Unlike others who used her full name only when they were upset or mad at her, Laydi broke out her full name often. It was her thing. When they'd met, she said Joey was a boy's name and declared she'd call her by her full and proper name. And she did.

Joey: *Seriously, Lay! I'll give you a call tomorrow. Luv u.*

Laydi: *You better. Luv u 2!*

Selena: *Luv u both!*

Joey shoved her phone into her satchel and walked out to the family room.

"Talon?" The television played loudly with movie previews, but he wasn't in the room. She shuffled into the kitchen to find him standing near the sink staring out the window. "Tal?"

"Hey." He turned, arms crossed over his chest. "I'm sorry, Joey. I should have known better than to barge into the room. I just got worried. With you passing out tonight and all, I don't know. I guess I didn't realize someone could take so long of a shower."

She smiled to reassure him. She wasn't upset and didn't want him beating himself up.

"No worries. And that wasn't a long shower. Not by a long shot." The rigidity in his face broke as a small grin split his lips.

"Not long? You're usually in the shower longer than fifteen minutes? What the hell do you do in there?" His eyes widened and his brows shot up. The smoldering look in his eyes hinted at dirty thoughts and warmth spread through her settling in her core.

"Wash." She quirked an eyebrow at him.

"I'm out in five minutes." He puffed his chest and his hands fell to his hips. Pride seeped from him as if quick showers were something to be proud of.

"So you don't wash yourself in the shower? You just wet yourself?" She placed her hands on her hips, mirroring his stance. She enjoyed their constant banter, particularly now. It helped ease the tension and the obvious attraction between them.

"Of course, I wash myself, smart ass!"

"Obviously not very well," she teased. "I mean how good can you wash yourself in five minutes? Do you get behind your ears? The back of your knees? Between your toes?"

"What's with your obsession with my feet?" He laughed, defusing any tension left between them. "Come on. I put on *The Hangover* since I know you like it." He walked toward her and put his arm around her. His heat permeated through the T-shirt, warming her from head to toe. Of course, she reacted to his nearness, but she'd come to recognize the warmth of being near him signified something deeper than just her attraction. Safety enveloped her whenever he was near—safety from the stalker and safety from her past.

"You look good in my clothes. I knew you would." Her cheeks heated at his words. They wandered into the family room and curled up next to each other on the chocolate colored leather couch. Less than twenty minutes into the movie, her eyelids grew heavy with exhaustion. She rested her head on his shoulder and closed her eyes. Sitting on the couch with Talon, consumed by his scent, his touch, his warmth—all was right with the world.

Chapter Three

Girl Code #6: Friends support your actions even when your actions are out of character.

A twinge in his neck roused Talon from sleep. He rarely woke in a fog unless he'd been in a fight the night before or had had an overly vigorous workout—the adrenaline release always made him fuzzy. Neither of those were the case. Nope. A restless night's sleep caused this morning's fog.

Restless for more than one reason. Every noise stirred him. Basically he slept with one eye open. He didn't know who Joey's texter was, but he didn't like it at all. The person had followed her around to photo shoots and quite possibly to her apartment or his house. That shit didn't settle right with him. He'd loaded his 9MM Glock while Joey showered last night, and tucked it under the couch—just in case.

But he'd also been restless because the woman he lusted after, the woman who made his heart race whenever she smiled, had fallen asleep, her warm body snuggled into him. He sported a hard-on despite his high alertness. All. Night. Long. Every moan, every whimper, every accidental graze over his lower abdomen had a new round of blood surging to his groin.

Joey hadn't even made it through the first twenty minutes of *The Hangover* when her breaths shallowed and her head rested on his shoulder. He loved the way she trusted him. Trusted him enough to let her guard down and fall asleep, knowing he'd keep her safe. The feeling was amazing. If he could bottle it, he would in a heartbeat.

His eyes crept open and he stared at the ceiling of his family room, the fan spinning at a mesmerizing pace. The sun peaked through crevices in the blinds. Yep, morning had arrived. His head lulled to the right to catch the time on the cable box. Seven a.m. On a Sunday. *Christ!* Sundays were typically his only day off, and he'd rarely opened his eyes before ten in the morning. He'd feel this early rising by late afternoon, for sure, but it was worth it. Tilting his head, Joey's dark brown hair tickled his nose. She nestled into his side, her head resting on his chest, his arm numb from the position.

She fidgeted, stretched her neck, and threw a leg over his thigh. A moan escaped her lips and Talon's cock went from half-morning wood to full hard-on.

Now what was he to do? If her leg inched up another few centimeters, she'd know exactly where his mind sat. And he couldn't ease out from under her because she would surely wake. She'd had a long, rough day yesterday, and needed her rest.

Another moan, and her body pressed closer to his, her hips rolling against his thigh. Was she dreaming? If so, he'd give anything to be in the dream if her movements and sounds were any indication. Her arm curled around his chest and her breaths puffed out in little gasps against his neck. His erection throbbed against his jeans, straining for release. A soft rumble bubbled in his chest, and despite his best efforts, he couldn't contain it. She startled.

"Talon?" The line between her brows displayed utter confusion. Her hand slid from his chest to the top of his jeans, making contact with his pulsing erection. The heat and pressure from her hand through his jeans caused his eyes to roll back in his head before he could meet her gaze. Three months of release by his own hand was no substitute for the girl of his dreams touching him there, even if by accident.

Her eyes widened like saucers and she yanked her hand away. "Oh, God! Did I do *that*?"

"How do you want me to answer that question, Josephine?" He didn't want to frighten her. He didn't want her to think the only thing he wanted was to get between her legs. Nothing was further from the truth, but a part of him wanted her to know what she did to him. How she turned him inside out. Yes, her presence, her smell, the feel of her next to his made him hornier than a stallion chasing a mare in heat. How she'd react worried him.

"Oh, God! I did!" Her cheeks turned pink. Absolutely adorable. She was gorgeous with her innocence and curiosity. It was the curiosity he wanted to explore if she'd let him.

"It's somewhat typical in the morning. But I'll admit, waking up with you practically on top of me didn't help matters."

She scrambled to her knees, grazing his balls as she did so. A jolt zipped through him from the contact. He didn't think he could be more aroused, but he was.

"Ugh. Hey. Watch it. I do want to have children someday."

"I'm sorry." She flung her leg over him and to the floor, standing next to the couch. Her teeth gnawed on a thumbnail.

"Joey, it's okay. Haven't you ever woken up with a guy before? Morning wood is normal." He kept his tone light, trying to defuse the mortification on her face. He didn't want her scared or embarrassed, certainly not with him.

"No, I haven't woken up with a guy before," she said with her thumb still in her mouth. Her face flushed again.

"Seriously?" He knew she wasn't a virgin. She'd openly admitted such one evening while they chitchatted at the beach, watching a sunset. Well, he had been watching her photograph the sunset. He'd also figured from her quick change of the conversation that night she hadn't been with a whole lot of men either, which was more than fine by him.

"Yes, seriously." Her fingers combed through her hair, and held the mass back from her face. "I've only been with two people, Talon. Neither one all that memorable."

His heart constricted a bit that no one had loved her properly. Fuck, he wanted to be the one. God damn this friendship barrier she placed between them. He could love her so well.

He pushed up from the couch. "Trust me, Joey, you deserve memorable." He placed a soft kiss on her forehead. "I'm going to whip us up some pancakes for breakfast. Go get dressed."

She relaxed at his command, as if his change in the subject alleviated the tightness of her muscles. "What? No bacon?"

"Of course, bacon, silly." He pushed on the ball of her nose with his index finger before scooting by her to get to the kitchen. "There's always bacon."

* * * *

Twenty minutes later, Talon sat at his kitchen table with her. Pancakes stacked between them. He could get used to this situation—going to bed with her in his arms and eating breakfast with her in the morning.

"So, I thought I'd ride back with you to your apartment so you can pack a bag." She lifted a forkful of syrupy pancake to her mouth. Her gaze rolled up to meet his as the syrup dribbled onto her chin. *Mmmm!* He'd bet syrup would taste even sweeter on her skin.

"Pack a bag for what?" Her eyes narrowed.

"So you can stay here for a few days until we find out who's texting you."

"I'm not staying here. You've got work. I've got work. I'll be fine." She shoveled another bite of pancake in. Oh, she was hardheaded, not afraid to stand her ground even if her decision might not be in her best interest. Luckily, he embodied the same trait. He wasn't backing down from protecting her, even if it meant she would be angry with him for a while.

He thumbed the dripping syrup from her chin before putting it in his mouth. Her breath caught. He'd been right. Sweetest syrup ever.

"I'm not letting you out of my sight until we figure this out. Have you reconsidered going to the police? At least file a report?"

She shook her head vehemently. "I don't want to get the police involved. It's some sort of silly prank and if it's not, this guy will have to get bored eventually. I'm not that interesting." She set her fork on her plate, and pushed it away. "You can't be everywhere I'll be, Talon. I have a photo shoot on Monday. You have work at the shop."

Her phone vibrated on the table. They looked at each other.

"Give it to me." She picked her cell up and laid it in his hand, reciting her password. Opening the text, his hand shook and anger rushed through him. Clenching his jaw, he ground his teeth and re-read the text.

He'll ruin you.

"Is it him?" Nervousness laced her voice, but he barely heard her. Blood rushed through his head, drowning everything except the pounding of his heart and a strong desire to hit the person on the other end of the text.

"Talon?" She wrenched the phone from him and gasped, covering her mouth. "He knows I'm here. With you."

"Fucking appears that way." He cracked his knuckles, then clenched his hands into fists, trying to contain the fury. Pushing from the table, he marched to the window over the kitchen sink. He scanned his backyard, looking for any sign of disturbance that someone had been on his property. Several large oak trees littered his yard, potentially providing great cover for a person not wanting to be seen.

"I'm going out back to check the yard." He trudged into the family room and grabbed his Glock under the couch, shoving it in the back of his jeans to avoid scaring Joey. But one could never be too careful. Whoever this was didn't know how often Talon visited the gun range perfecting his shot.

He walked into the kitchen, opened the door to the garage, and advanced outside. "Lock the door behind me," he said, pulling the door closed.

This guy had to have been on his property and it pissed Talon off. Not only did he threaten Joey, now he was trespassing.

It also bothered him this guy appeared to know him or of him. *He'll ruin you.* A warning to Joey. His gut wrenched.

He trekked through his backyard, Glock in hand, checking behind the large oak trees, around the side of the house, inside the large wooden container that housed his garbage cans. Nothing. Whomever had vanished, leaving no trace of his existence on the bone-dry ground. Frustration flowed through him. The guy had clearly been here, otherwise, how would he have known Joey was here? Yet, Talon couldn't find a single clue as to where he'd been or who he was.

Fuck! He reeled from the sense of being out of control. Since his father's death, he strived to keep command of his life, his emotions—everything.

He wandered to the house, sliding the gun in the back of his pants. She still sat at the table, gnawing on her thumb.

"I thought I told you to lock the door." Couldn't she just listen to him once? Her eyes bulged. *Shit!* He hadn't meant to come off so severe.

"It's daylight. And you were around the house. Don't be silly," she squeaked.

"There's nothing silly about these threats, Joey. Nothing. I don't care if I have to sub out the work on vehicles this week, I'm not letting you out of my sight. You can fight me all you want on this, but I'm not backing down and you won't push me away."

"I won't allow you to turn away business on my account. That's ridiculous."

"What's ridiculous is you thinking I'm not going to take this shit seriously." He ran his fingers through his hair. Damn, stubborn woman.

She pushed from the table, lifted her plate, and brought it to the sink silently. The tension in her shoulders shortened the length of her neck. Her sharp movements as she washed her dish made it clear she was upset. He'd deal with her being upset. He'd rather that than have to worry about not knowing where she was, or of her wellbeing.

He grabbed his plate and set it on the counter next to the sink. "I think the plate is clean, Josephine."

He gripped the counter on either side of her, caging her in. "I want you to turn around and talk to me. Tell me what's going on in that pretty little head of yours. Tell me why you're so resistant to staying here until we figure out who is following and texting you."

Goose bumps rose on her neck and her breath changed from soft and slow to harsh and rapid. The fact his nearness affected her altered his thoughts of concern and anxiety. He stepped into her, his chest and pelvis flush against her back. She dropped the sponge in the sink, rinsed the plate, and turned the water off before placing it in the dry rack on the counter.

"Are you going to kiss me or not?"

Her words smacked him in the face. *Huh? What?* She looked at him over her shoulder. His brow raised and his eyes enlarged. Had he heard her right?

45

"You want me to kiss you?" His voice wavered a little with a mix of surprise, nerves, and excitement. She turned in his arms and her expression had his knees buckle.

"Yes. We've been dancing around this for the last twelve hours—shoot—for the last twelve weeks and it's driving me crazy. This texting stuff is driving me crazy. I just want to forget about it. I want to take my mind off it. I want to take your mind off it."

Her hands slid up his abs and over his chest until they wound around his neck and into his short hair. A tingling sensation passed over the trail she blazed with her fingers. Pushing on her tiptoes, she pressed her lips against his and he all but lost his mind. Her lips were soft and pliable, moving over his in an unsure fashion.

He'd waited for this moment for some time. He imagined it would be him making the first move, lowering his lips to meet hers for their first kiss. But this was even better.

He clasped her hips in a tight grip as he inched closer. Flicking his tongue over her bottom lip, he savored the sweetness still there from their breakfast—remnants of maple syrup, buttermilk pancakes, and a saccharinity that was all Joey. She moaned. That little sound became the most erotic thing he'd ever heard and he wanted to hear it over and over again.

Her lips parted, summoning him in, and he seized the invitation.

Dipping his tongue into her mouth, he tasted her in long, leisurely licks. So fucking sweet and warm. A growl simmered from his chest and vibrated through him at the silky feel of her. *Fucking-A! Holy mother of God!* She tasted sinful, yet divine. His blood surged and headed south, making his cock hard as steel.

Her hands slid from his neck and grasped his shirt, pulling him closer. He pressed his pelvis flat against her belly and she groaned again. Interlacing his fingers through her long tendrils, he tilted her head to gain better access to her mouth. He continued the onslaught with more vigor than he'd ever kissed. For as little experience as she claimed, she met him with skill, brushing her tongue along his repeatedly until he was ready to explode.

They pulled back, chests heaving. His forehead rested against hers, and their breath mingled.

He cupped her face. "Jesus Christ. I've wanted to do that since the day I met you. The moment you walked into the shop. I wanted to kiss you."

His thumbs grazed over her jawline, relishing her smooth softness against his roughened hands.

"I can't wait to do it again. And again." He sealed his mouth over hers, dipping his tongue between her lips, licking. She clawed at his shirt, pulling and tugging as if she couldn't get him close enough.

Truth was, he wasn't nearly as close as he wanted to be. He wanted her wrapped around him, skin-to-skin. He wanted to hear his name fall from her lips as she came undone underneath him. He wanted everything with her, but couldn't rush things.

"Talon." She whimpered his name and pulled away. "I just don't want to screw things up. Aside from my sisters back home, you're the best friend I have."

He expected her words, but it didn't change the fact they and the reluctance in her voice still stung a bit. She'd given into her attraction—a means of distracting them from the tension of her stalker, but she hadn't quite given into handing over more than that. He wanted her too desperately.

"Josephine, there is nothing that would fuck anything up between us. We're always going to be friends. Always. No matter where this goes." He waved a finger between them. "I promise. I'm not going anywhere."

He kissed her softly on the lips. He loved that she valued their relationship so much. That losing him bothered her. The only person to ever make him feel that way was his mother.

"What happens if we get in a fight?"

"We get in arguments now. It hasn't ended our friendship."

"But once we cross this line, it changes everything."

With his forefinger, he lifted her face. Her milk chocolate eyes stared up at him with a mixture of worry and hope, but it was the hope that expanded his chest. All this time, he'd thought she hadn't wanted to be anything more than friends. He'd fought against his feelings for her, so he didn't ruin the only relationship he thought possible with her.

"You're right, Sweetness. It will change everything." A soft smile stretched his lips.

"I don't want us to change. I love our friendship, our relationship now. I love the way you make me laugh, listen to me, and make me feel safe." Her eyes fluttered for a few seconds before she met his gaze again.

"I know you're worried. Serious as shit, I'm a bit scared, too. I've never been in a relationship with anyone. I'm going to fuck up. We may get into arguments. But all the good stuff that comes with it will be worth it. Please give me a shot to prove it to you."

"I want to take this leap. I swear to you I do." Her big eyes stared up at him. "I don't know what I'd do if I lost you."

"Leap, Sweetness. Please fucking leap. I promise I will catch you and everything will be okay." He pressed a gentle kiss to her forehead.

Grabbing his face, she pressed up on her toes and kissed him. "Okay." She whispered so softly he wasn't sure she'd actually said anything.

"Okay?"

"Yes. Okay." Her eyes sparkled with joy. She was happy. He was ecstatic. Wrapping his arms around her waist, he spun her around before smashing his mouth against hers and kissing her with enthusiasm.

"So, can we go pack you a bag?"

She nodded.

"Good. Now go get your shoes on so we can get going. I thought I'd take you out four-wheeling this afternoon."

"Four-wheeling?" Her expression morphed into surprise. "I've never driven one."

"You'll ride on the back of mine. It'll be fun. We can expend some of our energy and get our minds off things for a bit."

"Okay. I think you're going to have to follow me, though. I have all the camera equipment in my car. I'm not sure there is room for you. I need to drop it at the studio before hitting my apartment. Do you mind?"

"Not at all. I'll follow you." She turned and walked out of the kitchen with a bounce in her step. He'd follow her anywhere—of that he was damn sure. He finished cleaning the kitchen and put the dishes away.

"T-bird." The front door creaked open and Jarrod clunked across the foyer toward the kitchen. Talon rolled his eyes and faced his brother. Jarrod didn't believe the rules applied to him. He came and went from his house as if he paid the mortgage. He never knocked. Just walked right in like he owned the place.

Talon needed to get his key back, especially with the possibility of Joey hanging around in his boxers and T-shirt.

"What's up, Jarrod?" Talon stacked the skillet in the bottom cupboard then made eye contact with his brother. Jarrod's dark hair lay disheveled, blueish circles darkened under his bloodshot eyes, and he wore the same clothes as he had last night. Hung over, no doubt, but he didn't appear to be drunk. No hair of the dog this morning. Thank God for small favors.

Talon inhaled and held it for a couple seconds before releasing through his mouth. "You look like shit."

"Thanks, dickhead." Jarrod opened a cupboard and pulled a glass down before tossing Talon a humbled smile. He filled the glass with water from the sink and chugged it.

Setting the glass on the countertop, he eyeballed his brother. "I wanted to apologize for my behavior last night. I had a couple too many drinks and well, you know how that goes." His tone was sincere, and, as usual, when Jarrod came to apologize, the guilt of Talon's anger weighed heavily on his chest. Jarrod had taken the brunt of things from their father as a kid. Being the oldest, he had to face their father's wrath first and for years until he became able to fight back. His spirit had been broken at an early age. Even though he turned his anger on to Talon for the better part of their lives, there were still hopeful moments where he would start being the big brother Talon had always wanted.

"I appreciate the apology."

"Why's Betsy parked under the Sycamore? You'll be cleaning the moss from the bed of your truck for months." Jarrod filled his glass with more water and sipped it this time.

"Joey's here. I had her park in the garage."

"So you finally nailed her?" Jarrod's voice was light and teasing.

"No, jackass. And don't talk about her like that." Talon shook his head. He hadn't meant to sound so defensive, but when it came to Joey, he just was.

"T-bird, you've never had a girl spend the night here." Jarrod eyed him suspiciously, as if he were lying about sleeping with Joey. Talon grimaced, mainly because the comment was true. He wasn't known for staying with one girl for much more than a night. He'd made it clear to every girl he bedded there wouldn't be any romance and roses. He'd bring girls home, fuck them, and then send them on their way. *Bastard.* Yes, he was. He simply didn't want any emotional connection. Girls who snuggled, cuddled, and spent the night typically grew attached. He tried to find those girls who understood a one-night-stand was just that—one night.

"Lower your voice." He didn't want Joey to hear this conversation. Even if Jarrod spoke the truth, Talon had changed his ways since meeting her, and he didn't need his past lurking around to ruin the opportunity she gave him.

"Are you afraid Joey won't let you in her pants if she knows how many girls you've actually been with?" Jarrod laughed heartily. In the old days they may have shared conversations like this, talking about each other's scores, but this conversation grated on his nerves.

"Go home and take a shower. And next time, knock before you come in. Let's not forget this is my fucking house."

Jarrod straightened. "Watch your mouth with me."

The apple sure didn't fall far from the tree. Even sober, Jarrod could turn cold in an instant when challenged, just like their father. "I'm still your older brother and the man of *this* family."

Talon snickered at the comment. *Shit!*

"I can still kick your ass."

The threat wasn't aggressive, so Talon laughed a bit harder. He and Jarrod had their rounds of fights over the years, verbal and physical. If there was one thing Jarrod knew, it was Talon could take him. Bigger, stronger and never hungover, he had the upper hand.

"You haven't kicked my ass since I turned sixteen."

"I know your weaknesses, little brother." Jarrod released a taunting laugh. The second time Jarrod mentioned this *weakness* thing. What was his brother getting at?

Jarrod enjoyed getting Talon charged, like it was a game, to see if he'd cross over the line. He knew it, but for some reason, he couldn't figure out where it came from.

Inhaling deeply, he crossed his arms over his chest and hoped to calm the impulse to deck his brother.

"Tal, I'm all set." Joey bounced into the kitchen in her clothes from last night. She noticed Jarrod propped against the counter and skidded to a halt. Her hair hung in thick, loose waves over her shoulders, framing her face. Her lips pulled into a tight line.

"Morning, Jarrod." She sidled over to Talon, and shrunk a step behind him. Joey wasn't Jarrod's biggest fan. She didn't like the way he spoke to Talon whenever he was drunk.

"Speak of the devil. Morning, Beautiful." Jarrod laughed. His gaze skimmed over her like she was a slab of gator meat and he hadn't eaten in days. Talon didn't like the way he looked at her. Sure, he'd ogled the girls Talon had hooked up with and had even snagged a few of them when he sent them packing. But the way he looked at Joey was altered from the way he'd looked at others—like Jarrod saw the same things in her he did. She was different. "Looks like I'm not the only one wearing last night's clothes."

Out of the corner of his eye, Joey winced and a pink flush rose from her neck. She tilted her head down. Talon entwined their fingers and gave a squeeze.

"Awe, how cute," Jarrod said with a hint of sarcasm. His gaze locked on their intertwined hands, eyes narrowing, and his mouth tight.

Talon recognized the jealousy. He was familiar with it. Despite all Talon had done—working extra shifts at the shop to cover for Jarrod, spending fifteen hundred dollars to bail him out of jail for a DUI charge or a fight at the local bar—Jarrod acted like he'd been slighted in life and Talon was the reason.

"T-bird's got himself a lady—for now. Watch out, baby. He's known for loving and leaving."

Talon's shoulders drew up taut, ready to lunge at his brother.

"Go ahead. Show Joey exactly what you're made of, little brother. Show her the ugly Manness temper. That angry side where you're just like me, just like the old man, needing to hit something—someone."

Joey squeezed his hand, reminding him of her presence, which calmed the bubbling of fury and shame in his gut. He hated that at times he hated his brother.

"Jarrod, head home." Talon's voice was stern. Blood rushed through his ears.

"Don't lie to her. It's not fair." He nudged his chin in Joey's direction. "You won't be able to settle down with her or any woman. It's not in your blood. You and I are like the old man."

He disliked—no, he despised—being compared to his father. Though Talon never turned to alcohol as a means of dealing with the shit life threw at him, he was like his old man in other ways. His anger. Turning to his fists first, more often than he'd care to admit. And the women—his father slept with every woman who spread her legs, even though he had been married to their mother. That fear rooted deep inside Talon. Could he have inherited that trait from his father, too? The inability to be faithful? He didn't think so. At least not since meeting Joey, but hearing Jarrod's words had him questioning it again.

Joey's thumb rubbed back and forth over his. The slow rhythm soothed him. His temper simmered and he released a breath. "We're heading out." Talon pulled Joey closer. "Mom mentioned needing some help with planting a few things in the garden. Why don't you head down there, clean yourself up, and give her a hand? I'm sure she'd appreciate it."

"You're Mom's favorite. Why don't you head over there and help?"

"Quit being a dip shit. We've got some errands to run." Talon waved his hand in the direction of the doorway, trying to shoo Jarrod out.

"Sure thing, little brother." Bending around Talon, Jarrod winked at Joey. "Catch you later, baby."

Talon flinched with annoyance and ground his molars, trying to keep his shit together. The vein in his neck thrummed with his racing heartbeat. Jarrod sauntered out of the kitchen and then the house, slamming the front door.

"Ass fuck." Talon growled and slammed his fist on the counter. The glass Jarrod left rattled from the vibration. He grimaced at the remaining tenderness in his hand from having punched the barn wall at the wedding. He'd forgotten to put ice on it and paid now. "God damn him."

Joey wriggled her hand from his, and resentment bubbled up that she might try to get away, that Jarrod had been right. He stiffened, every muscle taut. He hated any comparison to his father, but there was truth to it. Even when he tried to control his temper, it still could get the best of him.

Then, she slid her arms around his waist, interlaced her fingers over his belly, and rested her cheek against his back. The gentleness of her gesture melted him. She wasn't pulling away. Relief washed over him. He relaxed a little and sagged into her hug.

"Your heart's beating so fast. Relax." Her voice soft, calm, and soothing.

"Sometimes I want to kill him."

"I can tell. Do you want to talk about it?"

"And say what? I can't believe he turned out exactly like my father. He's a drunk." Talon's eyes burned with tears. What the fuck? He never cried. Never. Not even when he was alone and the craziness of his life got the best of him. But he certainly didn't cry in front of another person, and most especially wouldn't with Joey. He didn't want her to think Jarrod had any sort of power over him, or worse—he was weak.

With every beating, his father had told him tears were for pussies. After a few years, the tears stopped and nothing—not even his father's death—had brought them to his eyes again. Why now?

"I'm so sorry." She pressed kisses over his shoulder blades, and he tensed.

"I don't want your pity, Joey. I couldn't stand it." A lone tear escaped and ran down his cheek. He quickly wiped it away before she noticed.

"I don't pity you." More kisses. "I sympathize with you. You know my father's an alcoholic, too. He never hit me, but that may have had more to do with the fact I made myself scarce. He'd come home drunk after work, in a rage, throwing and breaking things around the house. Screaming. Yelling at the top of his lungs. God, I hated the yelling.

"Once, when I'd been in fourth grade, I'd made a paper mache volcano for school. I left it on the kitchen table to bring the next day. My father came home, drunk and angry because my mother didn't have dinner already on the table. He picked up the volcano and hurled it across the kitchen. When it didn't shatter completely, he stomped on it for good measure. I was up until one o'clock in the morning, trying to recreate that volcano for class. It didn't look anything like the original. I'd run out of some of the materials and my father wouldn't let my mom run out to pick anything up."

Her arms tightened around his waist. "If nothing else, you know I understand. There have been plenty of times where I've hated my father. It's one of the main reasons I left Ohio. I was afraid I'd spend so much time hating him, and my mother for enabling his problem, that I'd drown in the hatred."

"I'm already drowning in it and the guilt." Another tear fell. *Shit.* "I killed my father. And there are many days I wish to do the same thing to my brother." A soft sob rumbled through him. It was wrong to think life would be easier without his brother. He knew that, but a part of him fantasized about a life where he wasn't cleaning up his wreckage, where he wasn't dealing with his excuses. He'd had those same fantasies about his father.

"*You* didn't kill your father." She released his waist and circled in front of him, her beautiful eyes filled with so much understanding.

Her fingers grazed over his cheek, wiping away the stray tear. "He ran his car into a tree because he was drunk."

"He ran his car into a tree because I beat his ass." His hands clenched at his sides, remembering the rage when he found his mother banged up in the bathroom. "If my mother hadn't started screaming for me to stop hitting him, I may have beaten him to death. I wanted to kill him. Jarrod's right about me, Josephine. I'm no good. I'm angrier than a sack full of rattlesnakes. You don't want to be in a relationship with me. You were right to want to keep it as friends. Maybe that isn't even good for you." Self-pity ate from the inside out. His stomach turned over the pancake and bacon breakfast.

"Don't start telling me what I want, Talon Manness." She cupped his face, her thumbs brushing over his bottom lip. "You may be angry. You have every right to be. But don't tell me you aren't a good person, because I don't buy it. I've seen you. I've watched you. I've seen you do absolutely anything your mother asks of you, and I see the way the she looks at you when you do it. Like you're the greatest person she knows. You dropped everything to help Trevor when his mother found she had breast cancer and had to start treatment right away. I could go on for days of all the good things I've witnessed and I've only known you for three months. There's a whole bunch of goodness in here." She slid her hand down the front of his shirt and rested it over his heart. "A whole bunch."

His heart squeezed.

"You're too good for me. I'll break you. The goddamn text is right. I'll ruin you." He grabbed her hand and brought it to his lips, kissing the back of it. She was all the things he wasn't, but all the things he wanted. It would kill him to let her walk out of his life, but he had to give her the opportunity.

"Don't say that. We're actually good for each other." Rising on her tiptoes, she pressed her lips to his.

He cupped her face and returned the kiss, nibbling and licking at her lips until he slid his tongue inside. She tasted like minty toothpaste and something just her. The combination spun his head. He stroked his tongue against her own, exploring her mouth in a reverent manner. She grasped his shirt in little fists, holding on for dear life.

He pulled back and stared at her. "Now's the time to back out of this, Joey. I won't be mad if you tell me you don't want to walk down this road. I won't blame you. I don't deserve you. But if you tell me you want me, you want to try and make a go of this, I'll be damned if I'll let you go, Sweetness. You'll be stuck with me."

"I guess I'm stuck with you." She titled her head and a small smile stretched her lips. Drawing her into his arms, he held onto her as if his life depended on the connection. Maybe it did.

Chapter Four

Girl Code #9: Rescue plans will be implemented when a girlfriend is facing a challenging time.

Driving down Highway 301, she dialed Laydi's number. She needed to talk to someone. Not someone, but one of her sisters. She kissed Talon. She made the first move. Not at all how she envisioned their first kiss. She fantasized it would be him, pushing her against a wall or his truck or some hard surface to kiss the life out of her.

So many emotions floated through her. She'd given in to her attraction to him. Let it rule her actions, which were out of character. That explained the nerves tightening her chest and the butterflies fluttering in her belly. In the past, such courage wouldn't have surfaced, but despite all the anxiety surrounding the texting situation, Talon boosted her confidence.

Oh, God! She kissed him. Only one of her sisters would have the power to calm her down.

She thanked God every day for bringing Laydi, Selena, and Juls into her life. From the age of eight, their meetings at the pond in Pearl, Ohio were the only things that kept her sane. Some days, those girls were still the only thing keeping her balanced. Now, instead of sneaking through the woods at all hours of the day and night to meet up with her sisters at the pond, they'd do video chats, call, text, or whatever necessary to stay in touch. She talked to one of them at least once a week—sometimes more. They were her foundation, her base, the place she always came back to when her world tilted.

"Hey, Girlie," Laydi said with excitement into the phone. "I've been expecting this call since your text last night. It's been over a week. What's going on? And don't tell me nothing. You know I know you."

"Lay, I don't know whether to cheer or pee my pants. Can you conference Selena in? I'm driving, but I need your advice. God, I wish Juls still had her cell phone." Juls had sold her cell phone to score some drugs—heroin or something—months ago. It had been one of the many catalysts to get her into rehab. She was there now and doing well. Life had been difficult for her, but she was getting things together and would be stronger for it. God, she missed that girl.

"Joey, what's going on? You're scaring me a bit." Laydi's voice deepened over the phone, expressing her concern.

"I kissed Talon."

Laydi gasped. "What? Hold on. Let me see if I can reach Selena." Silence fell over the phone. Joey stopped at the red light just before Interstate 75. Talon's big Chevy Silverado rolled to a stop behind her. He wore his Rays' baseball cap backwards, which had been her favorite look of his since she met him. Something about it made her insides all mushy. His sunglasses covered his eyes and his thumb thumped on the steering wheel to the beat of some country song, she was sure.

Son of a biscuit, she kissed him! *She* freaking kissed Talon Manness. Where had her balls come from? More importantly, he did it back—more than once. For the love of God! Oh, the feel of his soft lips still lingered. Boy, did he know how to kiss. She'd never gone weak in the knees. Now? *All* she wanted to do was press her lips to his.

"Joey Lockhart. What is going on?" The familiar trill of Selena's voice had her laughing. It sounded like Selena had just rolled out of bed.

"Joey! Yes, tell us what's going on?"

Her eyes misted over at the rough sounding voice of Juliette Carrington. She hadn't heard Juls' voice since she'd entered rehab and it had changed—most likely from the tough road of detoxification. Juls hadn't been allowed to contact any of the girls until she'd shivered and shook her way through withdrawals, and came out on the other side. She had clearly reached that milestone. Thank God! Oh, she wanted to reach through the phone and squeeze her.

"Juls! Oh my God! Is that really you? How are you?"

"Yes, it's really me! Who else would it be?" Juls laughed. "Laydi called me at the clinic and told me you kissed the man who will finally prove you aren't frigid."

The girls laughed. Her dismal sexual experience had been a joke between them. After a few glasses of wine, Joey would talk about her singleness and how no man had ever brought her anywhere close to an orgasm, and the girls would point out all the times she'd brought herself to one in an attempt to prove she wasn't. They'd whoop it up until they were crying from laughing so hard.

"Obviously, I can't miss that discussion. So, a nurse was kind enough to let me use the phone in the office. I'm fine. I'm fine. I'll catch you up later. You needed us, so here we are. Now tell us what's happening."

A happy tear slipped from her eye and ran down her cheek. It had been awhile since the four of them had been on a call at the same time. In their younger years, they'd spent every moment together. Some of the townsfolk called them the bobbsey quadruplets because if you saw one of them, you saw all four. She wiped a tear away. Even living more than a thousand miles from her sisters, they still showed up when she needed them. She yearned to see their faces and hug them. It'd been months.

Talon beeped his horn behind her. The light at the intersection had turned green and she hadn't noticed—quite typical of her conversations with the girls. On more than one occasion, she'd lost track of everything else when they started talking. It had always been as if they lived in their own little world. Invincible. The four of them against the outside world—or at least, their little world of Pearl, Ohio.

One summer when she had been thirteen, they had been sitting on the edge of the pond after eating their picnic dinner of ham sandwiches, pickles, and Coca-Cola. All of them had finally discovered boys, or at least a curiosity of boys, and were rating the boys in their school on cuteness. They'd talked for hours, never noticing the sun had slipped behind the trees. It wasn't until Laydi's father, and a town police officer, shuffled through the trees with flashlights, yelling their names in a panic that any of them had realized how late it had been. Yep, lost in their own world.

She waved her hand in a shooing motion at Talon as she eased on to the gas pedal.

"What was that?" Laydi asked. "Is someone honking at our girl?"

"Girls, let me talk. It was just Talon. He's following me back to my apartment."

A few *oohs* and *ahhs* bantered about.

"It's still morning, Joey. Does that mean you spent the night at Talon's?" Selena shrieked into the phone.

"Yes." Her words came out like a whisper, but the girls cheered in unison. Joey laughed. Of course, her sisters would be thrilled at the possibility of her sex life moving from dismal to something resembling stimulating.

Heck, so would she.

"Did you fuck him?" Laydi asked. "I want to hear all about it. Did he give you a big O? I told you he was going to be your orgasmanator."

"Lay, I didn't have sex with him." Joey's face flushed at the mention of doing the deed with Talon. She wanted to—desperately. Every cell in her ignited. Feeling his skin against hers. His body above her. Him inside her. *Aagghh!* But she wasn't very skilled in that department. She worried she'd be a disappointment.

"Why not?" Laydi snorted. "I know you're dying to. Are you blushing on your end of the phone?"

Joey's face flushed. Damn Laydi for knowing her so well.

"She is." Juls giggled into the phone. "I can hear it in her voice."

"We kissed," Joey blurted. "That's it." Thinking of the softness of his lips against hers, she couldn't help but imagine how those lips would feel elsewhere on her.

"How was it? On a scale of one to ten—ten being the greatest kiss of all time." Selena's voice reached a higher level.

"An eleven."

More *oohs* and *ahhs* bounced about.

"An eleven?" The shock in Juls' voice made her laugh.

"You've never rated any of your kisses above a five," Laydi said. "Oh, this guy's going to rock your world in the sack. I can't wait until the day we have *that* conversation."

"Me neither." Both Juls and Selena chimed in.

"I should probably start from the beginning." Joey spilled all the details about the scary texts, Talon's protectiveness, staying at his house, and kissing him this morning.

"The kissing thing has me excited. You go girl. I'm so glad you grew some *cajones* and just did it! But this other shit about this creep, I don't like. And I'm a little pissed—make that super pissed—that this has been going on for a week, and I'm just hearing about it now. You need to go to the police." Laydi was adamant about it. Joey knew she would be. Exactly why she hadn't told her or any of the other girls. She knew they'd be all over her, especially Laydi, but now that things had escalated, she had to tell them and face the firing squad, so to speak.

"I'm going to call you tomorrow, and if you didn't go file a police report, I'm flying down there and doing it for you."

"Okay, Lay. I'll go to the police. It may just be a sick prank." Joey still hoped—even after this morning's text—whoever sent them was just messing with her, not meaning any real harm.

After the discussion between Talon and Jarrod this morning, she had wondered if the texter could be one of the women scorned by Talon. The saying "hell hath no fury like a woman scorned" flashed in her mind. She'd always assumed the stalker was a guy. Some of the texts would have seemed odd coming from a woman, but if that person wanted to scare her or get her out of the way. *Jiminy Cricket!*

She sat in traffic at the bridge heading into Bradenton. Talon wasn't letting anyone cut between them. His protective nature warmed her heart. When he said he wasn't letting her out of his sight, that this stalker would have to get through him first before he'd have a shot at getting to her, he'd meant it. He was an amazing man. So giving. So caring. So protective.

"You'd better bring your ass to the police station today. I'm serious, I'll fly down there."

"I agree with Lay, Joey." Selena chimed in.

"Me, too." Juls agreed.

"Maybe I won't do it if it will get you three down here for a visit."

Laydi released a sardonic chuckle and her tone was quite serious. "Don't even think about trying that, Josephine. I'll kick your ass when I get there. You know I will."

"Okay. Okay. I'll go to the police."

The girls continued their conversation until Joey reached Elegance Photography's studio. They agreed Joey would update them daily about the stalker situation, though Laydi had attempted to make it an hourly update. They talked about the next steps in Joey's progression with Talon, Juls' recovery, and the latest rumors spilling out from their hometown.

Joey pulled into the parking lot. "Girls, I'm sorry. I just got to the studio and have to unload all the photography equipment from last night's wedding."

"Gotcha, darling," Selena said. "Love you all."

"Love you, too." Joey's voice cracked and her eyes filled with tears again. This conversation had been exactly what she'd needed. The girls had a way of settling her, grounding her in the present and what really mattered. The last week had been stressful and left her off-balance. She wished she could hug and kiss them now. She parked the car near the front door.

"Much love." Laydi blew kisses over the phone.

"Love. Love isn't even a strong enough word." The truth of Juls' words floated over her. The four of them had seen many ups and downs. Yet, their faith and trust in each other only grew stronger.

They said their goodbyes, and Joey wiped her tears, tossed her phone in a cup holder, and opened her car door. Talon's boots crunched on the pavement behind her.

"You really shouldn't drive while talking on the phone." He opened the back door of her car and started unloading.

"I was talking to my sisters." Her hands rested on her hips.

He tossed one of her camera bags over his shoulder and turned to her. His sunglasses covered his eyes, disguising his intent, but a smile stretched his lips wide. "Well, you drive like a snowbird when you're on the phone."

"Excuse me?" She pursed her lips, trying to keep from smiling herself. He just called her a snowbird. Coming from Ohio, the term meant nothing to her after she moved to Florida. Come mid-January, though, traffic slowed to a crawl and almost everyone on the road had white hair. In essence, he'd called her an old lady.

"You heard me."

"Did you just call me an old lady?"

"No. I said you drive like one when you're talking on the phone." He stepped closer. "If you were an old lady, I wouldn't do this."

Bending to her with bags dangling off his shoulders, he brushed his lips over hers. Her hands fell from her hips and her defiant stance slipped away. She sighed.

"Let's move it, Sweetness. I'd rather be making out with you on my four-wheeler than in this parking lot." He pressed a chaste kiss to her lips before snatching the keys from her hand.

Butterflies fluttered low in her belly. This was really happening. By kissing him this morning, she'd opened their relationship beyond the friendship boundary. She may have no idea what she was doing, but she'd jumped with both feet and would give it a try—conclusively.

"Joey, get your ass moving." Talon strutted out the front door of the studio. His jeans hung low on his hips and clung to his powerful thighs. With his black T-shirt pulled tight over his chest, and his cap on backwards, her fantasy man stalked toward her in big strides.

His fingers slid into her tousled hair just as he sealed his mouth over hers. His tongue glided over her bottom lip, then nuzzled it before dipping inside. He licked into her mouth in languid strokes. Their tongues danced over one another. They moaned. He deepened the kiss and her knees wobbled. Heat coursed through her, settling at her core.

"Talon," she breathed against his mouth and sagged against him.

Dropping his forehead to hers, he broke their connection. His breath puffed against her cheeks in quick bursts. "Sorry. You just look so adorable. So fucking kissable. It's all I want to do."

"I know the feeling." Her chest heaved. Her hands rested on his hips. "Let's finish this up and get out of here."

* * * *

Riding in separate vehicles to Joey's apartment nearly killed him. He'd teetered on the edge with her since the day she walked into his auto shop. With her beautifully expressive eyes, and a smile that melted every brick he'd laid on the wall around his heart. But after her "are you going to kiss me or not" stunt this morning, he no longer teetered. He'd jumped right the fuck off the edge. A risk given his history, but she opened the door and nothing could have stopped him.

She'd wandered to her bedroom to pack a bag while he meandered around her charming living room. A black leather loveseat with bright green and blue pillows backed against a wall. A brown chest with black strap accents sat in front of the couch, posing as a coffee table. Books by Jane Austen and the Brontë sisters piled on the corner of the chest. Various frames housing photographs she'd likely taken at some point hung on the walls of the room, leaving very little of the white visible.

He perused her photography. Sunset at Siesta Key. Sunrise at an orange grove. The face of an old woman sitting outside an ice cream shop on Anna Maria Island. Kids kicking a soccer ball around on a sandy field. An old man helping his wife cross the street. A young boy skim boarding across the ocean's edge. All amazing. She had a knack for capturing a moment.

A red wooden frame drew his attention. Four girls—probably in their teens—stood at the edge of a pond in shorts and tank tops, water covering their feet. Their arms wrapped around each other as they giggled and posed. He recognized Joey. She was stunning, even then. Her long mahogany hair fell over part of her face. Her mouth opened in a laugh, and her eyes danced with silliness.

At first meeting, she seemed reserved, serious, perhaps a bit shy. In some ways, it was an accurate assessment, but once she got comfortable around people, he'd seen her let her guard down. Let people see the real Josephine Lockhart. Her warmth and loving nature, which beckoned a person to open up to her—to trust her. Her silliness, always quick witted with a joke, an entertaining face, a dance, or whatever else she could think of, made others laugh.

Her unbelievable strength in dealing with her parents and loving them anyway, but setting healthy boundaries for herself. Her determination—not only to make a name for herself in her photography career, but in maintaining her bond with her sisters. When she let her guard down, many were goners.

Though she talked about her sisters often and shared an occasional picture of one or the other, this photo told him everything. Those girls meant the world to her. Their bond exceeded blood ties. His chest tightened at seeing her so carefree, so comfortable, so happy. The need to wrap his arms around her overwhelmed him. He wanted to protect her from the stalker, but also from anything that could hurt her so she could be carefree and happy. So she could be the girl in the picture.

He glanced at the clock on her wall. She was taking a long time.

Walking down the short hallway, he pushed through the partially opened bedroom door to find her stuffing clothes into a duffel bag. She jerked her head up at his entrance, eyes wide with surprise.

"What're you doing?" She scanned the room looking for something. Her movements jittered as if nervous and she didn't want him in her bedroom. "I'm almost done."

"I couldn't wait a second longer to kiss you again." He strut over to her, cupped her face, and brushed his lips over hers. She whimpered, and it fueled his need.

He'd never been so out of control with his emotions for a woman. He always kept in check, but found that impossible around her. He caught sight of something behind her, propped up on her nightstand. A photograph. Black and white. Of him. Nudging her to the side, he grabbed it.

"Talon, don't."

She reached for his arm, but he already had the photograph. An eight-by-ten of him from the thighs up. He stood in his work jeans, ripped and dirty, and his black ribbed tank top. His hands pressed into his hips as he admired an old '65 Mustang he refurbished for Mr. Johnson. The headlight of the 'Stang peeked through the corner of the photo. Grease smudged the side of his face, his forearms, and hands. Below his backwards black baseball cap, beads of sweat pebbled his forehead waiting to leave a trail down the side of his face.

A satisfied smile stretched his lips. And she'd caught it. She'd caught the moment where he'd been proud of an accomplishment. That car had been a beauty. The body had been in almost mint condition, but Talon reconstructed the engine. Once in a while, he caught Mr. Johnson cruising the country roads in the 'Stang and it made him smile. He'd done that. He'd made it run.

Talon dreamed of working on an older car since he had been a kid. His father had promised to buy an old classic at an auction for them to work on, but alcohol made his father's promises unfulfilled. Finishing the car and seeing Mr. Johnson's excitement had been amazing.

"I don't remember you taking this." He held the photo between his thumb and forefinger, waving it. He cocked his head to her. Her hands fumbled with a T-shirt she had been trying to fold, but just balled up.

"The day you finished the Mustang. I was at the shop waiting for you so we could go grab a bite to eat. You were so enthralled with the car. I'm pretty sure you didn't even realize I was still there. I just walked around snapping some pictures." She raised her gaze to meet his. Emotion fluttered behind her eyes. "It's my favorite picture of you."

"Favorite? You say that like there are more." He scanned her bedroom. Several pictures were pinned to a corkboard on the other side, and a couple sat on the mirror of her dresser. She'd captured him in unsuspecting moments. One where he sat in the sand with his arms wrapped around his knees, staring out into the Gulf of Mexico. Another on the running board of Betsy with a huge grin, waving someone in his direction.

"Joey."

"I'm sorry." She lowered her head. "I should have told you I had taken those photos."

"Sorry?" He pinched her chin between his thumb and forefinger and lifted. "No one has ever made me feel so special. Is this how you see me?" He envisioned people saw him as hard, unapproachable, and temperamental. Those who knew his father assumed he was a chip off the old block. These pictures—*wow!*—he'd never seen himself as being content and happy, and yet, she captured just that. Part of him knew Joey played a role in it.

"See you how? As an amazingly handsome man with a heart bigger than the world? Yes. That's exactly how I see you."

Warmth spread over him. Women liked him. They found him attractive, but none of them made him feel more than a good-looking guy. None of them made him feel worthy of more than he'd been handed. Joey did. She didn't just see him physically. She saw what was on the inside, too, and stuck around. That meant something. *Shit!* That meant the world.

He bent and brushed his lips against hers. Starting off slow, he nuzzled her bottom lip, flicking his tongue to wet it, then nuzzling again. She dropped the balled-up shirt to the floor and fisted his T-shirt, pulling him closer, kissing him like he were the air she breathed.

* * * *

On the way back to Talon's house late that morning, they stopped at the Manatee County Sheriff's office to file a report on the mysterious texter. Joey's sisters convinced her to do it, and he'd thank them for that at the next opportunity. Any more suspicious texts had to be reported to the sheriff's office right away. They promised to start the investigation immediately. Fingers crossed, they'd catch the creep sooner rather than later.

They lost track of time on the four-wheeler. He imagined it had to be near five o'clock. Having her arms wrapped around his waist, her breasts pressed into his back—*Good God!*— her legs tight against his as he drove his Honda Four Trax

Rincon four-wheeler through the mud near the Manatee River made the ups and downs of last night and the morning all worth it.

Mud splattered their clothes and shoes. She'd yelped and screamed and laughed so hard he made her promise she wouldn't pee her pants. Now, Talon drove the four-wheeler back to his property. With the exception of the run-in with his brother and the fucking text on Joey's phone, this had been the best Sunday of his life and it wasn't over.

He pulled the ATV behind his garage near the hose. If he let it set for too long, the mud would dry and make cleaning it later a real bitch. Laying off the gas, he slowed it to a stop.

"Hop off, Joey," he shouted through his helmet and over the slight roar of the engine. "I need to spray her down to get the muck off." She stepped on the platform and swung her leg over. Lifting the black helmet off her head, her dark tendrils swung in a tangled mess over her shoulders. Her gaze lifted to his, eyes sparkling with delight. Despite her initial reservations about going out with him, she'd had fun. So had he. Mission accomplished.

Her mud-clad jeans hugged rounded hips and muscular thighs, showing her off in a way that had all his blood rush to his cock. Her gray tank top stuck to her torso from the mud, river water, and sweat. She wasn't one of those skinny girls who looked good in those ridiculous clothes on the cover of a fashion magazine. Nope. Josephine Lockhart had a rocking body he'd bet his entire life savings, his property, and his auto repair shop looked spectacular with no clothes at all.

"Hot damn, Josephine. You look gorgeous wet and covered in mud." The words escaped before he could stop them.

She eyed him through her lashes and her cheeks turned a deep shade of pink. Damn, he'd fallen for this woman. For the first time in his life, he had hope he wouldn't spend his life alone, even if, at times, he believed he deserved it.

Deep in thought, he hadn't noticed Joey inching her way toward the garage until it was too late. She stood in front of him holding the hose nozzle like she was about to shoot a pistol, with a shit-eating grin.

"Don't you fucking dare." His helmet muffled his warning, but the cocked eyebrow indicated she'd heard him just fine.

"Or what?"

He flipped off his helmet and tossed it away from the ATV so the inevitable water fight didn't ruin it. He turned off the four-wheeler and stashed the key in his pocket. "Do you really want to find out?"

"Maybe I do," she sassed him, and he chuckled. He liked this playful, ballsy side of her. He'd had a glimpse of it a few times over the months, but she always tried to keep it in check. Today—however, she was balls to the wall.

"Then go for it. I dare you. I triple dog fucking dare you." He stood with a foot on each platform straddling the ATV with his hands resting on the handlebars. She pushed the trigger. Hot water pelted him in the chest as the hose cleared the water that had been sitting in the line all day. Two seconds later, cold water showered him, hitting him in the face, the chest, and she even had the audacity to aim for his groin.

Hurdling over the ATV, his feet splashed in the mud created by her water escapade. Screaming, she dropped the hose and ran through his back yard. He followed. She had some speed. He'd give her that. All the running she did at the beach paid off, but he was faster.

In ten strides, he wrapped an arm around her middle. Her legs dangled in the air as he swung her around and walked her back to the garage area.

"Stop, Talon! Stop!" She kicked and wriggled attempting to escape, but he tightened his hold.

"I warned you, didn't I?" Still holding her with one arm, he bent and swiped the hose off the ground.

"Talon Manness! You wouldn't," she shrieked.

"You don't know me too well then, Sweetness." He held the nozzle as far as his arm could stretch so as not to hurt her from the force of the water. Squeezing the trigger, he sprayed her hair until not a single strand remained dry, and brown rivulets streaked her face and arms from the mud. Then, he targeted her tank top, before releasing his hold on her and aiming the nozzle at her lower body. She dashed in the direction of a tree, but wasn't quick enough to avoid getting the back of her pants drenched.

"Truce," she yelled from behind the tree. She peeked around. Her hair hung in matted clumps. Black smudged under her eyes from her mascara. He snickered, and sprayed in her direction again. Her head ducked behind.

"Come on out, Joey. This hose can stretch pretty far. I don't want to come out and get you, but I will."

"I'm already soaking wet." Her voice sounded shrill.

"Then getting wetter should be no big deal."

"I can't get any wetter. It's a waste of your time." She peeked around the other side of the tree, and he blasted her again. "Arrggh!"

He quaked with laughter. "I told you not to do it. I warned you. Now you're going to have to pay the price." He yanked the hose and started dragging it in the direction of the tree. Unlikely it would reach, but she didn't know that.

"Okay. Okay." She stepped tentatively from behind the tree, her hands in the air as if she were under arrest.

Hmmm, now that was a fantasy they could play out. Cop and robber. Handcuffs.

She sloshed with each step, both from the sopping nature of her shoes and of the ground around her. They certainly made a mess of his yard.

Her gaze pled with him, pulling at his heartstrings, and stirring his erection. *Uh huh,* that was the look he wanted on her face right before he made her come, made her lose her mind. One of surrender.

Twisting the nozzle of the hose, he switched it from its jet stream setting to a fine mist. Her steps faltered when she noticed his movement, but she didn't stop. Her eyes narrowed with purpose. He pushed the trigger, water spraying in a cone, misting her face and the front of her already sopping top. Water droplets ran down her face.

She'd been right—she couldn't get any wetter. Damn, she looked irresistible, all wet and determined.

He dropped the hose and stepped toward her until their bodies collided. His hands immediately speared into her wet, tousled hair, and he slammed his mouth on hers, on fire for her.

Her fingers gripped his T-shirt, pulling him even closer. Her slick mouth slid over his in a gasp, and his tongue penetrated. Licking, he tasted her as their tongues danced.

Erotic moans and whimpers seeped from her, making his cock unimaginably harder. He'd never had a boner like this.

He gripped the base of her head, tilting her so he had a better angle at her mouth. He ate at her like she was the source of his energy, his livelihood, his sustenance. Perhaps she was. All he knew was he couldn't get enough of her, of her taste.

She inched to the hem of his shirt and slipped underneath. The feel of her soft, wet fingertips gliding over the ridges of his abs ignited him. Plenty of women had touched him. None had ever felt so damn good. She edged his shirt up and broke the kiss, staring down at his revealed skin.

"You're so unbelievably perfect," she whispered. Her gaze met his and he sucked in a quick, tight breath. Dilated pupils left only a small sliver of her milk chocolate irises. All her innocence flittered away, leaving a sultry seductress in its place. He'd never seen *this* side of her, but he liked it.

Screw that! He fucking loved it.

"Perfect doesn't even begin to describe you," he said gruffly, watching her with burning intensity. His hands skimmed over her shoulders and squeezed, then caressed her upper arms.

She leaned forward and pressed soft kisses around his belly button. Looking up, their gazes locked. She flattened her tongue and licked him from the top of his belly button through the center of his abs. A ripple of pleasure washed over him, and his eyes rolled in his head. The heat from her mouth, so different from the cold of his wet body. All he could think about was her mouth, her tongue elsewhere on him, relieving him of the ache burning inside for her.

"Do that again." His voice broke. He hadn't meant to sound so demanding. He didn't want to rush things. Didn't want to scare her, or have her think the only reason he'd hung around was to get in her panties. Yes, he wanted in them more than he ever wanted anything in his life. More than that, he wanted every single part of her.

But he needed to feel her tongue on him again. He reached behind his head and removed his T-shirt in that way that was innately male. He dropped it to the ground in a puddle of sandy mud.

She drank him in and a soft smile of appreciation split her lips. Her hands flattened against his abs and moved up his torso in the same slow motion as her tongue. She pressed tender kisses over his pecs and collarbone. Her mouth heated his skin with each brush. Pushing to her tiptoes, she cupped the back of his head and crashed her mouth against his. The kiss was hard, carnal, and entirely out of control. Lips, teeth, and tongues mashed, her hands tugging and pulling his hair by the roots.

A ferocious growl ripped through him. Her hunger feeding his.

He touched her everywhere: over her arms, around her chest, down her back. This primal need to claim her, make her his in every way took over. He cupped her ass and lifted. Her legs instinctively wrapped around his waist. He carried her up the three small steps of the wooden deck he'd built two summers ago and opened the door that led to his laundry room. Clumsily, he kicked off his shoes, walked into the house, and kicked the door closed behind them.

He strode down the hallway to his bedroom with her wrapped around him. She pressed little kisses over his face, down his neck, and paused at the point on his neck where his pulse beat at a rapid pace. The warmth of her lips absorbed into him and coursed through him, causing his skin to tingle. He didn't think his cock could get any harder, but he was wrong.

"Tal, I still have my shoes on. I'm soaking wet and covered in mud."

"What are you worried about, Joey?" He pushed his bedroom door open and strode to the bed. Her arms still wrapped around his neck, her fingers still tugged at his hair, and she pressed soft kisses along his jaw.

"I don't want to dirty your house or your bed," she said between kisses. He tossed her and she bounced with a gasp and a giggle. Strands of wet hair clung to her face and her eyes enlarged in surprise.

"The plan *is* to dirty this bed with you. I want it dirty and defiled." Grabbing her foot, he yanked one soggy tennis shoe off at a time and tossed them across his room.

"Are you sure?"

"I've never been surer of anything in my entire life, Sweetness."

Chapter Five

Girl Code 2: Talking about sex with your girlfriends is perfectly acceptable anywhere and anytime.

Oh God! This was happening! *Oh God!*

Joey had been bold and brazen in the back yard, coming on strong—much like this morning. Her body took over as if this thing between them was as natural as the sun rising and setting. Maybe it was, but it didn't stop her nerves from fraying as she sprawled out on his bed.

His dexterous fingers undid her jeans and peeled them down her legs, pulling her socks off in the process. Goosebumps rose on her damp skin.

"Sit up." His command sent heat coursing through her. She'd never been with someone who had such confidence. Her first experience with her high school boyfriend had been a bumbling, fumbling mess. The only thing he knew was where to stick it. Then, she dated a guy in college who hadn't had much experience with the female anatomy, or how to use his own. He had been awkward, which—in turn—made her uncomfortable.

Joey pushed to sitting, listening to Talon's command. He gripped the edge of her tank top and hauled it over her head, leaving her in a pirouette pink and white striped demi bra and matching pink thong from *Victoria's Secret*. These undergarments provided her with a bit of confidence, even though they were wet and dirty from their adventures.

"Better than I even imagined." He cupped her face and brought his mouth down to meet hers in a worshipful manner. His tongue swiped over her bottom lip once, twice, then he nibbled it between his teeth and pulled. She moaned, flicking her tongue at his upper lip. He slipped his tongue into her mouth, sliding, stroking. It was a deep, lush kiss.

Her hand rested behind her keeping her upright, and the other sunk into his short hair, holding him to her.

He coasted his hands from her knees, over her thighs, and around her hips. They drifted along her waist until cupping her breasts through her bra. Warmth penetrated her bra and spread over her. His fingers kneaded and molded in a sensuous fashion. With one quick snap, he unhooked her bra, and it fell forward. Her nipples tightened at the feel of the cool air of his bedroom.

Breaking the kiss, he slid the bra down and to the floor. She was in nothing but her panties, feeling exposed and vulnerable, yet incredibly sexy at the same time. He stared at her in awe. Heat rose over her neck and cheeks as he thoroughly drank her in. She'd always been self-conscious. It wasn't like she had self-esteem issues—not really. She'd always considered herself average. What guy wanted average?

"Beautiful." His voice a mere whisper. That alone erased any doubts she had. If Talon found her beautiful, then by God, she was. He leaned into her, his hands on either side of her hips, and brushed his lips tenderly over hers. They were soft, yet firm, and moved along her jaw, down her neck, and over her collarbone.

Kissing down her chest, her breath hitched when his mouth surrounded a taut nipple. His mouth burned, and his tongue a soft lash against her skin. Heat coursed through her, settling in her core, dampening her panties.

He slid his hand up her hip and over her belly to cup her other breast, molding it in his hand, pinching the nipple between his thumb and forefinger until she cried in an ecstasy she'd never known.

"Talon," she said, his name like a prayer. His gaze swung upward as he released one nipple and latched onto the other, doing the same nibbling and lashing. His fingers tugged at the moist nipple he'd left behind, pinching gently. She moaned at the sensations. Every touch, every lick, every pinch a new awareness, a new experience.

He gripped her shoulders and raised his head, kissing her hard on the lips. He pushed until she lay back on her elbows, kissing his way down her. Over her breasts, lashing and sucking on each nipple again before he moved lower, over her abdomen. Murmuring sweet words over her skin.

"You're beautiful. So soft. So sweet. I can't believe how lucky I am."

His fingers hooked into the sides of her panties. With concentrated precision, he inched the silk down in a painstakingly slow manner, trailing kisses along the way, until they were completely off and tossed to the floor.

"Joey, oh Christ, you smell amazing," he growled between kisses over the soft hairs of her core. Seeing the top of his head between her legs sent another surge of excitement there. "My mouth is watering to taste you."

"I've never...I mean no one's ever..." Her voice gave out. Embarrassment and shame seeped through her, her skin flushing. Here she was twenty-five years old, had sex with two men, and neither had performed oral sex on her. Neither had even looked at her there, now Talon stared between her legs like she was a rare treasure.

His head lifted and his gaze met hers. "No one's ever tasted you here?" He ran a finger through her slick folds. Every muscle tensed at the feel of being touched there. It'd been so long, and it'd never been with such adoration.

She shook her head, unable to speak. His fingers continued to caress over her swollen cleft. She arched her back off the bed and moaned loud.

A lazy, but shameless smile broke on his face. "I'm honored to be the first." Separating her legs, he positioned between them, his face hovering over her pussy, his breath hitting her in tickling pants. "And I hope to be the last." His thumbs parted her lips. "You're so beautiful here. So pink. So swollen. So fucking wet." He stared up at her, holding her gaze as his tongue laved up her slit.

"Oh my God!" She tried to maintain eye contact, but couldn't. Her eyes squeezed shut and her head fell to the bed. Her belly quivered with a thousand butterflies. A sheen mist of sweat covered her skin. His tongue flicked over her clit and her hips bucked off the mattress.

"Fucking-A, you taste amazing." His forearms pinned her thighs as he ate at her, lashing his tongue over her clit and through her slit. Nothing had ever felt so amazing, so exhilarating. God, she'd been missing out all this time. His skilled tongue laved through her core, exploring every part of her before circling the quivering entrance to her. He penetrated her opening. Fucked her with his tongue. She whimpered. A growl rumbled through him, vibrating against her, proving he enjoyed this as much as she did.

She tingled and her core tightened, the first signs of an impending orgasm. She grasped desperately at the comforter, fisting it. He licked his way through her folds, delving inside between ardent licks. He circled her clit with the tip of his tongue. His forearms held her down despite the upward motion of her hips. His mouth sealed over her clit and sucked on the tight bundle as he slid a finger inside her swollen channel.

Ah, God! The walls of her pussy rippled with pleasure around his invasion. His tongue flitted over her clit, once, twice…and she erupted, sparks of pleasure shooting to all her nerve endings. She cried out. The orgasm ripped through her and she bowed off the bed. His mouth remained over her, tenderly licking and sucking as his finger drew out the remaining waves.

Her first orgasm by a man. No, not any man. Talon. She'd never be the same.

After several long minutes, she floated down from her high. Her body more relaxed than she'd ever remembered. He still lay between her legs, peppering the inside of her thighs and the soft hairs covering her core with little kisses.

Slowly, he climbed over her, kissing his way up until his hips nestled between her legs. His erection pressed against her belly.

"That was amazing." He pressed a soft kiss to her lips. "You're so fucking beautiful when you come. I could watch you all day long. The noises you make, the way you move. Fuck, Sweetness, I've never seen anything more stunning."

He dipped his tongue between her lips, sliding it against hers. She moaned at her own spicy flavor on his tongue, sucking on it. She'd never known her taste, but to taste herself for the first time mixed with his own flavor was a heady experience.

Her hands glided over his back, feeling the ridges and planes of his muscles. She loved the feel of him poised over her, his weight pushing her into the bed, his hips resting against the apex of her legs. The ridge of his erection surged against her during her continual exploration of his mouth.

"I want you to make love with me." Her words came out rough and filled with desire.

"You have no idea how bad I want that. No idea." He pushed off her and the bed. She whimpered a soft protest, and he stretched his lips into a sly smile. "Trust me. I'm coming right back, Sweetness." He stripped off his pants and lowered his boxer briefs to the floor.

In all the weeks leading up to this point, Joey had fantasized about Talon naked. She'd seen him with his shirt off. He took care of his body, had sexy tattoos. But to see him standing before her completely naked took her breath away.

His muscular chest and his chiseled abs glistened in sweat and dampness from their water fight with the hose. His erection bobbed from its weight, long, and thickly veined. *Oh God!* Apprehension and a little fear flowed through her at the thought of Talon filling her.

"Don't be scared, Joey. We'll take this at your pace. Even if I'm dying to be inside you, I'd never do anything to hurt you."

"I—I don't know if you'll fit. You're so much bigger..."

"You were made for me, Sweetness. I'm sure of it. Our bodies will fit perfectly. I promise."

Her gaze fixated on him as he stroked his cock in long, languid movements. The most erotic scene she'd ever experienced. So comfortable with his body, his sexuality. Laydi was right—he would rock her world, and the time was now.

"You're insanely beautiful, Talon Manness." His green eyes sparkled with desire.

He pulled his bottom lip between his teeth, and a growl rumbled through his chest.

"Beautiful is you. I've never seen anything sexier than you sprawled out on my bed." He crawled between her legs. "Are you sure? I need to ask you because once I'm inside you, Josephine, I'm pretty sure I'll go crazy if you change your mind. Don't get me wrong. If you say stop, I will. I promise. But I will go crazy.

"Right now, I crave you. Nothing will satisfy it, nothing will satisfy me but having you." He rested on his forearms.

"I've never been surer of anything in my life."

He smiled at her use of his line moments ago. She grasped his neck, pulling him toward her, mashing their lips together in a hard, greedy kiss. When she released him, he groaned and reached for the drawer of his nightstand, pulling out a foil package. He ripped the condom open with his teeth, sheathed his cock, and tossed the foil to the floor.

He slid the broad head of his penis through her swollen folds and over her clit.

"You're so wet. I ache to be inside you."

Her back arched off the bed at another swipe over her tight bundle of nerves, and a moan rushed from her lips. He pushed against her, parting her opening with the head of his cock.

"Oh, God," she gasped. He was so much larger than either of the guys she'd been with, and it had been at least a year since she'd had sex. Her eyes widened at the pleasure-pain sensation of being stretched, invaded. Muscles in his shoulders bunched. His lips pulled tight and a tiny muscle in his jaw twitched, making his restraint evident.

He pumped his hips forward another inch, and she moaned. "Please."

"Please what?" He pushed another fraction.

"I want you inside me, Talon. All of you." Desperation cut her voice.

He growled, the sound entirely primal, and caused a new rush of moisture to her core. Holding himself up by his forearms on either side of her, he surged his hips forward with some power and into her, the thick length of him burrowing deeply. She cried out and raised her hips, welcoming him inside despite the slight discomfort.

"Holy Mother of God. Fuck!" He buried his head in her neck, panting against her skin. He ground his hips against her, trying to bury himself deeper within. Her legs wrapped around his thighs, holding him to her. She dug her fingers into the muscles of his back as her hips circled against him, trying to accommodate as much as she could take. She wanted all of him.

"You feel amazing. Jesus Christ, Sweetness. You're perfect. This is perfect."

His lips brushed against her neck and over her jaw as he stroked into her in long, measured blows. She writhed against him, pumping her hips upward. She'd never been so full. He filled her completely, all the way to the end of her with every thrust. She whimpered, she cooed, she cried out, urging him on.

He dug his knees into the bed, plunging into her. He powered his cock over and over. His grunts and groans fueled her lust. Her core tightened. Another orgasm loomed in the distance, within reach, his cock rubbing over a spot inside her that had her toes curling with every drive.

"I want you to come again, Sweetness. I want to feel your sweet cunt come all over me." She squeezed her inner muscles around his cock, and he groaned.

"Oh God!" She closed her eyes, the build up to her orgasm almost painful. Every muscle in his body flexed with each lunge. Her sex clenched, clutching his cock. She exploded into another mind-blowing climax. Her orgasm radiated out to every limb as he continued to chase his own, pounding into her with a fury.

"I'm going to come. Oh fuck, I'm going to come so hard. Open your eyes. Watch me. I want you to see what you do to me, Sweetness. Fuck!" He went ridged, his head thrown back, eyes squeezed shut, his cock pulsing inside her. His brusque sounds of satisfaction rumbled through his chest before he collapsed on top her, breathing heavily.

* * * *

She watched Talon's naked backside flex while he walked into the bathroom and a soft whimper floated from Joey's lips. *Ahhh!* He was amazing. Simply amazing. He made love to her like she was the most desirable, most delectable thing on the planet. This was what her sisters talked about. What sex was supposed to be like.

She'd never felt so alive, so carefree, so happy.

Oh God! She had to tell Laydi, Selena, and Juls. Slipping off the bed, she tiptoed to her bag. She pulled her phone out of the side pocket and tapped a text to Selena and Laydi. One of them would have to call Juls at the clinic.

Joey: *We did IT!*

Selena: *Did what?*

Joey: *IT*

Laydi: *BOOM!* ☺ *I'm calling Juls to let her know.*

Selena: *OMG! Yay! How was it?*

Joey: *Boom is right, Lay!* ☺

Laydi: *Rocked ur world, didn't he?*

Joey: *YES! OMG!*

Laydi: *We need the deets.*

Selena: *Hahaha!*

Joey: *I'll call u later.*

Laydi: *LOL-u better*

"What're you doing?" She startled from Talon's voice behind her, his head peeking over her shoulder. She pressed the phone to her chest in an effort to hide the text messages. "Rocked your world, did I?" He chuckled softly.

"Oh, God. How embarrassing." Her face heated. Did texting her friends after the most amazing sex of her life seem childish? She worried her inexperience would make her laughable in his eyes, eventually he'd realize he wanted someone more sophisticated and skilled in bed.

"Can I do it again?" He pressed little kisses along her neck, rubbing his calloused hands over her arms.

"Do what?" She moaned despite her confusion. The feel of his lips on her caused a new wave of desire. He slid his hands around her waist and glided up her belly to cup her breasts. Her head fell against his shoulder.

Then again, maybe he could teach her everything she'd ever need to know.

"Rock your world?" he whispered in her ear, sending a surge of heat to her core.

She nodded, unable to speak.

"Tell your sisters goodnight, Sweetness. You can chat with them tomorrow. Tonight, you're mine."

Joey: *He saw our texts. OMG. I have to go.*

Laydi: *LOL – Go get him, tiger. Grrr!*

Selena: *U lucky dog!*

Joey: *Night. Luv u.*

She shut her phone off despite the vibrations of continued texts. She couldn't stop her smile, and tossed the phone on top of her bag. Talon flung her over his shoulder, and she yelped.

"What are you doing?" She fidgeted around and he slapped her backside. "Ow."

"I'm going to rock your world in the shower, Joey. And then, on the counter. And then, maybe in the bathtub. And then, on the bed again."

He carried her into the bathroom and deposited her in the tiled shower under the steamy hot water. She gasped in surprise, but he took advantage and sealed his mouth over hers. She melted into him yet again.

Chapter Six

Girl Code #5: All big moments should be celebrated with dancing.

Talon woke to the grumble of his stomach. It churned in hunger and rightfully so. He and Joey had been at one another for a couple of hours—moving their lovemaking from the shower to the stripped bed—until they passed out from sheer exhaustion. A smile cracked his face. Opening his eyes to little slits, darkness filled his room except for a slight glimmer of moonlight.

What the hell time was it anyway? He glanced over at the clock on his nightstand. *Shit!* No wonder his stomach growled. It was almost eight-thirty. They'd slept about an hour after the sex marathon. He'd have this grin plastered to his face for days to come.

He'd been a little nervous. Certainly not because of lack of experience with a woman. He knew how to please, how to make her come undone multiple times before he went after his own.

Joey was different. Not overly experienced, which was perfectly fine by him. That fact made him happy. He wanted to be her experience. This time was different. He'd fucked in the past, but there'd never been an emotional connection. He'd never made love with a woman. Uh-huh, he was in love with Joey. It was so obvious to him now.

He had wanted to cherish her, and yet, fuck her brains out at the same time. He couldn't be overly aggressive, but he needed it clear—she turned him inside out with desire, he craved her.

As it turned out, Josephine was a fox in the bedroom. No swearing—which he'd work on because he'd love to hear her with a dirty mouth behind closed doors—but she caressed, licked, sucked, and bit every part of him. Relishing and pleasuring him as much as he had her.

She curled into him, her head resting on his chest, legs tangled with his. She sighed and squeezed him tight. He'd trade everything he owned to wake up with her in his arms, in his bed, every day for the rest of his life.

"You awake?" His fingers skimmed over the soft skin of her upper arm.

"Hm-mmh." She tilted her head and pressed a soft kiss under his jaw. "How could anyone stay asleep with your stomach growling?" He laughed.

"I didn't think you heard it." Lifting his head, he pressed his lips against hers, and her lush mouth softened. Tender lashes of his tongue, then he penetrated her mouth.

Despite the multiple orgasms, his cock swelled again. Fucking-A, he wanted her. All of her. Her body. Her mind. Her soul. Her heart. God, he wanted her fucking heart.

"I might be a little hungry, too. We did skip dinner."

"I found the substitute to dinner to be quite satisfying." Even in the darkness, he could see her cheeks redden. Her innocence and embarrassment was adorable and an incredible turn on.

"Knock it off." She swatted his arm. "How about I get up and whip us up something to eat." Her fingers glided over his chest and arm, giving him goose bumps.

Grabbing her hand, he brought it to his mouth, and kissed the back of it, then each fingertip.

"Sweetness, I want you to know today was amazing. Incredible. You're amazing. Holy Mother of God, I don't know how to say what it is I'm trying to say. I've never done this before." His stomach flipped. He inhaled and released the breath before he continued, "What I'm trying to say is this isn't some one night stand to me. For the first time in my life, I have a sense of peace when I'm around you. It's like the world righted itself."

She brushed the side of his face. "Aw. Talon. I feel the same way. We have some similarities in our pasts. We understand each other. We balance each other."

"You're a safe place for me, Joey. I've never had a safe place. I've never felt like I could talk so openly to someone, or that I didn't have to resolve all my problems with my fists. The weight of the guilt feels less." He was glad for the darkness. His eyes burned with tears.

"Oh, Talon. I know you carry a great amount of guilt around. I know your dad's death weighs heavy on you, but you didn't kill him."

"I didn't run his car into the tree, but I did push him to get behind the wheel. And the worst part is when the cops came to the house to tell us he had been in an accident and hadn't survived, I didn't feel bad. You know what I felt? Relief. I felt fucking relieved he was gone. No more yelling. No more hitting my mother. No more fights. I was relieved." A strangled, wounded animal moan escaped, and his tears fell.

"Oh, baby. I'm so sorry." Joey wrapped around him, pulling him tight. He enveloped her in his arms, holding her as if she were his lifeline as he sobbed.

He had no idea how long they'd remained like that. She pressed little kisses on his shoulder and the side of his neck, whispering sweet words of understanding. God, he fucking loved her. Loved so much his heart overflowed.

Pulling back from their tight embrace, he looked at her. The moonlight provided a soft glow.

"Josephine, I'm so in love with you I can't fucking see straight. I love you. I fucking love you so much."

She gasped, her eyes wide as saucers. Leaning forward, he kissed her forehead, her nose, her lips.

"There. I've said it. You don't have to say anything in return. I've been wanting to say it for so long now. I've never been in love. I've never been so consumed with someone, wanting to spend all my time with them. But, Sweetness, you have me wrapped around your little finger. There isn't a single thing I won't do for you."

Her eyes glistened. "I love you, too." The words came out in such a soft whisper, he almost didn't hear them. But he did. He never felt more alive— happier in his entire life as he did in that moment. Sliding over her, he poised himself above her, his hips between her legs, keeping his weight off her by resting on his forearms.

"I love you, Josephine Lockhart, and I plan to prove it to you every single day." Lowering his head, he kissed her, smashing his lips hard onto hers.

* * * *

The tangy scent of stewed tomatoes wafted down the hallway from the kitchen. Talon's stomach roared at the smell. Another round of lovemaking pushed dinner to after nine o'clock. Not that he was complaining.

Florida Georgia Line's, *This is How We Roll* blared on his little kitchen radio. Sauntering up quietly, he leaned against the doorway.

Wearing nothing but his T-shirt and his boxers, Joey stood at the stove, dancing and singing to the music, periodically stirring whatever cooked in the large pot. Her hips swayed to the beat, her damp hair flowing down her back in waves. Belting out the last verse of the song, she did a little jig in her spot, and spun.

"Oh, God!" she screamed.

He laughed. "Carry on, Sweetness. I'm enjoying the show."

"Darn you. You scared the heck out of me and now I'm so embarrassed." Her neck and face turned a deep red. He strode over to her, slipped his hands around her waist, and rested them on her belly. He pulled her back against his bare chest.

"I think you're fucking adorable. Will I get a show like this every day we have sex? Because, girl, you got moves." He kissed the top of her head.

"Stop it." She swatted him. "Or I'll hit you with this wooden spoon." She lifted the spoon out of the pot to emphasize her point.

"You promise?" He laughed. "I'm not opposed to kink."

"Talon Manness!" Her blush deepened again.

"Okay. Okay. What're you making?" He leaned over to see tomatoes simmering in the pot and pasta bubbling in boiling water in another. An empty box of spaghetti sat on the counter next to the stove.

"What's it look like, smart ass?" She bumped her hips backward into him.

"Keep doing that, Joey, and we'll never eat tonight."

"Fiend."

"It's not me. It's you."

"Me?" She giggled.

"Yes." He tilted her head and kissed her hard on the mouth. "You." His cell phone rang with the familiar tone for his mother. He kissed the top of her head before separating to grab his phone from the table. "Mom."

"T-bird. I need your help. Mom fell and I'm having trouble getting her off the ground." Jarrod's words slurred through the phone. *Jesus Christ.* Was he drunk again?

"What do you mean, she fell? Is she all right?"

Alarm filled him. If Jarrod was drunk, had he done something to his mother in a fit of anger? Mom didn't have any issues with falling. For the love of God, she was only in her mid-fifties and in excellent health.

"I don't know how she did it. I was in the other room and I heard a crash. When I came in the kitchen, she was on the floor. She says her hip hurts. Just get down here and help me. You might have to take her to the ER."

"I'll be right there." Talon disconnected the call and tossed his phone on the table with a sigh. Thankfully, his mother's house sat a half mile down the road.

"What's wrong?" Joey turned from the stove.

"Jarrod said Mom fell in the kitchen and he's having trouble getting her up. He sounds a bit shit-faced, so I need to check it out." So many thoughts rolled through his head. He didn't think Jarrod would harm their mother. In his own way, he loved her as much as Talon did, but if he was drunk, it could have been an accident.

"Go. Go make sure everything is ok. I'll stay here and finish dinner. It'll be ready when you get back."

"Come with me." The idea of leaving Joey alone in his house niggled him. After the threatening texts, he didn't want her out of his sight—not even for a minute, but his need for her with him was even deeper than that. She settled him. Her presence calmed his mind. But he needed to check on his mother. He'd never be able to live with himself if he didn't. Maybe she had fallen. Maybe Jarrod told the truth.

"Go on. I'll be fine here. Go check it out. If you need to take her to the ER, swing back here and I'll go with you."

"I want you to come with me. I don't want you staying here by yourself. Not with the stalker still on the loose." He heard the desperation in his voice and hoped it was enough to convince her to come with him.

"I promise I'll be okay. I'll lock all the doors. You're less than five minutes away. Hopefully, everything is okay with your mom, and we'll be eating this delicious pasta dinner in less than fifteen minutes." She smiled, but her reassurance didn't make him feel any better.

"I'd really prefer you come with me."

"I'd prefer if you'd let me finish dinner so you can tend to your mom. I'd only be in the way." Pushing to her tiptoes, she kissed him softly. "Go!"

"You're a stubborn pain in my backside." He kissed her forehead. "I'll be back as soon as possible, and I'm checking all the locks before I leave. Don't you dare leave this house while I'm gone. Understand?"

She nodded and saluted him. *Smart ass.*

He chuckled.

"I'm serious, Josephine. You stay put. I'll have my phone on me. You call me instantly if you need me." He hustled out of the kitchen and down the hall to his room to pull on a shirt.

Cutting through the kitchen again, he kissed her, and slipped out the side door to the garage. He jumped in his truck, turned the key and it roared to life. He hoped his mother was okay and the fall wasn't serious. He didn't know what he'd do if anything ever happened to her, or what he'd do to Jarrod if he had anything to do with it.

* * * *

Stirring the tomatoes, Joey's mind wandered. She hoped Mrs. Manness was okay. The concern on Talon's face bothered her. She knew what he thought. Had

Jarrod done something to their mother? The thought sent a chill through her. Jarrod wasn't stable—least of all when he drank. He carried a lot of anger and it came out in many different ways—mostly directed at Talon.

She switched the burner off and carried the pot full of pasta over to the sink to drain. Steam rose, misting her face. She jostled the colander, trying to shift the pasta around and drain the water.

A loud vibration sounded from the table. She went still. She recognized the sound. Maybe it was Talon with an update on his mom. Or maybe her mother with an update on Daddy. It didn't have to be the stalker, but a chill roamed over her. She walked to the table, lifted her phone, and pressed the button.

Oh God! An unknown number floated over the screen, and panic seeped into her. She was alone in the house.

Ur all alone. I warned u to leave.

She gasped and dropped the phone on the table with a clatter. He was here. Whoever he was knew she was here and alone. Her hands trembled as she looked around Talon's kitchen. Rushing to the door that led to the garage, she twisted the lock. Talon had said he'd locked the other doors. She exhaled a small breath of relief at the thought that they couldn't get inside.

"He said he was going to take my key away, but he didn't." A deep voice sounded from the kitchen doorway and she went still. Goosebumps rose all over her. He was inside. She recognized the voice.

"Jarrod." She cocked her head, trying to make sense of what was happening. What was Jarrod doing here? Hadn't he just called Talon to help with their mom? His bloodshot eyes glared at her with some dark emotion that looked like animosity. His hair lay wild on his head. He looked like he'd been rung through the wringer.

In some ways, he resembled Talon. His nose. The structure of his mouth. But his eyes were sinister—nothing like Talon's.

"What're you doing here?"

"I'm here to ask you to leave. And if you won't go willingly, I'll make you leave."

She inhaled sharply. The loathing in his voice scared her. Jarrod stepped through the doorway and into the kitchen. She retreated against the door. He snickered at her withdrawal and the blood in her veins turned ice cold.

Something was wrong with him—like he'd lost his mind.

"So you're the person who's been texting me? Following me?" She focused on him between scanning the kitchen, looking for something, anything she could use to assist her in getting out of here or disabling him. With her hands behind her, she unlocked the garage door and grasped the handle.

"Isn't that obvious?" Sarcasm dripped from his rough voice.

"But why?" She twisted the handle. If she could get out, maybe she could run down the dirt road to Mrs. Manness's house. It was only a half a mile away. Jarrod was under the influence. Surely, she could outrun him.

He ran his fingers through his already unruly hair. "Talon's a prick. Always has been. I can't fucking stand him. He thinks because he doesn't touch alcohol he is somehow better than me. Better than our father. He's just a fucking pussy who somehow always seems to find a way to get what he wants. The business. This house. Our mother's love. My friends. The ladies. Now you. It's fucking unfair. I see the way he is with you. Happy. Smiling. Laughing. If he thinks you've left him, that you don't want to be in a relationship with him, it will break him."

His words slurred, but they were hard. It broke her heart to see how much animosity Jarrod had for the brother who did everything he could to take care of him and put him back on his feet every time he fell.

"I've already told him I do want to be in a relationship with him, Jarrod. He'd know it was a lie, that my disappearance was forced. He'd come after me."

"If he can't find you, then eventually he'll give up. Trust me. It runs through his head right now you're too good for him. You leaving isn't so far-fetched."

"Talon loves you. Why would you do this to him? He wants to have a good relationship with you. He just struggles with the fact you chose to follow in your dad's footsteps." Her grasp on the door tightened. She'd have to move quickly.

"My father was a decent man. He taught me how to survive in this world." He stepped toward her, staggering a little. He caught his footing and moved forward. "Don't think about it, darling. Don't think you'll escape out the door. It'll only make things worse for you."

This was her chance while he was slightly off balance. She yanked the door open and had one foot on the step when his fist snatched her hair and jerked her to a stop. *Fuck.* Her feet came out beneath her. He hauled her by the hair through the door, then slammed it.

"Ow! Jarrod, that hurts." Tears stung her eyes, but she refused to let them fall. Even in all her father's drunken outbursts, he'd never laid a hand on her. She'd never been manhandled, and it frightened her, but she wouldn't let him know.

"I told you not to do it. I knew you were stubborn, but seriously, Joey, I don't want to hurt you. I just want you gone." Wrapping her hair around his hand, he jerked.

"Stand up." He raised his voice, and she cringed.

She scrambled to her feet, anything to keep him from pulling out a patch of her hair or snapping her neck, even if by accident. Her heart pounded. She faced him. A fine sheen of sweat formed on her skin. What was she going to do now?

His eyes bulged and his lips curled with irritation. God, what was he going to do? Kidnap her?

Breathe. She inhaled, counting to four in her head, then pushed the air out her nose in a four-count exhale. She had already attempted to flee and that hadn't worked. If she didn't calm down so she could think clearly, she'd work herself into a panic, and that wouldn't help matters.

"Did you hurt your mother, Jarrod?" Risky to ask. It could easily provoke him—anything could.

"Ha! I'd never hurt my mother even if she does love Talon more than me, but I knew Talon would leave you in an instant and unprotected if I told him our mother was hurt." Relief washed over Joey. Thank God for small favors.

A glance at the clock told her Talon had been gone less than five minutes. It shouldn't take him too long to figure out his brother tricked him. She had to stall. Keep him talking until Talon got back. She couldn't let him take her from the house.

"You're just a fuck to him, but I'm sure you've figured that out."

"What're you going to do with me?" Her neck ached from the awkward angle of his grip on her hair. She rubbed her neck, trying to relieve some of the soreness, but he grabbed her hand and twisted her arm behind her. She grimaced at the sharp pain.

"That's a great question." He stepped forward, pushing his body against hers until he had her pinned against the door. A chill swept over her.

The sourness of his breath hit her, and she winced. He reeked of alcohol and something acrid, like vomit. Her stomach roiled.

"You know he had a new girl here every weekend since Dad died? Every weekend. He screwed his way through much of Manatee County. Lots of angry women walking around these parts. He thought he was so fucked up no one would ever really love him. He gave up on getting married, starting a family. All that shit. Then you walk into his life and there hasn't been another girl showing her face around here in months. He's got a bounce in his step and a fucking smile on his face all the god damned time. I can't have that. I can't have him getting his cake and eating it, too. He doesn't deserve any better than me. He doesn't deserve you."

She recoiled at his closeness. He'd definitely puked at some point—the scent permeated his clothes—and he apparently washed his mouth out with whiskey.

"Why don't you think you can be happy, too?" She tried to turn her head in an effort to avoid his rank breath, but he tightened his grip. A mocking laugh spurt from his lips, and her stomach turned from his smell.

"Happiness doesn't happen for us Manness men."

"That's not true, Jarrod. But it doesn't just happen. You have to strive for it. Want it."

He cocked his head and stared at her for a moment, taking in her words or what he could understand of them. "Shut the fuck up!"

"You don't want to do this. You don't want to hurt me. You don't want to hurt your brother."

"You know nothing about me," he snarled. "For once in my life, I want to take something that means something to him. Let him see how it feels." He took a breath.

Her breath stalled. *Oh God.* She closed her eyes to catch her breath. The smell of burnt tomatoes tickled her nose. She'd forgotten about dinner.

"If you won't leave willingly, I'll force you. Drop you off in the middle of the swamp or something. I don't know. I haven't figured it out yet. All I know is you just can't stay, Joey."

Her heart pounded. She couldn't get in a car with him. He was drunk. They'd end up wrapped around a tree like his father. Could she convince him she'd leave on her own?

"Okay, Jarrod. I'll go." His gaze snapped to hers, assessing. "If you'll just let me go, I'll get in my car and drive away from here—never come back."

"How can I believe you? You'd say anything now." Distrust and insecurity laced his voice.

Movement in the kitchen doorway caught her attention. Talon loomed, his finger over his lips. Relief filled her, but so did dread. His eyes narrowed on his brother's hand in her hair, his jaw tightened, and his fists clenched. He morphed into the fighter she knew he'd always been. His survival mode. Though she knew this, she'd never really seen it. He'd kept this part of him concealed around her, but the look in his eyes told her he'd kill Jarrod. His chest expanded with each breath.

She had to disarm Jarrod on her own to keep the brothers from tearing each other apart—literally.

"Talon." She said his name loud, staring at him. His face scrunched in disbelief. He stood immobile, but saying his name made Jarrod twist his head, distracting him. With all her might, she pushed him in the chest with one hand.

Losing a bit of his footing, Jarrod stepped back enough for her to bring her knee up into his groin—hard.

"Arrgh!" Jarrod's hold on her slipped and he doubled over and fell to his knees. Talon rushed in, pushing his brother face down on the floor. He gripped his hands behind his back. Jarrod squealed like a pig being hog-tied.

"The police are on their way. I called them as soon as I found my mother sipping tea on the back lanai and Jarrod nowhere to be found. Did he hurt you?" His gaze roamed over her with concern and trepidation. The anger in his expression softened. Harsh breaths surged from his lips.

"No." Joey leaned against the wall, trying to catch her breath.

"If he hurt you, I'll kill him." He pushed a knee into his brother's back. "You fucking asshole! How the hell did I end up with such an asshole for a brother?" he asked, voice cracked with emotion. He wrenched Jarrod's hands.

"Get off me, mother fucker." Jarrod struggled on the ground, but with Talon's knee, he wasn't going anywhere. "Get off me!" Jarrod squirmed again.

"I'm not moving, dickhead. Not until the police get here." As if on cue, sirens blared outside and driveway gravel crunched under tires. Car doors slammed and feet thumped down the hallway toward the kitchen.

"Police!" A young sheriff deputy rounded the corner and entered the kitchen, his gun pointing at the Manness brothers.

"He's all yours," Talon said, raising his hands in surrender. "He's my older brother, Jarrod Manness. He's been threatening my girlfriend."

"I don't think he meant to hurt me." Joey said softly, but her tone was firm.

"Are you kidding me?" Talon looked at her like she'd grown a second head. One of the deputies clicked cuffs on Jarrod's hands.

Talon lifted himself off his brother. In two long strides, he had his arms around her, squeezing her to him with such force, she thought he'd crush her. "I saw you pinned against the door. I heard him say he was going to take you away. Don't be kind to him, Josephine."

Jarrod resisted being brought to his feet by the two deputies, but eventually stood. He hung his head, his body slumping against one of the officers.

"Tal, he doesn't need to be locked up in jail. He needs rehab and counseling. He grew up in the same house as you, getting punched and degraded by your dad. He just chose to deal with it differently than you." She ran her fingers over his cheek. "I don't want to make his life worse."

"Worse? Your heart is too kind. Jesus Christ. When I realized what my brother was up to, I couldn't get here fast enough. It's such a short distance, and yet it felt like it took forever. I kept thinking I played right into his hands. What if he had taken you out of the house and into the woods? Or tried to drive with you in the condition he was in? I can't even think about it." He brushed his lips across her forehead. His embrace tightened around her.

"But he didn't. I wasn't going to let him bring me anywhere. He's messed up. I agree with that. But let's get him help. Sending him to jail isn't going to straighten him out. It'll just make him angrier. Can't we try to get him in a program for alcoholics?"

"He's going to jail tonight, Josephine." He narrowed his gaze on her, his brows drawing down allowing his scar to bisect his eyebrow.

"Talon! Jarrod! Oh, God!" Vicky Manness rushed into the kitchen. Her auburn hair disheveled, her hazel eyes wide with concern, she looked from Talon to Jarrod and back again. Her khaki shorts and navy blue blouse laid wrinkled over her, making her look frazzled. Joey's heart broke a little more. She couldn't imagine how Mrs. Manness felt, seeing her two sons shattered and tearing each other apart all the time.

"Mom! Relax." Talon released his grip on Joey, but left his arm around her shoulders as he pulled her toward his mother.

"What have you done now, Jarrod Michael?" Mrs. Manness' voice pitched as she stood in front of Jarrod, hands on her hips, lips drawn tight. "We can't keep doing this."

Jarrod's head bobbed a couple times before he lifted it and made eye contact with his mother.

"I'm sorry, Momma." His eyes filled with tears.

Her stern expression softened.

"Jarrod, I love you, but your self-destruction is killing me. I can't watch you do this anymore. It's so reminiscent of your father it breaks my heart."

A tear escaped and ran down Jarrod's cheek. Like a true mother, a sympathetic smile pulled at her lips. She brushed the tear away and cupped his face.

"Oh, baby! Let's get you some help." She kissed his cheek. "Where are you taking him?" she asked, turning to the deputy.

"The sheriff's department off three oh one. He can sweat things out in the drunk tank. If the young lady wants to press charges, he could be in there longer as he awaits arraignment."

All eyes turned to Joey, including Jarrod's.

"I'm not going to press charges. You all have been through enough, but I do think you need to get him into a program. You need help, Jarrod. All this anger and hatred is going to eat you alive."

"I'll come down and get him in the morning. Let him sober up." Mrs. Manness pressed a kiss to his cheek before the two deputies carried him out.

"Joey, I'm so sorry." Talon gripped her shoulders and stared down at her. "He did this to you because of me—because of his hatred for me."

"Talon." His mother walked over and put a hand on his arm. "Don't beat yourself up. You did nothing wrong. A lot of this is my fault. Your father treated you both horribly and I didn't stop it. Now, look at both of you. Ripping each other to shreds, physically and emotionally." She pressed a kiss to his cheek. "I'm going to go talk to the police before they take off with Jarrod. I'll be right back." She walked out of the kitchen, leaving them alone.

"Your mother is right. You haven't done anything wrong. From the day you walked into my life, you've done everything right." Lifting on her tiptoes, she pressed a chaste kiss to his lips. Her fingers fisted his shirt.

"Do you really think rehab will help, Jarrod? What if he gets out and just winds up back on the bottle?" His shoulders slumped. His posture screamed defeat. It broke her heart.

"All we can do is try." She stroked his cheek, his jawline. "Juls is going through rehab now. It's working for her. I talked to her today. She sounded amazing. And look what alcohol has done to my dad. He's falling apart physically. We need to give Jarrod an opportunity. Otherwise, we may lose him completely." He closed his eyes at those words and his chest expanded with his breath. Now that the anger at Jarrod subsided, fear and worry lined his eyes. Her thumb glided over his bottom lip.

"We need to have hope. Hope we can get your brother the help he needs. Hope you will forgive your father and brother for their mistakes. And most importantly, hope you will forgive yourself. It's so hard to watch you suffer under the weight of something that wasn't your fault."

Tears filled his eyes. "I love you." He enveloped her in his arms, his body shaking with a sob. "God, I love you." He pressed kisses to the top of her head. "I was so scared. Afraid I'd be too late. I can get through anything with you by my side, Joey, but I can't imagine my life without you now."

"I'm not going anywhere." She laid her cheek on his chest and hugged him around the waist. She felt the vibration of his heart pounding.

"You've given me the greatest gift, Sweetness. I never had it before you." He cupped her face and kissed her hard on the lips.

"What's that?" she whispered.

Pulling back from the kiss, his eyes filled with emotion. "You've given me hope. Hope for a future. Hope someday you'll be my wife and we'll have this amazing brood of kids that will be as warm, and loving, and spunky as their mother."

Oh, God! Did he say wife? She may only be twenty-five years old, but just thinking about marrying him, becoming his wife had her heart filling with joy. So. Much. Joy.

She dreamed of being a wife and having a family—being the kind of mother she wished her mother had been. She started to believe those things wouldn't be possible—perhaps growing up an only child in an alcoholic home made her incapable of loving someone in that way—or worse, made her unlovable. But she loved him so much, and he loved her.

"I have those same hopes."

"You do?" He gave a small grin, eyes lit with excitement.

She loved the look on his face and she loved even more she put it there.

"I'll marry you any day of the week, Talon Manness."

"Tomorrow?"

She burst out laughing, and so did he, before he pulled her into his embrace again and held tight.

"I'm going to marry you, Sweetness. I promise you. When I said you were stuck with me, I meant it." With his thumb and forefinger, he tilted her head to look at him.

"I have hope." Pushing on her tiptoes, she kissed him with every ounce of hope she held until his stomach grumbled loudly. She pulled back and laughed. "I think dinner is ruined. You aren't going to eat *me*, are you?"

"Mmmm. That actually sounds delicious." His eyes danced with mischief and his voice roughened.

"You fiend."

"It's not me. It's you." He chuckled.

"Me?" Her voice rose.

"Yes. You." He pulled her into a hug and squeezed her tightly. "Let's clean this place up and I'll order a pizza."

"Perfect." She rose on her toes and kissed him again.

Epilogue

Girl Code #1: Friends will guide and support each other in all endeavors.

Eight days later...

The hospital machines beeped in a constant rhythm. Joey thought for sure she'd never get the *beep, beep* out of her head. God, she hated hospitals. Despised them. The sounds of coughing, sniffling, and gurgling. Antiseptic, bleach, and the indescribable stench of illness. Being here made her restless.

Her father lay completely still in bed, his hands resting at his sides. With pale skin and sunken eyes, he looked almost skeletal. His dark brown hair stood on end like he'd stuck his finger in a socket. A bandage on the side of his head covered the thirty stitches he'd received after lacerating his head on the side of the curio chest when he fell in a drunken stupor.

Joey shook her head. The head injury was the least of his worries. The doctors had told her last night his organs were at risk for shutting down. His liver was decimated. His heart struggled under the stress. His kidneys worked sluggishly due to an infection. He'd drunk himself into a broken body at only fifty-five. He'd been warned. The weeks leading up to his fall filled with doctor appointments and warnings to stop the drinking because his liver couldn't handle much more. Now, he lay in a hospital bed.

Her iPhone buzzed in her pocket. Pulling it out, Joey breathed a sigh of relief at the sight of Laydi's name. She'd only been back in Pearl, Ohio for less than twelve hours, but visiting her hometown always brought a swirl of memories—some good, some not so good.

"Lay."

"Hey, Girlie. How's the old man?" Laydi's voice laced with concern.

"Not good. He's not conscious. They have him heavily sedated. His body may shut down. They're administering antibiotics to help with the kidney infection and are hoping to wake him this afternoon." Joey's voice cracked. "He whacked his head good in the fall. They want to check his cognitive function."

"Oh, sweetie! I'm so sorry."

"I know you are." Joey stood and stretched. She'd been sitting in the chair watching over her father for the last several hours. A two and a half hour flight in a cramped airplane to then sit in an uncomfortable hospital chair wreaked havoc on her.

"Where's your mom?"

"She went home to sleep. She needed the break. She'd been at the grocery store when he fell, so she found him passed out and bleeding in the dining room next to the curio chest. Scared the bejesus out of her. I haven't been to the house yet, but I imagine there's a mess there. He'd never come home that drunk and not throw a drunken tantrum. I'm sure there's all sorts of things strewn about."

"How are you holding up?"

"I'm okay." Her eyes filled with tears and she cleared her throat.

"Joey, it's okay. It's me you're talking to. You don't have to pretend to be the strong one."

A sob burst free, and she walked out of the room and down the hall to a small alcove.

"Lay, I want to shake him or slap him. I'm so angry. After all these years, Jack Lockhart still can't pull himself together, even after the doctors told him he was killing himself.

"Then there's this side of me that wants to crawl into the bed and curl up beside him like I did when I was a little girl. No matter what, he's still my daddy and it kills me to see him like this."

"I know. I wish I were there with you."

"I do, too." She wiped her tears with the back of her hand. Laydi and the girls had always been her foundation. Knowing she could rely on her sisters for support made facing this situation with Dad bearable. They'd never let her fall on her face.

"How'd things go with Talon's brother? I know you said he was entering a program."

"I think things may work out for all of them. At least I hope so. Jarrod seemed extremely remorseful. It's so sad, Lay. He's lived all these years with so much anger and hatred in him, and all the alcohol in the world wouldn't drown out his pain. They put him in a twelve-week program. The last several days have been rough, especially on their mother, as Jarrod detoxes. I only know about that process because of Juls, but from what I understand, it's rough.

"And Jarrod isn't allowed any visitors until he's through the detox. Talon's mom is beside herself with worry. The hardest part will be getting him to open up and getting all the buried angry out of him. After seeing my dad like this, I don't want Talon to lose anymore. Or Jarrod. Or their mother."

"You've always had a big heart. It's one of the many reasons I love you."

"I love you, too. I should get back to his room. Mom will be back soon to relieve me."

Ducking out of the alcove, she walked back down the hall when she recognized a figure coming off the elevator at the far end. A six-foot tall, leanly muscled man. His baseball cap was turned backward, his dark blue T-shirt clinging to his chest and arms, and his jeans sat low on his hips—walking toward her in long strides. She'd recognize Talon anywhere.

"Oh my God!" She stopped in her tracks, staring at him in disbelief.

"What is it, Joey?" Laydi's voice sounded with alarm on the other end of the phone.

"Talon. He's here. Oh my God! He wasn't supposed to come until this weekend. He's two days early." Her heart lifted at the sight of him. Leaving him yesterday had been difficult. Their relationship was new and they were still trying to figure out exactly how it worked since neither had any real experience in that arena.

He was going through a lot with his brother and helping his mother deal with things, so she understood he needed to stay behind when she'd received the call about her father. To see him here now filled her with so much happiness and relief, tears overflowed her eyes.

"Oh, that! I knew that!" Laydi laughed.

"What? You knew he was coming?" Joey responded, confused.

"Of course. He called me last night to get information on the closest airport, directions to the hospital, what type of clothes he should bring for weather in Ohio in October. He's really a Florida cracker. Ha! He texted me a few minutes ago to tell me he arrived at the hospital. So go to him, Joey. Since we can't be there for you right now, he's filling in. He loves you tons."

Before she could end her conversation with Laydi, Talon reached her and swung her up in his arms. She shrieked, and tears streamed down her face.

"What are you doing here?" She wrapped her arms around his neck.

"I'm not going to let you go through this alone, Sweetness. We're a team. You're helping me with my family shit. Now I'm going to help you through yours." He pressed a kiss to her forehead and she melted into him.

"Hey, guys! Helllloooo!" Laydi's voice squealed from the phone.

"Oh, Lay, I'm so sorry," Joey said into the phone.

Laydi laughed hysterically. "Call me when you get an update on your dad. Shit, call me whenever you want, sweetie. I love you. I feel better knowing Talon's there. Much love."

"I love you, too." Joey disconnected, and slipped her phone back in her pocket. "I can't believe you're here." Her eyes welled with tears she couldn't contain.

"Sweetness, you couldn't possibly think I'd let you do this alone." Talon brushed her hair out of her face and stared down at her with such adoration. He wiped her tears away with this thumbs. "Come here." He squeezed her into him and held her, her tears continuing to fall and wet his shirt.

"What about the shop? Jarrod? You couldn't have possibly straightened everything out by now." She tilted her head up.

"There's nothing more important than being here for you. Mom's taking care of Jarrod. She should get to visit him tomorrow. When I get back, we're going to do some family counseling. The doctors seem to think it would benefit all of us. And I have Trevor covering the shop for me for a few days. I needed to be here. With you." He wiped more tears still falling down her cheeks.

"What's this?" Noticing a bandage on his wrist, she grabbed his arm. "Did you get hurt?" She'd left Florida in such a hurry yesterday afternoon to get up to Ohio to be with her parents. She knew Talon still struggled a bit with his feelings surrounding his brother. When his emotions jumbled, he worked them out physically—mostly hitting his punching bag—but he'd been known to hit other things, and she worried that might be the case.

"I got a tattoo." He smiled at her.

"Really? In just a few short hours you got another tattoo?" A tattoo sleeved his entire left arm and he had a large eagle on his back. Both of which she'd found incredibly sexy, but she couldn't imagine what he'd come up with in the short time she'd been away. What he'd want permanently inked on him in the midst of all the chaos that had been their lives over the last week.

"Let me show you." He peeled the bandage back, revealing a puffy— somewhat scabby—replica of her "hope" tattoo. She inhaled, her fingers covering her mouth that had dropped open. Her eyes filled with tears all over again.

"You got the Zibu Angelic symbol of hope on your wrist."

"I hope you're not mad. Afterward, I wondered if I shouldn't have asked you first since I know it holds a great connection with your sisters, but at that point, it was a little late." He chuckled. "I wanted a connection to you and I couldn't think of anything more perfect than what you brought into my life. Are you mad?"

"Mad? I want to jump your bones right now." She grabbed the back of his head, pushed up to her tiptoes, and smashed her lips against his.

"Jump my bones, eh?" He laughed against her mouth. "I could go for that as well. It has been almost twenty-four hours. That's a long time for me to have to wait to be inside you again. Is there a utility closet nearby?"

Heat rose to her face, and she swatted him. He closed the bandage back over his wrist and chuckled.

"You're the most amazing man I've ever known." She entwined their fingers and pulled him in the direction of Dad's room. "I'm so glad you're here," she said over her shoulder.

"I wouldn't want to be anywhere else." He kissed the top of her head as they walked.

* * * *

Three days later...

"Ms. Lockhart?" A middle-aged man in a white doctor's coat sauntered into Dad's room.

"Yes," she and Mom said at the same time. They both stood from the uncomfortable *faux* leather chairs near Dad's bed. Talon stood behind her, his hands resting on her shoulders—letting her know he supported her.

"It appears the antibiotics are doing their job. The kidneys are not as inflamed as they were four days ago, which will increase their functionality."

Joey released a breath of relief. "Well, that's good news."

It had been the longest four days of her life. Alternating shifts with her mother, she watched her father's body go through the painful process of withdrawal. The shakes, the groans of hurting and nausea, and the constant transfer between pouring in sweat and having the chills. His angry outbursts at the nurses, which sometimes morphed into sobs, to get him a drink, medication, or something to stop the horrible pain. The nursing staff did their best to keep him comfortable, but addiction had its repercussions.

She'd spent every night curled up in Talon's arms, shedding tears over the things she'd witnessed, and then feeling bad because Talon's brother had experienced the same thing. He had to be thinking that, too.

"He still has a hill to climb. His liver isn't functioning at half capacity. The good thing is the liver has this amazing ability to heal itself sometimes—when and if the abuse stops. Once we have him over this kidney infection and we feel confident his cardiac issues are under control, we will need to focus on getting Mr. Lockhart into an alcohol program to assist him with sobriety. That's not an easy task for most alcoholics—staying sober. His next visit to the hospital may not be so lucky."

Joey nodded and tears welled in her eyes. Talon squeezed her shoulders.

"I may be sick, but I still have my hearing, Doctor," Jack Lockhart croaked. A fit of coughs followed.

"The oxygen tube will it make it tough for you to talk, Mr. Lockhart. Your throat is probably dry. But it's good to see you awake again."

"My throat's drier than sandpaper." His hand rubbed his neck.

"I'll have one of the nurses bring you some water." The doctor exited the room to the nurse's station.

"Jack," Joey's mother approached the bed and squeezed her husband's hand.

"Daddy." Joey stood next to her mother.

"Josephine. You're here."

"I am. I've been here for days, Daddy." She gave a small smile. She hadn't seen Dad in almost a year. She'd come home for Thanksgiving the year before and they'd gotten into a fight when he came home from the office Thanksgiving party obliterated. It had broken her heart—again.

"And who's this tattooed boy behind you? I don't know him." Dad craned his neck to get a better look at Talon.

"Daddy, this is my boyfriend, Talon Manness."

Talon stepped forward and extended his hand.

"He's a charmer, Jack." Joey's mom smiled at her.

"It's a pleasure to meet you, sir." Dad reached for Talon's hand and squeezed it briefly. It was clear her father's strength was diminished.

"Are you taking care of my daughter down there in Florida?" he asked gruffly.

"I am, sir," Talon replied. "She means the world to me."

"Are you a drinker?" Dad asked, eyeing Talon.

"No, sir. I don't touch alcohol. My father was an alcoholic and my brother is a recovering one." Talon's voice was strong, but gentle.

"I'm sure she's told you I'm an alcoholic. For the better part of my adult life, alcohol consumed me—still does, by the sounds of my medical reports. I want something better for Josephine than what I've given my wife all these years."

Mom whimpered at his words, leaning forward and placing a gentle kiss on his forehead. "We'll work through it."

Joey flinched at her mother's words. The same words she always used when her father came to apologize to her after some outburst. Joey had to take charge of this situation. Her mother wasn't strong enough, and her father—well, he wasn't in any state to take care of anything.

"Mom, he needs help. We can't work through anything until he gets help. No more excuses. I can't take it anymore. I need you to want him to get better, too. I've talked to the doctors about a few facilities that can help him, but you and I need to be on a united front about this. The doctor doesn't think Daddy will last another bout."

She stared at Dad. Talon laced his fingers with hers, offering her his undying support. "I love you both very much." Her voice cracked with emotion. "But this cycle has gone on long enough. My whole life, in fact. You both need counseling. I don't want to lose either of you, but I can't stand to watch this anymore."

"Josephine," Mom cried. Tears spilled down her cheeks.

"Stop talking about me like I'm dead already," Dad barked.

"I'm talking like this because I don't want you to be dead, Daddy."

"I've already decided to get help, Josephine. I'm not ready to die. This scared me. I want to be able to walk you down the aisle when you get married, to see my grandchildren. It's not going to be easy. I realize. But I have to try. I've still got some life left in me—for Christ's sake, I'm still young. And thank God, because I have a lot of forgiving to ask for." Dad's eyes landed on Mom and they stared at each other in a way she'd never witnessed. Perhaps this incident had frightened them both enough to make some changes. Only time would tell.

"You do have to try, Daddy. If not for yourself, then for Mom and me." She bent and kissed Dad on the forehead. "Let's give them some time."

Pulling Talon's hand, she led him out of the room. "Why don't we go get some dessert across the street at the bakery?"

"Mmmm. Dessert." They entered the empty elevator. Once the doors closed, he backed her against the wall. His fingers tangled in her hair. "I'd like you for dessert." Covering her mouth with his, he kissed her thoroughly with deep, lush licks.

"Okay. Let's skip the bakery," she said against his mouth. Her fingers curled into his hair and she pulled him into her.

"I knew you'd see things my way." He smiled against her mouth. Pulling back, he looked at her, a crooked smile on his face.

"I love you, Joey. I can't believe how lucky I am to have you. You're so beautiful. So strong. So fucking amazing. I can't wait for you to be my wife. "

"Me, too."

"And I hope we have a little girl at some point because I already know what I want to name her."

Her eyes widened with surprise. She always thought guys were afraid of these conversations.

"What?"

"Hope. Hope Josephine Manness."

Her eyes bubbled with tears and one escaped down her cheek.

"I love you, Talon Manness—more than words can ever say." She pressed her lips against his and they stayed like that until the elevator doors opened and let them out into the world.

~The End~

~LIVE~

By

Lea Bronsen

~Dedication~

To Sid. You're *"Something else"*.

Big thanks to D.C., Cait, and Jessica for believing in me and giving me the chance to collaborate with you. Love you girls!

Thanks to Mallory for your insight, deepening each of our stories and the book as a whole.

A bear hug to Jay for the fantastic cover. You are a true gem.

Special thanks to Julie Ann for your support and touching words.

As a French, I want to give my most humble *merci* to the 'Poilus', men of immense heart, for your 1,500,000 lives lost and 1,500,000 wounded and scarred for life during WWI. Each sacrifice for your beloved fatherland, *la patrie*, is inestimable. Dear husbands, fathers, sons, brothers, uncles, and sweethearts: a hundred years later, we still talk about you.

~Lea

Chapter One

Girl Code #12: Your girlfriends' opinions matter more than your family's.

Juls wandered to the back of the bus. Once she found a seat and the engine roared to life, she looked for her diary. No time to waste. Two weeks ago, she went off methadone, going from thirty-five grams to cold turkey. It was crucial to keep her mind busy.

The bus hit the main road and picked up speed while she rummaged in the black duffel bag next to her. It contained all her belongings, those she'd managed to keep from petty thieves and cops at night, and those she'd refrained from trading for dope. A worn sleeping bag, a hoodie, spare underwear, a pair of wool socks, a bottle of water she'd filled in a public bathroom earlier... Yep, that was about it. And her diary. She fished it out, and, from a side pocket, a tiny glue stick.

For a moment, she caressed the notebook's beautiful flower wrap, so soft and shiny it felt like silk underneath her callused skin. A boost of warmth made her heart swell. She loved this wrap. When looking for food in a trash bin outside Walmart last year, she discovered the colorful piece of gift paper and knew it was *the one*. Maybe someone who'd just bought it had second thoughts, deemed it too tacky, whatever—people could be crazy like that—but this particular wrap gave her diary shelter, a home. Within that frame of beauty, she could hide her darkest thoughts and most daring dreams, and forever keep small things she collected through the journey of her life.

She opened the notebook and turned the pages. Calmness washed over her like a hit of something she tried not to think about. The urge to get high was omnipresent. Here, she found a food coupon a super cute guy in a tux handed her on a cold morning by the metro entrance. There, a cigarette paper roll a smoker dropped beneath a bench. On this page, gum wrap, and on the next, a few doodles she'd made while waiting on a doctor appointment. Adorning the second-to-last page, a pink rose petal, just beginning to fade, from a park she'd slept in two days ago.

The kind of evidence an investigator would look for at a crime scene to determine a suspect's doings and whereabouts. Except her diary told the tale of a twenty-four year-old homeless ex-druggie. She'd always kept a secret journal as a kid, but it was after her overdose that she thought important to collect daily proofs of her existence. They reminded her of the life she had to leave behind.

To her 'documentation', she solemnly added the bus ticket, moistened with sweat from the fifteen-minute-wait in her palm before the bus arrived. The paper had crumpled and probably wouldn't adhere to the glue. She would use tape then, and grabbed a small roll kept safely in the inner pocket of her black leather jacket.

After taping the ticket, she found a pen and wrote underneath, *'Ticket to home'*. She looked out the window, but having taken this road once, when leaving at seventeen, she didn't recognize the flat, never-ending farmland scenery.

Home...? Well, what she used to call home in her better days. The city of Pearl, Ohio—a nice and perfectly snobbish community where she grew up, before the call of 'the Concrete, the Steel, and the Needle' became too strong.

Home meant family, too, and, in her case, anonymous dinners with everyone silently staring into their plates, bothered verbal exchanges, and a cold shoulder instead of much-needed hugs. It didn't take abuse to shove a kid out of a family house. Lack of attention and affection could be an equally strong incentive.

Juls wouldn't have travelled back if dear Granny, her warmhearted and unusually tolerant grandmother who treated her more like a daughter than Mom did, hadn't died last week, at age eighty-four.

A sharp rush of hurt burned a path from the pit of her stomach to her throat. But she forced it away, would deal with the inevitable, ruthless grief later, upon arrival at the burial.

The bus followed the curve of the highway, and the sun appeared at her side, heating the window and her leather jacket deliciously. Still, a shiver ran up her spine. Fucking withdrawals. Despite the heat, she'd felt frozen all morning, as if having slept outside mid-winter. But it was late October, and some of the golden field crops had yet to be harvested.

Hand cold and slightly trembling, she placed her pen in the middle of the notebook and patted the warm, velvet-like seat between her and the glass pane. So soft, like the fur of a newborn kitten. Almost too good for someone living on the street.

She wouldn't remain homeless much longer. As soon as Granny's burial was over, she would seize the opportunity to knock on every door until she found a job. And if she didn't succeed, she would try the neighbor towns. Anything and everything to make a little money, make it another day. To no longer be hungry or have to sleep outside.

Turning a few pages back, she found the ones indicating a new chapter in her life. On one side, the word *DRUG* in big, capital letters, filled the entire page, and connected to the word *FREE* on the opposite side.

Yes, she was drug free, for the first time in seven years. A miracle.

Pride filled her chest. She took a deep breath, savoring the sensation of strength and courage. Quitting had been a long, winding road, probably the toughest she'd ever walk in her life, but she made it. Despite the horrible abstinence she suffered every minute of the day since her last dose, she was on track. Determined to stay there, living as a free person, looking ahead, and never returning to the dark nothingness.

She wished she could say her family would be proud of her, too, but doubted they would. It took them a long time to find out about her 'disease'. When she left Pearl to attend high school in Columbus, no one suspected anything about her growing addiction to stimulants—booze, and Mom's valium pills. She lived on campus, and whenever Mom and Dad offered to visit, she managed to hold them off, pretending to be too busy preparing for exams. They didn't insist, undoubtedly happy she gave them a reason not to travel.

Though leaving her dreaded home and starting a new life in high school should have eliminated the need for mental getaway, her abuse spiraled out of control. It had long become a physiological problem—her body's demands constant and unquenchable. One day, an unfortunate mix of chemicals and alcohol sent her into a coma. She died in a speeding ambulance, before being brought back to life minutes later by a team of medics who refused to let her go.

It was only then her parents came to see her at the hospital, bringing along her older brother Connor, and discovered she'd fooled them for two years. "God, what a deception," they whispered to each other by her bedside, believing she couldn't hear them. "What a disgrace."

She'd always been the black sheep, but the news of her drug abuse forever left a stain on the Carrington family, sealing her reputation of the bad child and weak chain link. Had she not been proclaimed clinically dead, her parents would probably have disowned her. That knowledge did little to encourage her to regain control of her life.

In sharp contrast, the image of her three best friends in the world, who called themselves sisters—Laydi, Selena, and Joey—remained burned on her mind. Eyes red-rimmed, holding hands, they sat around her hospital bed and watched over her for as many hours as their busy schedules allowed them. Neither asked questions, but since she'd never had the guts to inform them about her dependence, the news had to have been a shock.

The only person she confided in was Granny, but not until years later, when life had become a complete hell and she needed someone's love and support to avoid a second lethal mistake.

Shortly after the overdose, the principal threw her out of high school. Dad sent money each month so she could rent a room, but she used it on drugs. The money transfers stopped after he found out she was unable to spend it wisely. With nowhere to go, she ended on the street, sleeping alternately between squatted buildings, shelters, parks, and back alleys. Cocaine and quaaludes became a lifestyle, and after some experimenting, heroin. When she didn't have enough money for a daily dose, she would steal it or sell her belongings, one by one—and when too stoned to care, her body. A stranger even seized his chance to rape her 'for free'.

"Well, fuck that!" she exclaimed, anger taking over, and slammed her open palm on top of the seat in front of her.

A few heads turned. Were they wondering who spoke such a foul language, and why, had she gone mad? Not that she cared. She was used to ignoring other people's perception of her.

She looked down and whispered to her diary. "Yes, I'm homeless, but I'm clean, and I'm gonna get myself out of the gutter."

She may have done her drug time, experimenting and leading a wild life for years like her punk hero Sid Vicious of the Sex Pistols, but she refused to die young and be destroyed like him. She owned a white shirt with a picture of the black-haired rebel doing his famous smirk. A constant reminder of the fate awaiting if she fell back into bad habits.

Her brother Connor once asked, disdain lathering his voice, "Why are you a fan of a junkie from the seventies who couldn't even play his instrument? Aren't there enough contemporary bands to choose from?"

To that, she replied, chin in the air, "He was the only true punk rocker." Sid invented the outrageous, larger-than-life punk lifestyle, and with his attire and extreme behavior and opinions, adhered one-hundred-percent to every aspect of it. He was the *embodiment* of his generation's cultural revolution.

She wore Sid's shirt today. Of course, she would have preferred to dress better for Granny's burial, but didn't have much of a choice since she owned only four shirts and this one was the least worn. The three others were folded in her bag. One from the cult movie *The Shining*, with a demented Jack Nicholson pressing his snarling face through a hole he'd hatched into a door; one with *Eddie*, the iconic man-sized puppet walking the stage during Iron Maiden concerts; and an inappropriate black singlet that revealed too much cleavage.

"Hey, Sid," she murmured, picking up the pen and scribbling his name in capital letters underneath the bus ticket. "I remain a dissident. I curse the fucked-up world my parents' generation is leaving us, I really do, I swear it to you. But I deserve to live. I deserve to be happy. Like you did, too, poor fool. Why the hell did you have to—"

A lump built in her throat and tears rushed to her eyes. It wasn't his fault that he died. He wasn't a bad person. He was a disillusioned kid who could no longer stand reality. Just like her.

Swallowing hard, she drew a heart around his name. He didn't die for nothing. Thanks to him and all the others who overdosed as the years passed, and *for* them, she would continue to live.

The catalyst for her getting clean was a video conversation with her sisters two weeks ago, when she borrowed a kind nurse's office at the methadone clinic. Seeing the three beautiful, sane women she loved so much on a big computer screen and listening to them chat about their lives opened her eyes to the reality of her own ruined one and probably saved it. The following night, alone, freezing, and exhausted under the concrete underpass of a bridge, she decided to quit for good.

She owed Joey, Selena, and Laydi more than they would ever understand.

* * * *

"Mom's gonna kill you." Connor glowered as Juls sat in the passenger seat of his shiny gray Fusion Hybrid and closed the soundless door.

The interior reeked of leather and detergent, and with all the lit buttons on the dashboard panel, the car looked like a NASA aircraft bound for space. Not bad for a thirty-year-old accountant.

"I missed the ceremony because of you." Connor leaned toward her and offered his cheek in a semblance of a hug, though not so close their skin touched.

Maybe she smelled of the street, her clothes gave a too-filthy impression, or he was afraid she'd pass on some viral disease. Knowing him, he was probably embarrassed after their lengthy separation. Six years her senior, he was supposed to take care of his baby sister in the face of their parents' coldness, but had failed, never standing up for her when she was lonely. Once she overdosed, he visited the hospital *one time* during her recovery.

Why didn't he ask how she was doing?

He'd grown big, barely fitting into his dark gray tux, and like his body, his voice had thickened. A prematurely receding hairline made him look older than his years.

"I'm sorry." She sighed and fastened her seat belt. "There was an accident. Took them forty-five minutes to clear the road."

"Couldn't you have caught an earlier bus, just in case?" He started the engine and pulled out of the parking lot, his movements strangely energetic for the meek, characterless man she recalled from the past. Now he was practically a stranger. "All that time I had to wait for you at the bus station. You can imagine what Mom and Dad are thinking."

As if she needed to be reminded. She frowned and stifled a groan of irritation. "I said I'm sorry. There aren't many buses to Pearl."

He drove in silence, although he glanced at her a few times as if intending to speak before he refocused on the road.

What did he think of her? And what did he see? A skinny girl with pale, dirty skin and shoulder-length dark brown hair, black eyeliner intensifying her rebel attitude? That's how someone who gave her a dollar bill last week described her. The man probably pitied her, and she loathed begging more than anything, but his money provided enough food for that day.

Connor stopped at a red light and turned to her again. "You haven't changed."

"No?" Surprised, she lifted her brows. She *had* changed, she'd become a totally different person. Couldn't he see? In just two weeks, she'd gained a little weight, and the kind woman who found her asleep slumped against the post office door yesterday said her skin looked healthier.

He shrugged, as if unable to notice the difference.

"I've quit," she declared.

"You have?" He gave her a once-over, but his facial expression remained the same. Neutral.

"Yeah. For good."

"Amazing, if true." He didn't seem to believe her.

"It is, I promise." There'd been broken promises before, but this time, she would not fail.

He sent a nod to her shirt. "You gonna wear this at the ceremony?"

Bah. Ignoring the slight hint of contempt in his voice, she looked ahead. The street light had changed. "It's green."

"Shit." He bit his lip and pressed the gas pedal, propelling the car forward. After a moment, he glanced at her chest again. "Sid Vicious." He huffed. "I can't believe it. You were born what, twelve or so years after his death? How can you still—"

"C'mon, you know I've always loved his music... And his political opinions are still actual." She gazed out her window, squinted from the blinding sunlight, and smiled. The sun's warm, generous caress on her face was in perfect symbiosis with her feelings. You didn't lose a teenage love with a snap of your fingers.

Connor chuckled, looking ahead again. "You're aware he killed his girlfriend, right?"

That stupid, old argument. She frowned. "There was no evidence at all. Besides, the guy was too stoned on Tuinal to hurt anyone. According to a police report, he had to practically have been in a coma."

To that, Connor shot her a sideways glance full of accusation.

He must be thinking about her overdose, but, being the non-confrontational type, he didn't dare bring it up. It was okay. This one time, she didn't mind his lack of integrity and will power. Not only was she uncomfortable discussing anything drug-related with someone unfamiliar with the subject, it was crucial she stayed positive-minded, left the past behind, and focused on the future. *Her* future.

At a corner down the street, an enamored couple leaned against a wall, enlaced as one, kissing. Just like Sid and Nancy once did. Her vision fogging, she swallowed a lump in her throat. It wasn't jealousy, she'd never cared for crushing on a guy, but Sid's happiness touched a chord inside. "Plus he was in love with her. I refuse to believe he was able to stab her."

Connor grimaced and shook his head at the same time, making his fat cheeks wobble like a bulldog's. "Pfft. You're naïve."

The stone church loomed ahead. Almost there. She sucked in a breath. Soon, she'd have to face her entire family, after what seemed like a lifetime of separation. Death, too, because she'd been on the other side. As cold and lifeless as the person she was about to bury.

Her chest constricted, and she held the inhaled air for as long as she could. Grief lurked, waited to jump out from deep within and devastate her, reveal her mental and emotional fragility. Slowly exhaling to appease her dread, she prayed she would be strong.

Connor pulled into the parking lot and braked, tires screeching. About eight hundred feet from the church, on the green cemetery, a group of people dressed in black looked up.

She bit her lip. Stiff from tension, she climbed out of the car, grabbed her bag in the passenger seat, and headed toward the gathering. Instead of walking next to her, Connor stayed a few feet ahead. Thankful, she focused on his back and worked up the nerve until reaching the deep, rectangular hole with a wooden coffin at the bottom.

Hey, Granny.

Beneath the coffin top laid the sole family member who'd really cared for her. A wonderful human being, as goodhearted and generous as they came, all shrunken and wrinkled, but beautiful nonetheless. Granny had always had time for Juls, a shoulder to cry on, attentive ears, words of encouragement. She'd kept the gates to her heart wide-open even in the most tumultuous and shameful moments of Juls' life. Granny had *loved* her.

Juls' stomach knotted like a wrung-out towel and her throat dried. She tried to swallow, but couldn't.

Around the gaping wound of dirt in the grass stood Dad, Mom, distant relatives, friends of Granny's, and a few neighbors. Solemn, with their hands crossed and eyes lowered, pretending to mourn. They wore a mask, for none cared about the ageing woman, seldom visited her as the years went by and she deteriorated, alone in her center of town apartment. Even Dad, her only child, deemed his free time more important to spend at a shooting club massacring live pigeons or hunting wild boars in the bush with his stupid pals than checking on his mother.

When Granny took her last breath, no one held her hand. Not a single soul was aware she passed. Not even Juls, too busy crawling out of her misery.

Eyes blurry, Juls stopped a few feet from the grave and studied the line of attendants. In turn, they gazed up in her direction before quickly looking down again. Even elegant, poised Mom and Dad avoided her.

Must be her worn leather jacket. Sid smirking at them. Her unruly black hair, dirty skin, sunken eyes. Or just the fact that they hadn't seen her in seven years. Well, except from her parents and her sisters, no one did much to stay in touch. Neither did she, but she'd been too wasted to care.

In all fairness, she was the one who left Pearl, so she couldn't expect them to run after her. And she'd exchanged her cell phone for a week's worth of dope early on, making it impossible for anyone to reach her—she was the one calling from pay phones here and there in town, during short lapses of sobriety.

One after the other, starting with Dad, they threw a flower on top of the coffin or a handful of dirt.

While waiting for her turn, Juls stood in line next to Connor. The sun heated her black leather jacket without mercy. Unlike earlier, in the bus, the methadone withdrawals made her boil inside. Sweating, needing air, she removed the jacket and carried it over her arm, revealing the scarred tissue of repetitive punctures in her veins. Just like a self-cutting teenager she'd met once baring the grotesque scars on his arm, Juls didn't mind that proof of her 'disease' was in plain sight.

When it was her turn to step forward, her chest lifted and she sobbed. Every month or so, she'd spent a few bucks collected with difficulty to call her favorite person in the world, always promising to clean up, and, of course, to come visit. That last thing, though, she never did. Maybe in a desperate attempt to save her granddaughter, Granny had offered that she stay with her, but Juls politely declined: she simply couldn't burden an old woman with having a drug addict in her apartment.

Granny's grayish, limpid eyes appeared in her mind. Drooping. Was she sad, disappointed? Did she lose faith in her little Juliette? What a cruel way to die: lonely and deceived.

Wrong. Granny was the one blood relation who loved her sincerely and would never lose faith.

"I'm clean n-now, Granny," Juls murmured. She knelt in reverence before the grave, dug into the freshly upturned earth with her trembling fingers, and threw some on top of the coffin. Tiny pebbles hitting wood echoed in the grave. Hot tears spilled over the rims of her eyes and flowed down her cheeks, burning like acid. She sobbed and fought for control, but her throat was so constricted she could barely speak another word. "I'm c-clean, like I p-promised."

Only it was too late now, wasn't it? Granny was gone and she'd never know Juls kept her promise, suffering a torturous withdrawal hell.

As if reading her mind, she went from burning hot to freezing, turning the sweat on her skin to a thin, chilly layer. She shivered.

* * * *

After the burial, Mom and Dad invited everyone to a reception at their house. Juls stood alone in the parking lot, leather jacket over her arm and duffel bag at her feet, watching cars fill with people. Doors slammed, and a long convoy left. Connor offered to drive a couple of neighbors who'd arrived to the ceremony with Mom and Dad, so the back seat of their polished black Bentley was empty.

Now what? If she wanted to attend the reception, she had to go with her parents. She could choose to turn her back to them and walk in the other direction, to the town center, once more leaving them and everything they represented behind. Luxury, vanity, and their miserable personal traits.

Dad held Mom's door while she sat in the passenger seat, then circled the car and hesitated at the driver's side. Hand on the handle, he sent Juls a sideways glance. "Need a ride?"

She took in his strong build and chiseled, square face, the lawyer's typical sharp eyes gleaming.

Did she travel all the way from Columbus only to attend Granny's burial, or would she seize the opportunity to make peace with her parents, too? If they saw the new type of person she'd become, they might respect her. If she left without giving them the chance, she'd never know if it was worth trying or not.

Damn, the hesitation. With a short nod, she walked the few steps that separated them, opened the back door, and threw her large bag onto the seat.

Dad started the car and sped out of the parking lot, gravel spraying, the sudden speed forcing Juls against her seat. Something irritated him, but knowing him, it was likely something other than his mother's death.

It's my presence.

Mom sat immobile with her short, brown hair, woolly cardigan, and nails impeccable as always. A fine representative of the rich suburb of Pearl. As Dad joined the convoy ahead, she turned to Juls and gazed at her. Dark diamond-rimmed sunglasses concealed her eyes.

Juls had always hated talking to someone whose eyes she couldn't read. A person's look said everything, and not being able to study their "window of truth" made her feel cheated, as though they weren't playing by the rules.

That familiar stare. What was Mom concocting? She and Dad often spoke with subtle irony, that, whenever asked, they called "gentle teasing among educated, worldly people". It may be a common way of conversing in their inner circles, but Juls had never tolerated their condescending tone, and Connor's self-esteem had suffered greatly under their criticism.

"Juliette," Mom asked, voice seemingly neutral, "where are you sleeping tonight?"

Juls held her breath, wasn't sure what was the smartest answer. Why had she not anticipated this question?

Mom gave an exaggerated sigh. "You don't know?"

Before Juls had time to think, Dad's voice rose. "We don't want a junky in the house."

What? His words punched the air out of her lungs, and for a couple lengthy seconds, her heart seemed to stop beating.

Mom turned to him, mouth agape.

He nodded. "Obviously, we have to accept that you attend the reception, or else we'd make scandal. That's the last thing we want. With your outrageous addiction and lifestyle over the past years, our reputation is tarnished enough. But once this is over, you'll have to leave."

In disbelief, Juls gazed at him in the rear view mirror.

Mom stared at him, too.

After a theatrical silence, he met Juls' look in the mirror, eyes hard and spiteful. "You heard me."

She swallowed to keep the pain in her throat down, didn't want him to see how deeply he hurt her.

He was wrong, the asshole. Drugs were no longer a part of her. She was going to beat them and win. Taking on her most confident attitude, she straightened, inflated her chest, and delivered the most important statement of her life with as much pride as she could muster. "I'm not using anymore."

He didn't answer. Mom turned to look out her side window.

"You heard me?" Juls insisted. "I've quit."

Dad finally muttered, voice almost a growl, "I don't believe you."

Oh! His distrust stung, as though a knife bored into her chest. She gritted her teeth. "You know I've been on methadone for two years, right, so I would stop using the other stuff? Well, I've quit that, too, now, and I'll never use again."

"Not possible."

Fuck him, the bastard. But she'd heard his words before. On the street, in cafés, at the metro restroom, even in her doctor's office. People who refused to believe in miracles. And like them, Dad was wrong. The whole world seemed to think she was a helpless case, doomed to die at a young age like Sid. They were wrong, and with the unconditional support of her sisters, she would show everyone else, prove she had it in her to live.

Stronger and more determined than ever, she tossed her hair back and raised her voice. "I don't care what you believe."

In the passenger seat, Mom gasped loud.

Juls was glad to have struck a chord and looked from one to the other. "I know what I'm doing."

Dad huffed. "A junkie will always be a junkie."

"Juliette," Mom whispered. "For God's sake, your father's a lawyer. He's seen so many cases. He should know."

Something exploded inside Juls' head, blinded her. Fists clenched, she bent forward with her face between their seats and sneered, "Go to hell."

Another gasp escaped Mom, and she put a shaking hand over her mouth.

Dad sent Juls a hard look in the rear view mirror. "We've been there all right, your Mom and I, and back, a few times. Thanks to you."

Oh, the nerve. Juls was two seconds from punching the back of his seat so his head would be projected forward, but refrained. Instead, she took a few deep, calming breaths and stared at his reflection, drilling a hole into him with her eyes.

He held her look.

She wanted to sneer, 'I spit on you,' and 'I've always hated you,' but that wouldn't help. Nothing would.

He returned his attention to the road ahead.

It hit her. The bastards' opinion didn't matter. She wasn't detoxing for them or anyone else. No, she was making a new, drug-free life. Because she deserved that much. She deserved to live and be happy—become a normal person.

* * * *

Feeling moody, Juls went down the large, winding stairs to the first floor. She'd kept to herself during the reception, spent the whole two hours trying to doze in her old bedroom turned office. Following Mom and Dad's attitude in the car, she preferred to stay away from them so as not to "offend" anyone by her presence.

Besides, her body itched as if a million ants roamed beneath her skin, and, despite the air conditioning, sweat prickled and ran down her temples, from her armpits, between her breasts… Fighting the abstinence wore her out, but each minute was a small victory.

It didn't help that she hadn't eaten anything since last night—a half sandwich fished out of a trash bin in the park, with the owner's tooth marks still on it. Her stomach growled.

At the bottom of the stairs, Mom straightened a large medieval painting on the wall that someone must have moved accidentally. *Oh, the crime.* Her black ankle-length dress sparkled in the hall light from a multitude of shiny paillettes. The woman knew how to combine grief and elegance. As if that were necessary.

Juls floundered down the last steps with an inward snort of disdain and bent to put her bag on the floor, with her leather jacket folded on top.

"There you are." Mom turned to scrutinize her, cool brown eyes giving a once-over. Her nose twitched. "When is the last time you had a shower?"

Fuck, the same tone as when Juls was a teen. Not much had changed in seven years.

Juls shrugged, couldn't remember. Three, four days ago, maybe? Going slightly crazy from the itching, she passed Mom and walked through the family house, or the palace, as she liked to call it. She may have grown up in this luxurious mansion, spent a number of years here, but felt as out of place as before. Luxury wasn't meant for her. She'd fled it, and all that entailed. The fancy dinners, the posh friends whose lives revolved around owning more expensive things than their neighbors, the hypocritical laughs and exaggerated compliments…

"Juliette," Mom said behind her. "Even if you don't live here, you may use our bathroom."

How generous. Scratching her arms, Juls passed the closed kitchen door and went to the living room.

Mom followed, her high-heels clonking on the hardwood floor. Juls imagined the fifty-something year-old woman's large hips swaying, and snorted.

Dad and Connor sat in ornamented armchairs with their chins up, backs straight, and legs crossed like a couple of royals, probably chatting about the usual bullshit and making it sound important. Their well-kept hair glistened. They didn't bother to look at her or Mom. The same indifference and coolness as ever.

Behind them, large windows offered a unique view of the vast, neatly trimmed green garden bathing in sunlight, and in the distance, a patch of sparkling blue.

The pond. Happy memories. Four girls singing and dancing. When she was seven, she ran into Joey and Laydi one summer afternoon as they sat underneath a tree chatting. They were one year older, but accepted her as one of theirs. Selena joined, too, and soon the pond became a safe haven where the foursome met to seek and give advice, lift each other's spirits, and nurture sisterly love.

Intense warmth rushed through Juls, sending her brain a tiny spark of euphoria, much like the one a first hit of crack used to provoke. She couldn't wait to go through the garden to her childhood place of solace and rejoice, young and innocent again.

As soon as I get out of here.

Then, after immersing in the past for an hour or two, she would move on and work to achieve her top priority—getting a job.

But first, she had to say goodbye to Mom, Dad, and Connor. Though everything about them pissed her off, her conscience warned not to walk out of their lives without leaving them something. What exactly, good or bad, she had yet to figure out.

The two men picked up their meaningless chatting while she continued on to the open terrace. Her stomach gnarled and her treacherous lungs took deep breaths against her will. She couldn't help it: cooking smells sneaked from underneath the kitchen door and seemed to follow her, crawling along the floor like a lustful snake before reaching the terrace and swirling up in the air, a dancing fume of temptation teasing her nostrils.

Fuck. She didn't know what Mom planned for dinner. She never did as a child, either, never permitted to assist or even watch that egoistical woman at work, not once, but with a smell like that, it had to be a dish of wonder. Meat and cooked vegetables and gravy and… A third growl escaped her belly, as if a starved beast were locked inside, chewing at her intestines.

But no, she wasn't going to stay, couldn't eat with them. There was too much between them, too much and too little at the same time. All of it, the blacks and whites with a palette of grays in the middle, the extremes and their opposites. How to put it into words?

In fairness, she'd never been abused or physically hurt. It wasn't a house of violence, unlike the one of an alcoholic neighbor whose son, Reef, kept making excuses for his cuts and bruises. No wonder the kid became a drunk and left at sixteen, when Juls was ten. She didn't have much to complain about, in comparison—never starved or lacked anything material in Mom and Dad's household—but still, staying here was impossible.

At a loss for what to do or say before leaving, she sucked in a breath, slowly swirled, and went back inside the living room.

Mom waited with her hands on her hips, eyeing her. "Go have a shower. Dinner's in a half hour."

Juls frowned. How could a mother treat her twenty-four-year-old daughter like a little girl?

Mom's disdainful gaze went from Juls' shirt to her holed jeans. "Do you need clothes?"

"No." Juls wanted to reply she would never need anything from her again, but held back. She wouldn't sink to Mom's level of spite.

Was Mom going to add the usual, 'So you can cover that horrible tattoo?' This time, she didn't. Maybe she knew her daughter no longer listened, no longer cared.

Juls passed her annoying mother and the heavenly smelling kitchen, picked up her bag, and continued on to the bathroom at the end of the hall.

Mom was dreaming if she thought Juls was staying another minute. Instead, she would take a swim in the pond and wash there. Wasn't that an excellent idea? Then, leave this residential area.

With the bathroom door locked behind her, she opened a tall cupboard, scanned the contents, and located supplies on the bottom shelf. Shampoo, soap, toothpaste, and two rolls of toilet paper went into her bag. Sanitary pads and an old box of tampons that surely Mom didn't need anymore.

She glanced at the row of deluxe beige and brown fluffy towels hanging from metal bars on the white-tiled wall. She could almost smell their flowery scent. Damn, taking one was tempting, but that would be too much, it would be stealing. The other items were just cheap supplies in comparison that Mom would have given her if she'd asked. But an expensive towel?

Juls was done stealing. Possibly today, definitely tomorrow, she would find a job, make her own money, and never, ever need to steal again.

She zipped her bag and stood to study her reflection in the mirror. Bleary, hazel eyes that had seen enough for a lifetime could use a little make-up. Except from the cheap eyeliner, she'd never afforded any. The first thing she wanted to buy with her *own* pay was a deep red lipstick that'd make her lips full, wet, and sexy.

She'd never been attractive in her entire life. The few boys who'd screwed her did when she was desperate for dope, and, thankfully, too baked to remember.

Damn, her whole body itched from within, as if lice travelled up and down her veins. Nothing she could do about it.

Connor's voice sounded in the hall. Then the front door opened and closed. Was he going to have a smoke? His sole crime, albeit minor, the only thing he dared do against Mom and Dad's will. What courage such a challenge must cost him.

Time to go. Juls put on her jacket, picked up her bag, and went out of the bathroom.

Mom stood halfway in the now-open kitchen door, studying her nails. "So, are you ready for dinner?"

Regarding her maybe a last time, Juls pulled the bag over her shoulder and sighed. "I'm gonna go. I'm gonna find myself a job and a place to stay."

"You?" Voice higher-pitched, Mom looked up with eyes full of laughter. "You're joking. No one in their right mind wants to hire a drug addict."

Oh, the bitch, she hit where it hurt most.

Before Juls could react, Dad jumped out of his armchair and eagerly, like wildlife on the prowl, joined Mom at her side. "What's going on?"

Cackling as if having heard the funniest joke, Mom tilted her head toward him. "Your daughter wants to find work."

He rolled his eyes.

Throat tightening, Juls looked down in an effort to conceal her disappointment and bit her lower lip. This was precisely what drove her away seven years ago. The beast had several names. Superficiality. Indifference. Worse, even: rotten fucking contempt.

All the contrary of love.

Juls drew a profound breath and said with a croak, "When I said I kicked the drugs earlier, I forgot to point out I was doing it for me, not for you."

Dad grunted.

She waited a beat to gather more strength, looked up, and stared at them, holding their self-pretentious and self-sufficient gazes. She wanted to say something that'd crush them forever, and then she would turn on her heel and never come back.

Mom opened her mouth, but Juls interrupted her, voice hard. "Did you ever ask yourself why I left?"

From the sudden shine in Mom's eyes and Dad's pursing of his lips, the question stung.

Bingo. Juls nodded and spun, leaving them behind with their load of dirt to handle.

* * * *

Juls opened the front door and had to blink from the sharp, blinding sunlight that blocked her view of the street. Sucking in a breath, she adjusted the bag on her shoulder and stepped out.

This was it—freedom. She slowly breathed out and refilled her lungs with warm air smelling of flowers, green grass, autumn heat…and yes, cigarette smoke.

A blurry shape waited at the bottom of the stone stairs. She squinted to focus and took another step on the porch.

Connor. A half cigarette in hand, he busied himself digging holes in the red gravel with the toe of his shoe. Always the kid, so subdued he never really became a man. When the door closed behind her with a *clank*, he looked up, eyes flickering with the usual nervousness and low self-esteem.

Juls snorted. "Mom's gonna kill you for that."

His eyes widened. "For what?"

Laughing, she nodded her chin to the traces in the gravel, uprooted dirt mixed with the small, red pebbles.

He shrugged as if pretending not to care, but his face took on a redder hue than the ground. After sending a glance up to the house to search the windows, he pulled clean pebbles over the holes with his shoe and evened the surface, eliminating the evidence of his crime.

She disliked him. The feeling in her gut wasn't hatred, but distaste. Connor had always been weak, daddy's little dog that would comply and obey, never dare speak up or argue. It wasn't his fault. He was born weak. Fragility repulsed her. Though to be fair, she'd had her share of that vice commanding her every decision in the past years, along with a disappointing lack of will power, loss of initiative, and self-loathing.

She dreaded saying goodbye. Moving to Columbus, she left her twenty-three-year-old brother behind, too. Left him to deal with Mom and Dad alone, since he didn't have enough initiative to get his own place. It couldn't have been easy for him. At least, when she was home, she spoke up and argued for both of them, even if he was six years older. The poor boy didn't have to say a word. Fighting for herself included fighting for him.

Well, she couldn't stand up for him anymore. She had her own battle, every goddamn second of her life.

With his free hand, he pulled a thick wad of dollar bills from his pocket and handed it to her.

What the hell was that about? Was he teasing her, or pitying her?

"C'mon, take it," he said, the look of sincerity in his gaze seemingly genuine, and took a drag from his cigarette.

Why help her? Was he trying to make up for their lost years as siblings, especially the ones when he let his baby sister addict slowly die, alone, in the gutter?

But the temptation. Imagine all the stuff she could buy with that money. Not to mention, enough drug supplies for the rest of her life. The old, diabolical craving roamed at the bottom of her stomach, worse tenfold than the hunger raiding her bowels. With the bills Connor wiggled in front of her nose, she'd satisfy that need in a matter of minutes. The need to surf high, to escape, to forget.

No—she grimaced and almost slapped her forehead—she was no longer a druggie, but a responsible twenty-four-year-old looking for a way to support her decision to get her life on track.

Swallowing hard to keep the carnivorous urge down in the pit of her stomach, she shook her head. "I'm not a beggar."

He lifted his brows and chin in a slightly condescending way—Mom and Dad's way—as if to say that she, the poor, helpless junkie, should know better than refuse the gift of a wealthy and generous man. He waited a beat, regarding her, then with a nod, insisted. "Take it."

Did the douchebag think he could buy his way to respect, from her or anyone else? He was the worst loser. Her past might not be something to boast about, but at least, today, she could keep her head up.

She held his look, clenching her teeth before releasing the tension in her jaw. "No. I want to make my own. But thanks."

His brow lifted, then he feigned not to care, eyelids half-lowered over his pupils. But it obviously bothered him she refused his 'alms', and that alone gave her a sweet boost of pride.

"Well." She shifted her weight from one foot to another. It was time to say goodbye, but she didn't know how to without hurting him. She might despise him, but she'd never want to hurt him.

"Where are you going now?" he asked.

"Getting myself a job."

He gave an exaggerated sigh, the kind Mom did earlier, as if this conversation weighed on him. "Can I at least drive you somewhere? I hate seeing you walk around like this"—he threw her clothes a glance of disdain—"in the neighborhood."

Oh, he'd just given her an excuse to leave. What a prick. She laughed whole-heartedly, throwing her head back, and savored how the laugh released her inner tension and guilt.

"What's so funny?" he asked, brows furrowing.

"You sound like dear Mom and Dad. What a nice boy you are." Shoulders dancing, bad mood alleviated, she swiveled and walked away from the house. The gravel crunched underneath her sneakers.

Bye, Connor. Have a good one.

As soon as she could sit by the pond, she'd write these very words into her diary…and begin the journey of her new life.

Chapter Two

Girl Code #15: No matter when a girlfriend calls, you pick up the phone.

The long, dark blue pond twined like a gigantic snake tail, the end out of view from Juls. Flat and blank, the surface reflected white dots of clouds in the azure sky like a mirror. Now and then, bugs landed on the still water, leaving miniature circles in their paths. A carpet of fresh, green grass flanked the shore, as did white-barked trees and pine trees with patches of copper-colored earth at their feet. If not for sporadic quacks from the other side of the pond and a few bird chirps up in the trees, pure silence would reign.

Juls dropped her duffel bag on the hard dirt ground, tilted her face to the burning sun, and closed her eyes. Focusing on the peaceful surroundings, she drew deep, calming breaths of forest air, and several scents filled her lungs—a sour-sweet mix of algae, mud, fungus, grass, leaves, pine needles...

How long since she last visited? It had to be seven years, when her sisters threw Selena a going-away party before she left for Andrews Air Force Base in Maryland. An unforgettable day. As countless times before, they met at their secret place of solace, bringing snacks, drinks, and a portable CD player, and partied until late after the crimson sun descended behind treetops.

What made the occasion even more special was Juls convincing the sisters to seal their forever bond with symbolic tattoos. In spite of her young age, she'd already secretly had hers done a week earlier—three black birds flapping their wings on her wrist—partly to eternize her desire for freedom, and partly to provoke Mom and Dad, knowing they would hate it when they found out. They judged tattoos to 'make people look dirty and cheap'.

After think-tanking and throwing around ideas for a few hours, the other girls opted for Zibu angelic symbols imprinted on different parts of their bodies. The quiet and reserved, yet spunky Joey chose *hope*. The guarded, sincere, and loyal Selena *faith*, and the sassy, no-bullshit, and charmingly blunt Laydi *persistence*— each tattoo representing their respective personalities.

Juls sighed. Not only did she love and miss them, she felt terrible for not staying in touch as much as would have been natural for a sisterhood. The girls called often after she moved to Columbus, but since she traded her cell phone early on, they lost the means to connect with her. Later, she used pay phones once in a sparse while, but had neither the bucks nor the mental strength to hold lengthy conversations.

Her chest hurt. She'd failed them. The same way she neglected Granny over the years, she spent more time nursing her drug habit than caring for her sisters. Surely, there must have been times when they needed someone to talk to, weren't able to contact the others, and wished Juls wasn't so fucking selfish, unreachable.

Ugh, some friend I am.

To think they were the most wonderful, loveable, selfless women in the world. Despite being one year her senior, they were her biggest supporters, usually within reach—when *she* wanted them to be, mind you—and never with a harsh word. Of course, they worried about her addiction, but didn't voice their concerns too loud, as if afraid to vex her and provoke further distancing.

She wished they had. Maybe if they'd scolded her, shaken her, told their honest opinions and feelings, even threatened to dump their friendship, she would have quit earlier. But putting the blame on someone else was so typical, wasn't it, when the responsibility of her actions was hers.

Eyes sore, she gazed at the pond. She had lost a good chunk of her life and nearly lost her loyal friends in the process. Time to wash—not just her body, but her past and her conscience.

Though it was an Indian Summer day and the intense sunshine had to have heated the calm, blue surface, it was October, too cold to have a swim. But who cared about temperature? Perpetually homeless, Juls was used to adjusting and tolerating, sometimes gritting her teeth for hours on end in the biting cold, making sure to stay moving to survive another night.

A few of the street brothers she'd met in Columbus had died of hyperthermia in their sleep, too drunk or drugged to be aware. Stiff, livid bodies found in the early morning hours curled under a bench in the park, behind dumpsters, or on the steps of a back-alley door. If only someone had cared to look out for them…

A lump grew in her throat, as if she'd swallowed a too-large chunk of food. She took another deep breath to suppress the pain from her memories.

Look forward, always. The past is the past.

No one was in sight, so she didn't need to worry about her nudity. She took off her sneakers and socks and stripped off her clothes. After folding them neatly inside her bag—being a bum didn't mean she didn't care for her belongings—she grabbed the bottle of shampoo and piece of soap. The coat of grass, needles, and bark prickled her bare feet as she walked to the pond bank.

She dipped a toe into the limpid water and shivers went up her leg. It was as cool as she'd feared, but she braced and continued as fast as possible, her legs making small circular waves, until reaching waist-depth. Gasping from the cold shock, she stopped and clenched her hands, nails digging into her palms.

The soft bottom glued to her feet, but she knew where to step. Rumor had it the mud was deeper on the other bank, where children were warned not to play.

With the bottle of shampoo floating beside her, she washed and rubbed her goose-bumped skin red with the foaming soap, over and over, a heavenly scent of lavender filling her nose.

She hesitated at her hardening nipples, then the lips of her sex. Touching herself happened so seldom, once a week at most, it felt strange. Besides, she didn't like her body, couldn't remember anyone ever saying something nice about the way she looked. In her eyes, she was too skinny and child-looking, her figure lacking feminine curves, so why should anyone have a different opinion?

A few handsome guys did cross her path, causing her heart to flutter and her inner thighs to throb with desire. But each time, she gave up on building a relationship. The men were either too busy wasting their lives on drugs, or their behavior revealed abusive, calculative traits she steered clear from, or, being 'perfect', they were already taken. Every failed attempt indicated romance wasn't in the cards for her.

She didn't really mind. Having just jumped off the drug wagon, she had to take care of herself first.

Once her skin and nails looked clean enough, she threw the cube of soap onto the shore and grabbed the plastic bottle floating in the water. She dove below the surface to wet her hair, closing her eyes and holding her breath, then jumped out again with a squeal of delight, splashing water around. A déjà-vu feeling from happy childhood days with her sisters flashed. She could almost hear them squeal and laugh. Smiling from the memory, she washed and rinsed her hair.

So, she had adapted to the cold—how about a swim? She'd always been curious about the dangerous side of the pond, and, now being a responsible adult, she would check out the infamous place. With white bubbles of shampoo dancing in circles around her, she threw the bottle next to the soap on the shore and dove back into the cool water.

In no time, she swam the few hundred feet until her toes touched the bottom.

The soil felt soft, thick, and sticky. Quicksand. The worst danger around here. The kind that, if she applied pressure, would surround her feet and suck forever. And if for some reason she was unable to stay afloat, the quicksand would pull her into its gluing, bottomless entrails, inch by inch swallowing and enveloping her.

She swam closer, pulse beating in her throat from excitement. It was the appeal of danger. The promise of a slow death. Not that she wanted to die, but the rebel in her, the *fuck-everything-and-everyone*, couldn't resist testing how far her luck could be pushed. She'd survived so many dangers. Whatever fate had in store for her would happen anyway. If she wasn't meant to die today, she would live another day. This philosophy and she co-habited for seven years, hour after hour balancing on the fine edge between existence and extinction.

The *craa, craa* of a crow and abrupt flapping of wings sounded in the forest.

Moving her arms in wide circles to keep her head above water, she dipped her big toe into the mud. The swampy soil's reaction was immediate, as if calculated, a monstrous suction wanting more. Quickly, it could become a fight of the stronger. The starved beast at the bottom of the pond, having all the time, patience, and force in the world, against a frail, detoxing human body whose candle had already blown out once.

"Hey, watch out!" a male voice called.

Holy... She nearly jumped out of her skin. Pulse beating at a frantic pace, she ducked until the water covered her breasts...and slowly, methodically, scanned her surroundings.

* * * *

There. On the other side of the pond, about three hundred feet from her bag, a shirtless guy wearing a cap sat on the shore with his back against a tree. Looking at her.

Shit.

He had toned muscles and unusually dark skin for a blue-eyed man, making his clear gaze stand out like flashlights in his bearded face. An outdoors guy. Had he observed her the whole time?

"That place is dangerous!" He pointed a few feet ahead of her. "You don't wanna get your feet stuck."

"Oh, I know," she called back. He wasn't telling her anything new.

"Yeah?" His tone said he didn't believe her. Understandable, with her toe still dipped in the mud.

"Yeah." She pulled her toe out with a silent *pop*.

"How?"

As if she needed to explain. "I used to live here."

"Uh-huh? What's your name?"

Damn, what a busybody. She frowned. What a weird conversation to have with a stranger. Her business was none of his. Shrugging him off, she spun in the water and swam toward her bag.

In the corner of her eye, the guy stood and walked along the shore, in the same direction as she swam.

Fuck. Her heart hammered in her chest. What were his intentions? Did he have the potential to hurt her?

Of course, he was faster. When he reached her bag, she was still fifty feet away.

She slowed, treading the water with her chin lifted. "What do you want?"

"Pretty girls shouldn't be alone in the woods."

Though her instincts warned to be careful, she swam closer and sent him a hard look. It would take more to frighten her. Living on the street, she'd seen it all. She sniggered. "If you're planning on hurting me, I've already been raped front, back, mouth, every orifice you can think of. I'm beyond caring." That should shut him up. Who would want to further damage a wreck?

Except she wasn't a wreck. The rape didn't break her, neither did the amount of chemicals she had absorbed over the years. Nothing could.

Her toes touched hard ground. She moved a little farther, arms flapping, until she could stand on her feet.

He stared at her, clear blue eyes beneath the gray cap scrutinizing and thoughtful. She'd seen eyes like that before, but couldn't place them. He sat next to her bag, his gaze sweeping the grass around him. "Where's your towel?"

She stepped forward until the water sank to chest level. "Don't have one. Now, go away. Leave me alone." If he thought he was in for a nude show, he had to think again.

"What if I don't want to?" Brows lifted in nonchalance, he picked a grass straw and placed it between his white teeth, flashing them to her with a teasing grin. "This is my forest. You'll have to *make* me go away." He used good-natured humor, so he was a teaser, maybe not the kind of guy who'd hurt her.

"Oh, your forest?"

His smile widened.

She shook her head. "At least, *look* away." Covering her breasts with an arm and her pubic area with the free hand, she treaded toward the shore.

He *did* look away—into her duffel bag. "What's this?" Before she could react, his hand dove into the bag, rummaged inside, and brought out her colorful diary.

Oh, no. Her heart made a giant leap. He would discover the most intimate, sacred part of her.

She waded faster, water rushing like small torrents around her waist. Her breath picked up from the efforts.

Grinning again, he waved it in the air. "Bringing Christmas presents to the picnic, are we?"

Fuck him. "Don't touch that!" She stepped closer. The water reached her knees and splashed around.

"What is it?" He opened the first page, feigning deep concentration, then looked up. "What are these things? What're you keeping them for?"

"Stop! It's personal."

His brows lifted. "It is? How interesting." With a chuckle, he stood and took a few steps backward while demonstratively turning page after page.

What an asshole. She hated giving the impression she was desperate, but fuck if she'd allow a perfect stranger to read her diary. Still covering herself, she reached the shore and sprang out of the pond, water running down her naked body in rivulets.

He turned another page and squinted as if unable to see well.

Breathless, she hurried around her open bag and stopped in front of him. He seemed harmless, but she was so pissed and shocked, she could barely speak. "Give—it—to—me!"

He stood a head taller than her and twice her size in width. Limpid blue eyes gleamed beneath the cap. Chewing on his grass straw, he gave her a once-over and grinned. "You want it?"

"Y-yes." Cool water drops prickled from her hair and landed on her skin, sending a shiver up her spine. "F-fuck-head."

Holding her gaze, he closed the notebook with a *bang* and held it out to her.

Oops. In her hurry, she'd forgotten one vital thing. How was she going to take the damn thing when she needed both hands to cover her body?

He smirked. "Problem?"

What options did she have? Walk back to her bag and grab a shirt, or stay put and remove one of her hands? Damn, she hated him, hated the situation he put her in. Why the hell was he bent on teasing her?

His smiling eyes lowered to the diary.

"Fuck you." She sneered, and, exposing her breasts, snatched her more precious possession from his hand.

Before she had time to cover herself again, his gaze shot down and took her in.

Diary in hand, she put her arm across her chest. Her wet fingers would ruin the paper cover, but she preferred *that* to the bastard holding her diary one second longer.

He tilted his head. "What a dirty mouth."

"What a perfect asshole." She glared with all the anger she could summon. "Stop staring."

After a hesitation, he said, voice lower, "With that kinda body, you don't wanna be naked around here."

Oh? She studied him. His mouth made a straight line, and his eyes darkened. The only thing his gaze held was the kind of sadness some of the shelter personnel, those with a real heart, gave her from time to time.

It hit her like a slap in the face. He was seeing the bruises, the scars, the way her ribs showed, her lack of curves. Hurt rushed through her, caused her chest to contract. Even a stranger, unaware of her history, found her ugly.

Fuck that. This guy's reaction was nothing new, nor did it change anything. She didn't need anyone, didn't need to be attractive *for* anyone. Filling her voice with spite, she quipped, "*That kinda body* has been punched, stepped on, kicked at, spat on, broken, screwed senseless. Everything on the menu."

His pinched lips turned white and he tore his eyes from her.

"But what you see, stupid, isn't *me*. It's what they've done to me. Fucking abusers." She turned on her heel and headed to the bag.

"I meant to say you're beautiful," he whispered behind her.

She huffed. Such bullshit, the worst lie…

But his voice sounded sincere, so maybe he wasn't mocking her. Was he trying to be nice, then? And why, was he feeling sorry for her? She didn't need that—not back on the streets of Columbus, not out here in the woods of Pearl.

"That's bull." She knelt beside her bag, slipped the notebook with its crumpled wrap inside, and looked for her clothes.

A faint breeze blew over the pond, creating small waves here, and there. Goosebumps grew on her skin and raised the hairs.

She pulled Sid's shirt over her head, then sat to slide her panties and jeans over her wet and irritatingly sticky legs. Struggling like hell, she huffed and groaned.

"I meant what I said." His voice took on a sharper tone. "And then you can do what you want with that compliment. Take it for what it is, a nice compliment from a nice guy, or you can step on it, spit on it, do whatever those sons of bitches did to you."

She stopped moving. What a *bingo* moment. He'd found the right words to touch her.

"If that makes you feel any better," he added.

She swiveled.

He sat on the grass a few feet behind her and stared at the pond. His build was strong with long, naturally forged muscles. Beneath his cap, the rough skin of his face, licked by the sun, and a week-old beard made him look weathered. If she had to guess, she'd give him thirty years, tops. From the dirt on his brown combat pants and the blackness of his fingertips, he spent more time outdoors, like her, than the rest of Pearl's population.

She had definitely seen his features before. He must have been chubbier at the time, his skin paler, but her past was a blur, a fog, a dark place she refused to revisit, and so he would remain there, unidentified. She needed to move forward. It was the only way. Move forward or whither and die.

Needing to change the subject, she asked, "Where do you live?"

He frowned. "What are you, the police?"

"Just asking."

"Told ya the forest is mine, didn't I? I'm the king of the forest." He gave a short chuckle and eyed her. "You don't sound surprised. Or shocked."

She shrugged. Living outside was nothing new to her.

"And you?" he asked.

"Columbus."

"And?"

What more did he want? Did this stranger think she was going to draw him a picture of her life? She snapped, "And what?"

"That's it? You have nothing to add?"

Damn, he was pushy. Irritation shot to her head. "Like what? You wanna know what streets I sleep on? What trash cans I find my food in? How many times I'm insulted a day? How—"

He lifted a hand. "Stop." The blue in his pupils looked somber, as if storm clouds behind her reflected in his gaze. "I didn't know you were homeless." His Adam's apple went up and down.

Why did he care?

She turned to slide her socks on and grabbed her sneakers.

He sighed. "Well, where're you going? Staying somewhere around here?"

"No." She tied the sneakers.

"So where're you heading?"

Good question. She glanced in the direction of Mom and Dad's house. A chimney peeked between the trees. Her chest tensed, but that part of her life was behind her. The drugs, her family. She would never go back. "I don't know."

"Where're you gonna sleep?"

She shrugged, swept the perimeter around them. Trees, more trees. "I guess I'll find a fallen log to sleep underneath or something. Got a sleeping bag."

The old feeling of being the loneliest person in the world crept underneath her skin. She swallowed. It was hard to be brave. So hard, and her will so fragile. Every minute of the day, she walked a fine, fine edge between the druggie's constant craving and the ex-addict's resolution to live. Not just stay alive, survive from one second to another, but *live*. Lead a decent life. Not the kind of life Mom and Dad had. No, those morons could stick their materialistic shit up their fucking asses.

She looked over at their chimney again, her vision fogging with warm tears. No, what she wanted was a job that'd make her feel valuable, someplace nice and cozy to call home, and food on the table. Every goddamn day.

She took a deep breath, swallowed again to push the old, ruthless pain back.

"That's the place you're escaping?" the guy asked from behind her. He was smart. He had already figured her out.

She raised her shoulders. Now, she was making the decision. Not earlier, when she left the house, refusing her brother's money. Not this morning, when she climbed into the bus and taped the crumpled ticket inside her diary. Not two weeks ago, either, when, trembling with fear for her future, she threw the remaining meth into the toilet and flushed, watched the evil disappear. Watched herself come clean. Then, a few hours later, trembling harder, barfed into the same toilet.

Making resolutions was admirable, but often left the door open for changing one's mind and giving half-believable excuses. She couldn't tell exactly why, yet she was certain of her goal, and nothing would make her budge.

"Wanna eat something?"

The guy's voice snapped her out of her thoughts. Tired, shaking and itching inside, she turned to him.

He stared at her, tense eyes and a deep line in his forehead betraying his concern. Tilting his head a little, he insisted. "You hungry?"

She nodded. As if awoken from a deep sleep, a sharp-toothed beast raged inside her stomach and let out a growl, ready to feast on anything within reach to still its hunger.

She'd go with the stranger. He was trustworthy enough. Then, tomorrow, she'd continue to the other side of the forest, head back onto the streets of Pearl, and get a job for sure. Promise.

* * * *

This guy moved fast in the broad-leaved forest. A few feet behind, Juls did her best to follow, dodging branches, circling tall, moss-covered boulders, and stepping over rotting logs that emanated a sharp smell of fungus. The rustling of fallen leaves on the ground filled the otherwise eerie silence, along with the occasional snaps and cracks of twigs under the weight of their shoes. Strong muscles played in the man's large, tanned back as he walked, his moves swift and graceful. From behind, he looked indigenous in the jungle.

After a few minutes, they arrived to a clearing. Between tall trees stood a small makeshift hut made of aluminum sheets, wooden boards, and tarp. In the middle of the clearing, worn plastic chairs surrounded a fireplace. The flatness and cleanness of the ground indicated he had lived here for some time.

He turned to face her, and splayed his arms. "Home."

She returned his smile.

"You're not disappointed?"

"You're kidding, right?" She rolled her eyes. "Compared to some of the places I've seen, this is a palace."

A large grin spread across his features, making him quite handsome despite his ruggedness.

She slid the heavy bag down her arm onto the ground, rolled her aching shoulders, and knelt to open it. A sudden shiver caused her upper body to jerk. It wasn't the weather. The withdrawals were playing tricks on her temperature again. She pulled her hoodie and black leather jacket out.

He asked, "Are you freezing?"

"Yeah. It's chillier here than—"

"It's the abstinence, isn't it?"

Fuck. She sucked in a breath and looked up.

His head tilted to the side as though he measured her, and his clear blue eyes stared into hers. Demanded the truth.

She groaned. "How did you guess?"

"The punctures on your arms."

Shit. She grimaced. Wherever she went, the past followed. The hundreds of tiny needle holes in her veins screamed, *'Junkie!'* and would continue to reveal her crime, her shame, until the day of her death. A forever liaison, a forever pact, and a forever reminder of the addict she once was.

"It's okay." His tone warmed. "The cops check on us every now and then, but I—"

"I've cleaned up," she hurried to say, relieved that he didn't scorn her.

"I know."

She widened her eyes. How could he know?

"Your scars are old," he explained with a small smile, as if reading her mind. "Cool shirt, by the way."

"What?"

"Sid Vicious." He nodded to her chest. "Cool."

"Oh. Thanks." She couldn't help grinning. She didn't get that kind of compliment often.

"And the tat?"

"You noticed." She turned her wrist and showed him the three black birds. One for her as a little girl, yearning for freedom, one for the teenager, flying away, and one for the future adult, forever free. "The day I got this done, I flew out of my parents' nest."

"I get that."

Their familiarity and easy tone amazed her. It was the same that she experienced on the street, an intuitive fraternity. "What's your name?"

He scratched his beard, slowly, as if to buy time, then sent her a wink. "I'm the Recluse of the Boise Woods."

"No shit."

Another deep shiver rattled her. She slid the hoodie over her head and arms.

"I'll make a fire." He went to the edge of the clearing to pick up some twigs. "It don't matter how many layers of clothes you wear, you'll feel cold as a dead man 'till you don't know what to do with yourself. Then the worst sweat will break out, and you'll be so hot you wish you could shed your own skin. Or hang yourself."

She gawked. Here was someone who knew what she was going through.

"It's an untamable evil," he continued, walking at the edge of the clearing. Small twigs snapped and dead leaves rustled. "Follows you for months, sometimes years."

"H-how are you coping with it?"

"I've been sober for three years, four months and sixteen days. But..." He walked to the fireplace and threw his load of wood onto a pile of black coal. "Look, I've still got the shakes." He held his arms in front of him and turned his palms up. They trembled. "And I can't *think* of alcohol without having that fucking craving inside driving me crazy. It takes a man to be stronger and resist. Every day is a fight with the demons. My demons. The evils inside of me."

She frowned. "You don't look evil to me."

Features tensing, he squatted in front of the twigs and rearranged them. "My old man passed some of it to me. With the beatings he gave me over the years, it was bound to happen."

Her stomach knotted. Many years ago, a similar story had occurred in the neighborhood.

He shot her a glance, his eyes reflecting the blue-grayish light filtering through the trees. "You okay with canned food?"

"What?" His sudden change of subject confused her.

"Canned food, is that all right with you?" He pulled a lighter out from his pants pocket. "That's all I have. Or maybe you prefer some old, musty bread from last week?" He sent her a teasing wink.

"Oh, no, canned is perfect."

"Good." His lips curled in a smile. "Once I get this fire going, we'll make a nice dish and feed that skinny body of yours."

"Thanks." She smiled back, but the words he'd spoken about his father, '*the beatings he gave me over the years*', replayed in her mind.

A new shiver caused her body to shake, this time not from the withdrawals, but the cold air. She slid her leather jacket on and sat on a chair near the fireplace. The old, hard plastic cracked under her weight. "I used to know a boy like you."

Frowning, he gazed at the lighter and rolled its trigger, provoking crackling sparks.

"Funnily enough," she continued, "there were times when I wanted to swap with him. My life was the opposite of his. I was lonely. My parents gave me all the material things I needed, but they cared so little about me, I would've given anything for a little attention."

"Swap?" His brows furrowed deeper and his arm muscles tensed. "Swap what? Your lives?"

"Just for a moment…" Hmm, maybe bringing up this notion was a bad idea.

He shook his head, his thumb rolling the trigger frenetically. "I don't think so. You wouldn't want the kind of attention a drunk bastard gives a child, believe me."

Her throat and cheeks flushed. "I'm sorry. I didn't mean to—"

He gave the trigger a hard roll. A white flame shot out. "It's okay." He gazed at her, eyes shimmering in the low light.

"It's the stupid me talking too fast." God, she hated herself.

"Don't worry about it." He lifted his thumb, killing the flame. "Listen, once we've finished eating, would you like to meet my pals?"

Chapter Three

Girl Code #16: Only a girlfriend has the liberty to question your choice of lover.

By the time Juls and her new friend, if she could call him that much, arrived at a group of huts in the woods, the sun was setting behind trees, streaking the darkening sky with long, red flames.

Glassy, tired eyes, and backs hunched from invisible weights, six men and a woman circled a campfire. A few sparse sunrays filtered through the maze of branches, bathing half of the campers in a warm, reddish light. The other half sat in the shade, yet light from the burning heap of twigs and branches between them flickered on their faces, sharpening their drawn features. Some munched on a cigarette, others passed a cheap bottle of wine around. Crackling and snapping filled the peaceful clearing, and, occasionally, low chatter and the squeaking of hard plastic chairs.

They looked up to acknowledge the visitors, but didn't ask who Juls was. Like the inner-city homeless, these forest campers were probably used to people coming and going, with only a hard core of recluses staying in the camp.

Juls' friend found two vacant chairs and brought them to the circle. As the woman moved aside to make place for one, Juls sat next to her, while he mingled with the guys, two seats farther.

Long, unruly gray hair and a wrinkled, puffy face suggested the woman was in her late fifties, but it was more likely a hard life had aged her prematurely, as it did most women on the street. With that and a black trench coat and pointy boots, she had the kind of look that, centuries ago, would get her burned as a witch in Europe—one of the few things Juls remembered from school.

"Hi." The woman smiled, displaying a row of yellow-brown teeth. "I'm Connie." Her voice sounded hoarse and rusty, the one of a long-time smoker.

Juls smiled back. "I'm Juls."

"Glad to see you. Not many women around here."

Juls nodded. On the streets of Columbus, the female ratio was higher—prostitutes, mostly.

On the opposite side of the fire, a broad-shouldered guy in a khaki army jacket raised his voice. "Sorry, guys. We usually have some food to share, but not tonight."

"It's not our fault, Spur," replied a young guy with blond Rasta braids and a dirty flannel shirt, who sat beside Juls' friend.

Juls frowned. "Don't worry about it. We've already eaten."

Spur glowered at the fire. "There are a few places Alex and I usually go to"—he sent a sideways nod to the braided guy—"but they're on to us now, the cocksuckers."

"They don't want you to have the leftovers, right?"

"Exactly." Alex shook his head, braids swinging on his shoulders. "Two stores poured fucking bleach into their containers last week. Today, a third did."

Grumbling, Spur threw a twig onto the fire. It snapped, a yellowish flame shooting up and illuminating the circle of somber faces. "We have to go farther and farther to find food."

"And to think they throw so much away every day."

"They all do. Restaurants, bakeries…" Connie turned to Juls and squinted. "How do you know about leftovers?"

"Been on the street for some time. I can go *days* without eating."

Connie reached out and stroked Juls' hair, a kind smile softening her traits. The patting gesture was more maternal than anything Mom had ever been capable of. How absolutely tragic, having to discover motherly warmth as an adult, with a hard-living camper in the woods.

"Poor, poor girl," Connie whispered. "And so young."

Enjoying the woman's caress on her back, Juls returned the smile. "Not *poor*. I chose this way of life. But now I've decided enough is enough. I'm gonna earn my bread."

All eyes turned to her. An eerie silence ensued, only disrupted by the crackling fire.

On the other side of Juls, a guy in a big, blue bubble jacket mumbled, "You wanna work?"

"Yeah. I'm sick of depending on others' pity."

"And bad conscience," Spur added.

Juls nodded. "Exactly."

"Good on you." Connie smiled. "No one should—"

Two male voices erupted, and a chuckle. Alex gave Juls' friend a push on his shoulder, destabilizing him. Grinning, the bearded guy regained his balance and effortlessly shoved Alex forward, off his chair, so he fell onto his knees.

"Fuck." Swift like a wild cat, Alex spun, grabbed the guy's arm, and pulled, bringing him down with him beside the fire.

Laughing, a mess of arms and legs, they rolled and wrestled on the hard dirt ground.

"Woo-hoo!" The guy in the bubble jacket cheered. "Bring it on!"

Connie's happy chuckle transmitted to Juls, and she smiled.

After a few rounds of friendly fighting, the bearded guy lost his cap in the commotion, revealing short, blond curls.

Oh...my...fucking...God.

Juls had seen that head before, and from the strange heat and appeasement that washed over her from the childhood memory, he'd been more than an acquaintance. He'd been a friend, someone she trusted.

Reef.

The guy who mischievously coaxed her out of the pond earlier, invited her to his hut, and shared his food, was the pal from when she was a little girl, his features rendered unrecognizable by the cap and dark beard.

She gawked, unable to believe her eyes or understand his agenda. Why the hell didn't that damn fool tell her?

He got to his feet again with the cap in hand, glanced at her, caught her staring, and flashed a white-toothed grin that nearly melted her insides.

Shit. Her cheeks heated. She hoped no one would notice.

Alex jokingly bumped into his back. "One-O to Alex."

"Ha, get off." Laughing, Reef maneuvered away from him, sent Juls a wink, and steered back to his chair.

After both men sat, silence descended upon the camp. Since Juls last looked into the sky, the red streaks of cloud had turned black. A lonely owl tooted somewhere in the forest.

"So." Connie turned to Juls. "What brings you here, sweetheart?"

Juls wasn't sure how to reply. People had many reasons to become homeless. Health issues, mental issues... Abuse, violence... What was her excuse?

I used drugs 'cause I hated life.

Although the campers had to have seen more than the average person did, Juls didn't want to be too upfront about her drug habit. "I was tired of everything." She hurried to ask, gazing from one to the other, "And, you guys, why are you here?"

Spur tilted his head and eyed her. "I was fired."

"What happened?"

"You wanna hear about it?"

All eyes darted from him to her, excited, as if having already heard his story and anticipating her reaction.

"Sure." She nodded.

He leaned forward and lowered his voice. "I got fired 'cause I dared speak my mind. What a crime, right? You think you live in a democratic country, with the human rights and freedom of speech and all. But you better watch your mouth. Big brother's listening, and if he don't like what he hears, you're outta the system faster than you can draw your next breath."

She grimaced. "That's sick."

"Yeah. It is."

"What did you speak up about?"

"The unspeakable." He gave a sarcastic chuckle. "You heard of the new world order?"

She shrugged. "Some."

Alex puffed. "Pfft, you're a conspirationist, Spur."

"Shut up." Spur fixed his gaze on Juls. "There's this community whose name I won't mention, 'cause you never know who's listening up there"—he nodded to the dark sky above—"an elite that has this big plan. They want to create a new global order where they dominate other communities. There won't be countries and alliances as we know them today. But *before* that can happen, there's gotta be chaos. So with the help of powerful lobbyists, they get wars started here and there. If you think it's for the land or the oil, or to instate fucking *democracy*, as they'll tell ya on the news, you're wrong." He pointed a finger at her. "It's for chaos. Destroying the world as we know it. World War III is right around the corner. And *then*"—his eyes gleamed—"they'll be there with their dirty money and their dirty power and restore peace. On *their* terms. Under *their* governance."

Juls didn't know what to think. During her seven years of drug hell, she'd been incapable of following what went on in the political sphere, and she didn't want the campers to find out about her ignorance.

The guy in the bubble jacket laughed, the sound raucous and hallow. "No wonder they fired you, Spur. You're delirious."

"No, I'm not." Spur shook his head. "It's the plain truth, man. Open your eyes. Read. Be informed. Listen to the dissidents. Check out forums. They may have fired me, but the movement is global." He crossed his arms and sat back in his chair, its sudden squeak of fatigue creepy in the night.

Rant over?

Juls glanced at Reef, whose blue, pensive eyes gazed at the fire. The flickering light casted moving shadows on his rugged features, deepening his eyes and sharpening his nose and cheekbones. He'd aged beautifully. His protruding lips made her want to stare forever. And the stubble! Irresistible.

How did she not recognize him earlier? He disappeared fourteen years ago, when she was only ten and too young to understand the mechanics between man and woman. All that time, the years worked to forge and chisel the chubby teenage boy into a grown and very handsome man.

She couldn't wait to tell Laydi, Joey, and Selena about him. He'd been Connor's friend, though, about six years older than them—would they remember him?

As if reading her mind, Reef stood, passed the campfire, and stopped in front of her. His Western-movie-star smile caused the blush on her cheeks to deepen. Unashamedly, he bent to offer his hand. "I think we need to talk."

* * * *

A big, white moon reflected on the calm surface of the S-shaped pond. Miniature bug silhouettes flew in circles above the water, their buzzing occasionally disrupted by the splash of a trout jumping out to catch dinner.

Juls and Reef sat by the shore, shoulder-to-shoulder against the large trunk of a tree. She savored their closeness. Not only was the heat emanating from his large body keeping her warm, being near her old friend made her heart flutter.

"You silly, you." She bumped into his elbow. "How long did you know who I was and didn't tell me?"

He chuckled. "When you charged out of the water like a mad sow whose cub was being taken away."

"But why didn't you—"

"I wanted to see at what point you'd recognize me. And I'm surprised you didn't right away."

"It's your beard."

"And a few years of ageing." He ran a hand over his cheek and stroked the dark hairs. "You still should've recognized me. You used to have a crush on me."

"I did not."

"You did. You had eyes the size of saucers and followed me everywhere."

A huff mixed with laughter escaped her. "I followed Connor, stupid. He was the one running after you. And anyway, little girls can't crush."

"Oh, *you* did, all right." He grinned. "I was your hero, babe."

He was. She recalled an episode when she was about eight. A mean dog, a cat hater, chased her Siamese up a tree. Believing the barking beast would kill her cat and then come for her, too, Juls had run through the neighborhood with her hands covering her ears and screamed her heart out. Reef came to her rescue, simply threatening the dog away with a stick.

She shook her head. "Remember when you climbed up that tree to get my cat?"

"Yeah." He laughed. "That poor thing was so scared, it scratched me to blood."

"I used my scarf to bandage you."

"You did, and my dad beat me senseless when I came home, 'cause the blood ruined your scarf and your mom would be mad at *him*, which was bull."

She winced. "I'm sorry, Reef. I didn't know."

"It's okay, I would've done anything for you. Climbed to the moon." He nodded to the white circle hanging above them like a lamp, lighting the night. His eyes flickered.

"You would?"

"Sure. I felt like your big brother. Wanted to take care of you."

Oh, such heart-warming words. "That's sweet, but I already had a big brother."

He snorted. "That lame fat-ass? All he cared about was his pathetic Mario games. Day and night, he'd play. I'm sorry to say it"—he shot her a glance—"but he didn't feel an ounce for you, the dickhead."

Though she'd already figured that out years ago, these spoken words made Connor's negligence more real. Yet, he wasn't the only one. Mom and Dad were guilty of the same behavior. An old and ugly feeling made her throat tighten. No matter how far she fled its source, the feeling would never go away.

As if reading her mind, Reef added, "He wasn't a good friend to me, either, Juliette."

She nudged his elbow. "Hey, I'm Juls, now."

"To me, you'll always be little Juliette."

"That's what my parents named me. I hate it."

"Julie, then, is that okay with you?" He made an abrupt intake of air. "Listen, I promised to look after you. But I failed."

"You promised *what?*"

He turned to her, eyes clear and limpid as an endless pool of water. "To myself. I wanted to take care of you, make sure you grew up all right. It was obvious no one else was gonna do that. So I pretended to be your big brother, the one who'd defend you and protect you."

What a revelation. She had no idea Reef was such a white knight, and all for her? Heat invaded her, and she held her breath before slowly blowing out air. "Wow. I didn't know."

"I didn't *need* you to know." He shrugged. "I didn't have anyone else to care for. No brother, no sister. Just you, a lonely little girl down the road. You used to sit on the porch with your doll and play by yourself. Someone had to watch over you, right?"

She wasn't sure if he was asking a question.

"I didn't even think of you as Connor's sister," he continued. "Just the little girl down the road. Pretty, tiny, fragile..."

"Huh. I'm far from fragile." If he knew the things she'd done to survive on the street...

"Not anymore, you're not. And the blame for that is mine. I was gone before I had a chance to help ya stay on track. I was far, far away. Not physically, 'cause I was never so far you couldn't find me, but in here." He pointed to his temple. "And I left you unattended."

She shook her head. "It wasn't your job to take care of me."

"Listen, I didn't have anyone else. It had to be you, little one." His voice sounded pleading. He'd carried his load of guilt for too long, and now he begged for pardon.

"Stop hurting yourself," she whispered.

"No. I have to say this. I needed to be someone's hero. And you were there, needing me, too." He looked to the sky as if searching for something. His Adam's apple went up and down. "I'll never forgive myself for leaving you."

"Stop it. I wasn't *your* responsibility." She touched his knee. "Reef, with what was going on at home, I was bound to go wrong, whether an angel was watching over me or not." Her throat thickened. "I was bound to go away, too. One way or the other. I was pushed to."

He gasped. His warm hand landed on top of hers. "But I wish I'd been there for you. I'm so sorry." His voice cracked. "I was s'posed to be there, but I was so busy nursing my own fucking sorrows, so busy leaving the goddamn place. I just couldn't get out of here fast enough."

Their fingers entwined, clenched each other so hard, his pulse beat against her skin.

She wanted to say that if they'd been together, there was no way they would have been able to keep each other alive. One plus one made two, and adding their hurts would have made them more intolerable to deal with. Reef and she would've ended up killing each other. Passively, but kill nonetheless. It was better that they slowly died on their own. She in the gutter, and he in his hut in the woods.

She worked not to utter these words, however truthful they were. They would only pain him more.

A shiny trout jumped out of the pond in the distance and splashed back into the water. Disrupted, bugs zigzagged above the circles of waves left before calming and pursuing their nocturnal dance.

"Tell me your story." Reef took a sharp breath. "I ran into Connor last year, outside the mall, and he told me you moved to Columbus High. That's all I know."

"I was thrown out."

"Why?"

"I...overdosed." The moment she said the loaded word, she bit her tongue. Reef hated himself for not taking care of her, and her failure to do so on her own would add to his guilt.

He ran a hand over his face. "Fuck."

"Yeah." God, she wished she could erase this bit of conversation.

"Your dickhead of a brother didn't tell me that. Son of a bitch."

"Hmm, Mom and Dad probably told him to keep quiet. They were ashamed of me. I dishonored them. Them, their fine fucking neighborhood, the world they wanted to live in..."

"Like me. I was scum, waste, a loser."

"I *still* am, you know. I saw them earlier today, at my grandmother's funeral, and it wasn't pretty. In their eyes, I'm better dead than a bum."

He shot her a glance. "What do you mean?"

"They'd rather see me dead than know I'm a bum. Even though I've cleaned up completely and turned my life around. But I'll never be good enough." She spread her hands. "Sad, but what can you do about it? I'm just not the daughter they wanted."

"That's fucked up. A sweet girl like you." His voice cracked. He covered his eyes with a hand and gasped. *"They* fucked us up." His body jerked with a sob. "I'm so sorry, Julie."

She was about to say it wasn't his fault, but the momentousness of his reaction froze her. Was this strong, weathered man crying?

"Hey." Chest tightening, she squeezed his shaking arm. "It's okay, Reef. We don't need them. We do fine alone." Mom and Dad's faces appeared in her mind, heartless and condescending. So ugly, they made her want to gag. "Better than fine, believe me."

"I wish."

After a silence, she asked, "And you, how did things go? You never told me. You just disappeared."

He sniffed and looked down. "My dad beat my mom up, too, and when she couldn't take it anymore, after years of black eyes and broken bones, she left."

How heart-wrenching. Juls could only utter a meek, "Oh."

"She should've taken me with her, right? That would've been the natural thing to do. Save me from that demented monster."

Juls clenched her teeth, and didn't know what to say. His words made her throat tighten.

"When I was fifteen, she sent me a secret letter explaining that if she'd taken me with her, he would've hunted us down and killed her. So she chose life over me. She said she was sorry, and she loved me, but... You know what I did, then?"

Though he couldn't see her, she shook her head.

"Smartass I was, I started doing the same evil that he did. I drank, and the booze gave me strength. I was so strong and invincible, whenever he punched me, I punched back. And that's how the story ends."

"He stopped hurting you?"

"He sure did. After I almost broke his skull against the corner of the kitchen table. The cops agreed it was self-defense and let me go. But I was hooked on his evil. Needed my booze every fucking day."

The air punched out of her lungs. "Oh...my...God." Imagining the desperate teenager pushed to hit his father to death tore at her heart. No one should experience such horror.

"He destroyed me," Reef added with a croak.

"No, you're—"

"Yes." He tilted his head farther between his knees and sobbed, his torso lifting from the contractions and gasp-like sounds escaping his half-open mouth.

His pain hurt her, too, nurtured the one she fought so hard to leave behind. With hot tears filling her eyes, she stroked his hair. Soft, blond curls twined around her fingers.

His ragged breaths filled the silent forest while he cried his sorrow.

Not knowing what else to do, she stroked his back, and ended up wrapping her arm around his waist.

He groaned and wiped his wet face. "I'm okay, Julie." Eyes shimmering, he looked to the moon and fixed his gaze, as if seeking an answer he'd waited a lifelong to be granted and saying that the time had come.

"We'll always be okay," she whispered, holding him tight.

"Yeah." His breathing slowed.

After a beat, he turned and stared at her eyes, then nose, then lips…and cocked his head to kiss her.

Oh, such warm and soft lips. Juls jerked from the surprise.

Growling, Reef pulled away, got up, and within seconds disappeared behind the big tree trunk.

* * * *

Twigs snapped in the forest.

What the hell happened? Extremely tired, Juls stood on trembling legs and leaned her arm against the hard tree.

She never intended to push Reef away. Correction: she *didn't*. He was the one who left. Why? Because his kiss caught her off guard and she startled? She was unkissed, for fuck's sake. Surely you couldn't blame her for being a little surprised.

She let out a cry of frustration and slapped the tree. "It's not my fault! Give me a fucking break!"

In the distance, a toad croaked, followed by a second and a third. Soon, a cacophony of croaks played across the pond, enough to drive the most collected people crazy.

"Shut up!" she shouted and hit the bark again, a sharp pain spreading like electricity through her arm. "Shit."

Gritting her teeth, she circled the trunk and entered the dark forest. Each looming tree, each hanging branch, a black silhouette she could barely discern from another. She walked the path from memory, hands outreached, her stupid imagination inventing the scariest shades. Thankfully, none moved.

Reef's hut was a few hundred feet from the pond. Even blind in the dark, she would be there in less than a minute.

What awaited her? From Reef's reaction, he seemed to believe she rejected him. Was he angry at her? Sad? Should she apologize? She didn't mean to hurt him. On the contrary, the sisterly feelings she'd nurtured for him as a child revived in the course of the afternoon and evening, and from his words earlier, he considered her a sister, too. Which made his kiss inexplicable. It must have been the heat of the moment. He needed consolation, that was all, and now he regretted his impulsive gesture.

She inhaled strongly to calm the upbeat hammering of her heart. The smell of fungus had intensified with the humidity of the night. She strained to hear, but the only sounds to reach her hypersensitive ears were her own footsteps crushing fallen leaves and rotten twigs.

Or—

Was that rustling ahead? She stopped, froze to the spot, and held her breath. Her eyes concentrated, tried to pierce the deep blackness surrounding her, but could detect no movement, no unusual shadow. Although—she couldn't be sure a warm-blooded, sharp-toothed beast wasn't lurking in the dark, drooling, ready to jump out from its hiding place and feast on her. Were there wolves in Ohio? Fuck, she wished she hadn't talked to Reef about the mad dog that chased her cat, for the dreadful memory caused the hair on her neck to stand.

She slowly let out the warm air she'd held, clenched her hands to brace herself, nails burying in her palms…and took a careful step forward. Since when was she so easily spooked?

More rustling of dead leaves. Her heart almost jumped out of her chest, and her muscles paralyzed from icy fear, became useless. Even if danger charged at her, she couldn't move.

Was that breathing nearby? Snarling?

The blood drained from her head. She resisted closing her eyes, because it wouldn't change a thing. Her surroundings were as black as the curtains behind her lids.

Another sound, crackling, at her right. She swallowed a cry.

Color appeared in the distance between the trees. A small, yellowish light. She blinked, but wasn't hallucinating. It moved, upward and to the sides, dancing as it slowly grew and intensified.

Fire?

Reef!

All her muscles moved at once in perfect synchrony. With her sole focus the swirling light ahead, she leapt forward more than she ran, dodging every hidden threat, each step swift and effective, her breaths short and calculated.

She arrived at the clearing within seconds. Thank fuck, she'd made it. Her pulse pounded in her ears.

Wearing a hooded sweatshirt, Reef kneeled on the other side of the small fire, blowing at its base. A line of worry creased his forehead. The swirling flames bathed him, the hut, and the surrounding trees in orange light.

"It's getting cold." He sighed and looked up, clear eyes devoid of anything resembling anger. A little sadness, maybe. "Sorry I left you like that, Julie. I shoulda made sure you followed me. It's not safe in these woods. I don't know what the hell I was thinking."

He wasn't angry at her? Relieved, she smiled. His apology further alleviated her mood. "For a while, I thought there was a hungry beast out there."

"Nah. The only beasts around here are human."

"Really?"

"Yeah. That's what worried me for a while. But I wanted to start the fire before going back to save you." He gave a half smile.

Her heart skipped a beat. He was so handsome. Seeing him practically made her chest hurt.

Sisterly feelings, my ass.

But it didn't matter that she liked him. After years on the streets, she was ugly, skinny, filthy…a rag…and he would never want to be with her. His kiss was a mistake. Why else did he leave so fast?

She shrugged. "I made it here fine. And you know, I'm homeless, so I know what human beasts are capable of."

He looked down, as if her reminder of the wild life she'd led in the past years pained him. But he was wrong. Her fate as a druggie was not *his* cross to carry.

The fire crackled while he stared at his hands and rubbed them.

She changed her weight from one uncomfortable leg to the other. They sizzled and itched within, like every night since she quit the meth. Only movement could stop the odd, crawling sensation, albeit temporarily. Exhaustion wore her out, too. More so from the mental challenges of the day than the physical efforts. She felt like slumping to the ground, curling like a cat by the fire, and closing her eyes. Tomorrow promised to be a big day, though. She would scour the streets of Pearl and find a job.

"Hey," she said, voice soft.

"Yeah?"

"If you don't mind, I'm going to sleep."

He didn't answer, just held her look, face placid.

"Okay?" she insisted.

As he still didn't react, she sighed, bent her head, and walked toward his hut. What was he thinking? She wished she could read his mind. Tomorrow, she would leave, once more separating them. Was that what bothered him?

"You know," he said from behind, sounding tired.

She swiveled without thinking. "Hmm?"

"There are times when…" He scrambled up on his feet, movements slow, as if the weight of the world hindered his usual swiftness. "There are times when all I think about is getting high."

She gasped. Just hearing the words *'get high'* caused a surge of need to rush through her body. Brutal, demanding. "Ah, shit." She balled her fists. "Me, too."

Features tense, he stepped forward and closed the distance between them. "It's so tough to…to resist. And so fucking easy to give in." He stopped in front of her, towering by a head, and ran a trembling hand over his face and beard. With the fire behind him, she could no longer discern the details of his features. "Just open a bottle and…" His voice came out like a croak.

She nodded. The familiar drug monster roamed at the pit of her stomach, fierier and meaner than the worst starvation, threatening to blow everything she'd fought for in the past two weeks. Her entire body shook and ached at the idea of feeding the sharp lust with some substance or other. Anything would do. Anything would soothe, take her away, help her escape in a matter of minutes.

Fuck, this was the precise thought that struck her earlier: if together, she and Reef would add both of their addictions to an intolerable level and crush each other.

But she was stronger. "We won't, Reef."

"I don't know about that." His warm breath brushed the tip of her nose.

"You have to fight it. You have to *want* to fight it."

He shifted from one foot to another, restless, his blue eyes pleading. "It don't work, Julie. I need to get high and forget. The stuff we talked about, our past, the things that've happened since, are messing with my mind. I don't know what to do. I need help. It's urgent."

"Is that why you kissed me?" Immediately regretting the stupid question, she bit her lip. Heat spread over her cheeks. Why couldn't she keep her damn mouth shut? What would he think of her now?

"No." He drew an audible breath and cocked his head. "I did that 'cause I'm in love with you."

"You're *what?*" She gaped.

"In love with you."

The steadfastness of his declaration made it sound real, but she'd seen and heard too much in her time to believe anything at first try. "Y-you're kidding me."

"No, I'm not."

She stood paralyzed. How could this handsome man develop such feelings for her? She, the ugly duckling, the society outcast. Surely, life would never give her love.

"Sweetie, I've been watching you since you ran outta the water. You're the same girl I knew, but you've changed, too. You've become a beautiful woman.

Gorgeous. Desirable." He spread his arms in front of her upper body as if to explain what he meant. "I can't imagine not—"

"It's not possible. You're making fun of me."

"No." Reaching for her waist, he leaned forward and without hesitation kissed her hard, his warm, full lips clamping over her mouth. His beard grazed her chin.

A violent rush of need invaded, tenfold stronger than the urge for a fix moments ago, from her sex through her womb to her starved brain. Her legs turned to liquid. She would melt into a lifeless, barely breathing lump on the ground, a pool of pure bliss, like when heroin swam up her veins and hit home.

Instinctively, and unashamedly, she moved toward him and molded her curves to the hard front of his body. Every inch fit, from her breasts against his chiseled chest muscles, to the crevice between her thighs where his bulging length lodged and throbbed.

Groaning, he let go of her lips. "Get inside the hut." With firm hands, he pushed her backward, adding, "Please," as if to not give the impression of using force. "Help me."

* * * *

The interior of the low roofed, one-room hut smelled of aluminum, painted wood, and earth. A lit brass oil lamp hanging from a rope across the tarp ceiling casted dancing shadows on the makeshift walls.

Juls lay on a thin mattress that took up most of the space on the dirt ground. Reef closed the door, and an unusual mix of fear and excitement filled her as he turned to her and took his sweatshirt off over his head.

Fear, because unlike the other guys, he wasn't going to rape her. He was going to sleep with her, yes, but not brutally, and she had to return the fervor—not just brace and close her eyes. Was she up to the task? Making love, giving pleasure, and satisfying someone who cared for her were new concepts. Opening up, too. Her heartbeat jumped out of rhythm at that thought.

Yet excitement coursed through her at the sight of the strong, bare-chested man who knelt at her side, eating her with his gaze. The soft, yellowish light from the lamp flattered his hard chest and stomach muscles. Already, the anticipation heated her, and she removed her heavy leather jacket to fold it at the end of the mattress.

As soon as she looked back, Reef dove toward her and pressed her down with his weight. She gasped and kept her hands in the air for a moment before daring to wrap her arms around his back. Groaning, he bore his hard crotch between her thighs, separating her legs, and attacked her lips again. Oh, so rough, so fast. A new gasp escaped her, but she clamped her mouth closed.

Having only had short relationships based on unhealthy combinations of drugs and forced sex in the past, she'd never kissed amorously, never known what to do, how it would feel, how to respond.

Let him lead the dance, that's the only way.

Wet and hungry, his lips ate hers, feasted on her mouth, nibbling and sucking, before his tongue thinned and pressed through her lips. She let him in, and he dove inside with a grunt, tongue roaming like a…like a… Damn, she was so overwhelmed, she couldn't think straight. He continued grinding his stiff cock into her inner thighs, moves insistent and confident. Her pussy muscles clenched with lust. She whimpered from the sharp contractions and raised her hips to meet him. How did he turn her on like that? It had to be the first time it happened to her sober, conscious. She was so aware, her arousal wetted her panties.

He stopped moving, broke the kiss, and lifted his head. Unfocused blue eyes revealing the tension within searched hers. His breaths came out short, ragged, and the warm scent of musk emanated from his naked torso. "Julie."

"Yeah," she said with a blow of air.

"I don't wanna hurt you."

Oh, but he wouldn't. She shook her head. "I'm a big girl."

"I know, but I don't wanna do what the other guys did to you. Promise me, if I hurt you, you'll stop me."

His thoughtfulness touched a chord. Never had a man cared for how she felt during sex. Not once. You just didn't worry about a dirty street girl whose mind was far off in Heroin Land. She swallowed to hold the hurt down, but couldn't prevent hot tears from sneaking to her eyes, fogging her vision. Ugh, now was not a good time to be sentimental.

He shifted. "For fuck's sake, Julie. I can't wait." As to make the point, he pressed his erection harder against her and groaned, features pained. "Promise me!"

No need for promises. She trusted him fully. He was her white knight, her hero, and he'd never hurt her. "I know who you are, Reef." She reached for his belt between them and unbuckled it. Next, the zipper. No briefs.

With his hands resting at the sides of her head, he lifted his lower body, allowing his cock to leap out of his combat pants and tap against her jeans. She didn't see it but fisted the warm, thick rod, stroking its veined length and caressing the tip of its velvety mushroom head. How many times had she masturbated a guy?

Too many to count. Only this time, it wasn't coldly for money or dope, but to please her best friend.

Reef growled. "Oh, you're a pro."

"Told ya not to worry about me." With her other hand, she cupped and gently massaged his soft balls.

"Fuuuck." He sounded torn. Short breaths blew on her face, hot, moist. "I can't wait, Julie."

She removed her hands, unzipped her jeans, and pushed them down her thighs along with her wet panties until everything bundled at her shoes.

Meanwhile, Reef kept his hips raised to give her maneuvering space. "I don't have a condom."

"I've been tested at the clinic. I'm clean."

"And I haven't gotten laid in years. Which tells you how long I'm gonna last." Despite the obvious tension in his body, he chuckled. "I'm gonna come like a randy teenager."

That, she questioned. Unlike the others, Reef was going to take his time and please her, make her scream. He was the kind to give a girl multiple orgasms, something she'd never experienced during sex. The strongest physical sensation she'd ever known was the other-worldly hit of a heroin dose reaching her brain, provoking a bliss so pure, so complete, she nearly climaxed from its strength before collapsing into unconsciousness.

He spread her thighs with his knees and lowered so the tip of his cock poked between her nether lips, seeking entry.

Holy shit, she'd never been fucked sober. Her heart hammered, and a cold hand of fear curled around her throat, long fingers squeezing until she could no longer breathe. She clenched her legs to Reef's. Would the penetration hurt now that she knew what was going on? Had her rape-induced fear made her frigid? Would he notice her inexperience?

He didn't give her time to think, and since his deep, sensual kissing had worked her up, she was moist enough for him to enter. A little pushing of his hips had the thick, hard shaft slide in easily, filling her inch by inch, thrust after thrust.

She breathed out and relaxed her muscles, the cool pressure on her throat lifting. It was okay—the penetration neither hurt nor made her panic. Maybe the love she nurtured for Reef outweighed her fears. She raised her ass to meet and help him farther in.

A low groan escaped his parted lips. He closed his eyes and withdrew, thrust into her wetness, pulled out, dove back in, establishing a quick and efficient rhythm. "Mmm, you know I'm not gonna last." Sweat pearled on his forehead, reflecting the yellow lamp light.

"Yeah, just don't come inside me."

"I won't."

She smiled. Even if he came too fast and she didn't have the time to build her own climax, having sex with him felt great. She loved the regular friction of his cock against her vagina walls and the sensation of fullness he induced. If this was making love, she wanted it every day. She arched her back to facilitate his gliding.

Diving deeper, he groaned. "Fuck, I can't believe how good you are." He kissed her hungrily again, not giving her the chance to respond as his wet lips and tongue moved on to her chin, cheeks, temples, then down to her ears, beneath them, over her throat, kissing, licking, and nibbling. Wherever he went, his rough beard grazed, heating her skin and sharpening her senses.

She moaned and writhed underneath him, concentrated on achieving both his and her satisfaction. His breathing increased with his quickening thrusts, the rubbing of her inner walls so fast and intense. Warmth spread inside. Still, she waited for her own climax.

"Ooh." Growling, he jerked back, pulled out of her, and lifted his hips away.

She gasped from their sudden separation, would have preferred him to stay forever.

"Oh, oh, oh." With a grimace of pain, he moved a hand to his cock and pumped his discharge between their stomachs. "Ooooh…fuck."

Damn, so soon. Too early for her. She closed her eyes, didn't want to see him jerk off.

Breathing hard, he retrieved his hand and lowered himself onto her stomach again, deflating like a lifeless puppet. "Holy shit. Couldn't stop it."

"It's okay," she whispered. The saying 'All men are the same' sounded in her mind, but she shook the thought. Insinuating Reef was like other men couldn't be farther from the truth. Worse, it was an insult. The poor guy just hadn't had release in a long while.

He nuzzled his sweaty face into the crevice of her throat and worked to catch his breath. His body trembled. "And now I've soiled your fancy clothes."

Oh, the goof. She gave a half-smile. "Fancy clothes, my ass."

"Heh. Sid wasn't exactly known for his taste in clothing." With each word, hot breaths blew on her skin.

"Ha ha!" Her sudden laughter relieved the disappointment in her chest. She opened her eyes.

Reef raised to his elbows and gazed at her, clear blue eyes still feverish. "Rather the opposite."

"He did dress well on occasion. Give the guy some credit."

"And you, will you give me credit?" He feigned a frown.

"What do you m—"

Before she could do anything, he rested his weight on one arm and snuck a free hand between them…underneath her shirt…and up her ribs, to her breast. Oh, what a surprise. She widened her eyes as the palm cupped her boob and molded, kneaded gently. "W-what are you doing?"

In response, he kissed her and forced his wet tongue into her mouth, coiling around her tongue like a snake while his fingers played with her hardening nipple. A sharp contraction of her pussy muscles made her moan and arch her back.

"That's my girl," he said to her lips. He deepened the kiss as if taking possession of her mouth. All she could do was follow the movements of his tongue, dancing with him while breathing heavily through her nose. He pinched and rolled her nipple between his thumb and index finger. Heat shot out of her sex, and her body trembled.

Kissing her hungrily, tongue diving in and out between her teeth, he moved a hand to her nether lips and inserted a finger into her wetness.

No—she squirmed underneath him and broke the kiss, didn't want him to touch her down there. A homeless girl seldom had the luxury of shaving. The bush would repulse Reef, and he'd never sleep with her again.

Lips red and swollen, he removed his finger and silently questioned her.

All she could see in his dreamy eyes was love, genuine affection. She swam in his tender gaze and relaxed, confidence and trust in him taking residence.

After reading her a while longer, he moved backward on the mattress and dove down. His face disappeared between her legs, curly hair tickling her thighs. She held her breath, but when the tip of his tongue slipped in where his fingers did earlier, a squeal escaped her. Oh, that. No one had done *that* to her.

His hard tongue went out and in again, mimicking the thrusting of his cock. He knew what he was doing, for delicious arousal coursed through her. How could she have believed he would disappoint her?

He pulled his tongue out, and, replacing it with a probing finger, licked his way to her clit. Whimpering, she squeezed her thighs against the sides of his head, pressed him to her needy spot. He obliged. While a second finger joined in to rub her inner walls, he found the bead and rolled it between his lips, back and forth, round and round, until she writhed and lost control. Hot liquid gushed out of her. With each roll of her clit, her inner muscles contracted, causing rush after rush of burning heat to traverse. Sweat broke out all over. He sucked the bead into his mouth. She grabbed his hair and squealed as a stronger wave washed over her, taking her to a height she'd never known. Frantic, sucking in air, she moved fast against him, rode his fingers, pressed against his mouth, chased her orgasm, and…screamed pure delight as her spent body finally exploded, jelly-like legs shaking and hot juices squirting over his hand.

Chapter Four

*Girl Code #18: No matter the directions you take in life, your girlfriends will be
there for you.*

Barking filled Juls' ears, waking her and sending a glacial rush of fear through her chest. Unable to breathe, she sat up on the mattress, wide eyes searching the small room. Morning light flowed in through the open door. She blinked. Outside, shadows hurried back and forth, their movements determined. Male voices, sharp, angry. And a dog barking. The hair on her neck stood. She hated dogs. They scared the living shit out of her. What was going on?

Worse, the hut was empty. *Where the fuck are you, Reef?*

A tall male silhouette wearing a cap appeared in the door, backlit and faceless, startling her. "Hey you, get out of there!"

Oh, she'd heard that cold, commanding tone before. On the street. Cops.

What to do, rebel or obey? She hadn't done anything wrong. And what the hell did they want? Had they hurt Reef, arrested him? Maybe he was wanted? It hit her—she didn't know a thing about him.

"Get out!" Not giving her the time to react, the big man dove inside the hut, grabbed her arm, and pulled her up.

Her sleeping bag knotted around her legs. She fell onto her knees.

The lock on her arm tightened and lifted again, sending pain through her muscles. "You don't want to cooperate?"

"You're hurting me," she wheezed. Struggling to hold her balance, she stepped out of the sleeping bag.

Outside, the barking continued, excited.

The man glanced around the floor, his hand clamping harder. "Got any dope in here?"

"No. I'm clean." Wincing from the pain, she took a step closer in the hopes that he'd relieve the pressure.

He smelled of cologne, leather, and outdoors. The polyester of his dark blue uniform brushed her naked arm. Déjà-vu images from similar encounters with Columbus policemen flashed in her mind, adding to her unease. Back then, she'd been drugged practically senseless, yet conscious enough to loathe the handling, the interrogations, the humiliation.

"Get out." With a single movement of his arm, the cop forced her to step around him and shoved her out the door.

She nearly tripped. Ice-cold morning air bit the skin of her face. She sucked in a breath and sheltered her eyes from the blinding light.

Loud voices filled the forest clearing. Uniforms moved around and upended things, narcotics dogs sniffed, searched.

Oh, fuck. Dogs. The blood drained from her head.

There, surrounded by two-three guys, Reef, his blond curls contrasting with the dark caps. He wore a brown leather jacket, but she couldn't see his face.

Someone pointed at her, shouted a command. From nowhere, a black-eyed German shepherd charged her.

Nooo! Lifting her arms, she stopped breathing. Her chest choked. She stood still, paralyzed. Nausea rose to her throat while the growling beast circled her legs, sniffed her up and down. It was going to bite her.

With a scream, she forced her frozen legs to move. One step, two.

Ears flattening, the dog snarled, flashed its teeth, and blocked her way.

Coldness invaded her. Unable to draw breath, she gave a silent shriek, nearly peed herself.

A voice behind her. "She's hiding something."

No, she mouthed, cool tears rushing to her eyes. *Your dog is going to bite me!*

With a bark, the beast stood on its hind legs and tapped its front paws on her chest. Rapid puffs of fog escaped its open, sharp-toothed mouth.

Icy fear ran in her veins and bile clogged her throat. She swallowed, forced the vomit down. Couldn't look at the threat, couldn't take any more sensations. Covering her eyes, she turned aside.

The paws clawed at her shirt and slipped off. Two sharp barks filled her ears.

"No, Julie!" Reef's voice was alarmed. "Don't move, it won't hurt you."

He didn't make sense. Legs heavy as lead, she staggered away, had to flee.

The dog circled her ankles and unbalanced her. With a shriek, she tripped over the low, muscular body and landed on her knees and elbows. The shock punched air out of her lungs.

"Julie!"

Barking loud, the dog jumped on top of her back, its weight flattening her stomach and breasts onto the hard ground. Clawed paws dug into her shirt and jeans.

Nooo! Face down, she drew a breath through her mouth, and got the taste of earth on her tongue.

150

"Don't move!" Reef again, closer.

The dog jerked, yelped, thrashed on top of her. Its weight lifted. Commotion at her side, more yelps, and Reef shouting.

What the hell? She looked up.

Raging, he rolled on the ground with the ball of black-orange fur in his hold, one arm around the large beige chest and the other across its throat. The dog fought to free itself, barking, flashing teeth, and turned its head to try to bite him.

Sharp orders behind her.

"Stop it!"

"Let go of the dog!"

In rapid succession, three men jumped on Reef and overwhelmed him.

Oh God, please, don't club him! Or shoot.

One grabbed his arms from behind while a second tore the growling animal out of his grasp and a third shackled his wrists. So fast, so professional.

Reef didn't struggle to get free, probably knew it wouldn't help his case. Nostrils flaring, his blond curls ruffled, he shot Juls a glance, wild blue eyes telling her so many things.

Her view fogged. She couldn't move, couldn't think straight.

A new command, "Heel!" flared the sudden silence.

Ears lifting, the dog jumped around and sat at the handler's side, short pants coming from its mouth.

"Right," a voice called from the other end of the clearing. "Take him to the station. Assault and obstruction of justice."

Rustling of leaves sounded at her side, and a human breathing.

Seconds later, someone kneeled on her lower back and shoulders, pinned her to the spot.

She gasped. First the crazy fucking beast, now a cop.

While a strong hand pressed her face down into the dirt, another searched her clothes and intimate parts.

She slowly breathed in, dust sneaking into her nose.

"Nothing." The weight lifted.

She raised her head in time to see the other men pulling Reef on his legs and bringing him out of her vision.

Oh God, Reef. Shaking, breathing fast through her dry lips, she managed to scramble on her feet.

In no time, the group of men and dogs disappeared on the path toward the other campers' huts, leaving complete carnage behind.

Then, nothing. Just eerie silence.

Nausea cramped her stomach. She wanted to puke, but couldn't. Instead, loud sobs shook her chest. Cries escaped her trembling mouth, and her eyes filled with burning tears. "R-Reef!"

The police had arrested him and would press charges. Thank fuck he didn't hurt the dog, let alone kill it, or they'd never allow him out of jail.

What to do? He got busted for protecting her—now it was her turn to help him. She looked above the rooftops the same way he, her hero, did last night, and stared into the infinite grayish morning sky. "I swear," she wheezed, throat choking, "I'll do what it takes to get him out."

But how, and where was the goddamn police station? They'd relocated it since she moved from Pearl. Maybe she should ask Reef's friends.

Knees weak, she staggered to the hut, took in the desolating sight. Everything lay upended and trashed around. Her bag opened, its content spread on the dirt ground.

She swallowed. In a daze, warm tears rolling down her cheeks, she bent to collect her belongings. Not the first time she'd been searched.

A bird chirped a merry tune up in a tree, seconds later joined by another. While chaos reigned on the site, life around Juls resumed.

In slow motion, she shook her dusty clothes and folded them into the bag. Next, the shampoo, the soap…all the supplies from Mom's cupboard.

Something was missing, but what? She stopped moving about, dug into her fuzzy mind and concentrated.

Her diary.

Fuuuck. A cold, rotten feeling creeping into her chest, she scanned the perimeter, but couldn't spot the colorful notebook.

Her head buzzed. Clearly, someone had stolen her dearest belonging. It contained the story of her life, the one she was struggling to put behind to start anew. It was crucial she had this junkie memoir nearby so she could look back and reaffirm that getting off the drugs was the right decision.

Did one of the campers steal it last night? The cops? Why be so rude and take it anyway? Who in the whole fucking world could be interested in the pathetic life of a homeless?

Weaker than she'd felt in a long time, she slumped to her knees and cried like a child, lamented sorely, clawed at the earth, hot tear after hot tear rolling down her face. They'd broken her, taken her willpower, pride, self-confidence, and strength. It didn't take that much more to destroy a vulnerable ex junkie barely recuperating from years of addiction, and condemn her to lose the fight of her life. Who, they? Her parents, Connor, the cops, fucking society.

If only Reef were here! Her white knight would sweep her into his arms, and, with words of love whispered to her lips, brush this unimaginable pain away.

Reef.

Gah, first things first. How could she feel so insanely sorry for herself when his situation was even worse? Locked in a cell like a trapped animal, he must be losing his mind.

Exhaustion coursed through her. She wiped her wet face and sniffed. Not only did she have no idea where the station was located, she didn't have the strength to walk all the way to town. She needed help, fast.

* * * *

"You've been crying." Brown eyes widening, Mom stepped aside in the open doorway so Juls could walk in. She paled beneath her immaculate make-up.

Juls took a deep breath to calm her nerves, the familiar, flowery scent of Mom's perfume filling her nostrils. She could have sought Joey's help, too, since she was in town, but her parents' house was closer.

In the hall, she threw her heavy duffel bag to the floor, folded her leather jacket atop it, and steered toward the living room. Her tense muscles ached, and, as usual, the withdrawals made the flesh beneath her skin itch.

"What's happened?" Voice higher-pitched, Mom closed the door and trotted behind her.

As Juls entered the wide, luxurious room with a view to the pond, old resentment teased beneath the surface of her consciousness. Bad timing. She pushed the ugly feeling back. She yearned to slump into an armchair, but worried her dirty clothes would stain its expensive fabric. Instead, she chose a plain wooden chair at the dinner table, crossed her arms over her shirt, and gazed up at Mom. Would she scorn her for using the same clothes two days in a row—or more, right, because you could never know with a homeless?

The middle-aged woman stood a few feet away with her hands clenched in front of her black silk dress, a pained expression marring her face. "A-aren't you going to talk?"

Did Mom really care about what happened to her daughter? What a surprise. Juls debated whether to snicker or be kind, but she didn't have the strength for either. She was still shaken deep inside, and her eyes burned from all the tears.

"Can I at least get you something?" Mom twined her neatly manicured hands on and on, as if seeking consolation. "A hot chocolate? Tea? And then we can talk."

After hurrying through the darned cold forest, Juls would die for a hot beverage, but Reef was waiting. She gave a short shake of her head. "No, thanks."

"Then say something." Mom's voice thinned, pleaded.

Juls stared at her, a mix of astonishment and relief seeping. She may have disliked her mother for years, but today, her concern seemed sincere, and Juls could only respond accordingly. That much, life had taught her. But how to start? She bit her lip and hesitated. "Is Dad at work?"

"Yes, but, don't change the subject. You look like someone's given you a beating."

"Hmm." Wanting to give her words as little impact as possible, Juls murmured, "I've been attacked by a dog."

Mom's hands flew to her face. "Oh my God, how horrible."

"It's okay, it didn't bite me."

"Oh. Thank the Lord. You gave me a start." Mom closed her eyes and dropped her hands with an audible gulp of air. "How did it happen? Where?"

Juls hesitated. She didn't want to say it was a police dog and give her an excuse to berate her about getting into trouble with the law, God forbid. What would the neighbors think, right? "Um, can I just use your phone? I need to call Connor."

Mom opened her eyes, wetness reflecting light from the large windows. "You're not answering my questions."

Juls shrugged, didn't know what to say.

"What do you need to talk to him about? Does it have something to do with the dog?"

"Kind of. I need to ask him a favor."

Mom nodded. "You know what? You can have my cell phone. I'll take Granny's old one instead."

"What are you talking about?"

"We've inherited Granny's phone."

Juls shook her head. "I still don't understand, but I don't need a phone. I just want to make a call."

Mom went to a low rosewood cabinet in a corner, picked up her shiny new cell phone that sat atop a white napkin, and returned to Juls. "I insist. I want you to have it. It's too fancy for me, with all these apps and notifications and whatnot. Granny's has bigger buttons, too, and it would be easier for me to type on it."

"Mom, I'm telling you, I don't need a phone."

"Yes, you do." Her voice sharpened. "I want to be able to reach you."

Juls widened her eyes in disbelief. Mom had never hinted at such a notion.

"I do. You know, since you left yesterday, I've had time to do a lot of thinking. You asked Dad and me if we knew the reason you left us, and quite honestly, that question has been plaguing me. I couldn't sleep last night." She paused and inhaled deeply. Ticks caused a corner of her mouth to twitch. "I've come to the conclusion that I haven't done enough. I've neglected you, neglected our relationship. And I'm...I'm sorry about that, my Juliette."

Oh, Mom hadn't said *'my Juliette'* since she was a toddler. What was going on with her?

Mom's eyes shone, and she fiddled with her phone. "I want to be in touch with you and know how you're doing. But you'll have to talk to me, too."

Juls nodded. She could do that.

"Like telling me what happened to you today. I need to know. Please."

The sincere tone in Mom's plea touched a chord within, so Juls would return the frankness. Being honest didn't cost her much. "Okay. I met an old friend in the woods. The alcoholic neighbor's son. Remember him?"

"Yes, of course. He became one himself, the poor soul. Your dad and I always wondered what to do to help him, but you just can't help a drunk."

Juls' breath caught. What? Had Mom and Dad wanted to help Reef? She would never have thought they'd think about someone lesser than them, even for a second.

Mom cleared her throat. "What's his name again?"

"Reef."

"Yes, that's right." She nodded, looked aside as if needing to think for a moment, then glanced back at Juls. "So… What happened?"

"This morning, the police came with dogs, looking for drugs. But both Reef and I are clean."

"You spent the night with him?"

Oh, the directness. But Mom's intense look coaxed the truth out of Juls. "Yes."

"A-are you fond of him?"

Of course. Very, very fond. Reef was one-of-a-kind. Juls' hero. Warm tears threatened to invade her eyes.

"Oh, my God, the two lost souls have found each other." Mom's gaze watered. "I always wondered what would happen if the two of you met. You were so alike." She stepped forward, arms extended, and offered Juls a hug.

The moment to forgive had come. Swallowing to stop the tears, Juls stood, wrapped her arms around Mom's warm body, and rested her chin on her shoulder.

Mom's insistent perfume filled her space, but it was perfectly okay. They hadn't hugged since fuck knew when.

After a moment, Mom sniffed, released Juls, and held her at arm's length. "My Juliette. You've become such a beautiful grown woman. How did I miss that?" A tear spilled over the rim of one of her wet eyes and rolled down in a single streak.

Again, Juls swallowed. She didn't have the answer to that question.

"So, go on, then. What happened?"

"One of the dogs jumped on me, and Reef just…attacked it, and pulled it off. I don't really think it was going to bite me, but you know me, I've always been afraid of dogs." Juls gave a wry smile. "I panicked."

"He fought a police dog to protect you?" Mom put a hand to her mouth. "Dear God. What a brave young man. Who would have thought—"

"But because he did, they arrested him. So I need help to get to the station. I figured Connor could drive me, if he can take time off work."

"I'm sure he can." Mom cleared her throat and handed Juls the phone. "Here. Take it. But you'll have to change the subscriptions. I don't know how to do that."

"It's easy. If you could get me Granny's phone, I'll exchange the chips now."

"Yes, but you'll have her phone number, then. How bizarre."

Juls shrugged. "Doesn't matter. I can get a new one later."

"Excellent. By the way." Mom tilted her head. "Where are you going to sleep tonight?"

Juls hadn't expected that question. She gaped. "Um, I don't know."

"Would you like to use Granny's apartment?"

What the—? Juls widened her eyes.

"Your father and I have talked about selling it, but in the meantime, you're free to use it if you want to."

Juls glanced down at her hands. They were dirty, callused, nails cracked, and her clothes worn and stained. An apartment? Just like that?

Come on, who the hell was she kidding? Too much luxury for a homeless girl. She didn't deserve that much. Besides, after helping Reef out of custody, her primary mission was to find a job and *earn* a place to stay—a room, simple as that.

Juls let out a long breath and looked up. "Mom, it's very generous of you, it really is, but I can't accept."

Mom gave a smile that lit up her face. Radiating beauty—and maybe even a tad of genuine happiness—she cooed, "Yes, you can, Juliette. There's no reason we should sell it when it can be of use for you. Granny would have said the same thing. She loved you dearly and would ask for nothing more than to help you in one way or the other.

* * * *

"Hey, Dad." His shiny car idling at a red light, Connor spoke into the handsfree. He wore a white shirt with wet stains under the armpits, every movement causing a whiff of sour sweat to emanate. "Yeah, I'm good. Took an hour off work. And you?"

Juls sat on the edge of the leather passenger seat, body tense, knotting her hands. The loss of her most precious belonging was driving her half-nuts and the idea a stranger had access to her innermost thoughts irked her. Yet as much as she yearned to go back into the woods and search the campers' huts in the eventuality one of them were the thief, she needed to focus on getting Reef out of police custody first—and that meant treating her brother nicely. He had the means to get her to the station and the money for an eventual bail.

Gaze darting from the red light above, Connor nodded. "I'm with Juliette."

She wished the news wouldn't spread so fast. Despite promising not to, Mom would end up talking to her posh friends, Dad to his colleagues, Connor to his pals, and too soon, the whole population of Pearl would know Juls, the druggie, slept with the drunkard Reef and had a bout with the police. How would anyone give her a job? She should have kept quiet and found a way to help Reef on her own.

"She's a bit shaken up," Connor replied. "Remember my old friend Reef? The boy who used to hang around our house?" The light changed, and the car shot forward, motor growling like an angry lion. "Well, he's in custody now—" He listened and nodded. "Yeah, apparently he stopped a police dog that was a bit rough on Juliette. Uh-huh. And I figured since you're a lawyer, you could make a call and… Yeah, in Pearl."

Juls stifled a groan. She hated when people used their contacts to obtain favors, but since the time had come for her, she could only swallow her pride and thank the heavens she actually knew someone willing to place strategic calls.

"Okay, thanks," Connor said. "In the meantime, I'm driving her to the station." He hung up and focused on the road ahead.

They entered town. Narrow streets flanked by tall buildings replaced the quiet, low-roofed suburbs. Juls' heart raced. She loved the city, loved its smells of concrete dust and metal, loved its variety, life, colors… And she would always know how to survive on the street.

Connor's phone rang. He shot a glance at it and took the call. "Hey, Dad. Did you talk to someone?"

Juls stared at him, ears strained. The news she was about to hear were of mountainous importance.

"Are you sure?" he asked.

She held her breath.

"They'll let him out today? That's great."

Oh, the world was a good, good place after all. Warmth seeped into her veins and she slowly breathed out. She shouldn't have worried so much.

Connor nodded. "Yeah, I figured there'd be a bail. Did they tell you how much?" Reaching a crossroad, he put his blinkers on and turned to the right. "What did you say? Twenty grand?"

Shiiiiit. The blood drained from Juls' head. She took a deep breath. Twenty thousand dollars was a *lot* of money, more than she'd ever...

Connor straightened the car and shot her a glance. "Yeah, Dad, we got it covered." Holding the steering wheel with his left hand, he pulled the thick wad of dollar bills out of his right pocket and waved it in front of Juls' face. The money she refused yesterday. She'd hoped he would renew his offer on his own free will today so she wouldn't have to beg, and *bingo*, he did. Sweet relief washed through her, as if she'd swallowed a few mouthfuls of liquor. Her brother might have been an ass growing up, but he did have a heart.

She took the wad from his hand and counted the precious bills, incredulous at having so much money within reach. Three, four, five thousand...

Connor shook his head. "Honestly, Dad, we have the money. No worries. Yeah. But thanks. Exactly. It was self-defense, after all."

Ten, eleven, twelve...

"Okay, talk to you later. Thanks. Yeah, bye." He hung up and glanced at Juls' counting hands before concentrating on the road ahead.

Eighteen, nineteen... Reaching twenty thousand, she pocketed the bills and gave Connor the remainder, a wad even thicker than the one she kept.

"Keep it," he said. "There's fifty K, and it's all for you. Told ya yesterday."

"I can't take it, Connor. I want to earn my own money." She pushed the wad of bills back into his pocket. "Please don't insist."

He made a pouting face. "I'll just have to find another way to give it to you. By the way, Dad said he'll represent Reef in court. For free."

What?

"He will? For free?" Juls lifted her brows in utter surprise, unable to believe Dad's sudden generosity. What was going on with her family today? Why were they suddenly so understanding and helpful?

While he drove on, she fished out her new cell phone and entered Joey, Selena, and Laydi's phone numbers into the contact list. Mom's gift would be of great use: finally, Juls would be able to call the sisters from her own device. She sent them a quick text each notifying them about her new number.

Connor slowed the car, parked into a vacant space, and let the motor run. "There's the station." He pointed at a tall stone and black glass building across the street.

"That's the new one?"

"Yep. You just tell them you're here to pay his bail, sign a paper, give them the money, and they let him out."

"Okay. Aren't you coming?"

"No, I gotta get back to work."

"Oh." She gazed at the building. Disliking the idea of walking into the police station on her own after what happened this morning, she'd hoped Connor would handle the administrative stuff for her. She sighed. Time to put her big girl panties on and face the challenge. "Okay, thanks for the money. We'll pay you back when we can."

Heat spread across her face. Did she just say 'we' about Reef and her, as if insinuating they were already a couple? Wasn't that a little premature?

Connor shook his head. "Don't worry about it."

She swallowed to suppress her embarrassment. "What do you mean?"

"Just take the money. That's the least I can do for an old friend."

She gaped. "You're *giving* him twenty thousand dollars?"

Sweat making his face shine, he nodded and stared at the dashboard. "I wasn't there when he needed me. He was my friend, but it was too easy, too comfortable to look away and hope someone else would deal with him. Like with you"—he turned to her, eyes bleary—"I let you down, too."

How strange, to hear him talk like this. Both Reef and she had perceived him as a careless idiot. Had they been wrong the whole time, not seeing his potential?

He cleared his throat and went back to staring at the dash. "I know it sounds like I'm buying myself out of my bad conscience, but hey, you need the money, and I want to make it up to you, so…"

Touched by his openness, Juls put a hand on his arm and squeezed the clammy fabric of his shirt. "Thank you, Connor. It's very generous of you. I'll never forget it."

159

Red-faced, he shifted in his seat, sending a stronger whiff of sweat in her direction.

Time to go. Reef was waiting. She grabbed the door handle. "Don't you at least want to see him, and give him a chance to thank you in person?"

"Um, no, I gotta run. Need to get back to work." He turned and hastily kissed her cheek—full contact, this time.

She accepted the sticky touch of his skin. He'd just saved Reef's ass. But why wouldn't he see his old friend? Maybe he was too shameful to face him, and feared revisiting the past would give him a giant psychological slap in the face.

"All right." She pulled the handle and opened the door, cool air whooshing in and blowing up her hair. "I'll tell him you're the one who paid his bail. Thanks again." She stepped out of the car, grabbed her bag in the back seat, and prepared to cross the busy street.

Vehicles zoomed back and forth between her and the large building.

Reef. I'm coming to get you.

She couldn't wait to see him, and hold him. Her heart palpitated as his dancing eyes appeared in her mind, exuding warmth. What to expect of their futures? Only time would tell, but in the meantime, she would return the huge favor he did her this morning and thank him.

Behind her, Connor's car gave a loud roar and tires squealed as it sped away, mingling with the inner-city traffic.

* * * *

After Juls signed the bail form, handed over the money, and pocketed her driver's license, she waited in front of the long counter while the officer in charge went to retrieve Reef.

Only a few minutes, and they would be together again. Delicate butterfly wings fluttered in her stomach. At the same time, being inside a police station made her jumpy and uncomfortable. Whether she was guilty or not, cops always made her feel like she'd committed a crime. To make things worse, her skin itched from the ever-annoying abstinence, and had she not been in a public place, she'd scratch herself half to death.

She sighed and scanned the large room with multiple desks, milling uniforms, and low buzzing voices. Finally a little alone time to focus on the theft of her diary. Maybe she should seize the opportunity and ask someone. Of course, her notebook contained no information of value to the police, but if the officers who searched her believed she was a drug user, they'd also suspect her to keep notes and phone numbers.

Behind the information desk sat a forty-something year-old female police officer with square glasses beneath a buzz-cut, nose deep in her computer screen.

Juls hated to disturb, but saw no other choice. She headed to the desk, put her bag down, and cleared her throat. "Excuse me, may I ask you something?"

The woman, whose nametag said *Anderson*, looked up over her glasses. "Yes?"

Juls took a deep, calming breath. "Um… This morning, officers searched my bag, and then I noticed my notebook was missing. I wondered if you could check—"

"Where did the incident occur?"

"In the Boise woods, behind the large pond in—"

"What kind of notebook?"

The woman's briskness confused Juls. "Um, it's letter-sized," she said and lifted her hands to demonstrate the length, "and it's wrapped in flowery paper. Kinda like a gift wrap."

Through the glasses, Anderson's sharp eyes followed Jul's hand movements, a small smile at her mouth revealing amusement—at Juls' expense, no doubt. "And…why would they have taken it?"

Juls lowered her hands. "'Cause it's…um…a diary…"

The smile grew. "So…?"

Fuck. Juls cringed under the woman's arrogant scrutiny, hated having to explain something to the police—and, what pushed her buttons more, loathed her own fucking fear of authority. But she'd do anything to get her notebook back. "They were from the narcotics division. I don't know, maybe they thought it contained information or something."

"About what?"

Juls hesitated, reluctant to say the word *'drugs'* aloud as it placed its user on the lowest possible rank in society, below illegal immigrants, prostitutes, felons, you name it. In certain contexts, that loaded word paved way for contempt, abuse, and even forceful incarceration.

Anderson sat back in her chair and crossed her arms over her uniformed bosom. "Miss, you'll have to explain why these officers had reason to consider the content of your diary such value to their investigation, they thought important to confiscate it."

Ugh, explaining *that* meant admitting to this piece of shit that Juls used to be a druggie, and then hastily adding that she had sobered up, but, now knowing said piece of shit, the last part would be ridiculed.

Juls balled her fists. Heat invaded her face, a mix of anger and humiliation. She'd always been despised, looked down upon, judged as a low-life. The policewoman probably made up her mind on first impression. It was Juls' worn clothes, the hair, lack of make-up, the tattoo, dirty nails, the large duffel bag—each detail a flashing sign giving away its proprietor's social rank.

What a blow. No matter how much effort Juls put into starting her life anew, she was doomed to be a loser. Her chest constricted.

But you haven't tried yet, a calming voice in her head said. *If you wear nice clothes, a little make-up, and—*

Movement at her side. The officer's eyes shot sideways and widened in surprise.

Confused, Juls turned aside.

A serious-looking and freshly shaved Reef joined her and put his arm around her, as if to demonstrate his support.

Oh, Reef. Delicious warmth washed over her and drove her dark thoughts away. For a second or two, she closed her aching eyes and savored the consolation. He smelled of faint musk…and soap. The cops had been nice to him.

She opened her eyes.

He stared at her, a deep frown across his forehead. "You okay?" With his firm hand on her waist, he pulled her to him, pressing them hip-to-hip, and placed a chaste kiss on her temple.

His small gesture of affection caused her stomach to sizzle. She stood too close to see much of him, but enough to be enthralled. Without the beard, he was the teenager she crushed on many years ago, only older, his features sharper, and he oozed pure, unfiltered male sexiness. His clear blue eyes contrasted with the rough, tanned skin of his face, their beauty and sparkle of intelligence mesmerizing. Juls' breath caught.

Anderson gave a short cough. "Isn't he the one who was brought in this morning?"

Oh! The crude question brought Juls out of her semi-daze. She glared at the grinning woman and resisted the urge to deliver a long line of obscenities, which wouldn't help her case.

Breathe deep. One last try.

"Please," she said, containing all hints of spite, "would you check your files or ask the officers who searched—"

162

"Suuure." Gaze ping-ponging between Juls and Reef, the woman gave a curt smile that held no frankness, no sincerity.

Reef pulled Juls away, his look cold and sharp, and she had no choice but to follow him. With his back to Anderson, he asked between gritted teeth, voice almost a growl, "What's wrong, Julie?"

She wanted to give in and cry in his arms, but bit her lip and controlled the impulse. "Ugh, I'm tired. Let's just get out of here."

He puffed, dark gaze wandering to the other counter. "I gotta wait for the officer to get my stuff first. Why don't you wait outside?"

"Sure, I can—" A familiar ringing tone from her jacket interrupted. Whose was it again? Seven years of drug abuse had reduced her memory to a vegetative state.

Reef returned to the bail counter.

Heading to the front door, Juls searched her pockets and pulled out Mom's cell phone, with the blinking video call icon on the screen. Ah, yes. She rolled her eyes from her stupidity, took the call, and held the phone up.

Selena, Laydi, and Joey connected, three small videos appearing one next to the other. Juls' spirits lifted, and she held back a squeal of joy.

Three simultaneous, "Hi, Juls!"

"Hey, girls! Hold on a sec." With a hard shoulder, she pushed the door open, went out, and walked down the large stone stairs.

Mist filled the fresh air. Traffic whooshed by, busy as ever.

"What's up? You're lookin' good." Lay's grin told her she suspected a guy was responsible. Sharp as her cop dad, that girl was always spot on.

How were they going to react upon seeing Reef? He may have the looks of a Western movie star, but he carried an aura of rebellion and anarchy. It took character, a certain kind of personality, to want seclusion. The sisters had accepted Juls' status of homeless because they loved her, but, even though Reef wasn't a stranger to them, they would probably not approve that she chose a boyfriend who held her down, and kept her captive of the street.

She let her bag slide off her shoulder and swiveled so they wouldn't recognize the police station and ask questions. The reason Reef spent half the day in custody was a story for later, not when the events drained her of energy.

"You've changed." Selena tilted her head, blonde hair dancing.

Juls gave a small smile. So much had happened lately, she wasn't sure whether to feel good or bad. "I have?"

Joey laughed, big, brown eyes sparkling with happiness. No doubt, being with Talon did her a world of good. "Is there someone we should know about?"

Lay flashed her teeth. "Spit it out, girlfriend."

Juls filled her lungs with cool air. "Do you remember—"

The door opened. Carrying his folded leather jacket over an arm, Reef stepped down the stairs and joined her at the bottom. Her pulse pounded. Was that drop-dead gorgeousness really hers? Features inscrutable, he stepped up behind her and gazed over her shoulder. His now-familiar scent of *male hotness* drifted to her. When his free arm circled her stomach and pulled her backward against his warm, heavenly body, she nearly fainted.

"Oh, lookie!" Joey's excited voice had Juls focus back on the screen.

"Who's that?" Selena, equally eager.

"Can you see him?" Juls turned to Reef again, now cheek-to-cheek with her and peeking at the phone with interest in his gaze. "You remember these girls?"

While he squinted to discern them, Selena replied, "Of course we see him. The two of you make one."

Lay chuckled.

Reef's soft breaths brushed her nose and lips. "Hi," he said to her sisters. "I'm not sure we've met. If we have, it's gotta be more than fourteen years ago."

"Wait," Joey asked, "Aren't you the boy Juls' brother used to hang out with?"

He nodded. "You have a good memory."

Juls glanced back at the small screen. "He's Reef. The hottest guy in Pearl." She stuck her tongue out.

Lay widened her eyes. "Oh, you're Reef? Really?"

Selena smiled. "Yeeaah, I remember."

"We were little girls, then." Joey gave a slow nod, eyes dreamy, as if taking a dive into the past. "How did the two of you find each other?"

Lay grinned. "How long were you going to keep that from us, Juls?"

"When is the wedding?" chirped Selena.

Jul's head spun from her sisters' bombarding.

"Um," Joey said with a wink, "maybe you shouldn't invite us..."

Lay's grin widened. "With a guy like that..."

"We couldn't keep our hands off." Selena giggled.

Laughs all around.

Reef shook his head. "Ladies, ladies. It was nice to see you again, but there are a few things I can't wait to say to this one in private." He turned to Juls and just like that, placed warm, soft lips on her cheek.

Oh! So damn inviting. Need raced through her like hunger for a hit, causing the image of a needle to flash in her mind. But sex with Reef was better. As a choir of excited squeals came from the phone, she spun in Reef's arms and encircled his neck.

* * * *

Reef held Juls so hard and kissed her with such evident passion, she forgot where they were standing, and to breathe. She could only cling to his strong shoulders and hang on for the sensual ride.

Voice like a growl, he said to her mouth, "I've been waiting since last night to do this." While he pressed his crotch against her, an unmistakable bulge grew in his pants, sending flames to her sex.

Whimpering and squirming, she molded to him. Kissing was no longer prohibited in public, right? When his hand moved down to her ass, she opened her mouth and sought his wet, velvety tongue. Their teeth clashed from the hurry. Never, never had a guy turned her on like this. She loved his ruggedness, his scent, his taste, his undying hunger, and the way he made her feel alive, so full of vigor and excitement. This was worth quitting all the drugs in the world.

He let go of her lips and groaned, eyes pained. "You wild cat. I told ya I'm not gonna last."

A happy laugh rolled through her. She was in love, and this man would give her orgasm after orgasm for the rest of her life. His hand palmed and kneaded her ass, causing her inner muscles to moisten and burn. Eyes half-closed, she stared at his swollen lips and said with a low, sexy voice, "You, mister, are making me so wet I can barely stand."

With a groan, he took in a sharp breath and closed his eyes. "Shut up." His hard length pushed against her stomach.

Again, she laughed, perfectly thrilled that she could provoke such desire to a guy. In the past, they only wanted to screw her because she needed dope. She'd never considered herself woman enough, never imagined the hottest man on the planet would be aroused from her behavior.

Something fell to the ground between them.

"Shit." Jerking back, he released her and looked at his feet.

His jacket had slipped from his arm and landed on the asphalt. When it unfolded, out slid...her missing flowery-wrapped notebook.

Fuck! Air was punched out of her lungs. She gasped and stepped backward. What the hell? She refused to believe it, but her diary lay at her shoes. Reef had kept it the whole time.

Looking bothered, he bent to pick up both objects, straightened, and handed her the notebook with a trembling hand.

She snatched it and refrained from slapping him, overreacting. She didn't want him to see her desperate because of a lousy notebook. Though despite her efforts to stay composed, treacherous tears snuck up to her eyes and blurred her view.

"Say something," he pleaded, face decomposed.

Oh yeah? He had stolen from her, lied to her, the bastard. Pursing her lips hard so she wouldn't yell the *Fuck you* that resonated inside, she picked up her bag, turned on her heel, and made for the sidewalk.

Her blood boiled, sour, ugly. She'd fallen for a guy who, at the same time as she gave him her heart, committed the worst fucking betrayal.

Across the street, a block down from where Connor let her off, tall, broad-leaved trees loomed behind a black cast-iron fence. A park. Not knowing where else to go—or what the fuck to do with her life, for now—Juls headed in that direction, dodging cars and angry bicyclists. Huh, no one was angrier than she was.

"Julie!" Reef's hasty footsteps sounded behind her, but she could care less and instead increased the speed of her strides.

She entered the park, the air cooling and smelling fresher. The mist had lifted, but a low pressure of gray clouds hung over the trees. Her chest hurting too much from the turmoil, she filled her lungs, blew in and out, and sought reprieve.

Farther, an old woman with white curls and a black coat sat on a bench dealing out breadcrumbs to pigeons and ducks. Shrieking seagulls jumped between the other birds, stealing their food.

Juls' stomach growled. She hadn't eaten since last night by Reef's campfire. And because life was being such a motherfucking bitch today, she didn't mind lowering herself to be the same as she was in the past years: a beggar. Who cared what she did, anyway? She walked into the group of excited birds and waited for them to flap aside before continuing to the bench.

Grayish eyes suspicious, the old, wrinkled woman looked Juls' punk rock attire up and down.

As countless times on the streets of Columbus, Juls held her gaze and asked upfront, without shame, "S'cuse me. May I have some?"

The woman's eyes grew to the size of saucers. "Some *what?*" She shot a glance to the plastic bag in her hand. "This bread?"

"Yes. Please."

After a lengthy silence, the old lady broke off a chunk of bread—which looked to be loaf, and wasn't it funny how birds in this town were better fed than lower-caste humans—and handed it to Juls.

"Thanks. Have a nice day." Juls spun and continued into the park, eating so many mouthfuls of the delicious, fresh bread, she nearly choked. Too much at once. Better save some for later. She stuffed the rest into a jacket pocket.

In her peripheral vision, Reef followed from a distance, wearing his jacket. She didn't acknowledge him. Eventually, he would let go and get out of her life.

To think, he hadn't even apologized. Well, she never gave him the chance to, but her conscience was clean. She refused to give him any more thought. This tactic had worked with other guys.

She passed a dark-watered pond full of ducks diving and chasing each other. Their splashing and enthusiastic quacks competed with happy birds chirping from the trees. Calmness washed over her. Being surrounded by greenery and wildlife always alleviated her mood. This was home. In the past years, she'd slept more nights in parks than indoors. And after today's series of events, she longed to lie somewhere and doze off.

On the other side of the pond, a disheveled guy sat underneath a willow tree with his back to the large trunk. Long, hanging branches hung over the water, enclosing him.

He stared into the air, unkempt locks of greasy brown hair in front of his glassy, hallow eyes. The sickly skin of his sunken cheeks, the long, too-sharp nose, and thin, crackled lips indicated malnutrition. After years on the street, Juls could recognize a hardcore junkie from a mile.

She couldn't pass a brother in need without helping in one way or another. Heart knotting, she headed in his direction, stopped at his holed shoes, and waited for his dark, blank eyes to drift to her before asking, "Hey, mind if I sit here?"

Mouth chewing as if missing teeth, he gave a slow nod.

"Okay." She dropped the duffel bag, placed her diary atop it, and sat on the hard dirt ground with her arms hanging over her knees.

Probably too smashed to process thought, he didn't say a word.

"You hungry?" She extracted the piece of bread from her pocket and showed him.

After some time, he nodded. She handed him the bread, and he lifted a trembling hand and closed long, black fingers around it.

The duck quacking from the pond behind her intensified. Then, seconds later, movement at her side.

She slowly turned her head. In the corner of her eye, Reef approached and sat beside her.

Son of a… Pain coursed through her chest, but she resisted the want to react on impulse. Or react at all. If she didn't give him a kind of response, he would abandon and walk away. She stared at her hands. Two distinctive breathing sounds reached her ears. The junkie's deep, throaty inhale and Reef's faint breaths, normal, and…familiar.

Ugh, they'd spent about twenty-four hours together, if you didn't count his time in custody. They'd talked, laughed, reminisced, cried together, made love, and he wrestled a dog to save her. In those hours, she'd grown fond of him. So, so goddamn fond. What a mistake. She bit her lip, needed to think of something else. But what—who—else did she care about? Her throat hurt. She swallowed.

His hand shot out and grabbed her diary on top of the bag, startling her.

So fast, and what nerve! Why wouldn't he leave that damn thing alone? Were her musings so interesting he couldn't keep his fucking hands off?

"Got a pen?" he asked.

"*What?*" Incredulous, she looked up.

His clear blue eyes entered her vision, demanding she focus. "A pen. You must have one, no?"

"Um, yeah." Why didn't she reply no? What the hell was wrong with her?

Too late to regret. Reluctant, she searched her leather jacket and handed him the pen. Why, a shrink would have to explain.

"Thanks." He turned the pages of her diary, not stopping once to read, until the first plain double pages appeared. Stretching his long legs, he steadied the notebook on his lap and wrote:

'Once upon a time, a sad bum was living in his hut in the woods with a bottomless bottle of sorrows. He fell in love with the most beautiful girl. She made him happy. She was smart and strong, and great things were in the cards for her.

Soon, she would embark on a new journey and leave the bum behind. He would spend the rest of his life alone in his hut, slowly drowning in his bottle. So the day she prepared to leave, he decided to do something to hold her back.'

While Reef's words filled the first page, Juls' heart knotted. She tried to focus on how each letter he put onto paper turned crooked, or the way his fingers trembled from years of alcohol abuse—anything to distract herself from the message he was writing her, for it held a promise of pain.

Taking an audible breath, he continued on the next page:

'The bum decided to take the girl's most precious belonging, because it would force her to stay. He knew if she found out he was responsible, she would

*hate him. But it was better to have the love of his life nearby, hating him, than far
away on her new, exciting journey, forgetting about him.'*

Aw, she understood what drove him to steal her diary.

Her eyes burned from the building emotion, and no matter how much she
swallowed to keep the hurt down, the choking of her throat wouldn't relent.

Epilogue

Girl Code #21: Your girlfriends will always forgive you.

A tiny sound at Reef's side, definitely feminine. A contained gasp?

He lifted the pen and glanced over at Julie.

As if having sensed him, she tilted her head to the junkie. Her abrupt movement made the dark brown locks dance before her face, and, like a convenient curtain, conceal her features.

Why so eager to avoid him, after what he wrote in her notebook? Hadn't she caught his message? Worse, did she even read his words?

Wrong questions. Whether she did or not, she turned her back to him. Refused him. The woman he'd loved for as long as he could remember was slipping through his hands, and who was responsible?

In the face of his ruthless, inexorable destiny, he struggled to keep his composure. The need for a drink ravaged his system. If he lost Julie, he would fight the thirst now, but what about later today, when the weight of loneliness became unbearable? And tomorrow?

He stared at the back of her head wishing he could kiss her with his eyes. He wanted to grab her shoulders, bring her close to him, nuzzle his nose into her soft, fluffy hair, and breathe in the scent of his woman. Because he loved her so fiercely, she had the capability to break him, but, as experienced several times since they met, she could drive him half-crazy with lust, too. How many times did he wake at her side during the night to eat her with his eyes and just barely contain the urge to stroke her sensual body, his own growing aroused and sweaty with need.

Everything about Julie attracted him, from her stone-hard will and uncompromising rebellious attitude, to her deeply rooted care for the weak and utter selflessness. Not to mention her looks. She radiated such beauty and feminine confidence. His heart cried and laughed at the same time. He loved her, simply. She was perfect for him. You didn't find that kind of match too often.

It was all for nothing, though. She made her choice the moment she discovered his betrayal.

Vision blurring, he glanced down at the crooked words he wrote in her diary, starting with *Once upon a time*. Ah, but their relationship wasn't a fairytale.

Happily ever afters were not in the cards for losers like he, those who'd given up on life.

The dice had been casted. Nothing he could do now, except add a few more words before the final goodbye.

His hand rattling worse than ever, he hurried to scribble beneath the last line, *'The bum hoped the love of his life would find it in her heart to forgive him.'*

Would she be able to decipher these hastily written words? A plea—but who was he to plead to a woman like her? She was a chosen one—her future shone with glory and esteem.

Maybe when she reopened her diary sometime in the next days or months, she'd re-read his apology and understand. But would it change her mind? Would it change a thing if she did? He would be long gone by then, enduring his miserable existence deep in a thin sleeping bag, slowly dying in his hut far off in the woods. That, he was convinced of.

She spoke at his side. "You look cold." Her words almost a whisper, as if speaking to herself. "Winter's right around the corner."

Surprised, Reef glanced at her. With her back still turned to him, Julie searched her jacket, pulled out a few items, and stood to slide them into her pants pockets.

The junkie at her feet had nodded off, the black-fingered hands twined over his belly livid. She was right. Regular tremors beneath his worn clothes indicated he was freezing in his sleep. After brushing her clothes of dust, she took her black leather jacket off, bent to spread it over his chest, and straightened.

"Not enough." With a sniff, she swiveled toward her bag and knelt abruptly in front of it, avoiding Reef, but finally showing him her tense, tear-stricken face, biting her lower lip so hard it whitened.

His heart missed a beat. He loathed seeing the woman he loved hurt. Was she crying for the unconscious guy? A weird mix of pride and jealousy raced through him. Julie was pure, infinitely generous, and loving her was right. At the same time, she bled for someone else.

As if having no patience for Reef, she tore the diary from him and closed it with a *bang*, the move so fast the tattooed birds of freedom on her wrist seemed to flap their wings. How symbolic—she was flying away from him.

Fuck. "Wait, Julie." He lifted the pen in an attempt to stall her.

She didn't reply, but opened her bag and dropped the notebook inside. Her breaths came out short, and her wet eyes shimmered with tension. She ripped the pen from his hand and pocketed it.

"Julie." He hated the pleading sound of his voice.

After a few seconds of searching, she pulled her sleeping bag out, and, without a glance at Reef, turned to the junkie. "This should help a little." She zipped open the fluffy duvet and slid it up the guy's legs, lifting one shoe after the other, groaning from the efforts. He mumbled something but never opened his eyes.

When the sleeping bag reached the guy's waist, she zipped it closed. "There." Chest heaving, she stood and contemplated him for a few lengthy seconds.

Behind her, the sun appeared between branches, a barely noticeable ball of luminosity through the grayish clouds.

Reef couldn't wait any longer. He wanted to respect her need to care for others, but his own needs sent pain racing through him. "Julie, please."

At last, she deigned to look at him. "I'm gonna go get myself a job," she said, voice low but firm, determination making her wet eyes sparkle like two bright stars at night. At chest level, a grinning Sid Vicious smirked to the world, defiant as the girl wearing his picture.

"Julie, I wrote you something—"

"But before that, I gotta find some nice clothes to wear. And fix my hair." She looked excited. More even, hopeful.

Her sudden change of attitude confused the hell out of him, and boy was he absolutely not ready for her to leave yet. His chest tightened as if compressed by vices. "S-sweetie," he stuttered, his vocal chords squeezed with nervousness. He pointed at her bag, where she put the diary, and his apology. "F-first, read what I—"

She smiled, her beauty and innate charm melting the last of his vigor. "I don't need to read any more."

"W-what?"

"I want you to come with me." She slid a hand into a pants pocket and pulled out a set of shiny silver keys. "Look, I got a place in town."

At a complete loss for what was going on, he could only shake his head. "What are you t-talking about? You're f-forgiving me?"

"I don't think I can get out of the gutter alone. I need your strength."

"My...my strength?" He widened his eyes, and, as the meaning of her invitation dawned on him, he suddenly found the ability to speak. "Sweetie, I barely have the will power to stay sober *one day*. It's gonna be one day at a time for the rest of my life."

"Me, too. The withdrawals are driving me half-nuts and it's too easy to get back into the circle. But the alternative is..." She shot a glance at the junkie, whose head lolled to a side, spittle drooling from his half-open, toothless mouth. "So, come with me."

Icy fear coursed through Reef's muscles. He wasn't ready. Never would be. "Baby, you don't know if I'll fall again. And if I do, *when* I do, I'll bring you down with me."

"I'm willing to take that chance. I love you, Reef."

His breath caught. Everything around him crumbled, the beliefs he'd thought safe to have, the feelings he'd begun to accept as parts of him. So it had all been wrong, but then, what was right?

"I can pretend to be fine on my own for a while," she continued, "but the truth is I can't do it without you."

His head spun. She didn't understand. "No, Julie." God, he was tired.

"Yes. Together, we'll be okay if we join forces."

"Forces? I have no forces. I'm weak. I'm nothing, a nobody." Moments ago, he was the one who begged her to stay, but the prospect of rebuilding a life with her and being responsible for her scared the living shit out of him.

She tilted her head with a small smile. "You're my hero. What you did this morning was pretty amazing, and as much as the cops hated that you interfered, they must have thought the same thing."

"No... I'd do it again, but it wasn't heroic." Her calm tone told him she meant well, yet it had double impact, did his self-esteem good and killed him at the same time: each praise, he countered with negativity, buried himself deeper into his own demise. He groaned. "No one in their right mind would see a dog hurt someone and not do something."

"Stop talking yourself down. You're the guy I want in my life. I need you by my side. What more do I have to say to convince you?"

His lungs ached. "Julie, what you need is someone stable, in good mental health, who'll help you stay on track. I'm a loser, just barely good enough to survive another day in my hut and hide from the world. While you—"

"No, Reef..."

"While you got big things ahead. Big things that will ensure you make the right choices, because they'll make you want to *live*."

Agile like a cat, she squatted and scrutinized him, brown eyes the beauty of jewels searching deep in his soul. "*Do* you want to live?"

He bit his lip, sucked in a breath, and needed to think fast. Julie's sincerity and profound kindness gave his heart a kick. She was the right choice, the only alternative. He swallowed the mix of pain, fear, and incertitude that had lodged inside for so long. Opted for love, hope, courage. "With you, yes."

"That's all we need." She extended her hand. "C'mon."

If he went with her, he would have to put a giant cross on everything booze-related, his dark thoughts, unquenchable thirst, and sudden pulses. It had been so incredibly easy and demanded so little resolution to live in the past and nurture his sorrows. With Julie, he would need to look forward to every remaining second of the rest of their lives. Never tread wrong, never destabilize her. Be positive, help her stay on her feet, and push her toward their future.

He reached out, *Quick, before I regret,* and grabbed her warm hand.

And on her end, Julie stood and pulled with the happiest smile, her frail but oh-so-determined spirit dragging him out of the dirt.

~The End~

~FAITH~

By

Cait Jarrod

~Dedication~

FAITH is dedicated to the men and women of the United States Arm Forces for their valor and immeasurable sacrifice. To their families for their unrelenting support and to the Wounded Warrior Project who aid in helping the warriors live their lives to their fullest.

THANK YOU!

Acknowledgements
Brittney O'Bryan, Patricia Smart, Neva Brown, and Norma Redfern, thank you for your valuable feedback and advice.

Writers In Crime—the authors of Girl Code—what a trip putting this anthology together has been. I can't thank each of you—Lea Bronsen, Jessica Jayne, and DC Stone—enough for the exciting journey. From the amazing edits to the support, I will never forget the interaction and camaraderie that went into the development of this wonderful book.

A special thanks to Julie Ann Walker for making this endeavor extra special with an introduction, and to Mallory Braus for her excellent craft advice.

A shout out to the talented Jay Aheer for the gorgeous Girl Code Cover.

~Cait

Chapter One

Girl Code #28: Never date a girlfriend's ex.

One phone call! One!—from General Ray Bodine three days ago stating he needed his daughter home to help him recoup from a car accident, had Selena's commander on a mission. Lieutenant Colonel Sullivan would do anything if it meant pleasing the general he admired, including ordering Criminal Investigator Staff Sergeant Selena Bodine to take leave.

Not her. She didn't bow to anyone, especially not dear ole Dad, a man who hadn't seen fit to act like a father since she'd turned eight.

She thumbed through the file on her desk, checking the final paperwork on a case before following orders to go to Pearl, Ohio.

Going to her hometown to help her father wasn't the internal battle she fought most. Seeing the place where her family fell apart gave her palpitations.

As much as she faulted Dad for his lack of parenting skills, her mother, Alice, held the award for worst parent. The day Mom walked out, the pain was so intense it numbed her from the inside out. She didn't wish that level of agony on anyone. Though the sensation lessened some over the years, she still hadn't shaken it. She longed for the days where love bounced off the walls as it had before Alice left.

Alice said, "I'll see you in a few days," as carefree as going to the store to buy a loaf of bread. Seventeen years ago!

The not knowing why she left ate at Selena. Alice didn't give a reason why she didn't want her daughter. Didn't explain why she'd stopped loving her or her husband.

She rubbed her chest to alleviate the pain. It didn't work. "I need caffeine." She tossed her pencil on top of a file folder and snatched her mug. Not even eight and she had drunk three cups. But who counted?

Not her. She'd need several more cups to have enough strength to face her father.

Reaching the break room, she took in the empty carafe. "Darn it." She rose on tiptoes and tugged down the coffee can from the top shelf. Times like these, she liked her above-average height. She worked on fixing the much-needed brew then rested back on the counter, listened to the hissing of the pot, and waited.

Freshwater Pearl subdivision may be a place she dreaded, but visiting Pearl gave her an excited rush to see her sisters. Any time she could see them was a good day. Pearl had gifted her with the three most amazing friends a person could possibly have. Their bond so strong and unique, she'd made up a saying about them.

Each sister fought demons, and fought them well. Yet together, their weaknesses turned to strength. They empowered, inspired, and set records to what girl code exemplified. What true friendship meant.

Joey and Juls lived in Pearl, not far from her childhood home. Laydi was available by phone. Having everyone together in Pearl, hanging out at their favorite spot—the pond—would be great.

She hadn't stayed at Dad's house since she left for the United States Air Force at seventeen, and hadn't intended to do so again. Yet…one memorable event lingered, replaying in her dreams.

The delicious night beside the pond.

Scared and unsure if the Air Force would help put her life on track, she dumped her fears on a guy she just met. Even though his body language revealed something worried him, he had listened. How they consoled one another was nothing short of fantastic. She left feeling more alive than ever. Her first time with a complete stranger still rocked her world.

Part of her, the one where the little girl within believed in happily-ever-after like in the movies, hoped that guy would be her knight in shining armor.

Fat chance, especially since she didn't get his name.

The coffee pot beeped it finished. She poured a cup and went to collect her keys. She might as well pack and locate her ride. She would catch a flight from Andrews Air Force Base to Wright-Patterson's base near Fairborn, Ohio. From there, she would ask Juls and Joey to pick her up.

"Bodine," Sullivan snapped as she passed his door. "Come in here."

She winced at his sharp tone. The supervisor of investigations had always been curt. This morning, he hit the angry bulldog stage.

She stepped into his office.

Sullivan had a rectangular face with a sturdy jawline. A pair of glasses perched on the end of his narrow nose, aging him at least ten years. As his slit-like eyes landed on her, she suspected he knew more about her apprehension to return to Pearl than she'd like.

"Yes, sir."

"What are you still doing here?" He pointed a file folder toward her.

The sloppy scrawl on the tab drew her attention. *A new case.*

Like a biscuit tempting a dog, a case yelled to her. She couldn't wait to sink her teeth into the meat of it. The drive for truth, not just in her job, became a part of her when life reeled with questions. Ones that remained unanswered. Solving a mystery gave her value. Gave satisfaction someone else wouldn't have to worry or wonder everyday about their love ones' whereabouts or what happened to them.

"I'm working until my plane is ready, sir."

When Mom disappeared, she did everything an eight-year-old could do. She searched the house, the yard, and the neighborhood.

She moved further inside her boss' office until she discreetly read the file folder. 'Homicide-suicide' followed by a question mark.

"I expect you on a plane by one-thousand hours," Sullivan's voice boomed.

"Yes, sir. While I wait, may I investigate the case in your hand?"

The lieutenant colonel bit the inside of his lip. The telltale sign a 'Your dad and I go way back' speech would commence. Anytime someone mentioned the retired general, Sullivan told a story of when the general, then a senior airman, saved Sullivan's life by exposing himself to enemy fire. While her chest swelled for what Dad had done, her admiration was no different toward him from any other military member who had put their lives in harm's way.

"Sir, if the case takes too much time"—she rushed to say before his long-winded tale began—"I'll pass it to someone else."

He removed his glasses and pressed a palm to each of his eyes. A tall man, standing over six-foot, no one berated or mocked the forty-five year-old officer. His bark brought results. As General Ray Bodine's daughter, she received special treatment. Not something she encouraged or liked, but if it got her on the case he held, she used it.

"Check it out." He angled the folder at her again, teasing her with its contents. "If it becomes time inclusive, then Senior Airman Flowers takes over."

"Got it, sir."

"Flowers," he yelled.

Airman Flowers, with a thin layer of hair covering his sun-kissed scalp, could bore anyone with his 'look-what-I did' stories. Gorgeous, tanned, but his egotistical attitude gave her a reason to say no to his many advances. "Sir." He stopped beside her.

"You and Bodine," Sullivan said, lifting the file before handing it to her. "Not sure if the crime is a homicide, suicide, or two homicides."

She opened the folder and perused the pictures. Two victims—one male, one female—each received a bullet wound to their upper torso. The female had an air of familiarity. Selena took in the name and address. For a split second, she let the sadness in for the lives lost, and then swallowed hard, shoving it away, and put on her blank expression.

As a plus one to a barbecue earlier in the spring, she met the Rodriquezes, but didn't know them personally.

"The bodies are still warm," Sullivan said.

Good. She'd get the opportunity to be one of the first on the scene. "Thank you, sir." She turned to Flowers. "Ready?"

"Always," he said, tugging her ponytail so the boss couldn't see, and held up his keys.

"Don't forget what I said, staff sergeant," Sullivan said. "You need this vacation as much as the general needs your help."

"Yes, sir," she said, when she really wanted to say, "butt out."

During the short ride to the crime scene, she gave Flowers the highlights. "Two victims. One male, one female, Hispanic descent. No sign of a struggle." She closed her folder. "And no tugging the ponytail. It's off limits," she said in a tone not harsh, but not gentle either.

"Yes, Blue Eyes." Flowers winked and parked the car. "I mean ma'am."

Used to the same routine and finding him harmless, she ignored his comments and climbed out. Truth be told, she didn't let anyone else close enough to flirt. Relationships meant heartache, something she learned from Mom and Dad's rocky marriage. An emotion she didn't want to deal with.

The house resembled most of the homes not far from base—two stories, groomed yards with little vegetation. Few airmen and their families invested time in a lawn they wouldn't have for long.

She nodded at Airman Freeman positioned outside and entered via the front door. Clean floors, no dust, and no sign of a forced entry. Both bodies slumped on the family room couch, next to each other. For the attacker to get close without one of the victims moving, it appeared they knew him. "A friend," she mentioned to Flowers and knelt in front of the victims.

"That's my guess." He stopped and wrote in his notebook.

The wide range of powder speckling the entry wounds suggested the shooter stood close.

She recalled the barbecue. Carmen Rodriquez laughed as she worked her way through company. While her husband, Juan, grilled and joked with his fellow airmen.

"Not long ago, I attended a gathering here." Selena straightened. "The couple and their son conversed easily with their guests."

"Son?" Airman Caron approached, his pupils darkening to match his hair. "They have a son?"

Since they'd been co-workers for the last year, she'd learned Caron did his homework and double-checked his findings.

"There's nothing in their personnel history to suggest they do."

"Check into it some more," she said. "I'm positive Carmen introduced him as her son. Dig past the usual background. Go deeper."

Her heart broke for the child. Losing a parent at any age sucked the life out of a person. She hadn't lost either of hers to death, at least she didn't think so, but she lost them just the same. "They introduced him as Manny. He's about twelve or thirteen."

"No sign of a boy living here during the house search," Caron said.

With every detail they uncovered, she grew more intrigued. She wanted to stay and work the case to the end, but no way would Sullivan allow it. "They introduced him as their son," she said to Caron as he rifled through papers on the kitchen table at the rear of the house.

"I got this," Flowers said. "You go pack."

She refused to pack until the last minute. Of course, he heard about her upcoming trip. Besides her commander talking loud enough to include the whole office in the conversation if they wanted, no doubt Flowers heard through the rumor mill. Whoever said gossip died in the eighties had never worked in her department. "I agree."

"Bodine," Caron yelled from the back of the house. "In the yard, at four o'clock, is that your boy?"

Selena moved to the living room window and peeked out. A young dark haired boy faced the woods. "Right height and hair. Let's go." She raced out the front door. This part of her job—confronting a child to inform his parents were dead—she loathed. "Don't rush him."

"Too late. He's a runner," Caron shouted, his voice fading as the screen door banged.

She bolted out the open front door and down the steps.

Flowers' boots pounded the ground behind her.

Keeping a hand on her holstered side arm, she raced in the opposite direction and darted behind the house. Sprinting down a slight slope, she headed toward the woods acting as a barrier between the yards.

A frightened boy would take shelter there. She would have, and had done so on numerous occasions.

Inside the dim area, she leaned against a tree and scanned the surroundings.

Sure enough, the boy blasted into the woods, breaking twigs and crunching rotten leaves. Fifty yards in front of her, he tucked behind a tree and peeked around the trunk. His hands pressed against the bark, his shoulders heaving with every breath.

She didn't trust his jerky movements. His body language didn't read a scared boy who possibly witnessed what had happened to people he cared about, but more a defensive one. Cautiously, she moved forward until close enough for them to have a conversation. Close enough to squeeze the trigger if warranted without a tree blocking her path. "Manny," she said in a firm voice.

He stiffened.

"Keep your hands where I can see them. I'm Staff Sergeant Bodine. We met at your barbecue not long ago. I need you to turn around slowly."

"Can't." The pitch in his voice was low, almost a mumble.

Concerned his argumentative behavior would carry through in his actions, she used the tree for cover and called her partner. "Agent Flowers."

Manny didn't move. His shoulders slumped.

"Got him," she said. "Line is open."

"On our way."

She hated not knowing if the boy would do something stupid, like resist arrest. "Let's talk through this before the others arrive." When the other agents arrived, if they thought Manny combative, they'd act quickly and restrain him before he confided. "Trust me, Manny. You want us to have this sorted out before anyone else joins us."

His right hand lowered to the front of his jeans.

Crap! The slim chance he'd talk fled. Instincts on high alert, she drew her gun and pointed it at the young teen. "Don't! I will shoot!"

He lifted his hands in the air and faced her with tormented eyes. Blood splattered the front of his yellow shirt. The butt of a gun poked out of the waistband of his jeans. "I didn't—" His mouth trembled.

Flowers, along with Caron, approached from behind Manny. If she could keep him talking, she could distract him long enough for one of the agents to apprehend him without too much of a struggle. She hoped. "What didn't you do?" She maintained a calm she didn't feel.

Tears fell as Manny reached for the butt of the gun.

"Manny, don't!"

"I'm sorry. I didn't want to return to the street," he said, his voice cracking. "They said they couldn't adopt me. Do you know what it's like not to have anyone in your corner?"

She had firsthand knowledge, but she wouldn't open her personal life to him. Holding back tears threatening to show her as weak, she said, "There are people who are willing to help. Let's make a deal, put your gun down, and I'll go with you."

"He esuchado las mentiras antes," Manny said. "No más." *I have heard the lies before. No more.*

This could go down a thousand different ways. In a shooting rage, he could fire on everyone in his path. Since he hadn't, she doubted he would. Or suicide by cop. Lord, she hoped not. "Manny, listen."

He jerked the gun out of his waistband.

"No!" Sweat pebbled her forehead.

"Drop it!" Flowers demanded, not a yard behind Manny.

With the gun held out in front of him, he didn't point it at her or the other agents. The barrel aimed at the empty woods. A good thing.

"Don't force me to make you drop it!" Flowers ordered.

"Manny, do as he says," she shouted. *Please, please don't do anything stupid.* "This will go a lot easier on you if you do what we ask."

His face fell, defeat reflecting in his eyes, as he dropped onto his knees, yet kept the gun at his side.

"Please." She detested for a teen to have his life cut short, especially when he thought there wasn't a better one. One flinch of his arm and she, Flowers, and Caron would have no choice but to shoot. "Drop the gun."

He wobbled, landed on his palms, and let loose a howl. The pain in his cry cracked open her chest.

Caron swooped in and snatched the gun from Manny's weakened grasp.

"I wish you'd shot me." Manny sobbed. "Put me out of my misery."

How did one respond to a request with such an open wound? Say things would get better? Nothing she said could soothe someone who time and time again had a dark cloud looming over him with no hope of a bright light. She knew. She'd been there.

The heat in the woods grew intense. Her lungs constricted. Her stomach roiled. She needed air and dashed through the sticks and leaves, pushing tree limbs out of the way. The edge of the woods morphed into a long, narrow path.

"Bodine!" Flowers yelled.

Answering him was out of the question. The empathy for Manny flashed her to a time where confusion and uncertainty ruled her life.

"Staff Sergeant." Caron caught up to her in the yard. "You okay?"

She sucked in a deep breath, filled her lungs with clean air, and cleared her thoughts.

"Lieutenant colonel likes it or not, you ain't going anywhere until we wrap this up."

Glad for the distraction, she stopped. "Stepping out of the musty smell for a second," she said in a firm, controlled tone, while her nerves roared in chaos.

"All right." Caron spun on his heels and disappeared into the leaves.

The sun heated her turned-up face, but she didn't get warm. No doubt, the bone-deep cold resulted from her emotions and the similarities of Manny to her own past.

Not minutes ago, her heart broke for this kid. She felt a kinship with him for not having parents. Identified with how hard his life would be all alone. Now, she didn't know what to think or feel. It was one thing to try to overcome struggles for what life tossed at you. Quite another to act like a coward and shoot people, if, in fact, he had.

"Sarge," Caron called.

Selena flinched and swiped a hand over her face. She didn't mean to stay out here so long.

He moved a branch and stepped out of the woods. "One call to Social Services and I got the info we need."

"Fast work." She blinked the fogginess out of her mind and focused. Receiving the information so quickly didn't bide well for Manny. The social workers must not have had to dig for his information, which meant they probably dealt with him often. "Whatcha got?"

"Manny's biological parents died years ago," Caron said. "He lived on the streets until the Rodriquezes found him and took him in."

"How did his biological parents die?"

"Mistaken identity. Wrong place, wrong time. Who knows? Lots of these cases go cold."

"Yes, they do," she said, thinking about her missing mother. She turned and went into the woods to help finish processing the scene.

* * * *

Hours later with tension gnawing at her shoulders, she headed out of her office and broke into a run toward her townhouse.

Manny confessed. A little pressure and he spilled like a child who'd never see his favorite pet if he didn't. His confession came easily and with lots of tears. So terribly sad. The whole situation stunk.

If he had listened, he would have learned the Rodriquezes wanted him. Carmen had said, "We can't adopt you," and Manny shot her. Then shot her husband. His hopeful parents had been working with Social Services to iron out the legalities. If he'd listened to everything Carmen had to say, he would have heard, "yet."

Why upset him? And how in the hell did Manny get a gun so easily? Questions Flowers and Caron would investigate. She filled out her paperwork and stepped away from the case to head to Pearl. Darn it, she wanted to see the case through to the end.

She needed her sisters worse than she needed a shower, to wash away the image of the boy's face. The one resembling hers when she peered into a mirror, the all-consuming look of someone lost.

Raw memories from her childhood encroached and weighed heavily. She'd been as desperate as Manny for attention.

The difference between Manny and her—she never thought about killing anyone. Still, she'd lived the pain he experienced, understood the desperate measures to feel loved. Her sisters had intervened, preventing her downward spiral, stopped her from misfortunes. No one had been there for Manny. But *lordy*, shooting people he'd supposedly loved. There had to be some way to help troubled kids. If only she possessed the strength and means to do something.

Today's incident, mixed with her father calling, ripped the scab off the wound she guarded so well. The scab that saved her from feeling the angst of what happened years ago.

She sucked in a deep breath, rounded the corner to her street, and pushed the video group button she'd set up for her sisters.

"Hey." Juls answered the phone quickly. "How are you?"

"Good."

"Liar," Laydi chimed in.

"Yeah, your voice is too tight," Joey said. "Don't try to kid a kidder. Your face is red, too."

She loved seeing their bright faces. "I'm coming to Ohio."

"As in Pearl?" Joey asked, her voice as tense as hers. "Or as in your subdivision, Fresh Water?"

As unremarkable as the question was, it was significant. When she came to visit her sisters in Pearl, she never came to the place she grew up. "Fresh Water."

She peered at the clear sky and blinked away the moisture. "My dad had an accident. He called me to help."

"You're kidding me?" Laydi's voice rose over whatever Juls and Joey had said. "Why?"

"I don't know."

"You can do this," Juls said, addressing her worries without her having to say a word.

"I had a case today. The boy wasn't any different from me, the same turbulent childhood."

"So sad." Joey's voice laced with concern. "What happened?"

"He shot and killed the people who wanted to be his parents when he thought they wouldn't adopt him. He'll have a rough road."

"Sounds like he deserves it," Laydi said in her police officer, matter-of-fact tone. "What's the problem?"

She couldn't stop her feelings from seeping into her police work where children were concerned. She admired Laydi's ability to categorize situations and keep them in their proper place. "I wish there were better programs to help troubled kids."

"You can't conquer the world," Juls said. "But you can reach out to children around you."

"Maybe one day. First, I have to conquer this visit with my dad. I'm putting you all on standby."

"You betcha." This came from Laydi.

"Call any time," Juls added.

"I'm right around the corner," Joey offered. "If you need a break from your father, come on over."

"Love you girls."

'Love yous' returned, and she disconnected.

She could do this—tend to Dad, be the dutiful daughter. As soon as he regained his strength, she'd get the hell away from Fresh Water.

* * * *

Detective Cullen Wilson knocked on the door of his kid brother's Northern Virginia apartment. During the last two hours, Todd had left two voice messages on his cell. The first one, Todd said he needed bail money. The second, he'd come across some and told him not to worry.

Asking Cullen not to worry was like asking him to stop breathing. He did it and would continue to do so, just as he had since their parents' death. Eight years older than Todd, he had acted like a helicopter parent and couldn't stop hovering over his younger brother. Every friend Todd played with, he checked out. In sports, he cheered him on. They were brothers, best friends, and parents to one another.

He knocked harder. "Come on, Todd, open up!"

If Todd went on another drinking binge or was off gambling, Cullen would beat the living shit out of him.

No answer.

He pressed his forehead against the cool metal. He didn't have time for this shit.

Worn out from pulling an all-nighter on a counterfeit case, he could barely stand. He eased away and pounded his fist against the door. "Open up!"

"Todd isn't home." A slow drawl came from the elevators.

Tension settled into his shoulders as he twisted toward Mason Baldwin. A short, balding man with a belly that made the buttons on his shirt scream, one he deemed pretentious and a user. His good friend, Congressman Alexander Kane, considered his attorney sincere and loyal.

Alex had been a neighbor and a good friend to his and Todd's uncle in Pearl, Ohio. Whenever they visited, Alex welcomed them as if they were his nephews. After their parents' freak hot air balloon accident, Alex stepped forward to help raise Todd. Cullen would always be in his debt. But with him came Baldwin, Alex's nosey-ass attorney. "What are you doing here?"

"I'm meeting Congressman Kane and Todd here."

Guilt filled him for not being able to help Todd. "I called the police station."

"Please," Baldwin said and waved a dismissive hand. "You don't need to explain. I went to the jail, bailed your brother out, and then escorted him to the Congressman's car a block up the street in case the media watched. He's taking your brother to a drive-thru for something to eat."

Chuckling, Cullen rested against the wall in the bright hallway and folded his arms. Only Todd could convince a health-nut like Alex to drive through a fast food joint.

"They should arrive any minute."

As if Baldwin's words were a preamble to Todd and Alex's arrival, the elevator hummed to life and they stepped onto the fourth floor.

The light in Todd's steel-colored eyes had disappeared, the area around them blackish-blue. He had a cut lip. His military cut had grown out in the last few months, softening his hard appearance.

Todd glanced at him before sticking his key in the door lock. "I need a shower and aspirin."

He agreed. Todd stunk of beer and rotten sweat. "We gonna talk about this?"

"Nothing to talk about. I lost a bet, couldn't pay up, and got into a fight. You weren't available, so I called Alex."

Todd shoved the door open and disappeared down the hall. A second later, the bathroom door shut, closing off any chance he would have of grilling him.

Cullen focused on the man who'd helped him and Todd countless times. Giving thanks with a head nod, he signaled for Alex and Baldwin to enter the apartment. "I'm surprised you're in Washington, D.C. I assumed you had returned to California."

Alex sat on the couch, facing the glass doors leading to the patio. "Todd has such a great view."

Cullen didn't think so. Buildings blocked the Lincoln Memorial and the Washington Monument. "Would you like some coffee?"

"Yes," Alex said, "thank you."

A man in his fifties, fit, and always well-groomed, he looked disheveled this morning.

Jeez, he hoped Todd hadn't gotten into more trouble than what he'd already confessed. "Would you like a cup of coffee, Baldwin?"

He could never bring himself to call Mason Baldwin by his first name. If he did, it meant he accepted him as a friend. He didn't trust polished, sketchy people and wished Alex didn't either.

"That would be lovely."

Cullen went to work on the coffee.

"I need to talk to you about a sensitive matter," Alex said.

From years working as a police detective, Cullen learned to read body language and subtle inflections in voices to know when someone had something on their mind, like right now with the sullenness of Alex's voice. "What's up?"

"A person very important to me died recently in a bathroom at a mental institution." Alex's tone was tight, as if he tried to keep emotion out of his words.

Although deaths happened infrequently in a mental ward, they did occur and weren't a concern. "Homicide or suicide?"

"The official report is suicide. I think it's a farce."

Cullen lifted a brow at Alex's determined tone. "How so?"

"My gut says so."

He understood. Gut instinct kept him alive more than once. "What do you want from me?" he asked as he presented Baldwin with a cup of coffee, along with the necessary condiments. Having already added the sugar and creamer to the other cups, he left one for Todd on the counter, and carried his and Alex's to the living room.

"Thank you," Alex said and took a sip before setting the drink on the table. He'd loosened his tie and unbuttoned his jacket.

Cullen relaxed in the armchair near the glass doors and waited for the rest of the story.

"I need someone I trust." Alex used his politician voice, smooth and easy.

Because of this, alarms sounded. He didn't use bullshit with Cullen. Never. "Spill."

Alex gave him a once over, his expression darkening as if he debated what to say. "The woman who died was a former lover."

Alex had several lovers before he married, so Cullen's uncle had told him. Again, the facts didn't arouse suspicion as much as the heaviness in his words. "Go on."

"Alice Bodine. She's from Pearl, Ohio. I need you to talk to her husband. Find out if he had anything to do with her murder." His gentle demeanor made it sound like an easy request, a no brainer, something Cullen could do in his sleep.

It wasn't.

After his parents' death, Cullen's aunt and uncle invited him and Todd to stay with them in Pearl to get away from the media frenzy. The reporters had asked questions: how does it make you feel that your parents died in a balloon? Better yet, what idiots guide their hot air balloon into electric lines?

The reporters hadn't asked the last one, but they might as well have since the question continuously nagged him. His parents were not idiots. The sudden gust of wind caused the freak accident. Still, how did Dad and Mom drift so close to the lines for them to be trapped? Each time his mind went down this path, he came to the same conclusion. They were in love. No doubt, his parents paid more attention to each other than where they were going. Bittersweet, but damn, it pissed him off. At eighteen, he became guardian to his ten-year-old brother.

When they arrived in Pearl, Alex had already moved to California. Feeling reckless and lonely, Cullen had mistaken a girl's attention for affection and fallen in love. That night replayed in his mind as if he lived it now.

He ran until his legs ached and he could barely stand. He flopped on the ground near a football-field-size pond. He heard girls laughing and hid behind a massive oak. When they dispersed, one girl stumbled upon him and kept him company. She didn't ask questions about his family, but talked about hers. Told him how her mother left without a word. He remembered the pain in her voice, how much the abandonment affected her. The similarities to Todd orphaned at almost the same age made Cullen more in tune with her troubles, with her. In that instant, something clicked between them and they bonded. They laughed and talked, and the next thing he knew, he lost his virginity and fell in love. They slept tangled in each other's arms. The first night since his parents' death, he got some rest. When he woke, she was gone.

Later, he discovered a piece of paper in his jeans pocket with some crazy design on it, but no phone number. She'd vanished, disappeared into thin air. He left Pearl grief stricken and dejected. Every time he contemplated visiting his aunt and uncle, his sensitivities and vulnerabilities from that night surfaced. Not wanting to relive the anguish of losing his parents nor the stupidity he felt for falling for some chick, he stayed away. Hell, almost ten years later, he should be over it. Yet, he wasn't. "Pearl is a no-go."

"Pearl?" Todd's voice boomed from the hallway entrance. He wore jogging pants and no shirt. The shoulder injury responsible for getting him booted from the Army healed into a wicked scar. It stretched from the top of his shoulder to his right pec. His short hair stuck out in every direction as if he'd shook his head to dry it. "You aren't going to Pearl!" The tension from his brother charged the room. "Maggots, venomous spiders, and women with no conscience, who'd rather rip a guy's heart out than treat them with compassion live there."

The sting of Todd's heated words hit him in the solar plexus. Todd, along with Alex, had listened to his grumblings for days after she'd left.

"Do it for me," Alex said softly.

"Aw, man, he's pulling out the heavy hitters," Todd said and went into the kitchen.

Arguing with the one person who had always been there for him and Todd gave Cullen a sour stomach. "Listen—"

"There's more," Alex said.

"There always is." He crossed an ankle over his knee and waited.

"I'm Alice's daughter's biological father. As far as I know, the girl doesn't know. I will tell her, just not yet. I want to have the issue of how her mother died resolved before I make contact. This is where I need your help. If the girl is around, besides checking into General Bodine, I want you to befriend her. She'll need someone to help her through the rough patches from learning her mother died and her father isn't who she thinks he is." Alex paused. "A few days."

"A general?" Cullen scoffed. "You think I can question a general without him knowing what I'm up to?"

"Allow me to interject," Baldwin said, moving toward them.

Damn, he wanted to tell Baldwin to shut the fuck up.

"I've written up a contract." Baldwin's smug persona gained momentum in the way he walked across the floor as if he owned the place.

"Since when do we need a contract?" he asked Alex.

"Mason feels we should have one in case—"

Alex didn't have the same issue with calling his attorney by his first name. He should! "In case what?"

"In case you become too involved." Baldwin paused and drew into himself a little, as if what he said next worried him. "And happen to mention more than you should."

Cullen bristled. "What are you talking about?"

"We believe—"

"Enough from you," he cut Baldwin off and shot Alex a glare. "What the hell is going on?"

Todd moved into the room and stood in front of Baldwin, blocking his view. Cullen appreciated the reprieve from having to look at the weasel.

"The case is sensitive," Alex said in his politician's voice. "Mason believes it's in my best interests to have you sign a contract to protect me."

"And you believe?"

"I believe he does."

"And you don't think I do?" Fury lit into Cullen. He clenched his jaw to gain control. Alex second-guessing his intentions shocked him.

"This is not personal, Mr. Wilson," Baldwin said, sidestepping Todd. "This is business. The Congressman is up for presidential party nomination. If word leaks out he had an affair with a married woman and denied his child, he'll never get the votes."

As much as Cullen hated to say it, Baldwin's explanation made sense. Still, he didn't like it.

"This investigation has to stay on the down low." Alex stretched an arm across the couch, appearing a lot more subdued than a moment ago.

"So why investigate then? Why not just let it go?"

"The girl's mother is dead," Baldwin interrupted. "The Congressman will win votes by reuniting with her."

"You lost me." Todd's dislike for Baldwin was obvious by how his mouth curled into a sneer as he spoke.

"We work on the human interest angle," Baldwin said, paying no attention to how Todd crowded him. "Father and daughter reunited. No one knows she's the Congressman's daughter, no one alive anyway."

Cullen bit his lip from saying, "That's convenient."

"But you denied her." Disgust reflected off Todd's expression, matching his tone. "You knew about her, yet ignored her. What the fuck, Alex?" Todd still hadn't lost his combativeness from war.

"Cool it, man." Cullen glared, reinforcing the warning.

Todd went to the kitchen and refilled his cup. All eyes focused on Alex.

"I didn't believe Alice when she came to my home accusing me of fathering her child. I used protection. Why would I think I had an illegitimate child? When I asked for a DNA test, she refused, said she wouldn't allow her eight-year-old daughter to be hurt by doubting who her father was. I figured she'd lied since I didn't hear any more from her until recently. A mental hospital informed me Alice Masters had passed. She listed me as the next of kin. Since I didn't know an Alice Masters, I had Mason check into it." A look passed between the two men that oddly enough, he couldn't read. "Her real name is Alice Bodine."

Cullen's mind clicked away...Alice Bodine...eight-year-old daughter...the girl by the pond...Selena Bodine. The heaviness in Alex's gaze, words, and body language became clear. "Selena Bodine! You're her biological father?"

"I have the birth certificate saying so," he said, but his voice didn't sound so sure.

He dropped his head back and stared at the ceiling. He never imagined Alex would use him. "You want me to get friendly with the woman who disappeared on me for your benefit? Did you take into consideration how this would affect me?"

"Yes. I did. I didn't think you had any feelings left toward her. I figured with the undercover work you've done, you could get through it."

He stared at the man who understood him better than anyone.

"I don't like it!" Todd snapped.

"The contract states if you take this case," Baldwin chimed in, "Todd does not have to repay the Congressman the bail money or the gambling debt he already covered."

"Don't bring me into this," Todd ground out. "I'm not my brother's problem."

"Please, Cullen." Alex rested his forearms on his knees. "I wouldn't ask if I didn't need your help."

He didn't like it. Didn't appreciate it. But he was his brother's keeper, for a little while longer, at least. If he did this, he could help him, maybe even give Todd an avenue to start fresh. Start a life without gambling and drinking. The downside, he would probably see Selena and possibly have to face feelings he'd rather not provoke. Would seeing her be that bad? He blew out a breath. He had no idea.

Selena or not, he had to help his brother. Until he got straight, found a job, and acted responsibly, he'd remain his problem. Todd was everything to him. The decision, while hard, was a no brainer. "I'll sign."

* * * *

The taxi stopped in front of her father's brick rambler. Selena stared at the house and wished Mom and Dad would rush out. Pepper her with kisses. Say how much they missed her and loved her. Good thing she didn't believe in holding her breath, waiting for something to happen.

An ache washed over her, stinging her body like bees. After all these years, she should have come to grips with not having a tightknit family.

Thank goodness, she met Juls and Joey for a late lunch when she arrived. Being in their presence eased her nerves. Otherwise, her skin would be crawling. They'd offered to give her a ride to her house, but with her arrival delayed a few hours and their tight time schedule, she called a taxi.

Her door opened and the driver waved her out.

Blowing out the heavyweight of anxiety, she got to her feet.

The sun warmed her back through her lightweight dress shirt and slacks, while a lump the size of a grenade filled her throat.

She slipped her sunglasses on and took in her surroundings.

Impeccable streets and well-groomed yards lined the side of the road, a regular Stepford Wives neighborhood. Flawless on the outside, and, as she well knew, hell on the inside.

Yet…one place offered refuge. At the end of the cul-de-sac, fifty yards through the woods, was her sanctuary. The place where she'd found home, and her sisters.

She loved them and they loved her. To this day, she still didn't know how she got so lucky to stumble upon Juls, Laydi, or Joey. One minute, she sat on the riverbank crying from missing her mother and feeling alone, the next, three girls surrounded her. No one talked. They played with sticks and tossed them into the water as if they'd hung out every day. Before long, Juls put her hands in Selena's curls, braiding it, and Joey patted her arm. Laydi kept watch as if she dared anyone to interrupt.

Selena laughed. Nothing had changed.

"Ma'am." The taxi driver stood next to her holding the overnight suitcase he'd retrieved from the trunk.

With the put-on-smile she'd adapted as a young child for nosey teachers, she tugged out her wallet and paid the fare.

The driver mumbled his thanks, climbed behind the wheel, and drove away.

With the wallet in her purse, she grabbed her suitcase handle and headed toward the house. The weight of the world settled on her shoulders. This was it. The moment she'd swore she'd never live. The moment she walked into her father's house and spoke to Dad.

The breeze kicked up, blew the boxwood's small leaves bordering the front of the house. The bush near her bedroom window had grown since she lived there. Her nightly escapes had played havoc on it. Tired of listening to her father's headboard banging session with the woman of the moment, she would slip out of her secret exit to run to the pond. Most times, her sisters were already there.

The porch screen slammed against the wood, plunging her out of the past.

Years of working as an investigator kept her from flinching.

She wanted to, though. She wanted to jump into the cab, seek out Joey and Juls for a couple of drinks, and return to Washington, D.C., as quick as possible. Resume normalcy and forget her father ever called.

A hiss sounding like a snake followed, outdone by feet stomping on the deck. A woman wearing a paint-splattered jacket moved away from the porch. A long, brown ponytail swung like a horse's tail. Hands on hips, her wild eyes zipped around the porch, the yard, in a way an animal under attack would when hunting for an escape.

Another pissed off woman, running out of the Bodine house.

As soon as the thought sailed through her mind, she realized only one woman had ever left the house mad. *Her.* If Mom had the same problem, she wouldn't know.

The women Dad had in and out of his bed left smiling and giggling.

Yuck! She shook her shoulders, rocked back on the heels of her flats, and waited to see what had angered the woman.

She opened and closed her mouth before she stormed over. The colorful garment—a nurse's smock—parted, exposing a white cotton tee. The panels flew at her sides as if she'd sprouted wings.

"He's a lunatic!" the nurse blustered.

Ray Bodine was many things. She could rattle them off easily, had often with her sisters. No one else—no one!—spoke poorly of him without hearing from her. She ignored the significance of what it meant to want to knock this woman

194

down a notch on Dad's behalf. She balanced her suitcase on its end at the edge of the driveway.

The nurse frowned. Stress wrinkles appeared and deepened above her lip. "I'd find a different gig if I were you," she snapped, finishing her approach. "Don't put yourself through the torment that bastard will dish out."

A lump gnarled in Selena's stomach. Any smart person would walk away. Avoid the conflict. Not her. Anger tight, she squared her shoulders. Like hell would she allow this woman to talk bad about Dad. He was a war hero! "Listen, that bastard, as you referred to him, is a retired general in the United States Air Force." She moved into the nurse's space. Taking up for him felt good, surprising her. "He's done more for this country in a few years than you'll do in a lifetime."

The nurse bobbed her head and gave her a knowing look.

Hells bells! The nurse was about to pity her. She'd seen the signs too often as a child, and had ignored it. As an adult, she wouldn't tolerate it. She held up a hand. "Don't!"

"You're Ray's child." The woman spoke as if her father and she were chummy. "This isn't the way I would have liked to meet you. Despite my smock, I am not your father's caregiver. He sent the nurses away. He says he only needs you."

She offered the woman the same lost look she'd given the house when she arrived. "I'm sure you are mistaken."

"I'm not. My name is June Barton, your father's fiancée. He has told me wonderful things about you, your accomplishments. Now that you're here, maybe he'll relax and let someone take care of him."

Selena's heart pounded and her gut twisted. *Dad talked about me.*

"That's unheard of."

A wide smile spread across June's face, an understanding one, a motherly one.

She didn't want to see a maternal look coming from this woman, from no other female. She had a mom, one that didn't know how to be one. Still if she couldn't have hers, she didn't want anyone to fill her place. It freaked her out. She stepped back. "Don't."

"Call me if you need anything." June pulled out a card from her pocket and handed it to her. "My cell is on there. You're not in this alone."

No, she wasn't. She had her sisters, but June touched her with how easy she offered support. "Thank you," she said as it occurred to her June introduced herself as her father's fiancée. Dad was getting married. Before she had a chance

195

to question, June had opened her car door, and hesitated. "Watch the man in the black truck."

Selena stuck the card in her purse. "Huh?" Not her best professional question. June's conspirator tone made Selena feel like she had a part in a detective show. She missed a beat.

"There. The black truck"—June tilted her head toward the house at the end of the street—"it arrived not long before you did. I wouldn't have mentioned it, but I hadn't seen the truck before."

An unfamiliar vehicle didn't mean anything suspicious. She eyed the house at the corner, then took in how the vehicle had backed into the driveway.

"Well, you should know the Wilsons moved to Florida some time ago." June tsked. "The house should be vacant."

Goosebumps rose on her arms.

Once June left, she'd hunt for the binoculars she'd played with as a child in the garage.

"They're not from around here," June said, easily, as if they were friends.

"How do you know?"

"I read the license plate," June said. "ACM-3892, I believe I'm right." She made a clicking noise. "Or it could have been ACN, hmm. Now, I'm confusing myself. I should have written it down."

"Did you get the state?"

"Yes. Virginia."

Selena took in the cut grass and flowers surrounding the white vinyl house. "Someone has been living there. The yard is trimmed."

"A lawn service comes once a week."

June had an answer for everything. Still Selena didn't believe poachers had moved in. From here, the truck looked to be a recent model, clean. The pilferers she'd seen didn't have nice vehicles. "Maybe they have a renter."

"Or they're trespassing and up to no good."

Selena laughed. "You do have a wild imagination."

June lifted a shoulder. "Tell your father, I'll be here tomorrow if he doesn't act like a child."

Anyone who could stand up to Dad was okay in Selena's book. "It'll be my pleasure."

June got into her car. Once she disappeared out of the subdivision, Selena darted to the garage for the binoculars.

Chapter Two

Girl Code #22: Girlfriends are always on standby with encouragement, a hug, and a voice of understanding.

Cullen thumbed through his cell phone messages, hoping to see one from his brother stating he was on his way to Pearl. The sooner Todd got away from the influencers who aided him in his downward spiral, the quicker he would get better.

No messages. Damn!

For the last ten minutes, he sat in his truck in his aunt and uncle's driveway, watching a short, petite woman talk to Selena.

The girl he met years ago hadn't changed. When he spotted her stepping out of the taxi and saw her blonde hair dancing around her shoulders, he recognized her immediately. Laying eyes on her slender back and firm butt, his body hardened. In all this time, his reaction hadn't changed.

How in the hell had she lived less than an eighth of a mile from his family and he not known it?

He dropped his cell on the seat and picked up his binoculars.

Holy hell! She stared back. Not only did she see him, she had a close up. Fucking binoculars! She discarded them to the top of her suitcase and stormed toward him.

His damn heart seized. The binoculars fell to his lap. The hope for an easy first meet, maybe a little flirting, flew out the window.

Taking Alex's advice, he used his undercover skills and plastered on a friendly smile. With unhurried movements, he slid on his sunshades and slipped out of the truck by the time she'd reached the driveway. "Hello, Selena."

Her bluish-gray eyes widened, her chest heaving as if it took effort to breathe. "You?" Her mouth formed a perfect 'O.'

He couldn't help but take a detailed appraisal from head to toe. A purple blouse covered round, high breasts and a narrow waist. Her legs went on forever. More womanly than he'd remembered, and definitely hot.

His body kicked in, wanting to get friendlier. Leaning on the truck door, he crossed his arms to keep from pulling her to him.

She blinked and rubbed a hand over her right eye.

Good, it appeared her nerves got the best of her, too. The thought gave him a satisfying rush.

"Why are you spying on my father's house?" The words were short, clip, to the point.

Not her father, he watched her. "I wasn't."

"You had binoculars." She stepped to the truck and shoved against him to peek inside.

He didn't move. "I like to bird watch."

Huffing, she stepped back. "I don't believe you."

"Revisiting the scene of the crime," he said off the cuff, referring to her disappearing act and putting off answering her question.

Obviously, it was the wrong cuff, since her eyes went electric and her face flushed. "Your name, what is it?" she asked, not missing a beat. He figured the comment might make her stumble and she'd stop with the questions, but she was good, real good to keep her cool. Not uncomfortable like he'd thought. Nope, he carried that burden.

The night he met her, he dreaded she'd heard about his parents' tragic deaths on the news. He needed a reprieve from the grief and didn't want to talk about it, and had chosen not to give his name. Actually, it had never come up. Once she'd told him hers, he had a second to decide not to give his before she switched to talking about tattoos. "Cullen Wilson."

She looked behind her at his aunt and uncle's house, then to him. "I understand."

Hell, she didn't understand anything. She might have connected the dots his uncle had lost his brother in a hot air balloon collision. Who couldn't forget such an oddity? But figuring it out didn't give her or anyone else the insight to understand. "I don't believe you do."

"Don't tell me what I know or don't know." Her eyebrow arched and she set her jaw. "I watched the local news, heard our neighbor had lost his brother." She jabbed her hands on her hips. "Hell, I cooked brownies and took them to your aunt and uncle."

She had?

"They're great comfort food."

The day after he met Selena, he found a plate of brownies on the kitchen table. His aunt said some pretty, young girl had left them. "That was you? When did you have time? You were with me, then disappeared." Damn, he already mentioned her disappearing once.

She blinked. The lines between her eyebrows vanished. "I'm not here to get reacquainted. I want to know why you're watching my father's house." Unfortunately, her tone hadn't lost its annoyance. "Cullen Wilson," she said his name as if to try it on for size and stepped closer. Too close for comfort. The same enticing mouth that mystified him years ago now tilted up toward him.

"Odd how you show up here the same day I do, and on the heels of my father's accident."

Baldwin or Kane left the tidbit out. *On purpose?* He made a mental note to check into it. "How do you know I just showed up?"

"I have my sources."

They needed space between them, but he refused to take the intimidating step backward, one revealing she got to him. Call him hard headed, but he wouldn't allow his past anger or his lust to seep into what he had to do. Knowing what she did for a living from the history he ran on her, he said, "You're a reporter," to throw her off the spying concept.

She studied him as if his face held the answer to whatever she debated. Then she made the difficult shift he couldn't do and put distance between them.

Phew!

"I'm a criminal investigator with the United States Air Force."

"Well, Investigator, did your source say I'm here to get the house ready to sell?" He spit out the lie without thinking.

She remained quiet. A plethora of facial expressions—extending from drawing her mouth into a straight line to biting her lip, ending with desire— stampeded across her gorgeous face. Chemistry circled them as if a living, breathing thing.

Just like when they were teenagers, he wanted her. Christ help him, he wanted her today as much as he did the day at the pond.

"Why are you here, Cullen?"

Damn, his tactic to change the subject didn't work.

She inched forward, waiting for him to answer. "It's not to sell the house," she said with the same sexy, goddess tone she'd used on him years ago when she said, "more."

That night, she'd gotten more. Not this time. This time, he could control his whims, his body's urges.

"Were you looking for me?"

He'd entertained the idea for years. Considered finding her and playing out his sex fantasies, the ones she'd starred in.

"You did come for me." The tough exterior she chose to use as a mask betrayed her. Her stern eyes peered into his soul, but the power behind the expressions cracked and softened.

The words 'come for me,' hung between them like they were his lifeline and she was the anchor. The idea of coming for her and ending his celibacy trek stole his ability to speak.

"Why?"

He blinked and plunged out of his musings. He had no idea where her line of questioning came from.

"Cullen?"

But...what better way to find out information? Not speak his thoughts, but act on them and kiss her. See where this flirty, combative chemistry took them.

Before he could talk himself out of it, he removed the distance between them and touched her arms.

Something along the lines of panic zipped across her face before she gave him an open mouth look of surprise.

He pressed his mouth to hers.

* * * *

It irked Selena to no end she couldn't back away from Cullen. His sunshades gave him a mysterious, forbidden air. His touch, his magnificent, electrifying caress sent her thoughts to where his hands had traveled before and where her body craved them now. And, oh lordy, his mouth, his sensual delectable lips curled into a smile when she hadn't backed away, the moment before they met hers. She hung onto his shoulders to secure her footing when she really wanted to run her hands through his thick, wavy ebony hair and pull him closer.

Then like the ice bucket challenge, reality stuck its nose in her way. Why was he here? Was he spying on her? On Dad? Why did he have binoculars? And why did he kiss so darn good, she couldn't leave?

She had to get rid of him, make him go. She slid her hands between them and touched his chest, ready to push him, when he groaned. The mating call of all mating calls grabbed ahold of her and held her hostage. It put her in deep kimchi and had her leaning into his body.

He tasted of spearmint and coffee, blasting her into a time machine, back to the first time they'd kissed.

The instant their lips touched, she wanted him, all of him.

Now, like then, she didn't know how to handle the electrifying sensation. Either sag to the floor or grasp onto him.

He wrapped his arms around her, holding her, and making her decision. His mouth moved over hers with a furiousness saying he had to have more.

All these years, the lust she held for him hadn't changed. Lust scared her. If it didn't die, it could morph into something more powerful, something she couldn't control. She would have no part of it. She'd learned firsthand how her family couldn't do relationships. First, her mother disappeared, and then her father left, not physically, but mentally.

She pushed him.

He didn't budge. No, he tightened his grip and eased her into his body.

Every hard inch stroked her.

His crisp, outdoorsy scent urged her fingers across the thickness of his neck and under the collar of his shirt. He was so damn desirable, she wanted to put her lips against the spot below his ear that she knew drove him crazy. If she did, there would be no turning away. She had no choice. Back away or end up knee-deep in a mess she couldn't recover from. Digging into her fortress of emotional ammunition, she did one of the hardest things she'd ever done. Moved away from someone who made her feel alive.

A spring breeze blew, drying her wet lips and cooling her overheated body.

He dug his fingertips into his scalp and searched the sky.

"What was that?" she asked, not liking the sound of her husky voice.

"I don't know." He pinched his lips together. A mood settled over his face. Dark, angry, distant…hurt, but he wouldn't look at her.

The night at the pond, he'd worn a similar expression.

Back then, she hadn't pried. Now, she couldn't resist. Something within registered trouble. "Tell me why you're here."

"Like you said, I'm here for you." His lips twitched.

"No, I taunted you to get the truth." No sooner had she said the words, she realized she wanted him to say he searched for her. Surprised at her unexpected thoughts, she kept her face neutral and ignored the feeling she hadn't considered until now.

Seeing him on a day that should have been difficult gave her comfort. Just like he'd done when she was unsure if she should follow through with joining the Air Force. Though she didn't have a choice, she'd signed the contract. Dad did, actually. But Cullen had lessened her anguish by letting her chat all night about her life. The stories she'd told about her family—the banging headboard for instance—should have embarrassed her. It hadn't then, and wouldn't now.

He had a peaceful way about him making her feel safe and secure, which didn't jive with the mysterious sensation she experienced when she first spotted his truck. Though she had no idea it was him, the hunch something was amiss stayed.

A slow, seductive smile crossed his face in a way a comic's would when ready to give a punchline. "Call it whatever you want." An underlying pain laced what he said, not matching his soft lips.

Through his sunshades, she could feel him watching her.

A shiver raced down her spine.

His intense gaze made her brain hurt, and her soul burned as if he extracted her every thought and planted his image in her dreams.

Then, without another glance in her direction, he walked toward his aunt and uncle's house.

Watching his perfect denim butt move away, she tucked her strands of hair behind her ear and straightened her blouse.

In her hometown for all of thirty minutes, she not only broke her commitment to stay away from the house which brought her so much misery, she delved headlong into a kiss with a man she'd never planned to have more with than a one-nighter.

Disgusted, she braced for the next distressing obstacle—her father.

* * * *

Selena hadn't stepped inside Dad's house since she was seventeen. So many things flooded through her. Sadness. Anger. Loneliness. All of them urged her to rush out of the house and run to Maryland.

Heavy breathing mixed with a low rumbling vibration brought her attention to the opposite side of the room. A whistle cut off each snore. Splinters of sunlight sneaked between the blinds from behind the couch, casting Dad in shadows. He stretched out on a hospital bed against the wall. A sheet tucked under his neck, and he had a remote control, pointing at the television on the opposite wall, in his hand.

She had a nose for scents, used them to help solve cases and save lives overseas. Here, the air reeked of antiseptics and bleach. She didn't have a clue how to react or what to feel. Should she pat him on the arm? Kiss his cheek?

The last time they met, two years ago in Washington, D.C., his broad shoulders and chest rose and fell with pride. Now, he seemed weak.

A rumble deep within sliced through her soul, resurrecting an anguish she'd long ago buried. The anguish scraped over her skin, spreading tingling then numbness from her fingers to her toes.

Gasping for breath, she brought her hands forward as if to push air into her lungs and then moved them away from her body on the exhale.

The meditation technique did little to stop the ball of emotions.

She snatched a change of clothing from her discarded suitcase by the front door and sought reprieve in the bathroom. Stripped to her underwear and bra, she splashed cold water onto her face and neck.

The pain lessened. With yoga pants and a T-shirt on, she returned to the family room. She picked up her purse, tossed it onto the couch, then flopped down beside it and took in her father.

He remained asleep, his breathing steady.

A framed picture of him holding her in his lap at her eighth birthday party rested on the coffee table between them. He wore a crooked smile and beamed. She faced the camera, her teeth flashing.

The distant memory of his love threatened to send her back into the bathroom for more cold water.

Not ready to give into the shocking, powerful need to touch him, to let him know she was there and would always be, she meditated some more.

Lifting her chin toward the ceiling, she breathed deeply and raised her palms side by side until they reached her throat. She rolled her hands as if they were petals on a flower blossoming for her to get a fresh breath, in this case, a lungful of antiseptic.

The pressure threatening to suffocate her disappeared.

Too bad, the breathing technique hadn't crossed her mind when she dealt with Cullen.

She touched her lips, reliving the tingle from his kiss. The sweetness. The tenderness of his mouth caressing hers. For those few precious minutes, her cares and fears vanished. The same as they did that special night.

She could relive it over and over in her mind and never get tired.

The air squeezed out of the mattress as her father changed positions in his sleep. Glad he hadn't wakened to give her more time to herself, she watched the news for a few seconds before focusing on the frames on a side table. More pictures of Dad and her scattered across the darkened shelves. Each one revealed the enthusiasm and joy they had shared until the day of her eighth birthday.

She braced her elbows on her thighs and caught her head in her hands. Too many days passed since Dad had looked at her with anything other than a wrinkle of disappointment.

She sucked in a sob and searched for a picture of Mom.

None.

Thinking about it, there were no pictures of Alice when she lived in the house. Dad had surrounded her and his world with just father and daughter. Until now, she hadn't considered how he felt. Hadn't measured his pain for his wife leaving. Of course, she didn't believe he could have any. After all, when she was eight years old, Daddy was invincible.

He winced in his sleep and his eyelids fluttered.

She held her breath and waited for him to awaken and send her a judgmental frown.

He coughed and cleared his throat. "Selena!" His light and excited voice confused her. "Darn, you're a sight for these old eyes."

"Um—" She didn't know what to say, what to do. The last several times they'd spoken, he'd been more relaxed than his time in active military. Still, she didn't know how to react. "How are you?"

"Good. I'm glad you finally made it. It took long enough."

There was the rough tone she knew. "You've been scaring the nurses off."

"You lived with me." He chuckled. "You know I don't run women off."

She did.

"I have fun with women," he said in a tone making her want to kick him in the shin.

"But that's not what your fiancée said."

"Ah, you met June. She says a lot." He pushed a button on the railing until the bed inclined to a seventy-degree angle. "You're staying fit. Glad to see it."

She worked hard for every toned muscle. Cursed with genes from her mother and not her father, she exercised twice as hard to keep in shape. Talking about physical attributes didn't rate on her 'to do' list. "You're not fit." She lied to get the upper hand of the conversation.

He twisted. The sheet fell to his waist and his unbuttoned, plaid pajamas shirt parted. The frailness disappeared with him waking. For fifty-five and being involved in an accident that fractured his pelvis, he moved pretty well and looked fit. His tight abdomen was still flatter than hers. Anything less than perfection didn't settle well with the general, but she wouldn't tell him how good he looked. It would imply a peace offering, not something she could do yet.

"Still tough as nails."

The teasing tone in his voice should have stopped her from running on, but she carried a lifetime of hurt. Her conscience screamed to throw Dad a bone and make peace. She shoved it aside and bulldozed through with the same determination she used to get through boot camp. Fake grit and arrogance had pushed her up the ranks quickly. "I had no choice. Either toughen up or—" Identifying that the *or* was *her crying* wouldn't do, not with the general. "You made me this way."

He pointed a finger at his chest and appeared offended. "Me? I made you snap at people, act rude. When?"

"The day Mom left. The day you scooted me out the door, and all the days in between." Her voice rose with uncontrolled anger. *Darn it!*

Ray slid a hand down his face. She couldn't tell what went through his mind, never could. That was part of the problem. After her mother left, he went to a desk job. Wore a poker face day in and out, and answered her questions with a shoulder shrug or, "I don't care." A few times a month, he gave her money to go to the store for food and clothes. "What else am I supposed to think, Ray?"

"No Dad for you?" His voice roared, rough and croaky.

"Were you one?" The distress on his face hit her like a slap. She'd pushed too far.

"Leave!" He shifted on the bed, not much, but enough to direct his full glower on her, the one that brought many men in line. "You know the way."

"Is this what you said to the nurses? They say something you don't like, so you kick them out? What happened to the man who charmed every woman out of their panties?"

"When did you get such a mouth?" He growled.

"When I had to listen to you in your bedroom."

He flinched as if she punched him. "I don't deserve shit from you."

She didn't need shit either. "Then what do you want? You called me. Why?"

He searched her face as if seeing her for the first time. "This isn't easy for me to say."

The sullenness in his voice extinguished her anger. "At least that's honest."

"Can it, kid," he said in a more moderate tone, with a touch of teasing.

One simple comment from her hard-ass dad bumped her back to a time when they were happy, like in the pictures. She would tease him unmercifully until he jokingly said, "Can it, kid." His way of letting her know she'd won the battle of the wits.

In recent memory, he hadn't even tried to joke. Maybe now, they could talk about the past.

"Can we put aside our differences?"

Lightness filled her, and an uncontrollable smile stretched her face. It died on the disgruntled lines giving him angry crow's-feet, sending a chill across her skin. "We can."

"What I'm about to say has to stay between us."

That shocked her.

"Don't repeat what I'm about to say to your investigative friends in D.C. or the group of girls you hang around. This has to stay in this room. Got it?"

Her father never talked so cagey.

"Agreed?"

Definitely unfamiliar territory. "Excuse me for being hesitant. I'm not familiar with you asking me to keep quiet. Is this you asking for my help?"

"You want me to say it?" A rhetorical question, since he added, "Yes," before she finished nodding.

Thrilled wasn't a word she usually would put to someone asking for help. This time, she did. "Okay. I agree."

"Someone caused me to crash," he said, his tone deadly.

Her hands shook and her mouth went dry.

Chapter Three
Girl Code #32: Don't leave girlfriends out!

Cullen yawned. With the sun barely awake, he'd been sitting in front of his computer for the last hour, searching for details on General Ray Bodine's accident.

The newspaper article stated a single car wreck and weather caused the crash.

A couple of things didn't add up. No police report. From his search in the police database, General Bodine had no other traffic infractions. Not having any didn't mean he didn't lose control of his car, but he wasn't buying it. Something was off. He couldn't explain why he thought so, he just did.

Selena's suspicion added to his questions. Why would she suspect him of doing something underhanded because he showed on the same day she had? And why mention he arrived on the heels of her father's accident?

At first, he figured she made the remarks to distract him. The heat between them revved up quickly. She probably wanted to throw water on it, but to accuse him...

He poured another cup of coffee from the pot sitting on the counter behind him and eyed the kitten on the deck. The morning sun sparkled off its white fur. He'd already given it a saucer full of milk.

Tired from the trip from Virginia to Ohio, and not able to stop thinking about Selena, he'd given up the idea of sleep at dawn. The sketchy details of the case had also helped with his insomnia. When he walked away from her yesterday, he planned to dive into the investigation. He needed to check out a few facts Alex and Baldwin gave him. Why would Alice Bodine not put her daughter as next of kin? From what he remembered her saying the night by the pond, she had a good relationship with her mother until she vanished. Had Ray Bodine searched? Or had he caused his wife's disappearance?

When he walked into his aunt and uncle's house late yesterday afternoon, he had to put his questions on hold. The cleaning crew extended to the exterior, not the interior. He couldn't live in the house with the layer of dust everywhere, much less think. By the time he had it clean, he'd hit the sack. The questions had festered in his mind ever since.

He jotted down his thoughts on a piece of paper, then typed in Alice Bodine, Pearl, Ohio on his laptop. He'd already checked the police database and come up empty. From the few pictures on the screen, he had no idea if it was her or not, but no other significant search results appeared. He needed to get inside the Bodine house. See if any images there could give him a clue of what life might have been like when she lived there, and feel General Bodine out.

Given the info dump on the day he met Selena, he didn't believe she had any knowledge of why her mother disappeared. Yet, when they'd talked by the pond, she didn't talk highly of her father. She mentioned he wasn't around much. Yesterday, she seemed protective of the general.

A motor sounded from the driveway. Todd. Last night, he had texted stating he'd be in Ohio today.

Cullen rose and went to the living room in front of the house and peered out the window.

Todd parked his truck, a black Ford F-350, beside his older model. In honor of the American Sniper, Chris Kyle, Todd had made some minor modifications to his truck. He'd replaced the Ford logo on the grill with a small chrome skull to resemble the man the Seals called The Legend.

He swallowed the lump occurring whenever he reflected on the soldier who'd given and done so much for his country, and opened the front door.

"Hey, bro." Todd carried a couple of plastic bags. "Brought you some groceries."

Todd staying with him brought a huge rush. Being away from his friends' gambling and drinking influences would go a long way in his brother's recovery. "Everything squared away at home?"

"Yep. Alex's attorney took care of things. Most of the charges were dropped." Todd pushed past him and headed into the kitchen. "Look, I get why you took this case, but I wish you hadn't. I don't need my big brother digging me out of trouble."

Todd hadn't wanted him to accept the case when Alex asked him, hell, he'd railroaded him to where he didn't have a choice. "I know," he said.

Backing off wasn't an option. He wouldn't sit idle while his brother floundered. One day, soon he hoped, Todd would get his shit together. Until then, Cullen would stay vigilant.

Todd nailed him with a glare and stepped closer. "You're clamming up."

They were about the same height, same eye coloring. It was like staring into a mirror, except the hell his brother lived in Afghanistan reflected in his dark circles.

"I'm telling ya, this is the last time you're bailing me out. After this, if I fuck up, you'll let me deal with it."

Todd's determination, while admirable, couldn't convince Cullen to agree. If he screwed up, how could he ignore it? It'd torture him.

"Cullen! Do you hear me?" Todd's eyes narrowed to slits. "Agree, or I walk out the door and you won't hear from me again."

Not having his brother near…damn…that would put a hole in his chest. Todd had his problems with a few vices, but having guts wasn't an issue. "I hear ya."

"Good." Todd patted him on the shoulder. "Glad you didn't push me. We have steaks to cook."

Cullen helped Todd unload the groceries into the refrigerator and cabinets before settling into the chair.

One name he hadn't searched. He typed in Alice Masters.

"Make any headway on the case?" Todd asked from behind him, chugging a bottle of water.

Like Alice Bodine, Alice Masters came up empty. "Nothing of interest. He closed the laptop.

"Let's head out to the front porch," Todd said.

Cullen snatched a water bottle from the fridge and followed. They each took a rocker. Just like he had done many times before when visiting his aunt and uncle, he relaxed, took in the fresh air, and enjoyed the quiet surroundings. Opposite of where he lived in Washington, D.C., Pearl's small population and few cars on the streets didn't compare to the number of people and traffic in the city.

He missed visiting Pearl. For the last several years, his aunt and uncle lived in Florida most of the time. When he called about using their home for a getaway, they were ecstatic and asked if he wanted the place. At the time, his immediate reaction had been no. Sitting here, he was glad he hadn't given them a final answer.

"Is she here?"

No need to ask Todd who he meant. "Yep." He pointed. "The brick one, between the two cedar-siding houses."

"You're kidding me," Todd scoffed. "As many times as we sat here, we never saw her."

"Or didn't pay attention. Aunt and Uncle kept us busy, so did Alex." The last time they sat on the porch was after their parents' funeral. They had stayed with their aunt and uncle for a week. Cullen couldn't take staying here any longer. Their relatives, while great, had a hard time dealing with the tragedy, which made Todd's and his grief worse. Coupled with his adolescent feelings concerning Selena, he had to leave.

"Do you think about Mom and Dad much?"

A day didn't pass that he didn't. The anguish from not seeing them had eased over the years, but he had his moments when the pain ripped through him. Those days, he stayed out of sight. "Some. Yes. You?"

Todd stared at the street. "When I returned from fighting in the war, wounded, I—"

Aware his brother required space to get himself together to say whatever he needed, Cullen focused on the kitten walking onto the porch.

"Let's just say, I really needed them."

The weariness in Todd's voice had Cullen snap his gaze to Todd's bloodshot eyes.

Missing a parent stayed on your conscious. When something significant happened, there was nothing like having parents to lean on. Todd was the one who'd gotten injured. Yet, Cullen remembered all too well how much he wished Mom and Dad were there not only for Todd, but also for him. "Me, too, bro, me, too."

Movement from in front of the Bodine house grasped his attention. From his spot on the porch, he didn't have a good visual. He bet anything Selena roamed around, at least he hoped so. He could use a distraction. The conversation with Todd grew heavier by the minute.

"Is that Selena Bodine?" Todd motioned to her house.

"Believe so." He drank some water in place of saying any more.

"Why do you think Alex ignored his kid?"

Todd quizzing him about her caught him by surprise. "He didn't believe she's his."

"I heard that," Todd said. "It doesn't add up. If he didn't think so then, why get the birth certificate now? Why not then? If an old girlfriend came to you and said she had your baby, would you assume she lied? To me, the reason Alice, whatever her last name is, gave Alex for not doing the DNA testing made sense."

Good point. Cullen wouldn't have. He would have checked into the paternity.

"All I'm saying is it doesn't add up," Todd said. "I don't like how suspicious of Alex I am."

Him, too. For that, he felt guilty.

"Another thing," Todd went on, "I don't want you involved with her."

"Since when do we butt into each other's personal life?"

"This situation is different." Todd crushed his plastic water bottle. "I was there. I lived what she did to you."

As a teen, Cullen didn't know some things were better left unsaid. He told his baby brother everything, well, not quite everything. He didn't tell him his first time with a woman had been more than he ever imagined. If Todd had been older, he might have.

"I saw your face when you couldn't find her. You went into a depression. Our world was already fucked up. Hell, we just lost our parents, then pulled away from our home not knowing if our aunt or uncle intended to keep us here or not."

"With Alex's help," he said. "I made sure that didn't happen. I got custody of you."

"I appreciate it, too. Even at ten, I was grateful you were the one I would live with. Even when Mom and Dad were alive, you had my back." Todd continued, "The reasons for her disappearing are unknown, but I have a sixth sense she's gonna mess with you again."

Cullen couldn't tell if he experienced heavy-duty lust toward her or something more. "You're a step ahead of me."

"Back then," Todd said, his voice eerily quiet, "I grieved my parents' death. Lived the pain inflicted on you because of her. All the while I prayed you wouldn't do something stupid."

Todd thinking he would harm himself in some way floored him. "I would never hurt myself."

"Try telling a kid."

He blew out a sigh. The pain from Selena's disappearance intensified the loss of his parents. It put him in such a dark place. He hadn't considered how his behavior affected his brother. "I didn't know."

"You do now." Todd eyed the cat playing with a fly. "I lived through a lot of shit overseas. Dealt with losing people, but I was never as scared as those few days after Prissy Pants vanished."

"Not her fault," he said. "It was me. I couldn't get my shit together."

"How about now? You got it together?"

He shrugged. "As good as I can, I suspect."

"Good," Todd said and rose. "Prissy Pants is on the way."

Cullen's heart gave a hard thump.

* * * *

Crisp air cooled Selena's face. The wind fluffed her hair and nipped her skin through her yoga pants and shirt as she headed toward Cullen.

Two people sat on the front porch in what appeared to be a deep conversation.

Yesterday, after Dad's recount of his accident, she'd grabbed her laptop and dug into the police records. There was none. No comment about a black sedan he said ran him off the road.

The newspaper article had a small paragraph stating the general had an accident, but no details.

She needed to see the accident site.

With no car, her father's SUV in the garage getting repaired, and unable to reach Joey or Juls, she had no other choice but to ask Cullen for help. Asking to use his truck to examine the crash area minus an explanation would be tricky.

She'd done her research on him. He was a police officer in Northern Virginia since the age of twenty-one. Their similarities in chosen occupations gave her a slight chill. Given his background, she may have to consider trusting him. Tell him a little without breaking her promise to Dad.

She filled her lungs with country air and the aroma of honeysuckle. The scent blasted her over the edge of nostalgia, to her sisters playing along the pond after a rainstorm. She stopped on the sidewalk before crossing the road.

Joey had her hands buried in the bank, making mud pies. The thought of dirt burrowing under Selena's nails irritated her as much as nails dragging across a chalkboard, but she'd jumped right in so her new friend didn't play alone. Juls and Laydi joined them. It didn't take long for brown-reddish splotches to cover them from head to toe. They had laughed so hard. Life was rough, their home lives not worth talking about, yet they giggled.

Nothing else meant as much to them as each other. She smiled, remembering how they jumped into the pond to get clean. Young, alone, and taking a bath in dirty water, she couldn't have been happier. That day, she realized, the girls would be in her life for the long haul.

"Are you okay?" Cullen's gentle voice drew her attention to him standing close.

It irked her she didn't hear him approach. She was about to ask why he snuck up when she locked gazes with him.

His eyes. Her mouth went dry. Her knees threatened to buckle.

They resembled the sky, just before sunrise, when the color turned from a deep bluish black to a lighter blue. Somewhere in all the variation was the perfect shade. The color she watched in the sky for hours when she lay near the pond as a kid. The hue, no crayon or paint could ever match. The one that had brought her peace on so many nights as the stars faded filled his irises, froze her in place, and stole her breath. She had no idea his eyes held the same rich color as the skies.

Shadows cast by the bright moon had hidden them the night they were together. Yesterday, his sunshades blocked the effects, but today...today... *wow, just wow.*

"Selena?"

Her pulse went into hyperdrive. Her speech failed. Emotions she put a stop to yesterday crashed to the surface again. She was losing control.

She wanted to press her body against his, taste him, and repeat their night of heaven, but she couldn't. The outcome of such desperation could do more harm than good, not only to her emotions, but also to his. Besides, she sought him out to ask a favor, not to lust over him.

In her dreams, he was safe. In the light of day, the fantasies disappeared and reality intruded. The lost, empty feeling keeping her company for years faded. In the oddest, most pleasurable way, his soul beckoned hers.

He touched her shoulder. "Hey."

She blinked.

His heart-throbbing, all-knowing orbs screamed to her. Tightness spread through her and swathed her in an emotion too powerful to contain. A choke-sob escaped.

Heaven help her...her teenage feelings remained.

No way could this be real. Her hand took on a mind of its own and inched up until her fingers clutched the front of her neck.

Bodines don't do relationships. Ever.

She retreated.

His hand dropped to his side. "Selena?" He moved into her personal space and the lustful sight between the panels of his unbuttoned shirt came into view.

Either he washed in tanning lotion or a magic wand sprinkled gorgeous-genes-dust over him. The golden color shimmered off his toned abs and muscular chest. Her throat, raw from lack of moisture, demanded water, and her thighs clenched.

Putting distance from a hot body was hard, but detaching from his intense gaze took more strength than she had.

"Are you all right? I remember," he said, paused, and sought out her father's house, "your comments about your dad."

His concern snapped her out of the daze. "I'm okay. Thank you for asking, but I'm here for a favor."

He shifted as if she'd goosed him. "A favor?"

"Yes. I need a ride. I believe I mentioned my father was involved in an accident. I would like to see the scene."

His eyebrows shot up. "Why?"

"No particular reason," she lied. "If you're busy, I'll wait for one of my friends to get home."

"I'm not. I'll be glad to take you." Buttoning his shirt, he moved toward the truck and opened the passenger door. "Ready?"

His crisp scent drifted by her on the way. Her insides burst to life. The deep kimchi metaphor came to mind. "Thank you."

* * * *

It took two minutes to drive out of the subdivision, another five to near the site. Cullen knew this since he eyed the clock to occupy his mind. Selena sitting in his truck inches away in her skintight pants and snug-cotton shirt had him wanting her closer.

Before he could act on what he craved, they had to talk about the past, the present. Reveal truths.

"Here," she said, pointing to a curve in the road.

He drove off the pavement to a grassy spot and cut the engine.

Nothing stood out of the ordinary. Trees, not five yards away, weren't damaged. Blades of grass stood tall, not a sign an accident had occurred recently. "You sure this is it?"

"Yes," she said, not explaining how she was so sure, and got out of the truck. "Over here." She moved toward the other side of the road to a fencerow lined with brush.

He waited for a car to pass, then joined her. A rectangle shape pressed into the grass, branches broken and disjointed behind the spot. "The SUV landed on its side?"

"Yes." She glanced both ways, then went to the center of the road. "He drove south when he lost control."

In most situations, when a family member came to an accident scene, their faces and voices exposed their thoughts. Not with her. Calling her General Bodine's loved one might be a stretch, but concern registered on her face. "How'd he lose control?"

"That's the thing. The sun settled in the direction he drove, putting the beam right into his line of vision. An awful time of day when you can barely see."

He hit it most days on his drive home from work.

"Dad said the sun blinded him. He hit a slick spot and spun off."

214

The newspaper article mentioned the weather was to blame. "Wait. You said the sun blinded him."

"It did."

"Do you have any idea why the paper reported differently?"

She moved to his truck, leaned against it, and studied the scene. "You read up on Dad's accident?"

He crossed the road and faced her. He didn't like having someone second-guess everything he said or did. "Of course I did after you told me about it." He waited a beat while what he said registered. "You questioned me about coming to Pearl. Accused me of having hidden motives."

"It's suspicious. I think everything is." She gave him her full attention. Her clip, almost rehearsed tone intrigued him.

He took the change as an invitation to move closer and draped his arms over the side of the truck.

She eyed his shoulder bumping hers, but didn't move. Maybe she'd trust him enough to confide why she asked him to bring her out to the scene and not wait for one of her friends. "Any idea what the substance was in the road?"

"No." The rich blue color of her cotton tee brought out the blue in her eyes. The color sparkled, danced.

The temptation to kiss her until she melted and gave up whatever information she withheld grew strong. Doing so would undoubtedly help him solve the case, but it would be wrong on so many levels. When he kissed her again, he wanted it to be all him, the case nowhere in his thoughts.

"I know you didn't come to the scene to see where he crashed. You have investigator written all over your face. You're examining the scene the best you can without using a forensics kit." He squared his shoulders to face her. "General Bodine wasn't in a single car accident, was he?"

She watched him for several seconds before she twisted around and faced the bed of the truck, same as him. "How do I know I can trust you?"

"You must already. Otherwise, you wouldn't have asked me for a ride. I'm also betting you've run a background and know what I do for a living."

"Said one investigator to the other." She lowered her chin on her folded hands. "Someone ran my father off the road."

That thought had nagged him. Selena's curiosity in the way she took in the scene strengthened this sensation. "There's no tire marks."

"I know. I can only surmise the substance Dad's tires hit stopped his brakes from working."

His opinion exactly. The road didn't appear to have much traffic. Since they'd been there, one vehicle had passed. Still, whatever General Bodine slipped on should have thrown at least one other vehicle off course. Which got him asking, "Who discovered the wreck?"

"Someone drove up on it. Found Dad behind the wheel blacked out."

"Yet, no police report."

"Crazy, I know. Dad said the police came and took a statement. The officer even administered a breathalyzer."

The short hairs on the back of his neck rose. Few people had enough clout to make a police report disappear. Unfortunately, as much as he detested the idea, he knew of one person who did. Not many people said no to Alex's charm and sincere eyes, but for him to act dishonestly… He groaned. He didn't think so. And why would he? The only connection between Alex and Ray was Selena. No reason for foul play. He tossed his thoughts aside and focused on her. "Do you have an estimated time for when the accident occurred to what time someone found him?"

"No."

With her talking easily, he pushed for information. "What do you know?"

"Um…someone said—" She hesitated and glanced down the road. "A dark sedan came up behind him and rammed his bumper." Her voice broke. "Twice."

He stroked her arm closest to him. "Has he ticked anyone off lately?"

She snorted. "He's a general. Of course he's made people mad."

"How about you?" He gave her a swift once-over. "I won't tell," he said, wanting a reaction. Given her and her father's history of not getting along, he had to get a read to see if he needed to pry further. Considering she lived several states away the day the accident happened, she couldn't have had a part in it. A detail he'd already checked on, but she could have hired someone. She wouldn't be the first disgruntled daughter to conspire to get rid of a parent.

"Why are you here?" She jerked her arm away, sweeping them out to her sides.

The same reaction he would have had if someone falsely accused him. "Helping you."

"No. Not here, here. Why are you in Pearl? The story about selling the house is a lie."

Had she talked to his aunt and uncle in Florida? Was she such a good investigator she could track them in a camping community?

Her gaze set on his, not wavering, unflinching. He could jump and wouldn't get a reaction out of her. She studied him, watched his actions, and picked apart every detail of what he said or did. The same as he'd done to her. She didn't know squat.

But being the center of her full attention was sweet.

"What do you want me to say?" He hooked a strand of hair that had slipped out of her ponytail and slid it behind her ear, letting his fingers linger. "Say after all these years, I came to find you?"

She leaned her cheek into his hand, eyes softening. "Did you?"

His focus intensified as the air around them snapped to life and brought possibilities of what could be between them.

He grasped her hand holding onto the side of the truck and gave her a gentle nudge.

She inched toward him and didn't remove his touch. "Tell me."

Outspoken and determined, she fascinated him more than any other woman he'd met in a long time. He had to answer her question, or, no doubt, she'd storm away, their new connection disappearing with her. To keep their conversation as real as possible, he decided to give her a partial truth. "My brother, Todd, arrived this morning."

"He sat on the porch with you earlier?"

"Yes. In Afghanistan, he received a shoulder injury. We came out here so he could..." He wasn't sure what to say without sounding negative. Talking about Todd's gambling and drinking problems was out of the question. "...get a break."

"Is he doing okay? Veterans can have a hard time adapting to civilian life."

He wanted to say, "Ain't that the truth," instead, he released his grip on her hand and cupped her other cheek. With a light touch, he stroked little fans along her cheekbones with his thumbs. "Why did you leave without a word?"

She rested her hands on his arms. "I had no choice. You were a one-nighter for me, a comfortable one."

He groaned in dissatisfaction. Was that all he'd meant to her? He hadn't felt the same. Still didn't see their connection as casual. To him, it had been anything but. Practically a stranger, what she said shouldn't have mattered, yet it did.

"I'm in unfamiliar territory," she went on to say, letting him off the hook from coming up with a reply.

He, too. It was hard to think with her scent and heat swirling around him, luring him in like a warm hug. This unknown feeling shocked and confused him. "We should go."

Chapter Four

Girl Code #30: Once you have the true blessing of a friend, they're always a friend.

Inside the truck, Selena stifled. Other than the hum of the engine, Cullen and she hadn't spoken. She left him thinking she didn't care about their night, dismissed if for convenience. As if he was at the right place at the right time. That part had been true. She often wondered if any other nameless guy had been there, would she have behaved the same way. Each time, she came up with the same answer without hesitation. Absolutely not.

"I didn't mean to say what I did." She paused. "That's not true. I did mean it, and what I said about a one-nighter is how I felt at the time. Mixed up and young, I didn't know what I wanted, who I was, or where I was going."

She twisted on the seat, took in his grim eyes and grimmer-mouth as he turned into Fresh Water Subdivision.

An unexpected panic punched her in the stomach, leaving her queasy. Had she said too much? Been too honest? It was the truth. Whether she liked her actions from that night or not, it was what it was. "Will you say something?"

With an elbow on the doorjamb, he ran a hand up his forehead and over his hair. She'd witnessed guys at work removing stress that way when wrung out.

"We were kids. There's nothing more to say."

"I don't want you upset with me," she said, realizing how much she meant it. She leaned forward to catch his attention, but he kept his focus on the road.

He slowed in front of Dad's house. "I'm not."

She didn't believe him. He wouldn't make eye contact with her, but she shoved away the urge to talk more about his grim mouth, and him not being mad, to figure out how to handle her father. If he heard the motor in the driveway, he'd immediately jump to conclusions. Fire accusations for spilling his secret that someone had run him off the road. In time, she'd confess, but their relationship had to reach stronger ground first.

"Can we go to your house please?" As soon as she asked the presumptuous question, she knew she better give a reason. Investigator she might be, but keeping secrets from family and friends didn't come easy. "Dad doesn't know I asked for your help. I'd rather keep it quiet."

"All right," he said flatly.

They pulled up in front of his aunt and uncle's house beside an identical truck. The man who talked to him this morning sat on the porch. He had the same dark hair and hard-edged expression as Cullen, just years younger.

Todd set his sights on her and his jaw tightened. The angry stare he sent her could have frozen a bear in place.

"Your brother, Todd, is he mad?" she asked as the guy who could be Cullen's twin stood and walked into the house.

He slid the gearshift into park. "Hard to tell." The motor died and he slipped out of the truck.

Hard to tell? For who? Whatever had Todd fired up would have to wait. She climbed out of the cab and caught him near the hood. "We need to finish our conversation."

He searched the area over her head before focusing on her. "If you want my help in investigating the accident, you got it." By his harsh tone, she surmised he didn't want to converse about the past.

"That's not what I want to talk about." She couldn't believe this. How did she get in a situation where she wanted to explain her actions, and cared what someone else thought?

He mumbled something under his breath and followed Todd into the house.

She rested a hand on the side of the truck to steady herself. Apparently, he was finished talking. Heat covering her from the emotional chaos developing between them, she headed home.

"Where are you going?" His voice boomed. The screen door slapped against the doorjamb. "Don't you want to talk?"

He stood on the porch between two rockers holding up beers. "Want one?"

A beer. He went for alcohol and hadn't walked away. "Could have given me a head's up."

He chuckled. "I said I'd be right back."

Wow, she'd been so deep in thought she didn't hear him.

He handed her a bottle and clicked his against hers. "To new beginnings."

Shocked and surprised he would suggest something new with her, but liking it all the same, she nodded.

He sat in the corner rocker, tipped the bottle to his lips, and downed several gulps.

She sat in the opposite chair and swallowed. "Ewe. What is it?"

Chuckling, he braced a foot on the porch railing and crossed his ankles. "Non-alcoholic beer. It's a new thing around the Wilson house."

Given what he said about Todd, she suspected he did have trouble dealing with being home. "It's good," she said, giggling and angling to be supportive, and took another sip. The second taste improved her opinion, or maybe it did because of how much Cullen went out of his way to help his brother.

Their laughter drifted off and she reflected on her one-nighter comment. Since she made it, he'd grown more cautious, reserved. She hated not feeling the coziness in his voice, the acceptance.

Explaining her thoughts the day they met was the only way to clear the air. Her only choice to help him understand. This barrier rising between them grated on her nerves, yet revealing her vulnerability stuck a lump in her throat.

"I lied to you." His voice was low and serious.

Her mouth dropped open.

"You asked if I looked for you. I said no. The truth is I hoped you were home."

Her pulse raced, yet his matter-of-fact tone gave her pause. His unemotional lilt should have numbed any sparks transpiring between them, but it didn't. "You did?"

"I hadn't been back here in years. I recently learned you lived down the street from my aunt and uncle. I can't believe I didn't see you before that night."

That night lingered in the air.

"That night"—she sucked in a breath as she broached the sticky subject— "you wouldn't tell me your name or what had upset you. You let me use you for a sounding board, yet wouldn't let me return the favor."

Chuckling, he winked. "Trust me, you returned the favor. More than I could have ever imagined."

Her already-warm face heated with the meaning. "Will you tell me what happened when I met you?" Their previous conversations had hinted at the facts of what troubled him, but no details.

He drummed his fingers on the arm of the chair. Just when she thought he wouldn't confide, he said, "A few days before I met you, my parents had died."

She couldn't stop the quick intake of breath. "I'm sorry." This she figured out when she heard his last name was the same as the Wilsons who'd lost family members. Still hearing him say it saddened her. "Why wouldn't you tell me then? I would have been there for you."

"You were." He grinned and winked again. "My aunt and uncle brought me and Todd to stay with them to get us away from nosey reporters."

She tried to remember exactly how he lost them.

"My parents died in a freak hot air balloon ride." His voice turned rough, tense. "They hit a power line."

"Foul play?" she asked in a gentle tone, feeling his pain. Having been a discarded child, she sympathized with abandoned children, by death or by parent's choice. At work, she excelled at helping them. She hated for any child, big or small, to feel alone or empty.

He shook his head. "Luck wasn't on their side."

She reached over the table dividing the rockers and covered his hand. "I really am sorry."

He looked where they touched, then her face. "There, right there, is why I couldn't tell you. I don't want sympathy."

She snatched her hand back. "Oh."

"It's fine now, but not then. I needed someone to talk to, hang out with, not because my name was on the news, or associate my family with the tragic accident. You did that for me." He sipped his beer. "Then you disappeared."

"Ouch." She relaxed in her seat. No matter how she tried to explain her actions, the result was the same. She had thought of herself, just as her mother and father had. But deep down, she wanted more, desired it. Sitting with him, this close, sharing with one another made her crave it. "Phew." How could she have something resembling a relationship without the risk of hurting him, hurting herself?

With the mouth of the bottle pressing against his lips as if he'd take a sip, his gaze didn't waver off hers. He stared until the lump in her throat shoved further down and moisture gathered behind her lids. How could she possibly have enough feelings to contemplate pursuing him? And why would she? His intense look made her feel the same thoughts ran through his head. "You'd better run," she said half-teasing, knowing she possibly opened herself up to a load of hurt. "I'm not relationship-worthy."

He swallowed some liquid and set the bottle on his thigh. "I'm not going anywhere." He spoke with determination, shocking her.

She laughed as if she hadn't been serious, as if she said the comment in jest and hadn't expected him to take her up on it.

"I'm not," he said, plunging into her thoughts and making her realize how serious he was.

Warm fuzziness spread through her. A guy she hadn't seen in years let her know he was interested. Wanting to dance and run simultaneously spiraled through her.

"But how about you?"

She blinked. What was he asking exactly? "Excuse me?"

"You neglected to tell me an important fact that night."

What had she held back? She'd given everything, from her body to her soul. Confused, she raised an eyebrow. Like earlier, his grim features reappeared, only darker. For the first time, she didn't equate him with sweet. The rest of the labels stayed intact—sexy, gorgeous, scrumptious—even more so, in a dangerous sort of way. Moments ago, he seemed receptive of her. Had she misunderstood? "Which was?"

He tipped the bottle to his lips and drank the rest. The glass clanked on the table. "You enlisted, knew you were leaving, and didn't mention it."

Double ouch. Their conversation kept circling to the same topic. She must have imagined him wanting to pursue dating. He hadn't named it, but still the thought…didn't matter. She shook her head and set her jaw. The direction their discussion headed, it could ignite into a heated one any moment.

If he wanted to rehash the past, then okay. Her reasons for leaving had made sense each time she said them, yet may be the problem. She didn't have a good one. Convinced entering the Air Force would offer the best for her, she'd joined without a lot of deliberation. It took her away from the sadness surrounding her parents' house. But mainly, the Armed Forces would keep her busy. Keep her day too full to think about dating. Otherwise, she'd leave herself open to anguish, like right now.

"You left me a piece of paper with no number."

The drawing she'd sketched. Emotions hit hard.

And just like that, insight about her actions all those years ago came to light. She hadn't blown him off. Subconsciously, she'd given him the one thing she'd never bestowed on anyone outside her sisters. The piece of paper didn't have a number. It held something she valued so much more.

It held her soul. In the lines, she'd drawn what she so desperately wanted while he slept. Faith. She wanted to have faith her world would be okay. She wanted faith in him. That night, she had a brief moment where she longed to have it all. Yet, history repeated itself. From the downward spiral of her parents' marriage, along with her inability to hold a relationship outside of her sisters, she and Cullen didn't have a chance.

One glimpse at him, and she recognized marriage material. Not that she had role models, but she had plenty of make-believe. Frightened by what could happen between them, she'd shoved the sensation away. So simple, and yet, so difficult. But her soul was smarter. It knew what it wanted. She drew the sketch, stuffed it in the pocket of his jeans, and left.

She trembled with the scariness of doing something so epic without being fully conscious of her actions. She let out a long breath. While ecstatic to figure out why she had done something years ago, how could she convey this to Cullen when she hadn't fully digested it?

The drawing on the paper replicated the ink on her hip. The tattoo linked her, Juls, Joey, and Laydi in sisterhood forever. "Oh, no." It hadn't occurred to her that she shared their bond with someone else. What would they say when she told them? "Life was complicated," she said, feeling a terrible itch to get away and talk to her sisters.

She closed her eyes and sucked in the indescribable ache hitting her ribs with a force of a jagged knife. Not only did she walk away from him, she crossed a line with her sisters. What must they think of her? "Thank you for the beer." She set her bottle on the table and rose.

He moved, blocking her path. "No," he snapped. "You're not walking away again."

She recoiled, gazed into the blue eyes she loved, and couldn't stop the quiver in her chin. "I'm sorry. I never meant to hurt you."

He brought her wrist up between them, and set her hand on his chest. "There's nothing to be sorry for." His words filled with such affection, such determination, tingles raced over her skin.

"This is messed up," she whispered, yet didn't remove her hand. She couldn't leave his comfort. Curling and uncurling her fingers, she spread her hand further to touch more of him. "I feel things that scare me. Remember things I didn't know I did."

He pressed a kiss to her forehead. "We'll take it slow," he said and tucked his chin until her gaze settled on his. "Okay?"

She nodded, and he pressed his mouth to hers in a feather-soft caress filled with gentleness and longing. His hand stayed against her lower back and the curve of her butt.

Through her yoga pants, heat radiated from his fingers. She prayed he'd move them lower.

As if he'd read her thoughts, he cupped a butt cheek and squeezed. His lips and tongue moved over hers like a fine-oiled machine, as if they'd kissed a hundred times.

She snuggled into him further, melted into the contour of his body, his hard plains aligning with her perfectly.

But she had to go. She needed time, distance, air. "I can't."

A low growl vibrated from him. She placed a kiss on his neck and laid her head against him, absorbing his comfort and warmth.

"The paper I gave you," she said slowly, unsure exactly how she would proceed in bringing up what she'd done and the reason for it.

"The sketch?" He lifted a brow, confusion and something else she couldn't name stretching across his features, and placed a hand on his pocket.

Her heart leapt so hard, she feared it would jump out of her chest, which made the raw emotions she faced harder.

"It may look like lines, a drawing, but it's more. It reveals what I want most from life." The pain of sharing something so deep, so personal with someone was difficult, yet with him, it felt right. "Research it. At the time, I couldn't give any more," she whispered next to his ear and kissed his cheek. Forcing a smile, she moved past him, down the steps, and headed home.

* * * *

From the porch, Cullen stared. Motionless and in awe. Years ago, Selena had rocked his world at a time he didn't think he could even feel. Then, she'd told him her fears, her wants, but she'd never mentioned what she craved. This woman, who felt so deep and had so much to give, blew him away.

Her admission gripped and snagged a part of him he didn't think would ever come to life. The part he thought had died with his parents' carelessness.

He admired her confidence. That she could figure out what she wanted, and had the strength to admit it, touched him in such a way his resolve weakened.

"You still have the paper?" Todd's tone fell somewhere between indignant and appalled from behind him.

Cullen twisted and glowered at his brother standing inside the screen door, looking out. "You listened?"

"How I could I not? You were loud."

He tugged his wallet from his pocket. "Yep." He passed Todd and ignored his downward mouth.

The case nagged at him, especially the part where a dark sedan ran General Bodine off the road. That stunk, but he had other matters driving him. For the first time in his career, he put work on the back burner until he figured out what Selena meant when she said research the design.

He plopped down in front of his laptop.

The kitten, curled on a blanket in the corner of the kitchen, blinked at him. "You let the cat in?"

"I found him in the kitchen chair," Todd said, sitting next to him. "I gave him a blanket."

He gave his brother a once over much like the kitten had thrown his way, a little disturbed someone could possibly think to bother him. Yet, he wasn't disturbed at all, far from it. Todd looked good. Besides the slight off coloring on his right cheek, his skin held a nice shade, healthy. Even the hue of his slate eyes deepened with his smile.

"Oh, shit!" Todd popped up from his chair. "I forgot the steaks," he said, rushing out the sliding door.

Cullen opened the laptop and gathered the piece of paper from his wallet.

"They're not bad," Todd said, closing the sliding door behind him as he balanced a platter in one hand. The aroma of steak and garlic filled the room. "A little more done than I like."

"Smells great." His stomach growled, confirming what he said. He rubbed a finger over the worn paper.

"I can't believe you still have the drawing," Todd said, coming up behind him.

He couldn't either. He'd carried it like a good luck charm.

"Tough guy is a romantic." Chuckling, Todd placed the platter of steaks and grilled vegetables on the table.

"That's me. A softy," he said, sarcastically. "I always considered the drawing chintzy, no meaning. Girls put hearts on everything." Yet, the sketch held more meaning than he wanted to admit or disclose. She could have scribbled a zero and he would have kept it.

Every day for a week after their magical night, he camped out at their spot and hoped she'd return. "I was lame."

"You'll get no argument from me."

He laid the paper above the keys on the laptop.

"It's a Zibu symbol." Todd picked up the image. "See the dots outside the outline heart, the squiggly line on the lower right corner?"

"Yeah," he said, not sure what it meant.

"Type in Zibu symbols," Todd said, and grabbed the plates and silverware.

The search brought up several links, the most popular on the top of the list.

"Click that one," he said. "The site has tons of info."

He tilted his head to the side. "I guess. I've never used it." He clicked the link. "Isn't this a chick site?"

"Hey, hey!" Todd teased. "You're in for a treat."

A colorful page of symbols with their meanings below appeared. He scrolled down, searching for one close to the image.

"There it is." Todd pointed to the screen. "Heavenly shorthand for faith."

"Heavenly what?"

"It wasn't all fun and games fighting in the war." Todd laughed. "I learned a few things when I debated getting a tattoo."

His brother had always been against needles. He reared his chair on two legs and folded his arms. "Did you get one?"

"Nah." Todd sat and spooned vegetables onto his plate. "It's getting cold."

Cullen scooted his computer and file folder out of the way, and filled his plate. They ate in silence. The only conversation was his moan as the succulent juices burst in his mouth. A little over done or not, Todd cooked a damn fine steak. "Delicious," he said, shoving his empty plate away and sliding his computer in front of him. "Feel like doing some police work?"

"Sure," Todd said, shaking his legs on the balls of his feet, excited as if it was Christmas and he a young boy.

He opened a file folder with the details he'd compiled on the case thus far, from beside him. "General Bodine was in a car accident several days ago, a day before Alice Masters/Bodine died. The general told Selena someone ran his SUV off the road. What's peculiar, there's no accident report."

Todd sucked in a breath. "Not good."

"Nope." His good friend might know more than he let on, but he couldn't ignore the niggling thought that Alex kept something from him, something extremely important. "I have a hard time thinking Alex had anything to do with Ray's accident."

"Baldwin?" Todd's voice rose with a questioning tone.

Since the day Cullen met Alex's attorney, he hadn't trusted him. The general's accident and his wife's death put the weasel on his short list of suspects. But what was Baldwin's motive? Being obsessive over Alex, while alarming, wasn't enough to find him guilty. Still it raised a flag to investigate. "Worth checking out. A few things we need to learn. Baldwin's, and damn, Alex's whereabouts on the day of the general's accident and the day Alice Masters died."

"Got paper?" Todd made a writing motion.

"Supplies on the dining room table."

Todd grabbed the paper and pen from the pile, returned, and jotted some notes. "Go on."

"My gut tells me Selena had nothing to do with her mother's incident or her father's accident. She hasn't even mentioned her mother to me. Something I'll dig into the next time I see her." Soon, he would pay the general and her a visit. Still tasting her sweetness and scent on his skin, he feared he'd have a hard time keeping his line of thinking where it belonged, on the case.

"I need to stay close and keep an eye on her." Not only for personal reasons, for safety. If someone killed her mother, attempted to kill her father, he feared they'd come after her. "She's a tough cookie, and, thanks to the military, she knows self-defense, but I don't want to go far away from her." Convincing her to allow him to act as her bodyguard was another matter he'd have to give some consideration to.

"I can dig into the stuff concerning Baldwin."

He jotted a name and number on Todd's paper. "Hugo Rivers was my partner."

"I remember," Todd said. "He came to my send-off party before I left for the Army."

"Yes. About six months ago, he moved to California to help his ailing mother. He now works for California Highway Patrol, has access to a helicopter, and has a wealth of resources at his disposal."

"Still the charmer?" Todd chuckled.

"You laugh," he said, "but his schmoozing abilities paid off. Hugo can breach areas most people can't. Contact him for the gritty work. I don't want Alex to know we dug into his life until we know for sure Alex or Baldwin committed a crime." The idea his friend could get involved in a horrendous act for political gain soured his stomach. And if he was wrong, the implications of his actions would destroy his friendship with Alex.

Todd tossed his pen on the table and rested against his chair. "Man, this is a lot to take in."

He agreed. A throbbing headache stabbed his forehead. "Remember, we know nothing. This is speculation. We have to find proof before we can go down the road of why."

"Alex involved in this would kill his presidential chances."

"That's why we're focusing on Baldwin." Cullen hoped to hell Alex, and by default Baldwin, didn't have any connections with either of the incidences.

* * * *

Selena rolled onto her side, wide-awake. Why had she told Cullen her deep secret? What would he do? Would he think her crazy for not knowing her own mind?

Ugh!

She tossed the covers aside and shuffled into the family room to sit on the couch. Listening to Dad snore was better than deliberating.

The low, muffled sound coming from him didn't drown her worries. They still rampaged over her. Was telling Cullen so bad? She trusted him enough to divulge her concern about her father's accident. Couldn't she trust he wouldn't hurt her the way Mom did Dad?

If she were to be utterly honest, she was glad she told him the truth and finally put words to her feelings. By doing so, she couldn't take them back, couldn't dismiss them. The more she thought about it, the more she didn't want to. That scared the crap out of her.

A chainsaw sound erupted, drawing her attention to her snoring father. His coloring returned to normal and he maneuvered around the house pretty easily. The urgent phone call insisting he needed help recovering was a farce. He hadn't needed her, never had, but one thing stuck in her craw. Out of everyone, she was the one he relied on.

Warmth spread through her. Dad and she hadn't had a chance to talk through their difficulties. Knowing he counted on her filled her with possibilities of having a family.

Soon, she would have a decision to make. Move to Pearl after her time with the Air Force ended or stay in Maryland. Wherever she decided to live, she planned to pursue the idea she'd had for some time now, open a recreational center for teens. Manny's situation had her thinking harder on it, but her conversation with Cullen cinched it.

She peeked around the living room curtain and took in Cullen's lighted driveway. What would he do? Was there a chance he'd move there?

Working at once on two relationships—mending the one with her father and developing one with Cullen—seemed daunting. Yet, the community she'd considered having a Stepford Wives persona felt comfortable, like home.

Home, a word she hadn't used in years, not even with her place in Maryland.

She released the curtain, twisted, and leaned her head against the windowpane. Wow. Just a short time ago, she considered her sisters as the only people to count on. Now, it seemed she had two more.

Waiting for sunrise to talk to Cullen about their conversation yesterday passed as slowly as a snail crawling. Not only did she have the situation to deal with, she should confess to her father she'd told his secret. When she returned last night, the muscle relaxer he'd taken made his speech loopy and he'd fallen asleep before they could talk.

Waiting was maddening.

She had to talk to someone, and knew who would answer the phone no matter the time.

She grabbed her cell, touched the sisters' contact icon. The quiet grew unbearable while she waited for them to pick up.

"Hey," a sleepy Joey said.

Grateful someone answered, she pressed two fingers to her lips, took a breath, and dropped them. "Hi!"

"Everything okay?"

"I needed to hear your voices and see your faces."

"What has you messed up?" Laydi eyed her and rubbed a palm over the other.

Here it was, the time for her to reveal what rolled inside her. Admitting aloud she didn't know what she was doing. "The boy I met just before I left for the Air Force. I've seen him."

"He's in town?" Laydi asked, her voice rising.

"Down the street, at his aunt and uncle's house."

"So romantic." Joey sighed. "You know," she lowered her voice, "there's nothing like a warm body lying beside you."

"Horse feathers!" Laydi barked. "The staying power of a dildo is better!"

She loved the energy coming off her sisters, lifting her mood as only they knew how.

The screen blinked with Juls' image. Her hair gave bed head a new name. "I always thought he was the guy for you." Her voice dreamy, as if she floated on a cloud.

"Wow, Juls, Reef has you glowing," she said. "Have you been to sleep?"

"Nope!" Juls slapped her lips together as if she'd eaten a tangy strawberry. "You getting together with this guy or what?"

"I'm afraid I messed things up."

"Why do you think so?" Joey asked through a yawn.

"Back then, I treated him like a boy toy—"

"Was he something more?" Juls inquired at the same time Laydi asked, "And the problem is?"

"Let me finish." She giggled. The laughter subsided as she remembered how she walked away from Cullen and what he must have thought. "I shouldn't have. To make matters worse, yesterday, I dumped my real feelings on him. I told him I wanted to have faith in him."

Gasps filled her ears, followed by a long pause.

After years of sharing, her sisters understood how hard it was for her to admit her feelings to anyone outside their circle.

Speaking of sharing, "Um, I have to tell you guys something else." These were her sisters. Why was she so nervous? "I gave him a drawing of my tattoo the night we got inked."

No one said anything. "Is the silence because you're upset with me or it doesn't matter?"

"Doesn't matter," Joey said. "He didn't get inked with us. Besides, Talon has one. I'm good."

"Me, too," Juls and Laydi said at the same time.

She let out a breath. Of course, her sisters wouldn't be mad, but still, she was glad she told them.

"Did you find out his name?" Joey asked, wearing a dreamy smile.

What is she doing? "Yes, Cullen Wilson."

"I'm gonna hand out some tough love," Laydi said in a low, gritty voice.

In spite of Laydi being the words of reason, she groaned. "Go for it."

"If you want him, go knock on his door," Laydi demanded. "Don't worry about the outcome, just do it."

"My plan once the sun comes up."

"Are you kidding me?" Laydi bulldozed through. "Don't wait!"

"It'd be romantic." Joey voiced, hopeful and sweet, like a woman truly in love.

"The sisters again?" a gruff, masculine voice asked. Joey scooted and shifted the phone until Talon appeared in the frame. "Hey, girls."

"Hey," went around.

Joey moved until she filled the frame. "Seriously, Selena, listen to Laydi. Don't put off what you want. When you realize the person you want to spend the rest of your life with is in front of you, you want the rest of your life to start immediately."

Everything about Cullen sent tingles through Selena. For the rest of her life? "I wouldn't go that far."

"With Talon, I would." Joey's eyes lit with humor. "Ah, got to go, girls. Love you." The phone fell to the side. "Talon." Joey giggled before her connection clicked off.

She glanced at Laydi's mouth twisting, to Juls, but Juls wasn't looking back. The side of her head filled the frame and fingers too thick to be hers rubbed her cheek.

Selena's chest filled with happiness for her sisters.

"Love you girls," Juls said between kissing sounds, and her frame disappeared.

"Just you and me," she said to Laydi, feeling empty that Cullen wasn't beside her.

"Go, Selena. Go get him. Do it for both of us," Laydi said, her voice a little softer, but determined.

Her pulse quickened. Laydi was right. She should go for it. "Love you."

"Back at ya."

She switched off her phone.

Her palms sweated and a tingling sensation traveled over her body. For the first time, she would trust faith. She headed to her room for a change of clothes and a brush before *just doing it*.

"Get me some water," her father gruffed out, stopping her at the entrance to the hallway. He'd pressed his hands on the bed and straightened a little. "Ice, too. And not that plastic crap. I want a glass."

She drew out a long sigh and regrouped. Talking with Cullen would have to wait until after her dreaded discussion with Dad. "Sure." She went into the kitchen and pulled out a brown, hand-blown glass her mother had bought overseas, and filled it. Funny how Dad kept Alice's things around, but no pictures. "Here you go." She placed the glass on the table next to him.

"Thank you." He drank half in one long gulp. After a brief hesitation, he finished it. "See anything at the wreck site?"

When she left yesterday, she hadn't told him where she was going. "How do you know I went?"

"June came by, saw you climbing into the truck she warned you to stay away from."

Like at work, rumors flew.

"So, who's the owner of the truck?" His strong voice sounded more like the general who dared anyone to cross him.

"He's Mr. Wilson's nephew. Cullen Wilson." Her heart gave a quick jolt saying his name.

"You don't say. Why is he here?"

She had the same question, but Dad asking aggravated her. "Is there a law saying he can't stay in his aunt and uncle's house?"

Dad tucked his chin and gave her a stern scowl.

She sat on the coffee table with her hands clasped between her knees.

One too many times, she'd played this routine. He'd glare. Expect her to cough up whatever answer he wanted. She'd cross her arms in defiance. It didn't matter he didn't speak the question. The question was there just the same. This time, he wanted to know if she told his secret.

Might as well go for it. What could he do, ground her? Didn't work when she was fifteen, it wouldn't work at twenty-five. "He drove me to the crash site. I saw no sign of foul play."

"What did your boyfriend say?" Suspicion laced each word.

Why did he have to make off colored remarks? "Not my boyfriend. He's a friend."

Dad went brows up. "What did he say?"

Cullen had said a lot, but he'd given no opinion about the accident. "Nothing."

"Uh, huh. You told him someone ran me off the road?"

With a return of the stern scowl, she nodded. "Yes, sir, I did. Without probable cause of why not to tell him, I didn't see any reason not to inform a veteran detective the facts. His input could be valuable. After all, I am close to the situation."

"Yet, he didn't tell you jack squat." Dad shifted on the bed until his bare feet touched the floor. He wore sweatpants and no shirt. He braced his hands on his thighs. "Do you know who Cullen Wilson is?"

"Yes. I just told you." So what if her voice sounded indignant?

"He's good friends with Congressman Alexander Kane." He spoke as if the name meant something and tasted nasty to say it.

"Am I supposed to know who he is?"

"No." Dad's shoulders slumped. "This is something you never want to tell your child."

Funny, how he spoke as if they shared confidences.

"Congressman Kane had an affair with your mother."

Breath exploded from her lungs. How could she have? "I didn't see anyone." They weren't in one location for any length of time. How could she have time to meet a man? "How?" she managed to ask, knowing how irrelevant the question was.

"Not long after your mother and I married, I went on a tour overseas. She stayed in the States and met him. I don't know the details."

Her mind buzzed. "How long have you known?"

"Well, that part is tricky. I knew, but I didn't admit it to myself until she became adamant about moving to Ohio," he said on a rough sigh. "I finally agreed I'd stay in the country and signed the deed to the house she picked out. At the time, I didn't give much thought about the house. Same as any other home, nothing extravagant. Easy to take care of. The day after I signed the contract, she told me she wanted to move to California. I refused and she disappeared."

He'd mentioned Mom had an affair before she was born. Around her eighth birthday, they had moved to Pearl, Ohio. A funny feeling went through her. If her mother had one, that could mean…

No! She and Dad had their differences, but he was her dad. "Um…" Suddenly she didn't know how to form a question. How could she ask him? "Eight years," she said tenderly. "You knew the affair lasted eight years?"

"Give or take a year, yes."

"Is there a chance—"

"Stop right there," he snapped. Instead of disappointment, his eyes held compassion. "Get the idea out of your head. I'm your father. I'm sure of it." The protective tone came out like a lion defending his cub.

His features—the shape of his eyes, his nose. No doubt, she was his. "Did you look for her?"

"I did," he said, bobbing his head. "Sources on base led me to California to talk to Congressman Kane. When I went to his home, he said he didn't know me and had never heard of Alice Bodine. I didn't believe the polished asshole. I wanted to punch him in the face. His wife coming to the door stopped me. A good thing, since he would have locked me up. After that, I stopped."

"Dad, I had no idea."

He snorted. "You weren't supposed to know, but hell. I should have told you. You were miserable. I was unhappy. I'm not above admitting being wrong. Consumed that your mother would leave me, I didn't handle things well."

His admission left her gaping.

The impassive façade Dad had worn as a protective buffer for over a decade dissipated before her. He gave a lop-sided smile. "Can you forgive me? I'm not perfect, Kid. I did my best and it wasn't good enough, not by any stretch of the mind. I have to carry the burden with me that I failed as a husband and a father."

An invisible clamp tightened around her chest. But why, after all these years, did he come to this miraculous conclusion? "Why now?"

"June. She's been good for me. Gave me crap when I needed it." Confessing had to be hard since he wrung his hands together. "I'm the type of man who needs a woman, companionship, someone I can trust. I thought I had what I wanted with your mother. When she left and I realized I didn't, I lived a life of not getting involved. June wouldn't have any of that. She showed me relationships can be good, then she got after me for not being a father to you."

She gaped in awe. Someone able to humble the mighty general earned her respect.

"I've missed you," he said, his voice raw and his expression sympathetic.

An emotive sphere the size of a grapefruit passed through her esophagus and snagged.

She couldn't have been more stunned if he rose off the bed and started to break dance. Neither his admitting how much he cared for her, nor his dancing, was something she expected to hear or see in her lifetime.

She'd missed him, too, every single day. "I love you, Dad. I always have, but this," she said and spread her hands slightly apart, "this is gonna take some time getting used to. I'm programmed not to rely on you." Harsh, but the truth.

He nodded. "I expect as much."

Her mind wandered to what started the conversation. "What does this have to do with Cullen?"

He studied her at length before shrugging. "I'm an old bird. I've seen a lot, done a lot. When my gut tells me something is up, I listen."

Coming from the same frame of mind, she understood, yet... "Have you always been able to rely on it?" Where was this instinct when his wife had an affair? If it slipped then, how could he trust it concerning Cullen?

"You're referring to your mother?"

Amazing how well she and Dad conversed since they hadn't held a conversation in years. "Yes."

"Like I said, with your mother, I didn't listen. I didn't want to believe it."

Their mending relationship made her head hurt. "Yet, you want to trust it on a man you don't know?"

"Let's leave it as I have my reservations. You make your own decision, but stay vigilant."

"Always." She kissed his cheek. "You're wrong about Cullen," she said and scooted out of the house.

Chapter Five

Girl Code #24: Always have a smile to lift your girlfriend's spirits.

The night whirled with fantasies of Selena. Each time Cullen fell asleep, seductive acts he longed for and desired played across his mind.

Giving up the idea of snoozing, he petted the purring kitten beside him and threw his bare feet over the side of the bed. The wooden floor chilled his soles and spread goosebumps over his skin. He slumped to the mattress and slipped on the socks he discarded during the night. Then padded through the shadows to the chair where he'd left his jogging clothes.

With running shorts, a cotton tee, and tennis shoes on, he headed outside into the dark.

The cool air nipped at his skin, but he didn't bother retrieving his jacket. The bothersome temperature would leave once his body heated. Until then, he'd welcome the distraction of something else to worry about other than this case he'd agreed to, and Selena.

The moon shone a nightlight glow over the houses and sidewalks on each side of the street. A flicker of light bounced behind the Bodines' front window.

He stopped and watched for movement or any indication that the ruthless night played havoc on her, too.

Crickets chirped, one would finish and another would start. A frog croaked. The sounds zipped him to the time he listened to an overabundance of chirps and croaks, the night he and Selena were together. He twisted toward the cul-de-sac, and further—at the darkened area, the woods.

Running again, he fell into pace and traveled north. Learning the truth behind the sketch she'd left him gave him hope and understanding.

At the end of the cul-de-sac, he slowed to a jog and stopped.

Darkness faded with streaks of orange, highlighting the black curtain as if the sky had a new-fangled dye job. The vivid glow illuminated the tree-covered path marking the entrance to the pond.

He lifted a sticker vine and shifted twigs out of his way. Walking under the cover of branches and leaves toward the place where he'd lost his virginity was surreal, such a beautiful, exciting moment. He never considered himself a type of guy to label a connection between a man and woman as beautiful, but here he was, thinking that and wishing for a repeat.

Breathing in the scent of pine mixed with honeysuckle, he wished he'd possessed more insight. He'd always considered his instincts keen. If so, he should have gone after her when she vanished. Searched for her home, found the women she called sisters, and questioned them about her whereabouts.

Part of him believed if he'd stayed close, been in her life, he could have helped her resolve the turmoil with her father. Maybe it was arrogant to think he could have solved her problems, but he wished he could have had the opportunity to try.

The pines thinned at the end of the path. He squinted against the bright morning sun's rays. No wonder she loved this place. It was a hidden treasure.

Pinks, greens, and yellows sprinkled the backdrop surrounding the water like an artist's canvas. Cattails and hollow reeds held their heads high in a grouping at the rear of the pond. Green grass grew in patches on the banks surrounding the water. Golden and reddish brown tones reflected off the water's surface like the gem tiger's eye.

He moved closer to the water, found a spot resembling the landscape where he'd met Selena, and plopped down on the grassy bank. Forearms on bent knees, he gazed in the direction of the glittering water, yet didn't see a thing but her pained eyes. The skin around the corners bunched in a vulnerable way.

As one minute slipped into the next, his eagerness to see her increased. He wanted to discuss her feelings, the note, take her hurt away. While he craved to console her, the case stayed in his mind. Soon, the hour would grow late enough for him to go to her house. By then, he expected to have a plan devised to convince her to let him stay close and act as her bodyguard.

He reclined on the ground and draped an arm over his forehead.

Later today, he should receive word on Baldwin and Alex's location on the day of General Bodine's accident and the day Alice Bodine died. Once he had those answers, he would know how to proceed.

A trip to the mental institution was necessary. Checking in to who visited Alice Bodine was paramount in learning more about her. Had she admitted herself? Who knew she was there? Her family didn't know. Her lover didn't know.

But going to California, he couldn't act as Selena's bodyguard. He groaned. He needed more manpower, which was out of the question. Three people investigating was two too many. The more people involved, the easier it would be for Alex and Baldwin to learn he doubted them. Something he didn't want until he discovered the truth and could confront Alex if necessary. He would have to figure out a way to take her with him, or maybe wait for Todd to return.

If General Bodine felt better, he would talk to him. The man had to know more than what he'd told Selena. Suspecting someone ran him off the road wasn't something he figured the general took lightly. Keeping it quiet amongst himself and his daughter spoke volumes on the man's suspicions.

Still, if he'd acted on his last idea and she learned he told her father before her, it wouldn't go over well.

He had to figure out a way to tell Selena her mother died in a mental institution she'd entered into years ago. He'd yet to determine her admission date, but had a good idea it was around when she went missing.

The heat from the spring day and the lack of sleep weighed heavily on his eyelids. He closed his eyes, and napped.

"Cullen?"

A sweet voice drifted over him. It was Selena, but he didn't peek for fear the dream would disappear.

"Are you awake?"

The scent of honeysuckle and warm breath blew across his arms and his face. His dick jumped.

He inched his arm higher on his forehead, squinted from the bright morning sun, and looked at heaven.

Sun-streaked hair softly framed her gorgeous face. Her blue-gray eyes sparkled with longing, need.

A fantasy that had played in his dreams was within reach. Selena kneeled beside him.

Excitement pinged through his veins. He wanted to pull her to him and never let go. Yet, doing so might scare her. He suppressed his smile and waited for her next move. "How'd you find me?"

She braced her hands on the ground beside him and leaned closer. "Your brother told me."

That surprised him.

"He called me Prissy Pants."

He chuckled. Todd must have grown a soft spot for her. "What's up?"

She pressed her lips together. "You're not going to make this easy, are you?"

He wished she'd say what bothered her, so he could get busy making her happy, make love to her until smiles stretched her face.

237

"I couldn't sleep," she said after a brief period. "I've thought of nothing but you since I saw you in your aunt and uncle's driveway the other day." She made a weird sound like a snort. "That's not true."

Something in him pinched. Was she lying? Had the attraction between them been inside his head? He lowered his hands to his stomach and waited for her to explain.

She sat back on her tennis shoes and sought out the water. "For years, I pushed people away."

"Except for your sisters," he said. She had spoken highly of them previously.

"Except for them," she agreed. "We made our own unique family unit."

The past churned his stomach. The sadness from when she'd left, the unknown answers to why she took off without a word fueled his questions. His next one was juvenile, but now, more than ever, he wanted to know. "Why didn't you treat me the same?"

"Simple. You were an impossible connection. From my father's behavior and my mother's," she said, her voice low, angered, "betrayal. I came to the conclusion Bodines couldn't do relationships."

He had his own skeletons involving commitments. Though not with her. With her, he wouldn't have ever put the brakes on his feelings. The fact she had stung. "You doomed us before we had a chance."

"I did. I could have given you my number. We would have seen each other. I would have loved it, but deep down I knew our relationship would fail."

"And now?" He prayed what she said next wouldn't send a blow to his ego. "How do you feel now? Are you willing to give us a try?"

"I screwed us." She pulled her lips inward and a tear fell on her cheek. "Because of the hateful way I left, you'll never know if you can trust me. I get that and understand, but"—a muffled sound escaped—"please give us a chance. I have no right to ask. None—"

"Selena." He blew out a breath and released the emotions bullying to tumble out of him. One crying person was more than enough.

"I'm sorry," she said between a mangled mess of sobs and tears.

A familiar band of grief for seeing someone upset knocked him off balance, but this time, it was different. On the brink of the angst lay a happiness he hadn't experienced. First, he had his own confession to make. "We have to talk."

* * * *

Selena walked hand in hand with Cullen. After he insisted he had something to show her, he hadn't said a word. His deep focus bustled with the air of irritability. Like a cougar after its prey, his strides lengthened. His grip on her hand tightened.

His behavior had her thinking about her father's concern—he was friends with Congressman Kane. When Dad made the comment, she didn't think much of it. Now, the increasing demand to ask grew. "Does this have anything to do with Congressman Kane having an affair with my mother?"

He stopped and his mouth fell open. His reaction could have knocked her over. "Why do you ask?" He regained his composure and quickened his pace, his hand still holding hers.

His actions should have made her a little nervous, but his secure hold didn't clutch her too tightly. She could get away if she wanted. "You're his friend."

"I've known him since I was a kid," he said in a firm tone, but his expression didn't give anything away, not like a second ago.

They rounded the corner and climbed the steps to his house.

"Hugo called," Todd said, meeting them on the porch, then stopped short.

Cullen bit his lip and Todd's brow wrinkled.

Their odd interactions weren't making sense. "What is wrong with you guys?" She tugged out of Cullen's grasp, surprised when he caught it again.

"I have to show you something." He held open the screen door.

She walked inside. From the family room, she could see the kitchen table and an open laptop, an image of her mother on the screen.

Uneasiness plummeted into her stomach as it did on an amusement park ride. She hated when it happened then, and loathed it now. She stormed across the room, peered at the screen, and took in the file folder with Alice Bodine/Masters written on the tab. A stabbing ache pierced her diaphragm. "W-what is this?"

"I'm out of here," Todd said, and the screen door slapped shut.

She sucked in much-needed air and leveled her sights on Cullen. Not a second ago, if someone said she would feel contempt toward him, she would have thought him or her crazy. Yet, that was exactly how she felt.

A piece of paper with handwritten notes sat on top. Under it, a picture of her in an Air Force uniform. One of her dad before he retired, and another of her mom, the age she last saw her.

Her legs grew weak and she slumped into a chair. "You lied," she said in an eerie tone foreign to her own ears. "You were digging into my family. Investigating...me?"

He thrust his fingers through his hair. "We have to talk."

"We should have already done so." Her world teetered off its axis. She didn't know how to stop it. Her police training, investigative skills; none of that helped when life dumped a pile of crap. She started to give her heart to him and he used her. She took a moment to let the blow slice through her so she could speak. "I have nothing to say to a person who continuously lies. No wonder you didn't give me a direct answer about why you were here."

He blew out a breath. "I can explain."

She popped to her feet and grabbed the folder. "Not gonna happen." She marched toward the front door.

"Dammit!" he bellowed. Halfway to the door, his rough tone stopped her. "You're doing the same shit you did before. You asked for my forgiveness for walking away. I gave it, but you're not willing to listen to me." He crossed the room and held the screen door open. "Fine. Do what you do best. Leave." His face was beet red, his eyes red-rimmed.

Oh, hell no. His lie wasn't the same as what she'd done. "I let you in!" She fumed through her sniffles. "Into my life!"

"And I didn't let you in?"

His voice held pain, but she wouldn't give into his emotional issues, not when hers spiraled.

The computer beeped. They both stared at the envelope icon revealing an incoming email. Damn, as much as she wanted to fume, she had to know what was going on more. "What is it?"

His sky-blue eyes roamed over her. Tenderness reflected in them and her anger slipped. No, she wouldn't let it. Couldn't. He lied.

"I'll tell you if you'll listen to what I have to say first."

"Go ahead." Maybe she ought to pay more attention to the nagging opinion from when she first saw him. He'd been watching her house with binoculars. "I started to trust you." Dear God, her head hurt so much, it felt like it would implode.

"You can trust me." His words trailed off.

"No!" She aimed a finger at him. "I can't." Before he grabbed it, she dropped her hand and stepped back.

"Sit." A gritty noise came from deep in his throat. "Down!"

She did, not because he demanded her to, but because her legs had grown tired. She dropped onto his couch.

Todd busted through the door, glanced at her, then at Cullen gathering papers off the table. "Oh, shit. You haven't told her. We've got to get a move on." He turned to her. "There's an explanation for this. Let me explain."

Red-hot fire shot through her. If one more Wilson brother told her what to do, she'd shoot them. "Explain!" She straightened. The folder and its contents fell to the floor. "Your brother lied!" She was being irrational. She knew it, but couldn't stop.

"I'm right here!" Cullen shouted.

"It's hard to understand," Todd said, ignoring Cullen's rant. "Trust me, he's looking out for you."

"No." She sneered. "He's looking out for someone. It's not me." For the first time since seeing Cullen, hope they could possibly have a chance together faded. "Whatever you're doing, you know where to reach my father, take it up with the general." She moved toward the door, dragging her heart behind her, and stepped on a handwritten note.

"Selena, no." His voice sounded desperate.

"No, not like this." Todd's tone wasn't any better.

Having a bad feeling she wouldn't like what was written on the paper, she picked it up anyway. 'Alice Bodine died two weeks ago—suicide in bathroom.'

Cullen said something. To her, his words were muffled white noise.

Her world swayed. The paper sunk to the floor and she made her way back to the couch before she fell. She had to tell Dad. Talk to him. See what he knew. If he knew Mom died. *Oh, God,* she ached all over.

Cullen knelt in front of her and held her hands clasping her knees. "Sweetheart."

She tried to assure herself his tenderness had no effect, and failed miserably. She wanted him to console her, but…couldn't. He came to Pearl with an ulterior motive—her mother. She couldn't, and wouldn't ignore the facts.

Tears spilled down her face. She had no more control over wanting him than she had over her heart breaking. All these years, she'd protected the vital organ. Understood she shouldn't get involved with someone. Not in Cullen Wilson's presence for a week, she'd lowered her defenses and became the perfect target.

She grasped his hands, pulled them off, and rose. Numb as an ice cube, she walked past Todd's shocked, red face and out the door.

The wood banged in her wake. She hit the porch steps running. An invisible force slammed into her, knocking her back a step. She sucked in a ragged breath and fought for control of the tantrum begging for release. He investigated her mother, her family for a reason. She would have to talk to him long enough to learn exactly why he came to Pearl. Then she could have an all-out-fit.

She twisted on her heels and marched up the steps.

"Hell's bells. I fucked up," he said as she swung open the door.

At least he got something right. "You did! If you think"—she hurried past a gaping Todd and glared at Cullen—"I'm gonna sit by while you do some sort of investigation on my family—"

His shoulders went rigid then relaxed before he faced her.

"—you're wrong."

His wattage smile cut through her thoughts and tempted her to lean into him and not stay mad. "I'm glad you're here."

Ignoring his soothing voice, she pushed onward. "Did you seek me out for the investigation?"

"The answer isn't a simple one."

The laptop's bright screen drew her attention to the message he'd received. The Department of Vital Records stretched across the top of the page. Underneath, her name. A million reasons came to mind why someone would research a birth certificate. The Air Force had done an extensive background check on her, verified her parentage. So why check her out? If she was good enough for the Air Force, she was good enough... An incomprehensive notion crossed her mind. Were her parents not her parents? "Why do you have my birth certificate?"

"Give it to her fast," Todd said. "We have to make tracks."

"In a sec." Lines stretched into Cullen's forehead. "This is too delicate of a situation for me to dump."

She shifted, suddenly more nervous than ever. "I like Todd's idea. Give it to me fast." She ignored the sexual innuendos of what she'd said.

He touched her hands and pulled out a chair with his foot. "Sit, please." Unlike earlier, his voice was easy, gentle.

"Okay," she said with a calmness she didn't feel and tried to sound collected. "Are you questioning who I am?"

His mouth went flat line, and she realized she was right. *Wait a second.* Her mother had died. He had her birth certificate. Was there some sort of inheritance? Receiving anything from the woman who'd abandoned her twisted her stomach. "I don't want it."

He added narrow eyebrows to his flat line lips. "Don't want what? What I have to say?"

"I don't want her money."

His thumbs stroked little circles over her hands. "That's not it."

One other way this scenario could go. "Well, I'm not the Congressman's child!"

"Agreed," he said and released her hand to open another email. This one had her DNA information, along with her father's on it. "You're General Ray Bodine's daughter. No question about it."

Relief washed through her. She knew the Congressman wasn't her father, not after the conversation with Dad. Yet a little tingle of doubt had stayed. Thank goodness Cullen squashed it.

"Like I said, make tracks." Todd's voice was as impatient as his footsteps pacing the wooden floor.

Cullen didn't respond. He clearly wasn't happy with his brother's curt tone, for he cut his eyes at him before softening his features to speak to her. "Short version. Congressman Alexander Kane is a good friend of ours. As you already said, he had an affair with your mother. Recently"—he paused and squeezed her hands—"Alex received a phone call stating your mother had died in a mental institution."

Hearing again of Mom's death wasn't any easier than the first time. "Go on."

"Although the police report ruled your mother's death as a suicide, Alex doesn't believe it and asked me to check into it."

She reclined in her chair and slid her hands from under his. Every angle went to him and those damn binoculars. "So, you were scoping out my dad and me?"

"Your father, by way of you."

"I appreciate your honesty," she said, stamping down on the sting that he'd used her. "What else?"

"Alex has a slime ball of an attorney."

"Yes," Todd cut in. "Hugo came through. I had him check on Mason Baldwin's vehicles. Since he has BMWs, the number of places willing to work on one isn't as long as say, a Chevrolet."

Goosebumps raced over her skin. Dad and she weren't alone in thinking weather hadn't caused his wreck. "You investigated my father's accident?"

"His accident happened a day before your mother's death," he said. "Too much of a coincidence." He focused on Todd. "And?"

"First off, Alex is clean. He was in a meeting the day of Alice's death, and having dinner with California's senator at the time Ray Bodine's accident occurred."

The air expelled from his lungs.

"Hugo got a hit. He tracked down a private technician who'd ordered a front bumper the day of General Bodine's accident. It didn't take Hugo long to find the car's serial number and its owner, Baldwin."

"Bingo! We've got him." Cullen jumped to his feet and paced the small confines of the kitchen. "Once I meet with one of Alice Masters', I mean Bodine's nurses, I'll confront Alex."

He said the name Masters as if it was common knowledge. "Who is Masters?" She inquired at the same time as he asked, "Do you want to go?"

The question milled over. She did want to face the person responsible for her father's wreck, and who possibly hurt her mother. Yet, there would be a conflict of interest. She was close, very close to the victims. Whatever she said and did could affect the case and her job. Right now, she'd lose control. "I best not."

"Understandable," he said. "Masters is the name your mother entered the institute under."

"That's why Dad couldn't find her."

A white kitten appeared out of nowhere and jumped into her lap, spun in a circle, and laid down. "Friendly much?" She petted the kitten, enjoying the distraction.

Cullen knelt in front of her and scratched the kitten's ear. "If what we think is true—Mason Baldwin causing your father's accident and harming your mother—then your life, as well as your father's, could be in danger."

As he spoke, his expression changed, hardness covered his face. She got a glimpse of his a-force-to-be-reckoned-with police persona.

She appreciated his concern. Having undergone her own police training, she could handle herself. "I'll be okay."

"Todd will stay with you."

"Yeah, I'll stay," Todd said and winked.

She could tell he didn't like the idea by the way he rubbed the back of his neck as if wanted the top layer of skin off. "No. Seriously, I'm good."

Cullen leaned in until their noses almost touched. "Baldwin is sneaky." He pressed his lips to hers.

A short, sweet kiss that left her body tingling.

"Don't think for a second the kiss changes anything," she said against his lips. "I'm still mad."

His chuckle vibrated through her. "Stay here as long as you want. Lock the door when you leave. And be careful."

"Yes, sir." She saluted.

He grinned and followed Todd out the door.

* * * *

244

It took one flash of Mason Baldwin's picture at the mental institution for the nurse to identify him as a frequent visitor. *Man,* that grated on Cullen's nerves. When he pulled out Alex's picture, a few nurses gushed over how sweet the Congressman was when he visited. He wanted to go ballistic. If it hadn't been for his old partner Hugo's words of reason, he would have.

"You coming or staying?" he asked his dark haired friend, before stepping out of the police cruiser in front of Alex's residence.

"Staying," Hugo said from behind the wheel. "I'll give you a few minutes, then I'll call for backup."

"Thanks, man."

"Good luck, buddy."

With tension coiling in his stomach, he moved to the intercom system. "Cullen Wilson for Congressman Kane." A beep sounded and he slid through the opening gate.

Alex's house looked the same as every other house along the Pacific, a mansion with an enormous pool and huge flower gardens. He used to think his friend got his dream home. With learning Alex lied about admitting Alice Bodine into the mental ward, his opinion changed. The house represented desperation, polished, and fake.

The few minutes' ride hadn't been long enough to process how messed up his friend was. Alex had given Alice a fake last name so no one could find her. By the time he reached the house, his anger gained momentum.

"Welcome, Mr. Wilson. It's been a while," Mrs. Goodman said and sent him a grandmotherly smile.

He hadn't been to California for some time. Whenever he and Alex met up, it was in Washington, D.C. "Yes, ma'am. It has been." He gritted his teeth to ward off the bite in his words.

"May I get you anything?" she asked and opened the door to Alex's office.

He stepped inside and swept the interior. Bookcases lined one wall. On the opposite stood a modest dark colored desk with a picture window. A fabric couch and dark cherry tables graced the other side. A cushioned chair and a coffee table finished the ensemble.

"No, thank you," he said and sat on the couch.

"The Congressman will be with you shortly." She closed the door behind her and it immediately opened.

He expected to see Alex. Instead, the weasel approached. He had a hand stuck in his pocket and the other loose at his side. Something simulating a rug stuck to the top of his head, loose strands from the mousy hair hung over his forehead. Baldwin's looks had changed since Virginia. "Congressman Kane didn't have a meeting scheduled. He's not able to meet with you."

Cullen scoffed at the comment. "Are you Alex's pit bull?"

"By being here, you're in violation of the contract."

He hadn't remembered Alex's residence being off limits.

Baldwin sat behind the desk, braced his elbows on the surface, and tented his fingers. "Which means your brother will not receive his get-out-of-debt ticket." His tone sounded as if he disciplined a small child.

Cullen held a grimace from the arrogance and entitlement flowing from the man and lowered to a seat. "Careful, Baldwin, you've got an edge to you like a dog in heat." He expected to get under Baldwin's skin where he'd spit out details about Alice Bodine's death. "Keep it up and you might need to check in the mental facility down the road for yourself."

Baldwin didn't flinch.

"You know the place. If it was a plane, you'd have a ton of frequent flyer miles to cash in."

"Thank you," Alex said to someone in the hall as Baldwin growled and moved out of the chair.

"I didn't expect you," Alex said, stretching out a hand.

The sight of his lifelong friend gave him palpitations. A coppery taste filled his mouth. He straightened. "I imagine not."

Alex's face tensed and he dropped his hand. "Did you talk to Ray Bodine?"

Cullen shoved aside his disappointment and gathered his wits. "The day of Mr. Bodine's crash, where were you?" Hugo already verified Alex had nothing to do with the accident, but he wanted to see what Alex did know.

"Huh?" Puzzlement covered his face.

"What about you, Mr. Baldwin?" Cullen slanted his head. "Or do you need a lawyer present for me to ask these questions?"

Baldwin snapped and snarled. Clearly, he was uptight. "What is the meaning of this?"

"This is the police asking questions about an attempted murder case involving Ray Bodine's accident. The case has recently been opened."

"You don't have jurisdiction here." The muscle in Baldwin's jaw jumped.

"You're facing attempted murder charges." He pressed, knowing Hugo filed them. First-degree murder charges would more than likely follow as well for Alice Bodine's death. He withheld that information until the authorities obtained more evidence.

"You're lying!" Baldwin charged forward, his hands fisted.

Waiting for him to swing, Cullen held his ground. Baldwin stopped a foot away. Since he didn't reach Cullen's shoulders, his intimidation method didn't come close to working.

"Am I? Evidence lifted off your car puts you at the scene of General Bodine's accident. Federal officers are in route." If they weren't, they would be soon.

Baldwin's face varied between a splotchy white to blazing red.

The motive stayed out of reach. Certain his smug attitude would have him boasting any minute, Cullen focused on Alex. Though he was partially convinced he had nothing to do with the general's accident, a tinge of doubt remained concerning Alice's death. "I don't know where to begin," he said, then pressed his lips together. Disgust, like a pungent bite of kale, filled his mouth. "You're willing to kill someone for a presidential nomination? Someone you claimed to love?"

"What?" Alex sagged to his desk chair. His elbows hit the hard surface with a *clunk* and he caught his head. "I didn't."

"But you were aware Alice Bodine would be murdered?" Hoping he was wrong, he pressed on. "You can be charged for knowing about a crime and not saying anything."

"No." Alex jolted out of his seat like a pogo stick. "I know nothing about a murder."

Some of his tension lifted. He believed Alex's reaction to be genuine. "The nurses sing your praises."

"I go there often." Alex lifted a shoulder. "So what? It cheers people up."

"You visited, yet you told me you hadn't seen Alice Bodine in years."

Alex shrugged, not acting at all like a confident politician.

Why would he go through all this trouble? Why would he lie? The presidential nomination was one thing, but he admitted Alice Bodine under a false name years ago. Then it hit him. "Your wife didn't know."

"Of course not!" Alex spun on his heels and stared out the window. "I couldn't tell her I had an affair with a married woman. She had no tolerance for adultery, and would have left me."

"So you hid Alice?"

Alex's jaw worked, but he didn't move. "That is the only thing I'm guilty of. If the press gets ahold of this, I'm washed up."

"You're already are. You lost Todd's and my faith." He paused, realizing what he said and remembering how much it meant to Selena.

"Don't say another word, Congressman," Baldwin said, moving to stand in front of the desk.

"What's in it for you, Baldwin?" He moved closer and slanted his head from side to side, doing his exaggerated curious dog act. "Money? You get some sort of treat?"

"If voted in office, Mason would become my Vice President," Alex said, his voice gruff and low.

"That doesn't mean I killed someone," Baldwin snapped.

Cullen sidestepped him, leaned against the desk, and stared at Alex with his face buried in his hands. If Alex asked him to look into the case thinking he'd cover up details out of friendship, he was sadly mistaken. "Did you think I wouldn't question people at the mental institute?"

"No. Your skills are the reason I asked for your help."

He hadn't asked jack shit. "Then why lie?"

Alex shook his head. "Alice's death had me not thinking clearly. If you knew the real reason, I was afraid you wouldn't take the case."

"How could I not, you held my brother's problems over my head, which was an asshole thing to do."

Silence. He had one more question. "Did you ask me to investigate Alice's death thinking I'd shut the case down? Either I'd be too taken by Selena or too loyal to you?"

"No," Alex said and rubbed a hand down his face. "I cared about Alice deeply. I wanted the truth."

No doubt he loved the woman, but he ruined lives. "I understand you were in a tough situation. Yet, you voluntarily took her away from her daughter and husband. Dammit, Alex, you knew what it was like for me not to have my parents, yet you inflicted pain to others. How could you dish out such grief on someone else?"

Alex didn't answer.

Cullen walked over to Baldwin. "I'm not a betting man, but I bet you're tied to Alice Bodine's death. Forensics is sweeping the ward she lived in now."

Like an adolescent teenage boy, Baldwin stuck out his lips.

"Why kill her? Why go after General Bodine?" He took in a deep breath, gaining strength. He still couldn't believe he was having this conversation. "How long before you came to Pearl and went after Selena?"

"It wasn't me!" The anger in Baldwin's voice sounded like he'd shattered.

Damn, he had expected to push Baldwin enough for a confession.

The door flew open.

"Sir, these men...they have warrants." The assistant's words broke off as uniformed police officers moved toward Alex and Baldwin. More than likely, Alex would be out tonight. The police didn't have anything on him to stick. Cullen hoped it'd stay that way, but his time for caring about Alex ended this afternoon.

"Cullen." Alex's weary gaze landed on him. "I should have never involved you, but I thought it was best for me and my daughter for you to talk to her."

He had forgotten about the birth certificate issue. "Years ago you didn't believe Alice, why question now?"

"I didn't. Mason brought it—" Alex nailed his attorney with a disgusted look. "You forged documents, too? You used me and Selena Bodine for the sympathy route?"

"That's the angle you wanted. I was making it happen." Baldwin shot back.

"I'll add forgery to Baldwin's growing list of charges." Cullen moved aside so the officer could take Alex out in handcuffs.

It wouldn't take long for the media to spin its ugly web. He thought back to the time Todd and he were in a similar media frenzy after their parents' death. His aunt and uncle, even Alex had helped removed them from the situation. A painful sort of tension spiked. Maybe one day he could forgive Alex, but not yet. Locking away someone's mother so her family couldn't find her had the same effects as a murder. It still took Alice away from her family.

"Cullen," Alex shouted from the doorway. "The contract stands. Your brother's debts are gone."

He wished those few words could make everything right again.

"Come on," Hugo said. "The helicopter that brought you over is waiting to take you to Pearl."

Chapter Six

Girl Code #23: Girlfriends don't backstab their friends.

Selena texted her sisters to meet at the pond later, fed Cullen's kitten, and went to talk to Dad. Sitting at the kitchen table, they munched on sandwiches while she told him about the death of her mother. His hard-core expression didn't falter. No flinching, no wincing, and no tears. He showed no sign the news fazed him.

Going from one conversation topic to the other, she said, "Cullen used me to find out about your accident."

Dad shrugged and said, "He had a job to do."

"Why the sudden change?"

"I know now what he was up to." He moved to the hospital bed and stretched out. "It makes sense."

She wished she could accept his actions as easily.

Dad transferred onto his side, offering his back to her.

No more secrets, though. From now on, she'd be upfront and hoped he would do the same.

Dad snored within moments. Sister time! She slipped out of the house toward the pond.

Stars sparkled in the sky and the spring-air cooled her skin. Thoughts raced through her mind about everything that happened since she returned to Pearl—seeing her sisters, her dad, Cullen.

The moon glimmered across the pond's still water like lighting bugs flashing. She dropped to her butt at the edge and recalled when she and Cullen met as teens. So many similar feelings had zipped through her—immediate attraction, explosive chemistry—all off the grid. Years ago, she'd walked away from him, knowing he was something special. His attentiveness and tenderness drew her in, yet she bailed.

Unsure of how to handle the churning acid in her stomach, she rested her head on her bent knees. This odd, sick sensation must have been what Cullen had experienced the night she walked away.

Over everything, one thought raised its head. Surprisingly, the sense he betrayed her wasn't it. He'd risked a friendship with the person who'd treated him more like family, by helping him out with his brother, than his aunt and uncle had…for her. To find out the truth.

A hand touched her shoulder, then a warm body sat beside her. Joey arriving so quickly touched her. Her eyes moistened.

Joey held up her cell.

Laydi's face brightened the screen. "Hi there."

Selena forced a smile. "Hey." She sniffled and clasped Joey's hand resting on her arm. "I'm a mess."

"Sweetie"—Juls approached and grasped her shoulders, kneading her stiff muscles with her magic fingers—"you look good."

Only her sisters would think her red nose and mascara streaked face highlighted by the moon's glow looked okay. They were the few people who saw past her flaws and dishevelment and loved her anyway.

"What happened?" Unusual for Laydi, her investigative tone was tender, sweet.

"Earlier, you were over the moon," Joey said.

The papers on Cullen's table contained details she couldn't process. To explain the reports and pictures to her friends would take more energy than she possessed.

"Cliff note version," Laydi said, somehow knowing her mind.

Despite being more upbeat with what transpired between her and Cullen, talking to her sisters would help. If they thought for a second what he did wasn't right, they'd tell her. "Cullen investigated me and my family." She mustered her detective tone to stop her voice from cracking. "He used me."

Joey placed a hand on her back and moved it in a circle, soothing her. "You know that's not true. Whatever he is up to isn't to hurt you. He may have, but I doubt that was his endgame."

Selena blinked through moisture to look at Joey's teary eyes. "How can you be so sure?"

"Because I know you. You would never let someone in who wasn't worthy."

Laydi made an odd noise. "You know she's right."

Juls finger-combed her hair as she sucked in a deep breath. The time they met flashed in her mind. Nothing had changed, not with her sisters' support. This she could count on.

She released Joey's hand and wiped her face. With a handle on her feelings toward Cullen, she brought up another life-changing situation. "My time is almost up with the Air Force. I'm thinking about opening a teen recreational center."

Juls squeezed her arm. "That'd be great."

"I can see you doing that," Joey said, smiling.

"Good idea," Laydi chimed in. "Where would you get the funds?"

She hadn't given much thought to the finances, but believed the general would help. "I'll talk to Dad."

"Wow, things have changed since you've been home," Laydi said and bit her bottom lip.

"They have." For the first time, her life came together. She'd found something the Air Force couldn't give her—herself. "I love you girls."

"We love you," Joey, Laydi, and Juls said in unison.

"Selena!"

She bolted upright, her breaths coming in short bouts. "It's Cullen."

"We should give you privacy." Joey kissed her cheek. "Good luck."

"Go get him, tiger." Laydi winked.

Juls ran her fingers down the length of her hair. "For once, listen to your heart."

Selena stared at Juls. Her smile was small, and her expression filled with empathy. Juls had been through so much, and she let someone into her life. Truly let him in. If her sisters had warning signs with Cullen, they'd tell her, not encourage her to give him a chance. "I will."

Joey and Juls wrapped her in a bear hug.

"You know I'm there, right?" Laydi grinned from the phone.

Their support gave her strength. "Together we can take on the world," she said, in a tone leaving no room for argument.

"Always have," Juls said, tenderness in her tone.

"Selena!" Closer, but the thickness of the woods blocked Cullen's shape.

"We're out of here," Laydi said, as if she controlled the phone.

She watched the true meaning of sisterhood hurry away—her two friends and a phone—before turning toward possibilities.

* * * *

Once the helicopter landed, Cullen couldn't get to Selena fast enough. To let her know her mother hadn't left her. To tell her the threat on her and her father was gone. He couldn't believe the lengths Alex had gone to reach his goal. Baldwin, however, he had no trouble wrapping his mind around his duplicity.

Thankfully, Todd waited near the helipad to give him a ride. After a couple of quick phone calls during the drive home, one to Selena where she didn't answer, and one to General Bodine, he had a good idea where she might be by the time Todd parked the truck.

With the moon lighting his way, he rushed toward the pond. At the opening to the path, an intense shift hit his chest, as if his next actions would be monumental. He swayed.

Regaining his footing, he darted through the woods. "Selena!" He approached the clearing, and his heart thumped so hard, a metallic taste rose to his mouth.

She and two other women stood near the water's edge.

Her sisters.

The women moved away, leaving her behind, and disappeared into the thicket.

He moved closer. "Selena."

She didn't respond, but she didn't take off, either.

The moonlight streamed over her delicate features.

Before he could pull her into his arms and explore the chemistry surrounding them, he had to come clean. She would demand it. Her fact-finding mind wouldn't let him close to her until he spilled all. One of her many traits he loved.

The fire in her eyes confirmed his suspicion. "What happened?"

"Mason Baldwin, Congressman Kane's attorney is the suspect behind your father's accident." He paused, waiting for her to take this in. When she only blinked, he continued. "My former partner is leading the investigation into your mother's death." Again, she watched him with no reaction. "If there is evidence of foul play, Hugo will find it."

"Why?" Her brows came together. "Why would Baldwin cause my father to have an accident?"

"Because your father knew you were his biological daughter. Baldwin wanted to remove anyone who could contradict the birth certificate's authenticity."

"For what purpose?" Her hard-edged investigator tone was in full swing. She crossed her arms.

"So Congressman Kane could use the reconnecting-with-my-long-lost-daughter issue as part of his campaign. Work on citizens' sympathies." Cullen cleared his throat. "Baldwin provided Kane with a false birth certificate. For a smart man, Baldwin let greed lead him to his own destruction."

He pegged Baldwin when he thought him polished, superficial. The man wanted name recognition, as if holding one of the most important jobs in the country could make people look up to him. "If Baldwin's plan had played out and

Congressman Kane won the presidential nomination, then Baldwin would have been his running mate."

"Vice President." She chuckled, her voice a combination of shock and disgust. "Does he have the qualifications?"

"Don't know."

"Wow. The lengths people will go."

His sentiments exactly. "I'm always amazed at how smart people think they can out-maneuver the law."

"This clears your friend of suspicion," she said with a calmness not matching her pinched lips.

"Ah, not exactly." This was the hard part. Telling Selena her mother hadn't left her when she believed it for so long. "Alex had your mother institutionalized to keep her away from his wife."

She recoiled.

The impact of her pain radiated to him. He sucked in a breath. Instinctively, he reached out to soothe her, but she flinched out of reach. "Alice had come to his home insisting you're his daughter."

"But I'm not," she said with more strength to her words than he expected.

"No, but he was afraid Alice would make trouble for him, so he had her admitted as Alice Masters."

"How? How can he get away with it?"

"I don't know," he said, shaking his head. "Maybe Alex pulled strings, coerced someone in admissions. I really have no idea."

He felt her loss. Angry from her mother abandoning her family, to learning she hadn't left after all, would be hard for anyone to process. She would have to cope with having accused her mother for abandonment and losing valuable time.

"All this time I blamed Mom." She placed a shaky hand over her mouth. "I never searched." Her fingers muffled her words.

He wanted to say sorry for what Alex had done, but he wasn't responsible. Just as he wasn't for Todd's trouble dealing with the aftermath of the war.

From the way she dealt with her life, she'd taught him he couldn't take the blame for what others chose to do. From what he could tell, she never held herself liable. That night at the pond, she hadn't. The other times she mentioned her father, she made no derogatory remarks that what he'd done was a reflection on her. She didn't criticize herself when her father had fallen apart. She put the responsibility where it belonged—on him. Still, he couldn't resist, "I'm sorry."

"It's not your fault." Her tone neither harsh nor hurt, but her eyes stayed distant.

And he knew. She still considered his motives and actions as underhanded. He clasped her arm, taking her hand from her mouth, and waited until she looked at him. Confessing his feelings wasn't his norm, yet he never felt more compelled to let someone know something than he did then. "I didn't use you," he said, fighting the ache from entering his tone.

Despite his anxiousness to hold her in his arms, he waited and watched.

She swallowed hard. "Didn't you? You acted like you went to Dad's accident scene to help me when you had ulterior motives."

Her weak response gave him confidence. "I went for you. The information you gave me put in motion Baldwin's arrest."

She searched her surroundings as if the woods had the answer to something else she could call him out on. "You're using your aunt and uncle's house to spy!"

Lame attempt to fire him up. He wouldn't argue or fight what existed between them and had survived for almost a decade. "You can't stop me from falling for you."

She lifted her chin. A tear fell. "I can't."

"No," he said in a low, firm voice. He glided his fingers down the curve of her face and wiped the tear with his thumb. "You've stayed a part of me."

She sniffled and wiped her nose. "I—"

"I'm not letting go." He lowered his voice. "Not this time. You're stuck with me," he said and let his voice drift even lower, going for a syrupy tone he hoped she couldn't resist. "Faith, remember." He echoed the note she'd left him years ago.

His heart swayed as it had done before he entered the path to come here. This time the shift was stronger, deeper.

"I want you in my future," he said with such earnest, he didn't regret how easily he uttered the words.

She parted her lips on a gasp. Yeah, they were on the same page.

Cupping her face, he bent toward her. She met him halfway.

The soft feel of her lips triggered an explosion through him. Every part of him stood at attention, even his toes. He nudged her closer.

She came willingly, snuggling her breasts against him, and opened her mouth on a moan.

He swept his tongue inside, tasting her sweetness, and eased away. She was so beautiful it hurt. Every fiber within him longed to touch her. "Selena…"

* * * *

The intensity in Cullen's voice sent Selena into a tailspin. She didn't have enough control to keep thinking of reasons to push him away. She had to stop. Her conscious had gotten its way forever.

She wanted him. It was time she got what her subconscious wanted.

She throbbed, ached in areas dormant for far too long. "I have to have your skin against me." She slipped her hands under his shirt and relished in what was about to happen.

He captured her lips, wrapped his hands around her, and squeezed. "I've wanted you since the first night we were together."

"Me, too," she said, and added eagerly, "I'm on the pill." She cringed at how that sounded. "It keeps me regular, not because—"

He kissed the tip of her nose. "You're adorable." He smiled lazily. Tingles erupted all over her. His warm hands went beneath her shirt.

She concentrated on him, his protectiveness, and the tender manner in which he stroked her. With him, dreams were within reach.

He nuzzled into the crook of her neck and traced the band of her bra, brushing her breasts. "You smell good," he said and moaned before flicking the hook.

They weren't teenagers trying to fill a void. No grief had them acting irrationally or jumping in without thinking. They knew and wanted each other. So right.

With ease, he whipped off his shirt and banded her in his arms. Her bra and shirt bunching between them didn't stop her nipples from getting their fill of his hard body. But she wanted more.

She crisscrossed her arms. Imitating a curtain rising slowly to reveal a prize, she lifted the hem of her shirt...exposing her stomach...her barely covered breasts...

His hands were on her in-a-got-to-have-her-now-or-I-die flurry.

The excitement of having him touch her stopped her movements, with her shirt covering her face.

He cupped both breasts, and stroked one with his tongue. She sucked in a breath and arched her back, giving and craving more.

The sensual rush flowing through her from not being able to see his face, mixed with the evening air, made the position wonderfully erotic.

When he had his fill with one breast, he moved to the other. Thrilled, she needed, demanded to see and take control. She finished tugging her shirt over her head and tossed it and her bra to the ground.

Spring, musty-ridden air hit her senses. She didn't care that someone could see them. This was their moment.

He growled. The look in his molten eyes hardened her already perky breasts. Liquid heat flooded between her legs. He gripped her waist and guided them to the ground, pulling her into his lap and settling her butt on his upper thighs.

Tenderness moved through her unlike anything she'd experienced, even more than the first time they connected.

He licked her nipple, blew on it, and drew the sensitive flesh into his mouth before giving the other one attention. He moved over her skin with precise detail, leaving her and her breasts happy he came to visit.

Heat curled, tightening her stomach. Craving him closer, she wrapped her legs around his hips and pressed her core in to him. Felt his hardening length. But it wasn't enough. "I'm dying here."

He crushed his mouth to hers and his hands glided over her thighs. His thumbs moved upward toward the spot craving his touch.

The single piece of clothing left on moistened even more.

His erratic breathing and the puff of air hitting her face revealed his excitement. She never dreamed she'd want someone as much as she did him.

"You're not wearing underwear." His seductive voice, a mixture of rough and barely audible, sent spirals of heat through her already excited body. He pressed his forehead against hers.

"No." Thank God, she didn't. "Take yours off."

"Absolutely, but"—he scanned the grassy surroundings mixed with sticks and pebbles—"maybe I'll just undo them."

"My pleasure," she said, smirking. She unbuckled his belt and undid his jeans. Holding her by the waist, he lifted her until she stood and removed her yoga pants.

She twisted to find he'd freed himself from his restraints and drew in a ragged breath. She didn't get to gawk long at how'd he'd grown nicely into a man, for he pulled her into his lap.

She grasped his velvetiness, savored its thickness, and stroked his length.

"Sweet Jesus," he muttered. "I'm gonna burst."

With her feet braced on the ground on either side of his hips, she held onto his shoulders and poised above the tip of him.

He held himself until the head found her warmth and moved his hand to join his other one in guiding her hips.

Unable to look away, she lowered, taking him in. Feeling his thickness. Warm-tingling pleasure seeped into her body, radiating through her as if she floated amongst the clouds. At the heavenly reaction, her eyes fluttered close. She remembered this—this mind-numbing awareness, greater than her. It was more powerful than both of them. The strong, unbelievable emotion that had scared her didn't anymore.

"Holy mother of God." He groaned as their sexes fused.

The emotions rushing stopped her from moving. She held his shoulders and waited for him to look at her. "You have to guide me." She puffed. "I can't move. My muscles are jello."

His tender, sweet face lit with heat. "Anything you want." He raised her by the waist until he nearly slid out of her, his biceps bunching and bulging.

The anticipation of him buried inside was almost painful. Digging her fingers into his arms, she hung on while he lowered her. The gentle act pushed him deeper inside, hit her G-spot. Urgency to release became unbearable. The tenderness of his movements so sweet, it touched her, but she desperately craved his thrusts hard and fast.

Whether from her brushing her breasts over his lips or his own driving need, he increased the tempo.

"Are you hot, baby?" His words a low growl.

"God, yes." She panted and wiggled on top. "Deeper. I need you deeper."

"Yeah." He obliged, holding her firmer and thrusting hard, driving further into her heat.

The thrill was so tight, so intense, her breath hitched.

He did it again.

The bottled sensation residing in her for years exploded on his name. She came…and came…and came more, until she slumped on top of his chest with him pulsating inside her.

* * * *

Engulfed by the intensity of the passion pounding through his veins, Cullen could only lay on the grass with Selena's body wrapped around him.

Physically, his muscles melted into one another. Mentally, his thoughts knotted into a mass of confusion. Where did he and she go from here? For him, there was no walking away. What would she want?

With a feather-soft touch, he trailed his fingers up and down her arm and listened to her steady breathing, savoring finally being with her.

"Wow." She propped her chin on his chest and clutched his sides, giving him a squeeze. "That was better than the first time."

Their first time had been out-of-this-world, too.

A twinkle lit her features he hadn't seen before. He didn't want to fantasize about their future. He wanted to talk about it.

"Do you ever get the feeling like you know something is about to happen? Or know there's more to a story?"

Her questions caught him off guard. "Do you?"

"Most times." She rose to a sitting position on top of him. He half expected her to accuse him of suppressing his thoughts. "This time, I'm still deciding."

Crunching his abs to raise, he captured her lips. "You're remarkable."

"You're delicious." She winked and pressed a hand on his shoulder, giving him a nudge until he lay down. "We need to talk."

"We do." But being inside her would make it more than difficult. "Except, something's coming up."

The vibrations from her laugh passed through her tight walls, squeezing him. His gut twisted. "I can't stay in this position and talk." Who was he kidding? He couldn't stay in any position near her to talk without being ready to go again.

He cupped her face and she leaned into it. "I'm in love with you."

Her face twisted and her mood dropped. The mischievousness evaporated into something resembling agony. She nodded. "I know," she said, but her head stopped bobbing and moved side-to-side. "I don't know what to do about it."

The admission pinched his soul and he closed his eyes. Her honesty hurt more than he could have imagined. She said relationships scared her, so why did he even consider they could have a possible future? He lowered his hand from her cheek and rubbed his fingers over the ache in his chest. It didn't work.

"Cullen," she said, her voice sweet. "Open your eyes, silly."

He snorted, did what she asked.

She wiggled with him still half-hard inside her. Her lush breasts bobbed in time with her movements.

Despite the blow, he wanted her so fucking bad that for the first time in his life, he didn't know what the hell to do.

"I want you to see something." She touched her lower right abdomen, just above her hip.

He spread his fingers over the symbol she'd drawn on the paper. "Faith."

She tilted her head and watched him touch her. "Yeah," she said, and her voice cracked. "I have it."

She lost him. One minute she didn't know what to think about him loving her, the next she found what she said she needed. "What?"

Tears slid down her cheek and she lifted a shoulder. "I'm scared. So very, very scared. But I want you. It hasn't been but a few days, and I feel like I've known you all my life." She gave a tepid laugh and wiped her face. "I guess I have in a way, haven't I?"

He rose to sit, but she slapped a hand to his chest. "Don't. I can't deal with you touching me and still talk."

Should he remind her that during her confession, he'd hardened again inside her?

She pulled her lips inward.

Maybe not.

She had to mull this over in her own time. Excitement raced through him. He could do this, let her figure it out on her own, and enjoy her coming to terms with the fact she didn't want to live without him. He linked his hands behind his head and watched.

The right side of her mouth lowered and her nose scrunched, as if she digested something sour. "I never thought I'd feel whole." She slanted her head. "I like how you go out of your way for the people you care about." To this, she nodded. "You're fun to hang out with."

"Thank you," he said, but his words fell on mute ears. Her attention was toward the water, as if she'd gone somewhere else.

"Sweet, kind to animals. Very important. Charming, I guess. Lord knows you're hot." She gazed at him. "And gorgeous."

He chuckled.

"Oh, that's rich," she said. "I'm in all my glory and you're watching me come of age."

Years ago, she'd done that when she'd rocked his world. "I was there, Sweetheart, when you came of age. This is something different."

She lay on top of him, pressing her breasts into his chest. "What are we going to do?" she asked, her voice quivering.

A treasure imparted on him. "Let's see what happens. Take it one step at a time."

"One step?" Her eyes widened as she rocked her hips, the friction hardening him even more. "What's the step?"

Bowled over by how much he wanted her again as if they hadn't just been together, he grasped her hips and held on.

Voices seeped into his sex-fogged mind.

"Oh, it's the girls." She scurried off him, much to his dick's dismay. He'd have blue-balls for days.

She slipped her clothes on more efficiently and faster than he could. Standing, he repositioned his erection, then attempted to zip his pants. No go. Releasing a breath, he gave it another try.

"I bet they're worried."

They were worried? Hell, he was in pain. "Damn."

She glanced at his bulge. "Oops." She slid a hand to his crotch. "I'll take care of you later."

"You're not helping my problem."

* * * *

Selena moved her hand away from his crotch as Cullen cupped her cheeks, a little smile playing around the corner of his lips. He was dressed, and still sexy as hell.

She melted.

"I want you. I'm gonna say this, and then you can catch up to me whenever you're ready."

Dipping her head, she bit her lower lip to hide her confusion. "Catch up to what?"

"I want you forever." He brushed a soft kiss on her lips. "I meant what I said. I'm not letting you go."

Forever. Could she do it? When she arrived in Pearl, she had every intention of helping Dad and getting out of town as soon as possible, but now...now, if this was where Cullen would be, she didn't want to leave. He filled a space within her she once preferred to leave empty. Not anymore. She didn't want it empty ever again.

His thoughtfulness, the way he protected her feelings when she didn't know they needed protecting. It wasn't betrayal, but thoughtfulness. He went the extra step for her. Put her before himself, before his friend. Her chest swelled. The walls she erected to keep guys away had already crumbled to half the size, but with him, they were nonexistent.

In the moment of all moments, this one was the cherry on the sundae. Without thinking, without dissecting any more possibilities of the 'what ifs' or the 'buts,' she let her heart lead the way as Juls suggested, and took a leap of faith.

She wrapped her hands around his neck and pulled him closer. Her yoga pants moistened from his intense expression. This was it. She was doing this.

Her mind did a slow, looping sort of dip, leaving fear and reservations behind. "Okay," she said through a smile and giggles. "I'm in."

He froze. "You're serious."

Goosebumps rose and a warm, gooey, comforting feeling flowed over her. "Marry me, Cullen."

"You betcha." His lips met hers. He kissed her with tenderness and belonging, a passion she didn't fully experience until now.

Several someones coughed and mumbled behind her.

She observed the women who meant the world to her. In the distance, Todd ran toward them.

"Your friends?" He kept a protective arm around her waist and squeezed her side.

"My sisters," she replied. "Laydi's on the phone. This is Juls and Joey." She pointed to each of them as she said their names. "Everyone, this is Cullen Wilson."

"Hi," her sisters said.

She blew out a breath. "He's my fiancé!" Her voice escalated by the time she said the last syllable. So not her. Nothing about her experience since she'd returned had been. It was great!

The sisters ambushed them with hugs and kisses.

"Man, I got worried something happened, and you're down here making out." Todd ruffled Cullen's hair and kissed her cheek. "He made a good choice, Prissy Pants."

She laughed, knowing Todd teased. Thankfully, he'd gotten over whatever bothered him where she was concerned.

"You know, I'm still there, right?" Laydi's voice rose above the commotion.

"I do." She grinned.

By the time the group walked to her house to tell Dad, she was in a puddle of tears and didn't care everyone saw. "I'm honestly, purely, completely happy."

"Words to live by," Cullen said. "Words to live by."

~The End~

~PERSISTENCE~

By

D.C. Stone

~Dedication~

In what Jessica, Lea, Cait, and I have dedicated toward this book, there are not enough words, or even enough gratitude that can be aptly described to thank those who sacrifice their lives in order for the rest of us to live freely. This encompasses a vast amount of men, women, and yes, children, because those kids have to face the daily worry and thoughts that their mother, father, grandfather, grandmother, aunt, uncle, or any family member may not make it home in one piece—if at all. Having a long line of family history serving in the military, along with myself and my husband serving, I understand the family-hood (because it isn't just a brotherhood anymore) and the daily push to get up, get your boots on, and make a positive impact to fight against those who want to do nothing but evil. It's about the dedication, the integrity, and the allegiance to doing what is right, to giving a piece of yourself so that others may rest in peace at night, so they may speak freely and of their opinions, so they can laugh and play, break the law, fall in love, have a child, watch a baseball game, cut someone off in traffic, go to the beach, spend time with their family, and live their lives.

So yes, there's not enough words to thank any of these brave and courageous veterans. Nor is there enough that we can do to thank them and their families for giving us the chance to experience life. So all I'll say is thank you for continuing to be you. None of you will ever be forgotten, nor will your sacrifice ever go without thanks.

And to my father…who is a wounded veteran himself, and just survived the biggest fight of his life against cancer.

~D.C.

Chapter One

*Girl Code Rule #41: When you're throwing up, make sure you have a girlfriend
to hold your hair back. Otherwise, it could get messy*

Laydi Michaels woke with a start. The glare of sunlight stabbed like a two-ton sledgehammer into her pounding brain, and she slammed her eyes shut. Not that a two-ton hammer existed, but with how she felt—headache, nausea, and alarmingly, yet deliciously sore in *certain* places—that was the only apt description.

She had the hangover of all binge drinkers. One that rivaled her high school days, where she would disappear with Dad's fifth of Jack, a bag from Burger King, and her best friends, until not a drop remained in the bottle and they'd mastered the latest Pop hit.

At the top of their lungs.

Forward and backward.

Her stomach recoiled at the memory, and away from any mention of alcohol. Keeping her eyes closed—because yes, her spinning vision didn't do anything for her nauseous stomach—she took stock of her surroundings. From the brief glimpse, she hadn't recognized the bare white walls, or the rose-colored drapes hanging in front of a large window.

This wasn't her room, where the walls were a sage green and the windows had blackout curtains—something required in her investigative line of work, due to her overnight surveillance cases.

Next noticeable concern? She was completely naked, just as the day she was born. The sheets against her skin—not that she moved much; no, her stomach revolted against that—were soft, smoother than the Egyptian cream-colored ones back home.

And the most alarming detail of all? The very heavy and thick arm wrapped around her waist. She lay slightly on her side, but her hip touched a warm thigh. From the uncomfortable poking sensation and the stillness of this male body next to her, something was up before the actual man was.

Raking her mind, she tried to remember anything, *something* from last night, a clue to explain where she was and *who* she lay next to. But all she could come up with was how she'd started the night by meeting, and then making an absolute blathering fool of herself to her boss, Andrew Cox.

She paused and gave a little girly sigh. Tall, well over six-feet, built like a Greek God, and not the ones learned about in History class. No, this guy had romance novel written all over him. Combined with the charm of a gentleman, and the resemblance to Chris Hemsworth; ladies fell all over themselves in his presence. And with his dating history, Andrew wasn't one to shy away from attention.

His hair was dark blond and a few weeks past needing a haircut. Bangs fell across his forehead when he typed furiously on his computer, or when he interviewed a suspect and got really into the story. His eyes changed colors depending on the shirt he wore. They could be either blue or green, and were wide-set, startling to the female population. She'd seen many women trip over their feet when taking in Andrew, and if his height, six-days-a-week I-work-out-at-the-gym body, hair, or eyes didn't do it, the silky velvet of his voice caused thighs to tremble with anticipation.

He should have been a radio DJ, or a phone sex operator, instead of the CEO for *Off The Record Private Investigations*.

He had a smooth southern drawl that spoke of being raised somewhere in the state of Georgia...sexy as hell. She shuddered at the memory.

Two things happened next: her stomach lurched and bile rose, her body's way of telling her she had indeed indulged in one or two too many drinks last night.

Second, as she snapped her eyes open and dove from the bed, she caught a glance at the mysterious stranger with her, who was really no stranger at all.

Gloriously sexy, sleepy—and familiar—blue eyes widened in surprised and concern before she bounded across the room for the bathroom, where she promptly regurgitated last night's fun.

* * * *

Andrew had a few seconds to enjoy Laydi's curves and parts that jiggled deliciously before the bathroom door slammed, cutting off his view. Unmistakable sounds of retching came and he sighed, remembering last night when he told her that no, she should not have a seventh tequila shot.

This was after she'd already downed a pitcher of strawberry margaritas—by herself.

He sat up and grabbed his briefs. Crossing the room, he winced as the retching continued. Beautiful as she may be, Laydi was not a pretty-sounding sickling. Not that it mattered—there were bigger issues to deal with. Like making sure she was okay.

He tapped on the door. "Lay? You all right?"

"Don't come in," she shrieked. "I'm not dressed, and besides"—she coughed and he winced, his stomach turning in sympathy—"this isn't pretty."

"Okay…Can I get anything for you?"

More retching. He laid his head against the wood and waited. When it continued, he tested the doorknob, found it locked. "Lay"—he tried to cajole—"open the door."

"No," she choked through what sounded like dry heaves. At least her stomach purged. They needed to get some fluids and crackers in her, otherwise, she'd feel like shit all day.

He shook the knob when the dry heaving didn't let up. "Open this damn door or I'm busting it down." Modesty damned, he'd get inside whether she liked it or not.

"Oh, God." She moaned as the toilet flushed.

"Sweetheart, open the door." He rattled the knob, hoping that somehow, some way the door would miraculously have unlocked in the last minute. No such luck.

"What...the...fuck?"

He paused, something in her tone alerting him of a shift in attention. Like she'd discovered that fat free ice cream really wasn't as good as the company wanted people to believe. He stepped back a second before the door whipped open.

Laydi in all her glorious nakedness.

He sucked in a sharp breath and fought against his immediate reaction to pounce—there was no pretty way to describe what he wanted to do to her—but jump on her like a caveman and ensure the human race's survival. If her expression was any indication, she wouldn't be up for some morning nookie. He winced inwardly. And especially after purging last night's drinks. Yeah, maybe he should give her an hour or so, get some food in her stomach and hydrated before he acted like a Neanderthal.

Her blonde curls popped in different directions around a heart-shaped face. He'd confirmed last night that her hair was as soft as it looked and tangled perfectly with his fingers. Five-foot-ten-inches of sculpted, curvy beauty: her handful breasts perky, waist tiny, yet with hips strong enough to hold on and direct her movement to his.

A colorful array of tattoos decorated her body. He planned to learn every one of them soon. A blue rose tattoo on her shoulder, the stem trailing over the generous curve of her cleavage. Two full sleeves decorated her arms from shoulder to wrist with enough different designs to make his head spin. A cheetah spread lengthwise on her right thigh, and another dazzling array of designs covered her left calf. And some sort of plain symbol on her right ankle. He had a feeling that tattoo was the most important.

Her nipples stood erect from the chilly air of the room, although he'd like to think they did from desire. But one look at her bloodshot hazel eyes, spitting with fury, and it was wishful hoping.

Her lips curved in a snarl, the color of them matching her areolas, before she bit out, "What the hell is this?"

His eyebrows went up and his attention shifted to what she pointed at. A sizable solitaire diamond wrapped her left ring finger, and below, a thin platinum band. He knew it was platinum and not white gold, because he'd purchased the rings last night.

Right before he married her.

"Um," he mumbled, unsure how to begin. *This* was a new situation. Did she not remember? He pushed his first reaction away to snap at her. Anger wouldn't do here. But call him Mr. Confused, because there was no way she couldn't recall just how acquainted they became with one another last night. The best night of his life. One he'd fantasized about for years. "Lay, what do you remember from last night?"

Her jaw clenched. She ripped a towel from the wall with enough force to send the holder spinning with a tinkling sound, and wrapped the cloth around her. Arms crossed over her chest, she glared at the ceiling before turning her spitfire gaze his way. "We went out to dinner at that Italian place in Dupont Circle."

"In DC, yes. Do you remember anything after that?" God, he hoped so, because this morning would go from confused to *what the fuck*, real quick.

If anything, her glare narrowed. He took a step back. She tracked the movement, then shifted her gaze to the side, looking out the hotel window. Her jaw dropped. "Where are we?"

From her question, no, she didn't remember last night. And wasn't that just his luck.

"Las Vegas," he answered cautiously, waiting for the impending meltdown.

"You said we were going to dinner." She turned her wary gaze to him. "For a business meeting. How did we end up in Las Vegas?"

He winced. "Well, after I fired you—"

Her back straightened, and didn't that just make certain parts of her move delectably. Her tits bounced, drawing his attention. "You what?" she shrieked.

He sighed and dropped his chin to his chest. "Look—"

A knock sounded at the door. He whipped his head toward it and wanted to growl. Actually growl. *Yeah, guess he was a caveman after all.*

"Mr. and Mrs. Cox," an unfamiliar voice said. "Your special delivery has arrived."

Laydi's eyes widened, her jaw gaped, and her face—normally a fair, pale shade matching the color of his grandmother's fine china—turned red. That couldn't be healthy. Was she going to faint? Get sick again? He took a step toward her, alarm coursing through him at the change before she made a strangled sound, spun on her heel, and slammed the bathroom door shut with a click of the lock.

"Fuck." This time he gave into the urge and growled. Loudly. He rubbed his forehead. How did one of the best nights of his life become one of the most confusing mornings?

Shaking his head, he answered the door.

* * * *

Mrs. Cox.

Oh God, she was married! Albeit, to a man she'd wanted for more than four years. The leader in many of her fantasies. But she'd never acted on that attraction to him because he was her boss.

Or—she frowned—her ex-boss, now.

Shit, she was fired, too. What the hell was she supposed to do? Her apartment wasn't the cheapest in her neighborhood, but she had wanted safety over saving money. Living alone in a city where she couldn't rely on anyone else caused a girl to make smart choices. And her taking the six-hundred-dollars-more-a-month apartment had been one of those.

But now fired? And married?

Weren't there laws for this kind of stuff? Sexual harassment? But even as she stepped into the hot shower, still flushing from her naked state, she knew there'd be no way in good conscience to take a suit against Andrew. In all truthfulness, this was a dream come true. Only she didn't remember everything. She wanted to not be cheated out of those sexy memories. How fair was that? And while parts of the night were hazy, she hoped things would clear up soon.

Several minutes later, she stepped out of the shower freshly scrubbed and wrapped the same towel around her. She grabbed an amenity pack and brushed her teeth, then took the small comb to try and tame her unruly curls. Keeping her hair from frizzing would be a lot of work, especially without her normal care products. She hoped the small amount of conditioner left in her hair did the trick. Otherwise, it'd be all over the place before they stepped outside. She took the extra time to prepare for what waited on the other side of the door, right on down to inspecting all of her moles—or as her father called them, "Angel Kisses"—just to be safe, not to keep delaying the inevitable confrontation.

They needed to have a talk she never dreamed she'd have with him, one that included the letters of M-I-S-T-A-K-E. There was no way, with his history and her distrust—*Thanks, Mom!*—things would work between them. Had her dear mother not taught her early on about cheating and shunning responsibilities and her word, then Laydi probably would have more faith in the actions of others.

Jumping into the world of private investigations where she'd learn the truth about why others made decisions certain ways, to get to the fact of the matter, wasn't lost on her with her past.

Not ready to face Andrew, she hesitated at the door. Her phone was on the other side, and the first order of business was to research ways to get their marriage annulled. They could chalk the night up to a drunken mistake, have a laugh, and move on.

They could remain on friendly terms. He obviously didn't want her in his life, otherwise why would he have fired her...and without any notice as to what she'd done wrong?

She bit her lip. Well, he *had* been warning her to pay more attention on her evidence tracking.

But that wasn't her fault...

Okay, it was, but she was working on it. As she "worked" on a million other things. She'd fucked up her evidence tracking, and would have to pay that price.

Cursing beneath her breath and calling herself all kinds of coward, she opened the door.

He stood across the room, his back to her, facing the massive window. The glass ran from floor to ceiling. He'd pulled back the curtains and bright sunlight glared in. Wearing the same charcoal pants from last night, no shoes, no shirt, he imitated the powerful stance and presence he normally did in a full suit. While she felt somewhat better after the shower, her head pounded a tune rivaling a dance club mix. Her stomach turned unhappily, reminding her she wasn't out of the woods just yet.

Andrew pivoted, and his gaze roamed over the length of her. His jaw tightened. "I had them bring up some Gatorade, coffee, and toast. If you feel up to it, there are eggs and fruit, too. You need to get hydrated, and get something in your stomach to soak up the acid."

She glanced at the cart with a silver covered plate atop, various liquids, and a single red rose. Her stomach rolled again, this time not because of the alcohol. While it was customary for hotels to provide flowers with room service, she couldn't help but be pleased at the rose. If she had to get flowers from any man for the first time, getting them from Andrew would be how she wanted it to play out.

She couldn't handle food yet, but needed the liquid replenishment. Tugging the towel closer to her chest, she searched the room for her clothing. Nothing lay on the floor, and she hadn't seen anything earlier either.

"Where are my clothes?"

Andrew's cheeks pinked. She cocked her head at the unusual reaction. He ducked his face, but not before she saw a smile. What was this? She narrowed her eyes, waiting him out.

He took a few minutes, drew in a breath, and met her gaze again. His eyes danced with humor.

Oh no, he didn't!

"Nothing is funny about this," she snapped. "I seriously want my clothes. Where are they?"

He chuckled, and she growled. His hands lifted, palms out. "I'm sorry, you're right. It's not funny, but it was last night," he started ominously. She frowned. "As you have figured out already, we got married last night."

"Something I plan on rectifying as soon as I can," she shot back, a little bitchy.

All traces of humor faded from his face and his eyes went flat, lips thinned. "Now," he drew out, "what does that mean?"

She rooted to the spot, even though she wanted to retreat to the bathroom. Sure, she'd seen that expression when he'd talked to suspects, but never her. His *"Don't fuck with me"* face. A little terrifying.

She cleared her throat and stared down the length of her nose at him. "Last night was obviously a drunken mistake."

His eyes narrowed, but he didn't speak.

"So we'll get an annulment," she offered with a wave of her hand. "Surely there's something we can do to erase this entire thing from our lives."

A muscle popped in his jaw and he stood eerily still. His blue eyes blazed with some unnamed emotion. What the hell was he about?

She swallowed and skimmed her gaze over the countertops in the room. Next to him stood a six-drawer dresser. On top, a Tiffany lamp and her black purse. He still didn't say anything. Time to take charge.

Crossing the room, she avoided his gaze, grabbed her purse, and took out her phone. Notifications filled the screen: thirteen missed calls from Selena—*thirteen*! She blinked at the number of those—eight from Josephine, four from Juls, and a dozen text messages. One missed call from Dad—a bit puzzling—the old man never called. Her finger hovered over the call back number, but she risked a quick glance at Andrew, then dismissed the thought. The faster she could get the information they needed, the better. Andrew was a temptation, and even though she had to put her foot down and step away, she wanted to lick him from the top of his head to his itty-bitty toe—with a thorough stop in-between to make sure she got the full package.

After ignoring what seemed like endless Facebook notifications, she pulled up her phone's Internet.

A quick internet search and a few seconds of reading later, she made a sound of triumph.

"Ah ha! See, here's a reason we can annul." She read. "'For want of understanding, if either of the parties were incapable of agreeing to the marriage.' It says so on the county court website." She smiled wide and lifted her eyes to his, then froze.

He stared at her with such intensity the air in her lungs left in a rush.

She couldn't breathe, the air in the room thick. His eyes glittered with a dangerous warning. Coiled, on edge, as if barely holding himself in check. From what? She had no clue, but being able to read people—after all, it was what she did for a living—she paused, trying to figure out what she overlooked.

Why marry her? What was up with him being pissed at the mention of annulment? She was so far off base from what he normally went for with women. Tall, thin, and gorgeous. Classy. Not short, curvy, and mouths without filters. The parade of women he'd had on his arm told her all she needed to know.

Him plus her equaled vinegar and water. The two didn't mix.

But damn, his mood screamed at her to get away fast, that he was seconds from exploding. On her or in general, she didn't know.

She tensed to run, but he pounced first.

One second, three feet separated them. The next, his unyielding frame pressed to the front of her and pushed her against the wall.

His hips fit to hers and he forced her legs to part while he settled right against her special place. A thrill ran down her spine as the thickness of his erection nestled between her thighs. Desire leapt to life, and warmth surged through her stomach, melting her from the inside out. He lifted one of her arms over her head and his other hand cupped her jaw, forcing her to look in his eyes.

Up close, he was even more handsome. Warm breath puffed against her lips. Cologne and masculine sweat filled her lungs. The scruff of a day's beard lined his face, high bones in his cheeks, and the plumpness of his lips. His very maleness against all of her femaleness. He pressed closer. If not for the towel and his thin layer of clothing, he'd feel the tight little beads her nipples constricted to.

"What are you doing?" Her voice came out husky, shocked, and more than a little breathy.

He didn't answer, but stared into her eyes, searching. She didn't know for what, but the longer he inspected, the closer she did.

While she couldn't read every emotion crossing his face, she recognized one. It was in the turned-down set of his eyebrows, the slight pull of his mouth, and the wrinkles on his forehead.

Hurt.

Why? What could she have possibly done to wound the ego of such a strong man?

"Laydi," he started, and she bit back a groan at the vibrations that rumbled through his chest and went to her nipples. The sound shot a direct line to her core, which swelled and dampened with further arousal. "You will not make what we shared into some mistake."

"What?" She struggled to keep up. What had they shared?

"It's not going to happen," he murmured, his grip tightening on her jaw.

His mouth closed over hers. She sucked in a breath and jerked back, but there was no place to go. Caught in his trap—pinned against the wall by his strong, hard body.

And what a nice one he'd set.

Not that she'd tell *him* that.

Instead, she tried her best to remain impassive as he kissed the ever-loving-shit out of her. Not that she didn't want to react—she did, with every fiber of her being. He was Andrew! The man who she'd fantasied about doing this very thing with, and a few other naughty adventures, for so long. Her boss, or ex-boss. And he'd taken one of the most important things from her: her job. Not to mention, she had no clue what this marriage business was about.

His tongue traced the seam of her lips so damn slowly she melted. As if he knew the effect, he slipped his free arm around her waist, yanked her closer, and urged her to part her lips with small nibbles and persistent licks.

"Laydi," he said through a soft breath.

Her name, that one word, undid her. In the words of her best-friend-forever, Josephine, FFS (for fuck's sake), this was her hottie boss who she'd imagined doing this exact thing to several times over.

With a sigh, she gave into temptation and opened. Surrounded by his arms, held captive by this strong man, she didn't resist. His tongue swooped in and tangled with hers. He invaded her mouth, leaving no part untouched, memorizing. He tasted of fresh mint, sex, and something identified as Andrew Cox. He pursued her participation with a single-minded focus that had her head spinning, her knees weakening, and her body blooming like tulips in the first month of spring.

Pushing her hips back, he wedged his lower body against hers and released her waist, only to grab her thigh and toss her leg over his hip. Lost in the moment, she wrapped her arms around his neck and submitted to her hunger for this man. His skin was hot, hard steel beneath a soft covering. Muscles jumped under her hands, and his cock pulsed against her, wanting in on the action, too.

She traced down his back, reveling in the strength he mostly kept hidden by shirts. When her hands met his waistband, she slipped under the small opening and found the pert curve of his ass. A thrill went through her, discovering skin-on-skin contact. Commando—the only thing standing between his hardness being inside her was the pop of a button and the slow drag of a zipper. Just thin cotton and her losing the will to figure out what happened last night.

Andrew ripped his mouth from hers with a growl. He spun her around, picked her up, and crossed the room in a few steps. Her back met the bed and she gasped as he loomed over her.

Lust drove a strong force in her veins, an aching kind of urgency that demanded to be set free. She couldn't object to anything, even if the smart thing would be to stop. And this time she'd remember every detail. She wanted it. But too many questions were unanswered. Why had he fired her? Marry her? And could she handle letting Andrew, a man she'd lusted over for years, into her bed? Would her heart be able to stand it when he undoubtedly let her go? He wasn't exactly known for commitment.

He didn't want her in his life; he'd made his point when he fired her.

Like the good little attorney she should have been, her conscious argued with her mind: *"But he's kissing you now…"*

Well, there was that.

"And he married you…"

That, too.

Her phone buzzed in her hand, the vibration singing a tune to *Jingle Bells* despite it being mid-May. That distraction and the latter thought had her turning her face away and going rigid beneath Andrew.

"Laydi." He licked a slow, warm path down the arch of her neck. Her name coming from his mouth again made her toes curl. A shiver went up her spine.

Be strong.

She glanced at her phone. Dad. Two times in less than twelve hours, a record for him.

"Stop," she said.

Andrew pulled back, his expression a tumbled mask of questions. "You seemed pretty into it two seconds ago, what happened?"

"We're not doing this. Can you get off me, please?" The buzzing in her hand stopped and started again. Three times—something was wrong.

She hit "accept" and put the phone to her ear. At the same time, Andrew moved in, his face and body sending all kinds of intense statements—half-mast lids, focus intent, tongue darting out to lick his lips.

"Lay—" he breathed against her mouth as she answered.

"Hi, Dad."

Andrew promptly rolled off her, heaved a sigh, and tossed an arm over his eyes. She barely spared him a glance as she slid off the bed and away from temptation, but the phantom of his touch lingered on her skin.

"Laydi, baby, how are you?" Dad said through the phone, voice deep and gruffy like the big brown bear he resembled.

Her father, Ben, was six foot four inches, a man who seemed much bigger than life when she'd been younger. He raised her alone after Lora, her mother, ran out when Laydi was two-years-old. And even when Dad found Mom's love letters, written to someone other than him, then the heartbreaking emails telling she hadn't been as committed to her vows as everyone thought, he still hadn't broken.

Nope, not her strong, larger-than-life dad.

Despite not having a motherly touch in Laydi's life, a female figure to help guide her through those troubling and self-seeking teen years, Ben made sure she had everything she needed to flourish and grow.

He made *absolutely* certain she had no qualms with coming to him, telling him anything that might be bothering her, and he'd started the conversations about what changes she might be experiencing early.

More, he talked about not only his emotional state and the betrayal of Mom, but of Laydi's feelings, too.

He was her best friend and her hero.

In her hand, her phone buzzed with another missed notification of some sort. *Geesh.*

She risked a glance at Andrew, sunk her teeth into her bottom lip to bite back a feminine sigh of appreciation at the sight of him sprawled out on his back, his chest and stomach muscles chiseled into his flesh, biceps bulging even lying at rest, the muscles at the vee of his hips calling to her. He shifted, and her gaze snapped to his face where she found one blond brow arched in silent question. Shit, she'd been caught.

She whipped her head back around and focused on her call as much as she could with the feel of Andrew's gaze on her neck. She wiggled her shoulders to get rid of the sensation...no such luck, and answered Dad. "I'm good. Tired," she added with a wince from the sunlight streaming through the large window, "but good. Is everything okay?"

Dad grunted. "Why wouldn't everything be okay? Can't a father call his long-lost daughter? His pride and joy? His one true reason for living?"

She rolled her eyes, but smiled and gazed out at the strip below. A few families walked down the street, a couple took pictures by a fountain, taxis streamed by in a line, some cutting across lanes of traffic to dart toward a raised hand. "Of course, but aren't you overdoing the dramatic a bit?"

"I have to keep you on your toes, baby-girl."

Laydi chuckled and stared ahead, not focused on anything. A niggling feeling worked at the back of her mind, something saying three calls in a row from a man who maybe called her once a quarter wasn't right. "Pops, what's going on?"

Silence met her question, before a long and heavy sigh drifted down the line. "I need a favor. I need you to do a solid for your old man."

Her heart gave a kick and she scrunched her brows. Distantly, she heard the rustling of cloth behind her. "Anything."

"I need you to come home for a bit. I wouldn't ask if I didn't absolutely need to, and I know you're busy with the job and all..."

Laydi winced as he trailed off, because technically she didn't have a job anymore, but quickly answered. "What's wrong?"

"I would rather you be in front of me before we have the next part of this conversation. All I'll say now is I'm okay, but I need you, would really like if you could come home soon."

Her breathing picked up.

Was he losing his house? Dying? Find her mother? Was Lora dying and trying for one last shot at learning who her daughter was? Doubtable, seeing as the selfish woman ran out on them years ago and hadn't looked back.

Her mind spun in a million directions, each thought worse than the next—unfortunately the way she was built. Since her mother left, the worst-case scenario for any child to experience, this is what Laydi did. That way, when something did happen, she wasn't surprised. Probably a smidgen dramatic, maybe even a bit morbid, but it was how she survived.

She wasn't a huge fan of—the thought of Andrew struck her, but she pushed that problem out of her mind—surprises.

"Jesus, Pops, can't you just tell me? You're scaring me." Her heart climbed into her throat and pounded out a dance club mix.

"Hush, baby-girl. No reason to get your panties in a twist." Ben offered gentle reassurance. She winced again—currently not wearing panties. "I'm still here and I plan to be for a long time, so don't go thinking the worse. Do you have enough money to get home?"

The switch in topics almost knocked her knees from beneath her. She spun and searched for her phone so she could assess her checking account balance, but it was in her hand. She glanced at the front. Dad was still on the line. She set it back to her ear. "Shit, I think so. Last I checked, I had enough, so don't worry about it. I'll call the airport and catch the next flight home."

"Okay, email me your itinerary and I'll pick you up."

"Sure thing, Daddy. You sure you're okay?" She couldn't help but worry.

"I'm alive." He quipped a goodbye and hung up.

Laydi stared at her phone. To lose Dad would destroy her. And something wasn't right.

A hand rested on her shoulder. She shook from her stupor and glanced up to meet the loveliest shade of blue ever. She'd heard women compare Andrew's eyes to the color of the Caribbean, but had never been somewhere so exotic. Now, she wished she could make the comparison herself.

"Everything okay?" he asked.

She could get lost in listening to his voice. Comforting, deep, and sexy. Just the right thing to calm her frayed nerves.

"Yeah." She took a step back, swiping across the screen to wake her phone up. "I just…"

She checked the notifications for her missed text messages. Before even opening the first one from Selena, she knew. *"How's it feel to be married?"* said the preview. Scrolling down, more of the same from Juls, Josephine, and a few coworkers.

"Shit," she swore. The dance mix was back and this time the beat broke out in her head, pounded through her ears. How had people found out?

"What's wrong?" Andrew's question went unanswered as she opened her Facebook account to check those notifications. How could people already know? Had they posted something last night? Had Andrew?

She clicked on the first notification, a picture she'd posted, and gasped. There, standing in the most god-awful pink colored chapel with Elvis to one side of her and Andrew to the other, she stood looking dreamily up at what had to be the groom as they both held their left hands in the air baring their rings.

The caption she'd posted on the picture read: *Mr. and Mrs. Cox 4 EVA*.

Her stomach rolled. "Oh, God, I think I'm going to be sick again."

"What are you looking at?" Andrew grabbed her wrist so he could see her phone. He dipped his head, froze, and sighed before dropping her hand and stepping away. She didn't want to tick him off, but it was a little late for either of them. Shit, what had she been thinking posting it on Facebook?

He lifted his head. A muscle in his jaw ticked, and his eyes were hard. Now why was he mad? It made her a little uncomfortable, and despite her chosen profession, dealing with conflict wasn't something she could handle. She needed to get home. Get on a plane and get home. Get dressed first. Yes, she needed a list to help keep her thoughts in order.

"Let me get this straight," Andrew started, "you mean to tell me you're upset because you posted a picture last night on Facebook? Or is it because you posted it under the influence, after you married me, announced it to the world, and now this morning are having second thoughts on fulfilling your vows?"

"What?" Air left her lungs. When he put it like that, she sounded horrible. "No...I mean, yes. But it's not like you mean. Oh, God," she said and wrapped her arms around her stomach. There was no way to keep this her dirty little secret. Everyone knew, save Dad, seeing as he wasn't on Facebook. But her friends, colleagues, and distant aunts and uncles were, and surely with as many likes as the picture received, word had spread.

Andrew raked his fingers through his hair, and damn if her greedy gaze and hormones didn't take in every second of his muscles bunching with each move. His hair fell back into the same position before he'd touched it...sexy, bed tossed, and oh, so seductive.

"Then what is it? Explain why you're saying you're going to be sick. Why you look ten shades of pale right now? And why you can't handle me touching you?"

She couldn't deal with this. Everything spun, her world like that song by *Dead or Alive*. She snorted at her thoughts and went around Andrew in search of her clothes.

"Laydi, what the hell? We're talking."

"I need to go home. That was my dad. I just…" She swirled in a circle, searching. Not a scrap of her clothing lay on the floor. "For the last time, where the hell are my clothes?"

Chapter Two

Girl Code Rule #37: "Figure out your group's 'man rules' before shit happens."

Andrew sighed and pinched the bridge of his nose. What he wouldn't give to go back twenty-four hours. He'd make different decisions, work to keep Laydi from that last margarita and tequila shot, and he'd have done things differently this morning, too.

But he wouldn't change marrying her. No, he was one hundred percent on board with that and accepted it as the best damn decision he'd made in a long time. And soon, given enough time on her part, and sufficient patience on his, Laydi would come to accept the inevitable, too. They were meant to be together.

"Andrew," she insisted with a bit of exasperation.

"In the closet." He swung his arm toward the double doors next to the bathroom. "That's what room service was doing at the door earlier. They brought back our clothing."

She threw him a questioning glance. "Do I even want to know why they had our clothes?" She crossed the room in a few long strides and yanked open the dark paneled door.

He thought back to last night and her smile, the way her eyes lit mischievously when they'd discovered the heated indoor pool. How her intent was written as clear as a summer's day across her face right before she tackled him into the water. They'd eventually stripped off every scrap of clothing and clung together long after the effects of multiple orgasms, and had been found wrapped in each other's arms going for round three when the hotel staff came in with a very ill-timed throat clearing. The woman from last night was a stranger compared to who he dealt with now.

"I'll give you two hints which involve water and our clothing," he said, and added when her face blanked for a moment before she ducked it from his view, "but from your reaction, I'm thinking you're starting to remember."

She wiggled and shook her way into tight leather pants. His groin tightened. All of her girly parts bounced again, reminding him of their extracurricular activities from last night when he took her pressed against the window behind him, over the table in the corner, beneath the spray of the shower. God, what he wouldn't give to relive it all over again.

She whipped out her black sequined tank top and put it on over the red lacy bra. He crossed to her, taking in every inch of skin showing, minus the fun parts. Not touching her wasn't an option any longer. She was his wife, dammit.

She whipped around and slammed back against the wall. He lifted a brow.

"What are you doing?" One hand fluttered above her chest. She held her boots in the other, but the expression on her face, just a tad bit aware, flushed, and a lot wary had him wanting to push her to talk…and do other things. Since she expected him to do something to her, and from the wariness in her eyes, anticipated it, he changed his plan. He needed to shift her focus to what she'd expect from him, keep her mind busy and off balance. That way he'd swoop in when she least expected it, and show her this marriage would work.

He reached in the closet and grabbed his sky-blue shirt. She watched the entire exchange with avid interest. He turned away, hiding his smirk. His wife wanted him, she was just too damn stubborn to admit it.

"If you're so keen on getting home, then we'll go. Once I get you on the jet, there's nowhere for you to run, so by all means, let's get going. It'll only speed up the time until we can sort this shit out."

He slid the material up his arms and looked over his shoulder. She still had her eyes on him. He wanted to puff his chest out, but fought the urge.

"I need to go home, Andrew. I told you. I can't play this game right now."

A game. That set him on edge—far from entertaining. "And I heard you. We'll be back on the jet and on our way to DC with the next available take off."

"Not DC, my home," she pushed. "Ohio."

Andrew paused in the process of tucking his feet into his shoes. He had meetings he needed to be in over the next few days, discussions about the case involving a special ops mission overseas, and calls to make. Work would be there for him no matter how long it took to get back to DC. In addition, with the digital age, he could work just as easily from Ohio, minus a few face-to-face interactions.

However, if he let Laydi go off on her own, especially now with their fragile ties, he had a feeling he'd never see her again. Not something he'd risk. Their connection, tenuous at best, but their bond over the years was anything but weak. Why didn't she see that? They complimented each other more than she realized, and she had been the only woman to make him feel like he was worth more than a checkbook, a nice body, and some trophy on an arm.

If she thought she'd get away, she had another think coming.

"Fine, we'll take the jet to Ohio. I'm coming with you, though. Exactly where in Ohio are we going? I'll need to tell the pilot."

"What?" Her voice went up about three octaves.

He grabbed his phone from the bedside table and turned to face her. Laydi's hair was in a mass of wild ringlets around her face. The sun bounced off highlights, sending gold patterns over the soft tresses. So damn beautiful, she took his breath away.

"What city in Ohio? Or rather, where do you need to be? We can always land at a private airport."

"No, no, I mean what do you mean you're coming with me?"

He eyed her, seeing her fight-or-flight response settling in. Like a skittish doe ready to bolt from its hunter's scope. He ground his molars, wanting to shake some sense into her...or kiss her, he couldn't figure out which. Probably both. "I'm not letting you out of my sight until we finish this."

"But your work, your life in DC. I can manage this on my own. We'll talk over the phone in a few days when I figure out what's going on."

Like hell they'd talk over the phone. He walked to her. She stood her ground and lifted her chin, as if daring or standing up to him. Either way, it was an absolute fucking turn on. He clenched his hands in his pants—perversely pleased—and resisted the urge to touch her.

"I can work where I please, and if you forgot, I own *Off The Record*. So, if I need to take a few days, I'll take a few days. Work can wait. You and I can't." She opened her mouth to say something, an argument for sure, but he cut her off by giving into his urge and reached out. He tangled his hands in her hair and gave a gentle tug, forcing her to look up at him. She gasped, and he bore his gaze into hers, searching for that wonderful, carefree woman from last night.

"Think about it, Lay...the jet is waiting, ready for us to get on it. Think of calling the airlines, waiting until the next flight, and paying last minute fares. I'm heading in that direction either way you look at it. I'll just accompany you to Ohio, and we can use some time management skills and talk on the way there."

* * * *

Two hours later, Laydi supposed Andrew was right. Not—she glanced at him looking smug in the leather chair, phone to his ear, a goblet of Coke in his hand—that she'd ever admit it to him. Once she'd agreed to let him "accompany" her to Ohio—*who even said it that way anymore?*—the entire process had gone down effortlessly. Andrew called for a car, then the pilot to let him know of the plans, and after clearing through the private airport security, they'd been ushered onto the Gulfstream and readied for take-off. She'd only flown with Andrew and Derek one time before last night on the corporate jet. Back then, she had wondered how a private investigation agency could afford such extravagance. Working for them for as long as she had, now she knew how they paid their employees so well, how they owned a nice fleet of vehicles for their investigators, and how they afforded multiple private jets to travel.

Derek was the co-owner of *Off The Record Investigations*. He worked directly with law enforcement, both local and federal, and was often contracted out to deal with the adultery cases. He liked being in the field, loved being caught in the action. Andrew handled the other side of the business, the more in-depth research and day-to-day operations. Together, they made a great team and ran one of the most successful private investigative agencies in North America.

The details of last night were a little fuzzy, but memories of boarding the aircraft came back, along with the tall blonde bombshell of a flight attendant and her all-too-attentive ways toward Andrew. The stewardess had barely spared her a word or two since they'd been on the plane. Meanwhile, Ms. Bombshell basically fell foot over head to jump at Andrew's every command, "Mr. Cox this, and oh, Mr. Cox you're so funny that". Laydi snorted beneath her breath and looked out the window. The aircraft started rolling toward the runway. Jealousy and ill will toward that woman certainly came back faster than anything else.

The jealousy was a new feeling, and Laydi didn't know if she liked it. Putting forth so much effort into something one couldn't control seemed like a bit too much work. And she didn't like how the feeling allowed others to influence what she felt. She preferred to be in charge of what was inside her. Not the stomach-turning nausea, so different from a few hours ago and the morning margarita that made its reappearance. Not when she wanted to claw another woman's eyes out for looking at a man whom she had checked out repeatedly.

The plane got permission to proceed with take-off, which, thank God, had Ms. Fall-Over-Myself buckling up in the front of the cabin. A few moments later, they lifted off. Laydi's stomach turned over again for a different reason as the plane gained altitude.

They were still climbing when the air next to her shifted. Andrew had crossed the small isle and sat next to her. He lifted the arm bar between them and turned to face her, one knee up on the leather, and his entire focus on her. Her breath caught as she took him in. To be married to him was a dream come true, but her emotions were all over the place, especially with him firing her last night. To be bound to a man—this man—after only being able to rely on four people in her life wasn't something easy for her to accept. Call her fucked in the head. Having a mother abandon her daughter at such a young age could do all kinds of weird things to someone.

And geesh, the guilt of not telling him she remembered last night ate at her. But like a bull unwilling to admit defeat, she couldn't bring it up first. She hoped he'd coax it eventually. Maybe she could even lead him into having her admit.

"The seatbelt sign is still on," she said, her gaze on his.

"We're fine."

"No," she responded slowly, "we're not."

His lips thinned, drawing her gaze down to them, before he nodded. "And she gets right to the heart of it, huh?" he murmured, almost to himself.

Anxiety in that one statement had pressure tightening her chest. "What?"

He shook his head. "Time to talk, Laydi." And *holy hell, call the cavalry for back-up*, because his gaze pinned her in place. "What's going on in that head of yours?"

She scrunched her brows, too tired, too anxious about Dad to try to explain what she felt with Andrew. How did one admit they'd had a crush on another for so long, when the word crush said anything but grown up? Yet on the heels of that, how could she possibly make him understand she may never be able to trust him? She didn't think she could, and not because of him, but because of the ugly lesson by Mom.

Dropping her head back against the seat, she sighed. "I can't do this. Please don't make me have this conversation with you now. I care about you as a friend, but I can't...I just can't right now."

He stroked the side of her cheek and she closed her eyes, basking in the tingling that shot from her face into her chest.

A memory from last night shot to the surface with sudden clarity. Him stroking her cheek while they stood at the altar. His eyes warm and bright, happy, as he said, "Hell yes, I do," just before he kissed her.

She gasped and snapped her eyes open, meeting his bright blue gaze.

He tilted his head and studied her face, before reaching over and undoing her seatbelt.

"Where are we going?" she asked. He pulled her up and led her down a short hallway to a room decorated in deep blues. Against the wall stood a single bed with a cream comforter, and opposite of that, a small, dark desk void of anything on top.

He drew her inside the room, shut the door, and locked it with a click, before turning and taking her gently into his arms. The feel of hard muscles against her—

bliss. Warm, hard, physical perfection. She wanted to forget he went commando, that only a few pieces of cloth separated them. That he kissed like heaven, and moved like sin.

"Tell me, Gorgeous, how last night could have been the best night of my life, but you're having a hard time remembering anything in your alcohol induced haze?"

Her stomach pitched and tumbled, on its own amusement park roller coaster ride just at his words. ...*the best night of my life*... "I remember...some stuff," she admitted, picking at a piece of imaginary lint from his shoulder.

His arms tightened around her and he walked her backward. She glanced over her shoulder a moment before her back met the wall. From the hold in his arms, to his slight lift of her body, they aligned almost perfectly. Hip to hip, chest to chest, mouth to mouth.

"What stuff?" he asked gruffly.

She shook her head. There was no way she'd be able to hold him off if he pressured her into talking. "I don't want to have this conversation right now."

"Why?"

"I..." She tried to come up with an excuse, anything to stop this. She needed time to think. A chance to figure out how to keep their friendship intact.

Apparently she took too long in answering, for Andrew went on the offense...in a sinfully, wicked way. "Do you remember screaming my name so loud we had hotel security come check on us? To make sure I wasn't murdering you in my hotel room?"

She snapped her gaze to his.

"Or how about how you couldn't wait to get me inside of you on our way from the altar and you popped a button on my pants trying to rip them off me?"

Her breath caught. A fuzzy memory. Had that happened?

"Or how about how you begged me to let you suck me off in the elevator? How I was two seconds from letting you when the doors opened and an older couple joined us on the ride up?"

"Or how about," he continued over her ragged breathing, "how much I've thought of you sucking me off all night and morning." He dragged his thumb across her bottom lip and pushed inside, gently, but insistently, until she opened for him. Masculine spice and salt exploded on her taste buds. "Suck me now, Laydi. Show me what that sweet mouth has tortured me with for years. Suck my thumb, Sweetheart."

Jesus, his words and the low, grumbly way he said them had her heated. She pictured every scene he explained with a surprising clarity. He wanted her to suck him, and oh, God, but she did, too.

He felt thick and rough in her mouth. She hollowed her cheeks and stroked her tongue against the length. His mouth popped open with a low gasp. He stared at her, focused entirely on what she was doing, on how she opened to stroke down his finger until the full length was inside her mouth and closed over it again.

Her mind blanked and surged with specific intent as he ripped open his pants with his free hand and let them drop. *This was madness!* His cock stood furiously erect, the head a striking purple against his olive skin. It was a thing of beauty; long, thick. She reached for him, but he grabbed her hand, popped his thumb out of her mouth, and tossed both of her wrists above her head, their fingers interlacing.

"God, what you do to me," he rasped. He changed his grip, and holding her wrists in one hand, moved swiftly, snapping open the button on her pants, ripping down the zipper, and pushing the cloth down. It caught on her hips, but with a bit of wiggle from her and a growl from him, the material slid down her legs. They didn't get far, though. Her black combat boots prevented them from coming all the way off.

"Christ," he rumbled.

With a glance over to the side, he pulled her from the wall, pressed his front to her back, and bent her over the desk. Her toes curled inside her boots, heat warming her from within just as hot as he was at her back. Knowing what they must look like, naked from the waist down and caught in a lust frenzy...hearing how much she affected this man who normally had such self-control, with his ragged breathing and warm breaths against her back, turned her on to a whole new level.

She did that to him. Her. Not the perfect bombshell out front. And she'd never seen him so out of his wits with anyone else. It was *her.* Another wave of warmth moved through her chest, and, between her legs, liquid trickled down her thigh. Her breasts achy and full, begged for his touch, rather than pressed against the dark wood of the desk.

She groaned as his cock pressed against her backside. Close, but not nearly close enough.

He touched his forehead to her back and took a deep breath—for control? She didn't know, and half didn't care. She just wanted him inside her. Wanted to hear him lose control even more.

"Laydi," he whispered against the middle of her back, and brushed a chaste kiss there.

She didn't answer, well, because it didn't seem as if he was actually calling her. Still, the sound of her name leaving his mouth, especially filled with so much heat, made her stomach flip and her sex swell.

"Tell me you want this, Sweetheart."

"Yes," she hissed and pushed against him.

"Tell me you want me, want us."

She shook her head, cloudy with lust, but clear enough to understand now wasn't the time to have that conversation. He wanted to fuck—fine with her. But when it involved more than her body, she couldn't deal.

"Tell me," he urged, voice gruff.

Irritation boiled in her chest like a geyser. Of all the times for him to use sex to get what he wanted! She went to move, but he rested a palm against her neck and urged her down, rolling his cock between the crease of her ass.

"Didn't say you could move, Sweetheart. You want this; you're going to get it. And when we're done, I'm going to show you exactly what I mean about us being together. You were made for me." He punctuated his words with a strong grip on her waist.

With her hips tilted to meet his, she would have thought he'd enter her in one stroke, because damn, even though it was mildly embarrassing, she wanted it. Instead, he shifted and the long stalk slid between her folds, right over her clitoris. She arched her neck and gasped as tingles erupted over her body.

He stilled and settled his hips against hers.

She peered over her shoulder, half in shock he stopped, and half-furious she'd let it get to this point. "What? What are you doing?"

"Tell me you remember this."

She blinked. "Now? You want to do this now?" Getting pissed, she bucked her hips backward, ready to take care of things herself. She'd mastered the art of giving herself a good orgasm. Of course, it probably wouldn't be as good as Andrew promised, but with the memories of last night, she wanted him. He tangled his hand in her hair, yanked her neck to the side, and pushed his weight over her back. She could barely move at all, and another delicious sensation rocked through her core. He had her fully dominated. She moaned. "God, Andrew, not now. You're running cliterferance and it's pissing me off."

"No…Now. Last night, you were very much a part of what we did. And not this pissed off woman I met this morning, but more of the Laydi I know. The one who acts impulsively, and goes with her decisions as if it defines who she is. One who was so fucking sensual and into what we did…" He dropped his head and finished with a murmur by her ear. "That I had a hard time convincing her to go to sleep. Because you see, she wore me the hell out.

"Tell me you don't remember. Begging me to suck on your pert little nipples as you rode me to ecstasy. Grabbing my hand and putting it between your legs when you couldn't wait. Wanting to suck my cock as if it were a drug you just had to have."

His words were shocking, a little dirty, and if she had to admit, damn hot. She liked her nipples sucked. It was one of her favorite things. And remembering earlier, when she saw his cock, her first instinct wanting to suck him off…

She turned her head, and he brushed his lips against her cheek. Her eyes closed. Memories hovered beyond reach. Little tidbits in time.

"Laydi," he called, questioning.

She clenched her hands above her head. "Stop. I don't remember. God, I want to, but I don't." *Liar.*

A few beats ticked by before he moved. Dropping his mouth to her neck, he licked a path up the side and murmured in her ear, "Then we're going to have to work on it. Perhaps replaying some of our scenes from last night will jog your memory."

She stilled. "What?"

He smiled crookedly, but didn't answer. Instead, he began kissing her again. First her neck, where he nibbled, then soothed with gentle kisses. He worked his way lower, over the curve of her shoulder and below, teasing a path down her spine. His cock slid between her nether lips, and she gasped again.

Instead of fulfilling that desire, he moved down and brushed his lips against the curve of her hip, dipped his tongue along the dimples just above. He shifted his hands to the sides of her hips and gently, but insistently prodded her legs apart until her pants wouldn't allow her to move anymore. His firm squeeze told her exactly what he wanted. *Keep them there, and don't move.*

She blushed. What must his view be with her bent over the desk, his face level with all her intimate parts?

The heat of him disappeared as he knelt. With the new position, she could only see his shoulders. Well, that, and his blazing blue eyes, which burned a path between her legs.

"Last night, I feasted on you." He trailed one finger down the crack of her ass before circling the entrance of her sex. She wanted his touch, burned for it. "Do you remember? Do you know how fucking good you taste?"

The cool air brushed over her skin, but his words caused a flame inside her belly to burn. Her thighs shook, so she gripped tighter, opened her legs wider, and tilted her hips more. So blatant, but screw modesty. She knew what she wanted—him. The problems and questions could be dealt with later. Right now, she had a primal urge that needed satisfaction.

He wrapped his hands around the front of her thighs and pulled her toward him. Without giving her any time to prepare—not that she complained—he dropped his head and gave her sex an open-mouthed kiss.

* * * *

Some men thought oral sex was a chore. There'd been times in Andrew's life where he'd believed the same thing. Not with Laydi, though. Not even close. She tasted of sweet nectar. One he couldn't get enough of, and considering they'd stayed up until the wee early morning hours discovering, learning, and tasting one another, he thought he'd had his fill.

Not quite yet.

Her moans spurred him on, making him feel like he was ten feet tall. From the hitching of her breath and quiver of her legs, she was close. Wrapping his lips around her hard bundle of nerves, he sucked and massaged it with the tip of his tongue. Her moans grew louder, so loud they'd get looks from Debra, the stewardess, but he didn't care.

Laydi tensed, her voice going up an octave, and as she crested, he stuck the same thumb she'd sucked earlier past the tight little pucker of her ass.

She screamed her release, which went on forever. One of her hands dug into his shoulder and held him there. *As if he was going anywhere else.* His cock kicked painfully. He wrapped his hand around his length, gave a few strokes to take the edge off and not come from the sound of her orgasm. No, he'd save his orgasm for being inside her.

Minutes passed as he eased her down, placing gentle kisses on her sex, small nibbles on her thigh, and giving reassuring words of his care. Once her hand released its death grip, he rose, turned her to face him, picked her up, and took her to the bed, where he laid them down and cradled her in his arms. Then, he waited.

She cuddled to him, soft and accepting. Her hair lay against his tanned arms in stark contrast.

He had to know. She had to remember. Last night couldn't be chalked up to a drunken mistake—he wouldn't allow it.

Laydi stirred in his arms minutes later. He had been content to hold her close, feel her breaths and heart sync with his, and, despite the raging hard-on between them, he'd been fine with having her in his arms.

She tilted her head down between them, and then up at him in question. Lust raged in her eyes, but more questions sat in her expression.

"Last night, you didn't seem like yourself." He watched her eyes, and damn if he wasn't falling head over heels for a woman who'd made his business life a living hell.

She stiffened. "So you admit it?"

He shook his head. "No, I mean before that. Thinking back on dinner, you slammed margaritas as if they were juice. I've been out with you several times. Never seen that before."

She shrugged. "Maybe I just felt like drinking."

He narrowed his eyes and tried to catch her elusive gaze. No luck. There was something going on with her, and it started way before last night. "Laydi, look at me."

She turned to him, and his mind spun. He'd wondered what was going on with her, and how he even dreamed of the fact that he'd be able to keep her as his. He couldn't let her go. He didn't have it in him. If that made him a selfish son of a bitch, so be it.

"Five years ago, I met a different woman than I know now," he started. "She was on point, sharp, and knew exactly what was expected out of each case." He shook his head, trying to wrap his mind around any idea of what could be affecting her work to where it'd gotten this bad. "I've asked you before; I'll ask you again, what's going on with you?"

She bit her lip, but didn't say a word.

He sighed and wanted to shake some sense into her. Too much had happened, and now that they'd been picked up to investigate a rogue agent with the CIA, he had to know. That case screamed all kinds of bad news, and it had the potential to bring war to America's front door.

"I didn't want to let you go," he said. She opened her mouth, but he cut her off. "I had to, you've become a liability. One I can't take a chance on, especially with the case we've been building for the past year, and with the new one coming down the pike. This could be huge for us, get us on board for taking large contracts. Tell me, Laydi, please tell me. Not as your boss, but as a man I'm hoping you'll grow to understand will be here for you, whether you're with *Off The Record Investigations* or not."

That got a response out of her. Her lips thinned and her eyes narrowed. "What if I don't want this marriage or this job?" she snapped.

He bit back an insult and moved closer. "Tough shit, I'm not going anywhere, and the sooner you get that through your head, the better off we'll both be, and the faster we'll be able to figure out exactly what's been going on with you."

"Get off me."

He acceded her request, for now. Rolling off, he grabbed his pants and shoved his legs inside. She moved around behind him, but he didn't turn until he buttoned and zipped his pants.

Arms crossed and holding a sheet in front of her body, she glared at him.

"Goddamnit, give me something to go off of here."

She glared harder, and if he'd been a lesser man, he would have tossed in the towel. Instead, he shot her a glare back. "I won't give up. On either topic." He wanted to see what had caused her downward spiral, and he wanted her to get the message they were married and would stay that way.

She clenched her jaw, tightened her fist, and sighed heavily. "Five years," she bit out.

He lifted a brow. "Five years you've worked for me, yes. I remember the day you walked in my office like it was yesterday."

She shot him a look that said she didn't believe him, but pushed on. "I love," she started and cleared her throat, "loved my job. God,"—she tore her gaze from his and stared out the side window—"I was like a sponge, soaking everything up. I couldn't get enough of it, wanted to learn more, and did hours and hours of research just to make sure I was the best. That I wouldn't let you down.

"I knew I was coming in as the underdog, especially with everyone else's experience with some sort of Special Operations in the military, or industry investigations, but I knew I could do it, this was what I was born to do. I knocked out my Private Investigations course in less than six months, and then tested with the state."

He tilted his head and crossed his arms. She recited what he already knew, but since he had her talking, he didn't want to interrupt. Her recount of those first days also reminded him of the woman he had become increasingly, and uncomfortably, attracted to. He had been her boss, and didn't need to lie in bed with an apprentice where he was trying to run a successful business, so he'd kept his desire in check. But to watch Laydi grow as an investigator and into being comfortable around them all had been a hell of a picture.

The only other who had called him on it, had seen his true feelings, was his partner at the firm, Derek Denny. Yet still, he kept things locked tight.

"Then a year ago I went to Derek and asked him to teach me more. I felt as if I had hit a plateau."

He arched a brow at that bit of news. Why hadn't Derek said anything about this?

"He put me on this case involving numbers and learning all about tracing the trail of money. I got so wrapped up in the research and pursuing that I would lose track of time and end up spending all-nighters looking through everything. It wouldn't be until my alarm went off that I realized I hadn't slept, hadn't eaten, and needed to start a new day. But I was so into the case," she stressed, her voice excited with renewed interest. Her eyes danced and her arms moved like someone who had tried candy for the first time, or sex, he amended, seeing her mused hair sticking in every direction around her heart-shaped face. Either way, she showed signs of someone who had discovered something they loved. What he wouldn't give to see that look directed at him.

He processed what she had said and shook his head, hating he hadn't expressed his concerns with Derek. He thought doing so would have brought even more attention to his unhealthy obsession with Laydi. "So you started showing to cases late, missing subjects leaving home, losing them altogether while trailing."

She nodded, drew her gaze back to his, and bit her lip. "I'm sorry I didn't say anything, but I really didn't want to disappoint you, or Derek, for that matter. I loved what I was doing."

Nothing added up. He narrowed his eyes. "What about when you broke your cover and let the subject, Matt Melendez, know he was being followed?"

"That was a mistake," she pressed and looked so stricken he didn't have the heart to push it.

"What about when you showed last week at the workman comp trial and brought the wrong video?"

She shook her head, her curls bouncing wildly. "I have no clue how that happened. When I left the office, I had the right video, I swear I did. It didn't make any sense."

He sighed and pinched his nose, not liking the excuse. He could almost laugh about the court incident now that his anger had simmered. She'd been working a huge insurance case where the guy claimed he injured his back too much to work. But Laydi had caught him on camera mowing his lawn, running marathons, and playing basketball with his friends. A solid case, and a client who'd promised them more money and work in the future.

Andrew had sent Laydi to court to show the video, but the video hadn't been the surveillance. It was a copy of some movie called *Legally Blonde.*

They'd lost the client and the potential for millions of dollars in assets, and Andrew lost his mind.

He wanted to fire her then, especially with the call from the government about the new case, but Derek had insisted on waiting, trying to identify her problem.

Only when they'd approached Laydi, she claimed nothing was wrong. Yet her actions hadn't changed, and now getting closer to solving a multi-billion dollar embezzlement, he couldn't afford another reputational hit.

He had to get rid of her.

At least from anything dealing with his professional life.

He didn't want that to get in the middle of them. Of what they could be as a couple.

"Will you get my bag from last night? My briefcase, please?"

A little taken aback at her sudden use of 'please', he knifed off the bed, arranged his pants so he was presentable, and left the cabin to retrieve her bag. He ignored the stewardess and her gasp, grabbed Laydi's black leather briefcase, and once back in the cabin, tossed it on the bed. Laydi didn't move and instead stared at his unbuttoned and untucked shirt, her brows drawn in a frown. Her gaze slid to the closed door, where she frowned deeper. He tilted his head, about to ask her what was wrong—a question he didn't know if he wanted answered, as there had to be plenty—but she beat him to the punch.

"I have some questions for you. You answer them fully and I'll think of answering yours."

He shook his head before she finished. "That isn't fair. You'll think on it?"

She shrugged. "Take it or leave it. That's my offer. I could push for an annulment, bring a suit against your company for sexual harassment, and walk away with enough to start my own PI firm."

A haze of red clouded his vision, and he took a step toward her. "We're married. I've got a certificate that says so."

"Semantics, Andrew."

They went into a stare-down. Hundreds of miles in the sky, in an aircraft several thousand miles from home, him half-undressed. Nobody else but the two of them in this small space. He had never felt so helpless, so alone, and so damn determined in his life.

He slapped his thighs. "Fine," he spat. "Ask your damn questions."

"You'll answer honestly?"

He took another step forward and pointed his finger. "I've never lied to you. Don't insult me by thinking I'll start now."

* * * *

Laydi hid her wince.

She had lied.

Not only to him, but to herself. She remembered everything about last night. Sure, it had come to her a little late, the details and erotic memories, the vivid reminder of how happy she'd been to give into the temptation that was Andrew Cox. But God, she couldn't turn back now.

He didn't see her for who she truly was. She worked hard, and yeah, sure, the whole *Legally Blonde* moment hadn't been her best, but she'd busted her ass for years to get to where she was. And she hadn't stopped working toward that goal, even when pulling double shifts; those Andrew gave her for their regular cases where she watched Johns try to get by on unemployment without truly being injured, wives skipping out on their husbands, employees selling secrets to competitive companies. And then the additional hours she'd given Derek in pursuit of trying to track this embezzlement case.

Millions of dollars had up and disappeared out of a client's account. Not in one shot, and not anything noticeable overnight. Instead, pennies for pickings from each investment the guy had made. The client invested in companies and stocks all across the world. From candy to furs, electronics and medicine. If the product looked to have promise, Mr. Alan Rodgers would write a check and be willing to pave—or in this case, pay—the way.

So when Derrick approached her, explained the case, and asked her to partner-up, she'd been so intrigued with how the crime happened, she'd jumped in with both feet. And now, a year later, she realized she'd been running ragged. Her work was her life, something she'd uprooted her entire being for: moving away from her sisters, from Dad, and from the memories of her mother's abandonment.

Andrew sighed and drew her attention. She held hers in, for reasons probably different from his. He was getting impatient, if the slight scowl, the tapping of his toe, and his hands on his hips indications. But he was so damn handsome, so deliciously disheveled, she wanted to see how much more she could muse him up.

Instead of acting on that impulse, she cleared her throat. "Okay, so you said you had originally intended to fire me last night?" Dammit, her voice cracked. *Hold it together, Lay. Girl code, remember, "no damn crying in front of a guy. They'd use it against you, or worse, feel sorry for you."*

He nodded, but didn't say anything.

Dammit, squared.

294

"Why?"

He heaved a breath as if forced to do something awful. Could this get any more humiliating?

"I told you. You're a liability I can't afford. Your work used to be superior, and damn it, you were one of my best investigators, but over the past few months, you've gotten sloppy. And you're on our biggest case. I can't have any more mix-ups happen. I'm already getting shit for the past court incident."

She crossed her arms, not something easy with the sheet wrapped around her chest, and damn if she'd have this conversation naked, no matter how much she still—*yes, still*—wanted to jump his bones. "I apologized for that."

"You did. But it happened again. Wrong surveillance, wrong case. It keeps happening, and I don't know why. You won't tell me *why*."

She ground her teeth, fighting to keep from lashing out at him. Shifting, she tucked the sheet beneath her arms. Keeping cool with this conversation would be the first step in keeping her job. Because ultimately, that was her goal. They'd put the marriage behind and move on.

"I've been paired with Derek on the Rodgers case for almost a year."

His eyebrows went up. Surprise. Body language one-oh-one gave her that much.

"Yeah, I see you didn't know," she continued. "I've been pulling in research, trying to track the money every free moment I got. I've lived and breathed work for the last year."

Derek had gone and started asking questions of witnesses, bank officials, and various employees of Mr. Rodgers.

She, on the other hand, dealt with the research portion of their operation. She could analyze a bank statement, dig up dirt older than her great-great grandmother, and had the ability to hack into just about any site in the world, including those with three letters and apparently unhackable.

Yeah, right.

"I've looked at the case, though," he said, and her shoulders went tight. Would he see everything she'd done as a benefit, or would he dismiss her based on the few mistakes? God, she could kick herself. "I can't find the link in your notes. You're not any closer than we were when we first got the case."

"No," she replied. "What we have is close to nine thousand individual investment accounts with pennies to nickels leaving the accounts daily. Nothing to tip someone off immediately, just small enough it's an overlooked nuisance."

"Daily?"

She nodded and slid off the bed, needing to move. Her nervous energy and adrenaline rush of digging into the case were too much to keep her stationary. She paced to the small window and back, not much room to move, but it was something.

It was like a puzzle waiting to be solved, and she'd finally done it. She'd hit the motherboard with it. "Daily. Do the math in your head. Now multiply that by twelve years and see what kind of figure you get."

His lips pursed. "Impressive. However, the bigger question is: what changed twelve years ago for the client? New accountant?"

She shook her head. "I thought the same thing, but that isn't it. Mr. Rodgers has had the same accountant for thirty years. They manage their investment accounts through a financial advisement company. You see, tracing the money is easy enough until it leaves the country."

"Cayman Islands, I take it?"

She wanted to shout and raise her hands in the air as if she was his cheerleader and he'd scored the winning touchdown. She didn't. Instead, she kept her face calm and went on. "The funds leaving the accounts are going to different beneficiaries. So while the wire may be easy enough to watch, I couldn't see what happened once they were in Cayman. I tried to get contacts down there, but they are clammed up tighter than an oyster with a million-dollar-pearl. Literally, in this case. I have one more contact I'm trying to get in touch with."

"This puts us still at square one." He didn't say anything else. Would he catch on to what she'd figured out? He could read people just as well as she could, and she wasn't holding in her excitement too well. His gaze roamed over her face and the side of his mouth tilted. God, this man was too damn sexy for his own good, and that smile made him irresistible. With the movement, his plump lips pulled taunt, tempting enough to bite.

"Earth to Laydi," he called, laughter in his voice.

She forced her gaze away from his kissable mouth. "Sorry, it's been a long twenty-four hours. You were saying?"

He gave a low laugh and shook his head. "Uh huh, I'm sure that's exactly why you zoned out." He sounded anything but sure.

Fuck it. "I traced it. I took a chance, put spyware on the computer of my suspected offender, and traced the money. Or, at first, it was just a transaction being perpetrated, but then, once I was in, I saw everything. Including some crazy communication with an analyst at the CIA."

She looked at the wall behind his head, remembering how she'd sent the investment advisor an email requesting a time to meet, saying she had to talk to him, seeing as they were talking to everyone, and the attachment to the email an innocent enough spyware. The feeling of finally catching this guy after so long sang through her veins. While they'd only found one account, they were closer than a year ago.

The weirdness started when she watched as the investor had contacted someone at the CIA right after doing the transactions. Every time he moved money, another communication went to this "Tom Smith" (if that wasn't a fake name, her name wasn't Laydi) where he spoke in code so thick, she needed a chisel to get through it. She didn't know what went on there, but whatever it was, it smelled worse than the skunks that had attacked her, Josephine, Juls, and Selena back in Ohio.

She smiled in memory, remembering how Dad had taken one look, or sniff in this case, at them, and promptly handed them all the tomato products he could find, refusing to let them in the house. So instead, they went to her backyard, stripped down, and painted their eight-year-old bodies in red goo. It still took days before the smell was completely gone.

Andrew said nothing, standing there, arms hanging by his sides, face slack, eyes wide and on her.

"You…what?"

She smiled, a slow curve of her lips that felt damn good. "I solved the case. I still have to find the other accounts, but I think we have enough to hand it over to the FBI for an arrest and prosecution. But to be honest, something doesn't look right with this inside communication at the CIA. I think we should hold on to that for a bit and keep digging."

He put a hand at the base of his throat. "A lot of things at the CIA don't make sense. And from my case to yours, that's evident. So tell me you aren't shitting me. My mind, Jesus, it's spinning in crazy directions right now. My fucking heart is about to explode out of my chest. Don't mess around with this, Laydi."

She giggled—actually giggled! "I'm serious." She walked over to the bed, opened her briefcase, and pulled out the file, laid out the case across the duvet, explaining each step she'd gone through. She showed him screen-prints of the account, of their perpetrator transferring more money, and her handwritten notes for the passwords to the accounts and wire transfers. When she was done, she stepped back from the bed and let Andrew take his fill. He picked up a few pieces of paper and took it all in. His silence made her a little uneasy.

"Where are these emails you're talking about?"

She swallowed, pulled out another thick file, and shoved it over to him. He rifled through, taking his time reading one, then another, before going back to the first.

Leaving him to do as he needed, especially since the embezzlement part of the case was solved, she grabbed her pants and put them on. Her mind wandered away from the case and her new marriage, to home, and she couldn't help but muse over exactly what went on with Dad. He sounded fine on the phone, though a bit anxious, and while he was a retired detective five years now, she couldn't think of anything big enough that he needed her home.

Her sisters weren't involved, seeing as Juls, Josephine, and Selena had been texting her nonstop. Dad and she weren't close to any other family members, although they'd attend the occasional holiday dinner. So there was no one else to check with.

Turning to face Andrew again, she let out a shocked squeal. He stood no more than a foot away from her. His eyes angry, face hard, and fists clenching at his sides repeatedly. She swallowed.

"You've been working yourself to the bone," he said through a growl.

She blinked. Why so angry? "Um, I've been pulling a few additional hours, yes."

"A few?" he spat. "A forty-five to fifty-hour work week is a few. From what I can gather and see," he said, flinging an arm out toward the bed where the case was, "is you've been pulling more like eighty-hour workweeks. What the fuck?"

She flinched. Not just from the not-so-happy grumble, but from the truth in his words. "I had a job to do."

"Not at the expense to yourself. Not when it makes me think you've been a clumsy fool!"

"Hey!" she snapped. "Watch it. I just solved your company's biggest damn case. You should be happy. You should be praising, not insulting me."

He came up on her so fast, she had no time to react. Just like before, in the hotel room—*dammit*—her back was to the wall and he crowded her space. No, correct that, he plastered his body to the front of hers. *Wow, that's nice.* She bit back a groan. *Traitorous body!*

"I could strangle you. I could kiss you. I could worship the fucking ground you walk on. And I do. I want to do it all. But dammit, why didn't you tell me?"

"I thought you and Derek talked," she said a bit snippily. *Hey,* he didn't have to use that tone. She'd give it as good as she got if he wanted to play this way.

Looking back, she figured she might have been wrong in not bringing it to the attention of one of the partners that she worked for both of them. *Shit.*

"You beautiful, giving woman. You," he murmured, and she lifted her gaze to his. His voice had gone soft, so much so, her knees felt like jelly. "It's all going to be okay now." He smiled.

Confused, she made a face. Did she have her job back? "What do you mean?"

He brushed his thumb over her cheek. "Everything makes sense now. And everything is going to be fine. I'll give you your job back, but you need to make sure you're only taking directions from one partner for now on. That'll be easy especially since I'll have to step out of the equation because we're married. You can report to Derek. Obviously, you're made for that side of the house. Your research says it all. You did it."

She blinked. "Just like that?"

He nodded.

She shook her head and pushed at his shoulders. "No, no, no. I don't think you understand, Andrew. I don't want that."

"What? You don't want your job?"

She tried to push him away again, but he didn't budge. It was like moving a brick wall, hard and impossible. Just like the man, set in his ways and stubborn. "No, I want my job."

"Then…what?"

She swallowed and drew in a deep breath. "I don't want to be married to you."

He grew impossibly still. He didn't blink. Several moments passed in silence, so quiet, even the beat of her heart sounded overly loud.

"What?" he asked, his voice calm.

"This was a mistake. You don't want me—"

"The hell I don't!"

She blinked and stared into his eyes. His face was open, but so hard it physically hurt to look at. To lose herself in this man would be everything she could want—had wanted for so long. But with the circumstances that brought them together, with how he'd been willing to fire her without getting the full story, without pushing to find out the truth, well…that caused pain to well in her chest. Plus, she didn't know if she could open herself like that to anyone. Not after the loss of her mother. It was too damn painful.

"Andrew," she started, making her voice soft, "perhaps last night would be better to just forget it ever happened."

"You stubborn, stubborn woman." He slammed a fist by her head on the wall and growled beneath his breath before dropping his forehead to touch hers. "Damn it, I can't just forget last night happened. I've dreamed of having you in my arms for years. I wish I could, and damn knows I have tried. I have tried to purge you from my system, but it doesn't work. You don't see it, do you? I wish I could forget you. I want to pretend you don't exist. Lay down and not dream of you."

Her heart hammered in her ears, like a rushing tidal wave from the ocean. His words bounced around in her head, echoing off endless walls. She couldn't breathe, the air inside her lungs frozen. Her body wouldn't move. She was surrounded by him, engulfed in his sweet, sweet words that sang to her soul.

"I can't," he finished on an angry whisper.

She sucked in air, and stared up at this wonderful man.

A knock sounded at the door.

"Excuse me, Mr. Cox?"

Laydi scowled, but secretly wanted to pound her fist in the air. She didn't need any more sweet words. She needed space. Away from Andrew. She couldn't think around him.

"Go away," he barked, not taking his eyes off hers. Laydi's heart beat against her chest hard.

"I'm sorry, Mr. Cox," the stewardess said, "but the captain has asked me to have you return to your seats immediately. We've got a rough batch of weather coming up."

"We'll be fine. Tell the captain I appreciate his concern."

"Mr. Cox, it's FAA regulations, I'm sorry. I must ask you return to your seats now or we'll have to divert."

A muscle popped in Andrew's jaw and he stared at Laydi. She wanted to shrink away, but refused to show him any weakness. He'd know he was getting to her and then he'd continue. He leaned down until his eyes were at her level. "We're not through with this, Mrs. Cox."

Laydi winced at the name and breathed out a sigh of relief, short-lived when he took her hand in his and led her out of the cabin. She stared at their connection, such a simple thing, when they'd done so much, but more intimate than anything else. He passed the attendant in the hall, who glanced down at their joined hands and frowned. Laydi wanted to say something, but Andrew was relentless, getting her to her seat and buckling her in before he took the time to do himself.

He stared out the opposite window, the back of his head in her view. She sighed. Once they got on the ground, once she got to her house and was surrounded by her friends and family, she'd be stronger. She could let him go. She had to for the safety of her own heart.

Chapter Three

Girl Code Rule # 44: Make every possible effort to deny the opportunity for drunken text, emails, and calls.

Andrew wasn't letting Laydi out of his sight. She might think she could get away, pretend this bond between them didn't exist, but he would be damned if he'd continue to play this game. And she was playing a game. Of that, he had no doubt.

Only what she played was the liar card. He felt the connection in her arms, in her kiss, in the way her eyes had gone soft when he'd been upfront about his feelings for her. And didn't that just chap his ass? The fact he played "chase his tail" with her? He didn't have any experience with going after someone; he'd always been pursued. Why did it need to be so difficult with Laydi?

After landing in Columbus, Ohio, they'd grabbed a car and made the eighty-eight-mile trek to Pearl. Apparently, from Laydi's short explanation, Pearl was a small town of about three-hundred-and-sixty. People didn't lock their doors at night, kids didn't have curfews, and her father had been the sole detective on the force for Pearl PD for years, until he retired five years ago.

Great, just what he needed; an over-protective cop father, and one he would be meeting for the first time after he married his daughter.

He hoped like hell this would go over well.

But he was a realist, and the optimism quickly dwindled.

Pulling up outside a one-level blue rancher, Andrew took in Laydi's childhood home. It sat on a large lot, the backyard fenced off with a three-foot white picket fence. A large oak tree stood in the front, its sole decoration one tire hanging from a tall branch. He leaned forward and peered at the tallest branch where the rope to the tire connected, and whistled through his teeth.

"Dad put it up with his partner when I was six. Almost broke his neck when he slipped off the second branch closest to the bottom there." Laydi pointed in the direction of the tree.

"How tall is it? It must be at least a hundred feet up?"

"It's an American Sycamore, and at last measurement is one-hundred-and-thirty-two feet high. We have a huge Australian Pine out back that's close to eighty-feet. I have no idea why they named it that. Dad said those trees came over a long time ago from Europe and Asia. It's anyone's guess if they actually originated from Australia.

"I grew up on these trees. Josephine used to give Dad a heart attack climbing all the way to the top without a harness. But then again," she said with a smile hovering, "that's Josephine. She always has to do something to shock everyone. It's in her nature. She likes to toe the line of appropriate."

He was fascinated with not only her smile, but also the insight into her childhood. She'd never spoken of it. "Is Josephine your sister?"

She shook her head. "Not by blood, but yes, she's my sister. As are Juls and Selena."

His brows drew down in confusion. "I don't understand. By blood?"

"Well," she said, shrugging, and went back to staring at the tree. "We did do a blood pact on the first day we met back when we were eight, but we're from four different homes. Juls is quiet, but fierce with her love to us. She had a rough start to life, and it got worse as she got older. But things are coming around." Her lips curved softly, and damn, that sent a shot of longing through him. What he wouldn't give to see that smile directed his way.

"Josephine is a goof, constantly trying to get a laugh out of us. She's the best listener, though, and always around to have fun and pull us out of hard times. Selena is more of a gentle creature, who had a lot of tough times accepting love, even when it came from us. But despite the time and distance, the differences between us all, we're still very close, and consider each other the sisters we never had. I would have never made it through my mother's abandonment without them."

Andrew stared at her, his entire being slammed by this information she willingly gave to him. It had to be good. She was opening up.

"I'm sorry about your mom. How old were you?"

She reached for the door handle. "It was a long time ago, but thank you. Let's go inside."

And like that, his insight into Laydi Michaels cut off. She was out the door and strolling up the walkway before he could react.

* * * *

Laydi stepped inside. Childhood memories, and the feel of home slammed into her. The old, ratty couch Dad refused to replace because Mom had loved it at first sight. The smell of stale coffee, and a hint of tobacco lingering (something she inwardly growled at, because wasn't Dad supposed to have quit?). And the soft setting sun coming through the open blinds along the back wall lit the house with the same color at six in the morning, just coming from a different direction, west, rather than east. She knew. She'd experienced it year after year.

"Dad?" she called and sensed, rather than heard Andrew come in behind her. How the big man moved without a sound was something she wanted to find out, but was too curious about what happened with Dad to ask now. And even after she figured out this latest puzzle with her family, she'd have to really examine if she wanted to know more about Andrew than she did, as she expected they'd be parting ways soon.

She had no idea why she'd let the little bit slip out about her past—perhaps feeling nostalgic she was home?

She didn't have time to scrutinize it anymore, for her dad, Ben, came around the corner with his bushy silver brows raised. The question on his face morphed from hope into happiness in a second and he opened his arms. She rushed across the room. The same scents of home wrapped around her along with an undercurrent of Old Spice and some sort of antiseptic.

"Pops." She squeezed him as tight as he did her.

"Sweet Pea, welcome home. Pull back and let your old man take a good look at you."

She smiled and did as requested, putting a little spin in to get a chuckle (which Dad did) for good measure. She went back into his arms, took his face between her hands, and studied him. He returned the favor, without the hands, taking in every detail, too. Her ring flashed in the sunlight against his face, and she stiffened. Shit, with everything going on, she'd forgotten to take it off.

He regained his loose grin and pulled away. Surprisingly, he didn't ask any questions. Knowing him, she hid her disbelief: he was just as nosy as she, took in details like she did, and had been paid for years to ask questions. That he didn't, said a lot, and increased her worry over him.

His gaze shifted over her shoulder, and now she had a whole other reason to go stiff. She turned and watched in avid fascination as her father shook hands with Andrew, the words they spoke lost through the *whooshing* in her ears.

Andrew had insisted he see her home, but she hadn't expected him to come inside. Now she didn't know how to explain his presence. The ring on her hand would tell a lot of things, many of which she wasn't ready to explain—if she ever wanted to, anyhow. First chance she got, she needed to get it off.

As if reading her mind—*damn the man*—Andrew shifted his attention to her, slid an arm around her shoulder, and pulled her against his side. All of his hard parts hit her soft ones, and she had a moment's thrill at the lovely contrast before going hard as a board and trying to push away. He didn't budge, nor did he let her move.

Grr.

"Laydi," Dad called, drawing her attention, "someone is out back waiting to see you. Why don't you go check it out?"

She pushed away from Andrew, and this time he let her go, but not before she saw puzzlement on his handsome face. She crossed the house in a few steps, threw open the door, and instantly had to brace to catch Bubba, her father's German Shepherd.

"Oomph," she grunted, taking a step back in order to handle his weight. "Hey, boy," she said, her voice a few octaves higher, and all lovey as she scratched him behind the ears. Bubba rubbed and head-butted her legs, and gave little doggy growls as he greeted her.

She made sure to give Bubba his attention and greeting, long enough for the sounds of Dad and Andrew's voices to pierce. She patted his hind leg, and brushed her clothes off as she made her way back to the living room.

Andrew sat on the right end of the couch, legs spread in a total alpha man way, angled to where he faced her father, but with direct access toward the entry points in the room.

Dad sat in his lazy boy, stool rolled up, as apparently it was too early to get comfortable around her...what was Andrew? Her friend, her boss? No way could she tell Dad she'd made a drunken mistake and married him. Nope. Not until she found out what was going on.

Bubba followed her into the room, did a hesitant sniff at Andrew, before falling on his side in greeting and presenting his belly.

"Come sit, Sweet Pea," Dad said. "We have a few things to talk about."

She narrowed her eyes at Bubba, the traitor, and sat in the only other seat available, the left side of the couch. As soon as her ass hit the cloth, she was moved, sliding toward Andrew until her leg and hip flushed with his.

Dad raised a brow at Andrew's move. She let out a heavy sigh, but didn't fight it, especially since he wasn't going to be sticking around for long.

"Okay, Pop, what's going on?"

Dad stared at where the two of them touched, his eyes lost in thought, before lifting his gaze to Andrew, dropping it to their hands now interlaced (by again, Andrew!) and then to her face. Yeah, he didn't miss much.

"Sweet Pea," Dad said, "I think I need to ask you first what's going on with you?"

She cleared her throat and tried to shift away from Andrew, without any luck. "What do you mean?" she asked, her voice an octave higher. *Dammit.*

Dad leaned back in the chair, tented his fingers over his chest, tilted his head, and pinned her with a stare. "Are you going to make this difficult, Laydi Marie Michaels?"

Andrew's hand spasmed in hers, and she winced at the use of her full name. "Dad…"

He shook his head once.

"Seriously, it's nothing. Andrew isn't staying. He's just dropping me off."

Dad's brows went high and his attention turned to Andrew, who had gone motionless at her side. The only thing that moved was a muscle in his jaw, ticking to the beat of her rapid heart.

"Andrew, do you want to explain why there's a ring on my daughter's wedding finger, why she's shown up with a man I've never met, and why she's as skittish as the bucks I hunt every fall?"

"I'd love to explain it to you, Mr. Michaels," Andrew replied.

She gasped. "No!" She jumped off the couch. Both men eyed her as if the next question she should be asked is if she needed to go to the looney bin.

"No," she repeated, this time softer in order to show some calm. "Andrew was leaving, weren't you?" She turned and gave him a look she hoped communicated *go-now-and-never-come-back-nor-speak-of-this-anymore-especially-to-my-father.*

Apparently, even though Andrew could read her mind, he couldn't read her facial messages. "Mr. Michaels," he continued.

"Ben," Dad said.

Andrew nodded. "Okay, Ben. Laydi and I are married."

Oh, jeez. She groaned and slumped back to the couch, where Andrew drew her to his side again. She crossed her arms, fists tucked beneath, so this time he couldn't grab her hand again. Childish? Of course. But he needed to *back off*!

He shook with something suspiciously like laughter, wrapped an arm around her shoulders, and pulled her tighter.

"When did this happen?" Dad asked.

"Just last night. I know this is unorthodox, but we found ourselves too caught in the moment to stop. I'll admit we were both a little inebriated at the time, but I don't want to place all the blame on that. So I'll just say I'm sorry, and you have every right to be angry."

"Hmmm," Dad said, and she found him watching her closely, but without any inkling of anger. Dad had always been over-protective, to a point where she'd given him the nickname of a drill sergeant. She expected him to flip out, blow a fuse, and chase Andrew out of the house.

"Hmmm? That's it?" she asked, without meaning to say it aloud.

He lifted his brows again. "What would you like me to say? You're already married, are you not?"

She opened her mouth to deny it, but Andrew squeezed her shoulders. She sighed. "Yeah we're married, but…"

"Does Andrew treat you bad?"

She snapped her mouth close, opened it. "No, of course not."

He looked at Andrew. "Does Laydi treat you bad?"

"Not even close," Andrew answered without hesitation, his words causing her a little pang and a whole lot of softening. "She's the best thing that's ever happened to me."

She whipped her head toward Andrew, her stomach summersaulting. An incredibly sweet thing to say, but she didn't understand.

"I know the feeling, son. I know the feeling. Whelp, now that that is out of the way—"

"What?" She jumped up again. "Just like that? I come home married to a man you've never met, you ask two questions, and that's it?"

Dad's brows went up yet again. "Would you like me to say something else, Sweet Pea?"

She sputtered, "Yes!" Her hands slapped against her sides. If anyone could help her escape Andrew, it was him. "Dad!"

"Good luck, son. This one turned my hair gray before I was thirty and gave me more than one heart attack. She's been watched over by half the police force and more than a quarter of the town, and believe me when I say it took the entire village to keep her out of trouble."

Andrew chuckled aloud this time. "I think I know what you mean, Ben."

"Ugh, you two are completely unbelievable!"

"Sweet Pea," Dad called, his laughing eyes softening and going serious all at once. "Please sit down."

Oh shit, this was it, wasn't it? The real reason he had called her home.

She sat again, this time next to Andrew, and reached for his hand. Andrew froze, but only for a beat, before his thumb swiped a circle against her skin. Even with the fear of what Dad was going to say, that touch was nice.

Dad took in Andrew and her again, nodded, and got right to the point. "I've got stage three lung cancer."

She sucked in a sharp breath, and her heart kicked against her chest.

"Before you go freaking out, Laydi, I'll tell you outside of that, I'm healthy, and both the doc and I agreed we're going to do some aggressive treatment here to get my body to kick cancer's ass."

She stared at Dad, her vision getting a little cloudy around the edges, almost as if she were going into a tunnel. White spots danced in front of her eyes. Andrew's concerned expression filled her vision and he gripped the sides of her face. When had he let go of her hand?

"Breathe, Lay, breathe!"

"Shit, push her head down between her knees," Dad said.

"Not going to help if she isn't breathing, Ben."

Someone tapped the side of her face. "Laydi, girl, you need to not give your dad a heart attack, breathe for me."

God, was it her, or did someone pull an Edward from *Twilight* and punch a fist through her chest to squeeze her lungs? While Edward typically grabbed for the heart of evil vampires, she wasn't arguing over the difference.

"Fuck, I'm sorry, Ben," Andrew said.

"What are you..." Dad asked right before Andrew laid his mouth over hers. He gathered her in his arms, and *yeah,* while her chest still hurt like hell, and her vision quickly faded, being held in his strong arms and pressed against his hard chest felt very, very nice.

His tongue swept inside her mouth, velvet coaxing her into action. His eyes were on hers and she would have laughed any other time, but panic rose in his gaze, urging her to grab ahold of something, anything, and get with the program. His beautiful blue gaze burned into her eyes while he kissed her deeper, extremely thoroughly and very intently.

"I'll just...erm, give you two a minute," Dad muttered.

Andrew trailed a hand up her back and tunneled it into her hair, tilted her head even more, and deepened the kiss. She had no choice but to respond. She tentatively touched her tongue against his, and the relief in his eyes was palpable. He pulled back, watched her breathe in and out for a few moments, before exhaling.

"Jesus Christ, Laydi, if you weren't so fucking gorgeous, so sweet, and the only woman I wanted, you'd be an extreme pain in the ass," he said against her mouth.

Her toes curled in her boots. Did he just say that? The only woman? *Hold up, wait a minute!*

She stiffened, and he gave her a grim smile. "Yeah, she's back."

Pulling out of his arms, she sent him a death glare as Dad walked back in the room.

He had three bottles of beer between his thick fingers. He handed one to her, to Andrew, then regained his seat. "You all right, Sweet Pea?"

She nodded and cleared her throat, ignoring the beer between her palms. "How long have you known?"

"About a week. Doc just got the biopsy results back yesterday, which is when I called you to come home. They want to start me on treatment tomorrow morning."

"What?" She leaned forward, her ass on the edge of the couch. A little more, and she'd be on the floor. "Why so quick? Is that normal?"

He nodded. "Yes. Like I said, they want to go in aggressively, and the quicker we start, the better chances we'll have at it not metastasizing."

She leaned back until she hit the couch. Andrew's arm came around her a moment later. She ignored it. "Okay. I'll go with you tomorrow morning."

Dad looked down at his beer. "I'd appreciate that, Sweet Pea."

* * * *

Several hours later, after they'd all argued over and decided on dinner, Laydi turned to Andrew and declared with a slap on her thighs, "Okay, I'm beat. Time for you to go. Thank you for making sure I got home okay."

He turned toward her. If she thought he'd leave, especially after all that happened in the past twenty-four hours, she was sadly mistaken. And that wasn't even including the little incident on the couch. That just gave him more leverage. She needed him to stand by her through this.

"Where exactly do you think I'm going?"

"Um…a hotel? Back to your jet?"

"You mean the jet which is powered down and parked on the runway about two hours from here? Or the hotel where the rest of the flight crew is staying, also another two hours away?"

"The jet?" Ben asked.

Andrew enjoyed the comical change of expressions on Laydi's face too much to look away. He knew she was thinking about not only the drive, but also the stewardess who he'd seen her get jealous over earlier. He answered Ben while continuing to watch her. "My company owns a jet. It's a needed necessity for work between New York and DC."

308

"Well…you could always stay at a motel in town and make your way back to the jet"—she winced—"tomorrow."

He shook his head; she was too fucking cute. "Not going to happen. We've only been married a day, but one thing you should learn now is, I'm not going to leave just when the going gets tough. If you think that's the case, I would've run for the hills long ago."

She gasped, and Ben laughed. "He's got your number, Sweet Pea. What exactly do you do?" Dad asked.

Andrew turned to him. "I own a private investigations agency that works domestic and government cases."

"Oh," Ben said. "Is that where you two met? Through a case?"

Andrew fought to hold back a smile. "Through the company, yes."

"But… That would mean you're Laydi's boss?"

It seemed, if Ben's confused facial expression an indication, he had a hard time wrapping his mind around this.

Andrew let out a breath. "Yes. I was her boss. I own the company with a close friend."

"Yes, yes, yes," Laydi interjected. "While this is great catch up story time, I'm tired. Andrew, it's time to go."

"Laydi, why in the world would you want your husband, your *new* husband to stay in town by himself?" Ben's face got a faraway expression, then turned red. Andrew fought back a laugh. Of course he'd picked up on why newlyweds wouldn't want to be in separate beds. "Actually, how about you *both* go and stay in the hotel tonight? Tomorrow I'll be staying overnight anyway, so it's not like I'll be around here much."

Andrew was a second away from taking Laydi down the hall to kiss some sense into her, when her father stopped speaking. Worry moved into her face, mouth tight, eyes alarmed. He had to act fast. She was close to her dad, and this situation must be hard on her. He probably wasn't adding any peace in her life, but he wasn't going to back away now. He meant what he'd said. He was sticking around.

"What if I want to stay the night with you?" Laydi asked, her voice softer than Andrew had ever heard before. Working close to her for five years, he'd heard her voice several different ways, and this soft, gentle tone with a slight tremor underneath was unfamiliar. He clenched his hands at his sides to resist the urge to take her in his arms. He had the right, yes, but he didn't want to put up a show in front of her pops. This sight of her, one so different from the normally tough-as-nails investigator, had peeked out on occasion before. Now, he saw her in her full glory…caring, vulnerable, loving. Each piece of the Laydi pie that made him want her even more.

"No," Ben answered a bit gruffly.

"Dad—"

Ben lifted a hand. "No, I'll be fine. All they're keeping me for is to make sure I don't have any kind of reaction to this"—he waved a hand in the air—"shit they're pumping me full of. Let your old man have his peace with this. You hover, it's just gonna piss me off. Sweetheart, I love you. I know you care. But seriously, I don't need you to hover. That's not why I called you home."

Laydi grunted and crossed her arms. "Okay then, why did you call me home if you're not going to let me stay with you?"

"I'm only going to be held overnight tomorrow, that's it. Then it's back home, where I will need your help. Plus," Ben added with a mischievous grin, "you never come home anymore. You don't call, you don't write," he said with a laugh, impersonating the Wolverine with a quote from *X-Men*. Laydi lifted her hands and waved them in the air.

"Yeah, yeah, yeah. Sorry, Dad, I've been really busy."

Ben lifted a brow and looked between them. "I'll say so. You come home married to a man I've never met before. I'd say you've been busy."

Laydi's face turned an alarming shade of red. "Dad," she whispered, horrified.

Ben's laugh boomed through the room. "I'm just saying, Sweetheart." He walked up next to her and laid a hand on her shoulder, giving it a brief rub before continuing down the hall. "I'm wiped, so I'm off to bed. You kids be good now."

"Night, Dad."

"Night, Ben."

"I'll see you in the morning," Ben replied with a wave over his shoulder.

Laydi watched her father while Andrew watched her. When a door shut behind Ben, she turned to Andrew and glared. "That was completely unacceptable." He popped a brow, but she went on. "You practically forced my hand there."

He chuckled. "Beautiful, I hardly had to say anything. Your father is the one who insisted. But," he went on when she opened her mouth, "you can bet your sweet ass I wouldn't have ended up leaving anyway."

She growled. "You're impossible!"

He crossed his arms. "Impossible that I want to stick close to you?"

"You're putting your nose where it doesn't belong." She matched his stance. Her eyes spit fire at him, and it was a wonder he didn't go up in flames.

"By insisting on staying with my wife?"

"I'm not your wife," she snapped, and *that* got his attention. He dropped his arms and took a step toward her. Her eyes widened and she moved back, matching the distance he tried to close. He took another, and another, walking her back until she hit the wall behind her. He bent low and got within inches of her face.

"Baby, I've got a marriage certificate that has both our signatures on it, a dozen pictures with witnesses, and a good chunk of cash gone from my account to pay for a ring on your finger. And I will add that we consummated the marriage several times last night, so if you want to sit here and play this little spitfire routine with me, go right ahead, because Lay," he called and waited until her gaze met his. "I can tell you it's not turning me off. In fact, I've never been more turned on in my life."

She gasped, and he dropped his focus to her mouth. She licked her lips, and he about pounced on her. It took everything in him to hold back, but accosting her in her childhood house with her father down the hall probably wasn't a great idea. If he started kissing her now, he doubted he'd stop.

He lifted his gaze again and met her eyes. "I'm going to go get our bags. Why don't you go get ready for bed and I'll be in in a bit."

Her brows went into a little vee and she nodded, looking away. "I'll get you a blanket and pillow and make the couch up."

He stopped walking toward the front door and whipped around to face her. "I'm not sleeping on the couch."

She frowned. "Okay, then I'll make it up for me."

He shook his head. "You're not sleeping on the couch either."

She slapped her sides, and mock-shouted a whisper. "Then where in the hell are *you* sleeping, and where will *I* be sleeping?"

"I don't give a fuck where we sleep. I just know I'll be sleeping with you. *We* can do that in your bed, or in a tent in the backyard…again, I don't give a shit, but at the end of the day I will be lying next to your sweet body. *That*, you can take to the bank." He headed for the door again.

"You will not," she hissed.

He pivoted, this time slower, and smiled the same way.

"If you make two beds and try to sleep anywhere other than next to me, Beautiful, there'll be consequences. You want to test me, go right ahead and try. But make no doubt, if you fight me on this, I will win. It'd just be so much sweeter if you gave in now." He tilted his head to the side. "But if you want to fight it, baby, go ahead. Like I said, that shit turns me on."

With that and her angry gasp, he turned on his heel and headed out for the bags.

* * * *

Trying to ignore the butterflies in her stomach, caused much by the fact that Andrew took a quick shower down the hall, Laydi powered up her laptop to check on her case. The little Windows icon spun, and she fought against fidgeting or locking the door to her room, especially with Andrew's sensual threat bouncing in her head.

"...but at the end of the day I will be lying next to your sweet body; that you can take to the bank."

What the hell was that? How had her life changed so much in such a short amount of time? She'd gone from doing surveillance work, going home to her lonely, but lovely, one-bedroom apartment that overlooked Chinatown, to sitting in her childhood bedroom, waiting on her *husband*, and fighting against her stomach and the anticipation of finally, finally having a boy in her room.

Well, Andrew was no boy, but still. She'd been too good, too nice in high school to go against Dad, and too by-the-book to even think about trying, for fear of being caught. Not that any boy from high school would have taken up the opportunity with her, with Dad being the lead detective in their small town.

A lead detective that could very well make their life hell, or make them disappear without a trace...

This was Andrew waiting for her, not just any man, but one she'd wanted for so damn long, one she'd imagined this very real fantasy with—although not necessarily in her childhood bedroom—many times before.

The door opened, and she did her best to keep her focus on the screen in front of her, when her attention was on the man walking in her room. The rustle of clothing, the zip of his suitcase, and his soft breathing. As she logged into the trace she had running on the banker's computer, she tried—and failed—to ignore her wandering mind going to whether Andrew slept naked or not. This morning, he'd woken as naked as she, but maybe that wasn't an everyday occurrence.

Was that a good or bad thing?

Her screen went bright blue. She bit her lip and frowned. A white lettering code flashed on her screen.

"Shit." Her professor in Cyber Warfare 101 had covered this the second week of class. Somehow, some way, *someone* had reversed her trace. She tried to input a command to stop the reverse Trojan.

312

"What's wrong?" Andrew asked, immediately at her side.

"Shit, shit, shit. No!" She typed faster, but not fast enough. Her computer's drives locked and became accessible to whoever traced her.

"Laydi," Andrew urged. "What's happening? Talk to me."

"I-I-oh hell. I can't even shut down now! No, no, no!"

"God dammit, tell me what the hell is going on."

She snapped her hands away from the computer, everything useless at this point, and drove her fingers through her hair, tugging once at the crown before looking helplessly at the screen. Whoever was in her computer knew of her, and could trace her. She powered her laptop down, hoping it'd stall the hack for a bit longer.

"I've been hacked."

Shit, shit, shit! The amount of data she kept on this laptop was unreal. Years of work, contacts to informants, and personal information on each of her suspects galore.

Andrew frowned between her laptop and her face, and really, any man who looked handsome even while frowning should be locked up. It wasn't fair.

"The trace I had running on our banker's computer shouldn't have been detectable, but apparently it was. Someone must have figured it out and reversed the trace, and now I'm being hacked."

Andrew's face hardened and his entire body stilled. "What will this hack do? Can they trace you to find out who you are?"

She bit her lip and focused on the dark laptop screen. "I think so. I'm really good at what I do, but whoever this was is better."

"What do you mean, better?"

"Better!" She tossed her hands up and slapped them back on her legs. "Better than me. I couldn't stop it. Hopefully, I've slowed them down, but now it's only a matter of time."

He took her by the shoulders, squaring her body against his. "Can they find you?"

She looked to the side, and he gave her shoulders a slight shake. "Lay, can they find you?"

"I don't know! Maybe. Sure! There's a possibility. Oh my God, I'm so sorry. I didn't think this would happen. Bankers operate in the world believing their networks are secure, and I didn't think anyone would contemplate they've been hacked by an outside source. I made sure that their security network looked at the trace as friendly, as part of their network security."

Andrew let her shoulders go, reached for his phone, hit one button, and put the phone to his ear. She didn't like the hard, dark expression on his face—he was pissed. She'd never seen him this angry, and if she were honest, it scared the shit out of her. Although he also looked very...*male*. From the tenseness of his shoulders, to the protruding veins along his arms, the firm set of his mouth, the wideness of his heaving chest, which tapered off to his trim waist. She tried—not very hard—to keep her eyes from dropping lower to the bulging package between his legs. Impressive. Hot.

"Derek," he said. "What the fuck do you have Laydi on?" Pause. "No, D, I'm talking about this fucking banker shit she's tracing." Pause. "Yes, I know about the case, but I don't *know* about the case, you feel me? All I know is what you've explained, what she's explained, and what I've read, but that still doesn't explain why her computer was just hacked in a reverse trace and now whomever she's looking into can find out not only who she is, but also where she is. Do you see why I have a tremendous issue with that?" Each word ticked off precise and lethal, like a whip cutting through the air.

"Andrew," Laydi called softly, definitely a little freaked out. Not because of the trace, granted that was a whole other ball game, but because she'd never heard him speak to his partner this way. They'd been friends since they were kids. It wasn't Derek's fault this happened. She should have been more careful.

"The CIA?" Andrew asked, his body, if possible, stiller than a few minutes ago. "Why is every damn case coming back to that alphabet agency lately? You wanna explain that to me, buddy?"

Uh oh, that didn't sound like an endearment. Laydi tried again. "Andrew..." She rolled to her knees and looked up at him standing next to the bed. His expression was thunderous, staring over her head.

"Have you ran him?" he asked into the phone. "Okay. Then how about you pick him up?" Pause. "Uh huh. Uh huh. Wait...what?" he roared. "You're telling me you have no idea where he is?" He took in a deep breath and pinched his nose. "No, Derek, I have a huge issue with someone looking into my wife, especially when those three alphabet letters are behind it. Yes. Yes. That isn't the point. I swear, Derek, we need to take everyone off his or her cases and focus on this... You should have thought through this the first moment you realized something didn't smell right. Having her use her own laptop isn't thinking it through!"

She sucked in a breath and hissed, "Andrew!"

His eyes snapped to hers, and she tried to shrink back. Maybe now wasn't the time. He grabbed her arm one-handed, held her in place, and spoke into the phone again. "Uh huh. That's right. Keep me apprised. I'll talk to you tomorrow."

With a flick of his thumb, he ended the call and tossed it on the nightstand, then faced her fully.

His face was harder than she'd ever seen. Wearing only black boxer briefs, the material cut so close to his body it was a wonder his blood circulation hadn't cut off. His broad chest should be bronzed, and spread just below her vision. She wanted to peek, but damn if she could tear her gaze away from his angry one.

"Do you have something you want to say, baby?" he asked, his voice measured, quiet.

Uh oh, they were back to *baby*. He only used that endearment when he tried to get a point across.

"Um…" she hedged. "It's not Derek's fault."

Andrew's lips thinned. "You're wrong."

She sucked in a breath. "Jeez. We've barely found out about the retrace and you've already made up your mind? You're not even going to listen to what I have to say on the matter. Just"—she dropped her voice—"you're wrong."

His brows lifted. "Are you sure this is the right response you want to give me now?" His voice held a lethal edge, as if he teetered on a cliff.

She dropped her chin to her chest and took him in. "Are you—are you angry at me?"

"I'm furious with you."

I wouldn't say I've missed that, Bob, she wanted to quote from *Office Space*, but, more than anything else, she wanted some distance for an obvious fight coming on. She pulled back to get out of his grasp, but he adjusted his grip and set a knee on the bed, bringing them closer.

"Why?"

"Why?" he asked, his tone hinting at surprised sarcasm.

She nodded, and he released her shoulders and put his arms around her. One went around her back until the edge of his fingers brushed the side of her breast. The other went beneath her shoulder blades. She was, by all means, effectively trapped.

"I'll tell you why, baby. And you better listen closely, because I swear to fuck, this is the last time you will find yourself in this position. I will not tolerate you in danger, nor will I stand by and do nothing while this happens again. You even think of doing something this stupid, I will be all over you in two seconds flat."

Her back went straight. *Of all the*! They needed to address this chauvinistic attitude, but first…"Stupid?" she hissed.

His eyes narrowed more. "I'm pissed at you because I've waited five years to be exactly where I am right now. Five years of standing back and watching you hand out smiles as if they were water. Five years of my hands itching to touch you. Five years of listening to your voice in my ear and just the sound of your laugh—Christ!—it can turn me on faster than your attitude."

Oh well, shit, that's nice. Still a bit pissed, as she could tell he was, too, but his words were very nice.

"I've finally got you in my arms, in my bed, and, baby, I plan to be between your thighs for many years to come—to have some unknown threat with only God knows who trying to find you, for only God knows why. It's a threat on the very thing I want to have, on where I want to be, and I'll be damned if I just wasted five years to let all that shit wash down the drain in a matter of days or weeks."

Her spine stiffened again, and she surged forward, right up in his—*yes siree*—face. "Wasted?"

He got close, too, until his lips brushed against hers. "Yeah, wasted. That five years I waited, biding my time, giving you time, and fighting against the chemistry we"—he squeezed her again—"have wasted. I know that now, especially after I've had a taste, and, Beautiful, I plan on tasting it a lot more, so yeah, you can say I'm a little pissed that something is interfering with those plans and threatening you."

"Shit," she said softly and stared at his throat, unable to meet his eyes. She hadn't realized earlier how big of a threat this could be. In her defense, she had no idea what was going on, but from his reaction and the way he had spoken to Derek, she didn't figure it was good.

"Laydi," he called.

Her back went straight as something else popped into her head. "Do you think…shit, if they are able to get a lock on me, they can find Dad?"

"Laydi."

"Oh God, he's already going through too much as it is." She gripped his waist, trying—and failing *again*!—to ignore the hardness she found there, too.

"Angel." He leaned down and gave her a chaste kiss, a brush of lips against hers, before he murmured, "We're going to take care of this. Your dad is going to be fine, you'll be fine, we're going to be fine."

"How can you be sure?" She should really be calling local hotels, hell, maybe even the new police chief in town. Get more protection, get Dad moved, and figure out what's going down. In that order.

"Lay, sweetheart, look at me." She hadn't realized her gaze slid away again until he called her. Strengthening resolve stood like a beacon behind his eyes. "I'm sure," he said once he held her gaze, "because like I said, I have you exactly where I want you, and when I say I want more, I'm not kidding. There's no way in hell anything is going to come between me and my end game here."

She frowned. "I'm not sure I like being referred to as an end game, Andrew."

He grinned. "Well, at least you aren't fighting being my wife anymore now, are you?"

Well shit.

Chapter Four

Girl Code Rule #34: Honesty is ALWAYS the best policy for "How do I look?"

The next day, Andrew paced Ben's front porch, alternately talking to Derek on his phone and waiting for Laydi to return. She'd been insistent that morning about taking her dad to the hospital herself, and while he hadn't liked leaving her to deal with that shit alone, she'd made every promise she wouldn't be. She'd have her "sisters" with her, which was a bit odd considering she was an only child, but he figured these were the friends he'd heard her talking to time and again.

That assurance, combined with her strong argument about having some alone time with her father, and explaining she believed her dad was trying to put a front up before him with this cancer business, and was worried more than he led on, had Andrew stepping down and staying at Ben's house.

But, that wasn't before he gave her explicit instructions on calling or texting him when she arrived, while at the hospital, and when she left. This, of course, led to her snapping off a sharp salute with a, "Sir, yes, sir," which in turn led to him kissing her long, hard, and wet.

She hadn't had much to say after, so he figured she got his point.

Plus, she had called him twice and texted him a half dozen times since. Some told him she'd arrived, that her dad had been taken back and started on the treatment, and another he was doing well. Others showed the sass he'd thought he kissed out of her, with messages informing him she was stopped at a red light, another asking if she could pull over and take a piss break, and so forth. He very much looked forward to his way of communication when she got back, and this would involve a lot of tongues, groping, and more of her breathless moans.

Trying to make use of idle time, he'd gotten on the phone with Derek to get a brief on any updates, only to have nothing but bad news.

"It's got all the prints of CIA on it, my man," Derek told him through the phone. "And what's worse is that analyst is now up in the dust. He's completely off the radar. Didn't show up for work, not at his apartment, and his phone's GPS is gone."

"Please tell me you're joking."

"Nope. Shit, wish I was, especially since this is coming on the heels of everything happening overseas. Unfortunately those guys have already gone black, so there's no way to pull them back at this point."

"Fuck," Andrew barked. "I don't like this. Having a rogue agent out there, a team elsewhere with targets on their asses while hanging in the wind, and now this, with all the connecting points cementing to the same analyst, don't give me warm fuzzies. Never, never in a million years did I think these two cases would be connected. What are the odds?" He scanned the horizon again for Laydi's car and tried to get a handle on his anger. He shook too much, worked up with concern about everything, the whole picture, not to mention Laydi's safety, that he couldn't seem to think outside of locking her away in a padded room, or disappearing with her to some remote island until all of this blew over. Unfortunately, with the deterioration of her father's health, that wasn't doable. He took in a deep breath, and swallowed against the tightness in his throat. "Talk to me about the trace on her computer."

"From what Scott could see, it's got the makings for some sophisticated tracking. He's not happy about it, and if the frown on his face and the amount of energy drinks he's taken in since are any indication…"

Andrew tightened his fingers around the porch rail and glanced over as Bubba gave a deep doggy sigh. The big dog hadn't a care in the world, lounging under the sun's rays.

Andrew focused on the call. Scott was their IT guy, so good he'd been recruited by every government alphabet, including a few the government denied existence of. Smart, and a little geeky if the games he played online and some of the comments that came out of his mouth anything to go by. Plus, the guy could quote lines from about any *Star Wars* and *Star Trek* movie like it was another language. Somehow, the quotes always fit the situation. How he did it—anyone's guess. But if Scott was bothered by the new situation, this didn't bide well for any of them.

"Shit," Andrew hissed.

"Yeah. He wants to get his hands directly on her laptop, so brace yourself for some company soon."

"The faster we know more, the better. Make it happen." Andrew pulled his head up as the crunch of tires rounded the bend of Ben's drive. *Laydi.* He kept his eyes on her and continued. "I don't like the feel of this, and the fact that this shit is coming on the heels of what is supposed to be Laydi's time with her dad, and right after I've gotten my ring on her finger, has me going from pissed to pissed the fuck off. I don't like that whoever can track her, and I don't like knowing that we're standing here with our dicks in the wind while they plot whatever it is they're planning."

Laydi parked the car and got out. Anguish drew a clear picture across her face. She wiped at her cheeks with angry movements.

She slammed the car door and stomped toward the house.

"I gotta go, Derek. Keep me updated."

"Will do."

Andrew pocketed his phone, meeting Laydi at the stairs to the porch.

"What's wrong?"

She stepped to the top and crossed her arms, not meeting his eyes, but turning toward the front yard, and in the next blink, exploded by tossing her hands in the air and slapping her sides. "Everything!"

"Laydi," he tried, but she cut him off.

"How about we start with the fact that my dad is sick, for one? And apparently he has been keeping this a secret for months. Not weeks, but months!"

He took a step toward her, but she lifted a hand, palm out.

"And then, oh no, things couldn't possibly get easier, right? The doctor started going through it while we sat in her office before treatment. And so instead of hearing this from him, I'm hearing it all, the whole ugly mess his body is going through, from her."

A tear leaked out the side of her eye, but before he could do anything, she swiped it away, thinned her lips as if she were fighting against some internal monster, and went on.

"Then they come and take him back to get the port inserted, and start round one of chemotherapy." She said the last word as if it tasted bitter, uttered it with such a soft whisper, he moved closer. Still not touching her, but he had a feeling he'd need to soon.

"Then she tells me after he's left the room that he has a twenty-percent chance of living past five years." She looked to the ground. "Twenty percent," she whispered, her voice raw and utterly broken.

That sound, one so far off from the strong woman he'd known for years snapped him into action. He moved forward, ignored her backing away, and took her into his arms. He threaded his fingers through her soft, blonde curls and pushed her head to his chest. He held her while her body shook with silent sobs. Each shaky movement of her frame against his broke his heart. He wished he could take it all away, the pain, and the uncertainty. If he could, he'd seize it and bear the burden on his shoulders.

He'd never understood when people had said they'd do things like that—throw themselves before bullets in front of their loved ones. But he knew, and even if he'd only been married to Laydi less than a week, he'd been close to her for much longer, and without a doubt was hopelessly in love with her. He'd guessed it before; now he understood. There was no amount of money he wouldn't pay, no place he wouldn't go, no person he wouldn't take on to give her five minutes of peace.

He didn't know how long he held her, but the sun had shifted a bit in the sky before she pressed slightly against his chest. Pulling back, he waited until she lifted her gaze to his. He'd try and move the moon, anything, for the helplessness to leave her hazel eyes.

"Sorry about that," she said.

"There's nothing to be sorry about." He loosened his arms, but didn't let go. Instead, he leaned against a post and pulled her with him until she rested her hips against his. "If I understand anything, I know your dad is going to pull through this."

She gave him a look as if she didn't believe him. "What makes you so sure of this? You just met him yesterday."

He tightened his arms. "Yeah, but I've known his daughter for much longer. And from what I know of her, she's strong and so damn stubborn that she'd take on the world before admitting defeat."

Laydi snorted. "Stubborn?"

He eyed her for a few seconds before lifting a brow. "Are you ready to admit you're my wife yet?"

She laughed softly and shook her head, then let out a deep sigh.

He tightened his arms again. "What's that?"

"Well, as if this morning wasn't fun"—she spat fun as if it left a dirty taste in her mouth—"I also have something else I've got to deal with before the day is out."

Andrew lifted a brow.

"You know," she said, eyeing his brow, "most people actually use words."

"Laydi," he warned.

"Oh, all right," she huffed. "Something is going on with Dad's paperwork, so they're sending someone over from the pension board to see if we can get it worked out. I need to go find a few papers before she gets here."

"What exactly does that mean?"

"One would figure," she said with no small amount of annoyance in her tone, "that all this paperwork stuff would be worked out before treatment started. But apparently not. Something is missing, or between the insurance agency and the pension department, some lines were crossed. So now they're sending over Renee Conish to sort it out." The distaste on her face when she spoke of this Renee person wasn't small, nor did he think he'd ever seen it on her face before. It looked as if she was trying to be as politically correct and nice as she could, while fighting some internal urge to find the right words.

Hmmm, there was something there, and he didn't know if he should push it.

"Renee stole my boyfriend in high school. She's this uptight, hootie-tootie, who thinks her shit doesn't stink, and managed to go against me in everything I did. It was as if she had some sort of competition going on with me and I wasn't brought in on the game. Juls said it was pure jealousy, especially considering I could hang out with the boys and fit in like one of them, when all Renee wanted to do was play the boys." She shook her head. "It's seriously all trivial, and really juvenile, but she ended up marrying my ex, and now that it's almost ten years later, I just don't know if I want my father's livelihood resting in this woman's hands."

"Why didn't this meeting happen at the hospital?"

"Because one, the pension department is in the next town over despite it being the pension division for this town's police department. And two, I didn't have all of Dad's paperwork with me."

"So while they fucked up," Andrew said, a low grumble of anger pitching in his stomach, "and while you should be dealing with your dad when he needs you, instead you're left picking up the pieces they couldn't get together before treatment started."

"It's not that big of a deal. I can handle it; I just don't like doing it."

He squeezed her again. "No, it is a big deal, and it's not right. What time is mega-bitch supposed to be here?"

Laydi burst out laughing. "Mega-bitch?"

He shrugged, giving her a small smile, and loving the sound of her laugh.

A wave of warmth rushed through his chest.

She looked out over the drive, then her eyes came back to his. "Soon, but there's something else I need to tell you." She bit her lip.

He eyed her mouth, contemplating the idea of using his own teeth on that plump lip. There might be a small chance she'd let him, and a picture playing out in his head. He'd bite down softly, but hard enough to let her know who was boss. Her breath would catch and flutter against his lips, but she'd make a tiny sound, a low moan almost too quiet to hear. And that moan would be his all-access pass to cover her mouth with his.

She took his silence apparently as indication to go on. "I've been getting…these weird calls all day."

His hackles lifted. "What do you mean weird?"

She shifted, but didn't pull away, nor did he let her go. "Well, at first I thought they were just wrong numbers. An unknown caller on my screen, I'd pick up, but it'd be silent on the other side before they hung up. Maybe it's the insurance company?"

He whipped his head around to take in the drive and Ben's yard before backing her toward the door. He'd been in the business too long to believe in coincidences. Having Laydi out in the open caused his skin to itch like hell.

Giving a quick whistle, he barely paid any attention as Bubba scrambled to his feet and passed them into the house. Andrew slipped inside, not taking his eyes off the landscape or his arms from Laydi. "What else?"

"What are you doing?"

"I don't like being out in the open. Now, what else?" he asked.

"But you were just standing out there earlier."

"Laydi," he started.

She pressed against his chest. "No, why all of a sudden did you move us indoors?"

"Lay, finish with your story. What else happened after they'd hang up?"

She eyed him for a few moments. "Sometimes there'd be back-to-back calls, all where no one would say anything on the other end before they hung up. The first few times, I brushed it off. Now I'm just getting annoyed."

"How many times?"

"What?"

"How many times did this happen?"

Her gaze darted away before coming back. She bit her lip again. He gave her a little shake and urged, "Laydi…"

"I stopped counting at twenty."

"You've been out since eight this morning. What time did they start?"

She scrunched her nose, and fuck him if that wasn't cute, too. "About twenty minutes after I left here?"

She said it like a question and a statement. The ball in his gut, the one that had warned him of his unease, tightened. "That's six hours."

"What?" she asked again.

He leaned closer and hissed, "That's six hours these calls have been coming through. You've sent me almost double that in text messages, and even called me twice, and this is the first I'm hearing of this?"

"I didn't think it was anything," she snapped, leaning right back into his face.

He stilled. She tried to pull away, but he tightened his hold around her waist. "No, just hold on. You mean to tell me that after everything that's been going on these past few days, from the shit we've learned going down with the CIA, to the trace being put on your computer, and now, these calls, and you think it's nothing?"

"Prank calls are naught but a nuisance. It's nothing," she said, her face turning away. If she could cross her arms, she probably would. Her position screamed for him to back off. No fucking way.

"Wrong," he snapped, and at his sharp tone, she turned her face back to his. Once he had her eyes, he said, "I know you haven't been in the business that long, baby, but that's where you're absolutely wrong. We have no clue if those are prank calls or someone trying to get a lock on your location. I'd rather not play Russian roulette with your pretty head, so please, next time this asshole calls your phone…matter of fact, next time it fucking rings, you give that shit to me, yeah?"

"You're really bossy, you know that?"

She wasn't telling him what he didn't know, nor would she get any leeway on this, so he didn't answer.

"Do you think this could have something to do with the CIA? Do you think whoever this is, is coming here?" Her eyes were wide, and although he hated it, full of fear. Good. He needed her to be afraid. This wasn't a game and a lot more was at stake, shit he suspected they hadn't even begun to scrape the top of yet.

"I don't know. But what I don't like is each of the different steps we've gone through, only to end up here. Derek's on it, so is Scott. Whatever it is, Scott will find out. In the meantime, I don't want to take any chances with your safety. Next time you leave the house, I'm with you. Okay?"

He phrased it like a question, when they both knew it was anything but. Her face scrunched, indicating she got the message loud and clear, before she mumbled, "Okay."

Laydi pouting and pissed was a whole new combination of cute. She did everything she could to tell him nonverbally she didn't want to be in his arms, but fuck if he was going to let her go.

She tensed. "Is Dad in any kind of danger?"

A small chance, but any chance was too much. "I don't think so, but I'll call a guy I know up here and make sure he's covered." The tension swept out of her body, some of the anger, too, for she melted into him and put her hands on his chest. She still hadn't looked at him again, but that'd change soon.

"When is your dad supposed to be released?"

"Tomorrow morning."

"Okay. When does he have to go back for his next round?"

She sighed. "Every Friday, two different rounds broken up for a total of twelve weeks of treatment. This round shouldn't do too much but get him nauseous, but the next one may mess with him a bit."

"We'll take care of him. Don't worry about that."

Her eyes came to his, bright. "We?"

He gave her a squeeze. "We're a team now, baby. I'm in this for the long haul. Through thick and thin. Get used to it."

She smiled. Small, but there. Her hands moved from his chest to cup the sides of his neck. "Thank you."

He matched her smile with one of his own. "Give me your mouth, Laydi."

"What?"

"Your mouth, baby. Give it to me."

"You're bossy," she snapped, a little prudish.

He didn't answer. Instead, he swept his head down and took what he'd asked for.

Chapter Five

Girl Code Rule # 46: "Chocolate, wine, and friends are required when a man fucks up."

An hour, a mini make-out session, a dozen knee-weakening kisses later, and lunch—because they couldn't survive on lust alone—Laydi rinsed the last plate and set in it the drainer when there was a knock at the door.

She grabbed the dishtowel, wiped her hands, and checked the clock. She'd been trying to get her mind calm and in order. Something she'd missed these past few hectic days.

But every time she thought of any of the issues going on—from Dad being sick, to her marriage to Andrew, and last, but not least, the issue going on with the case—her mind spun with all the ways things could go wrong.

She couldn't help it.

This was her, always looking at the bad in the situation, and trying to figure out how it could go worse, because it always did.

Every time.

From Mom leaving when she was a little girl, to her first love being stolen from beneath her nose in high school, to being fired from the first job she loved. The only good she had in her life, the thing that had stuck by her, were her sisters, and her father. These four individuals were the ones she'd been able to count on. And now, one of them was fighting for his life.

The other three—she smiled—at least had found their shot at happiness. Men whom she heard catered to their every whim, and even though happy ever after wasn't for her, she was over the moon for them. Her smile widened when she thought back to her brief conversation with Juls this morning, and how she'd caught her in a very compromising (read: blushing) position when she called.

The knock came again, and Laydi sighed before moving out of the room. She cuddled the warmth of love she had for her girls and held it tight. If anything, it was that love and happiness she'd need to get through the next however many minutes.

She crossed the hall toward the back rooms. The shower turned off, and she tried not to think too much about what water slicing off Andrew's body would look like.

Instead, with determination, she unlocked the front door and opened it to find Renee Conish.

Not a whole lot had changed about Renee in the time since Laydi had been gone. Tall, she towered over Laydi by about five inches, and yes, still wore her thin stiletto heels. Laydi couldn't figure out if Renee did this to have people look up when talking to her, or because she was trying to invest in the security of the medical industry with sore necks; but Renee's height and appearance caused turmoil to roll in her stomach. It may have to do with Renee being the pretty girl in high school, the fact to this day she was still beautiful, but none of it, or of Renee being in her home, sat well with her.

Renee wore a dark blue suit so tight it looked painted on, the skirt rising what had to be several inappropriate inches above her knee. The jacket was buttoned, and at the vee between her breasts, a hint of pink lace showed. Her makeup was seriously heavy, so much that it had to take acetone, a shovel, and about two dozen towels to get it off at night.

"Renee," Laydi greeted with a false smile and opened the door.

"Ms. Michaels," Renee answered with false serenity and stepped inside.

Renee looked around with no small amount of disgust, her upper lip curling, face scrunched with revulsion. Laydi fought back her rising impatience. She wanted to get this over with, move Renee and all the bad memories associated with her out of her life as soon as possible.

"Should we sit at the kitchen table?" Rather than wait for an answer, Laydi brushed past Renee and led the way. She didn't look, but heard the woman follow, and went straight to the papers she'd already pulled out from Dad's files.

She slid into a seat at the dark wood six-place setting table.

Renee brushed nonexistent crumbs from her seat before sitting. She held her black briefcase on her lap, didn't set it down, and couldn't contain her discomfort at being in Laydi's house.

Whatever.

"I've gone through and grabbed the papers your office said you'd need." Laydi slid them in front of Renee. "How long until this *snafu* gets settled and Dad's bills get paid for?"

Renee leaned forward and gingerly picked up the forms, scanning over the documents. "Once I get these loaded into the system, it shouldn't take more than a few days."

"A few days?"

Renee lifted a brow and her eyes to Laydi. "Yes, a few days."

"B-but, Dad is in the hospital now. He needs his bills paid now. They won't let him schedule another treatment until those bills are paid, or the insurance is worked out. A few days could delay that and he's already in the program."

"Then perhaps he should have thought about this before he went in."

Bitch. Instead of making a bad situation worse, Laydi took a deep breath.

"He thought he did. Everything was supposed to be set up, and in fact, everyone, including the hospital thought it was, but we showed up today and they discovered this missing form. Just this one," Laydi said with a pointed glance at what Renee held. "Can't you do something this once? Maybe fast-track it?"

Renee slid the papers inside her briefcase and picked at a piece of lint only she could see. "And break procedures? Surely you don't want me to put your dad ahead in the pile of all the other individuals I'm trying to get processed, too, do you?"

"Yes, actually that's exactly what I want you to do. This wasn't his fault. He shouldn't have to deal with this on top of everything else."

"Then he should have taken care of it before," Renee said pointedly.

Unable to stop her heavy sigh of disbelief, Laydi snapped, "He did. He even dealt with your office. They said everything was fine."

Renee checked her nails, as if Laydi wasted *her* time. "Well...it wasn't."

Laydi pulled her hands through her hair. "What happens if we don't get this fast-tracked?"

"Well, then either you can pay his bill directly to the hospital and wait for insurance to reimburse, or you can take the chance that he'll miss a treatment."

"Pay the bill?" Laydi said with no small hint of exasperation. "Do you know how much something like that costs?" From the glee in Renee's eye, she did. "I can't afford something like that! And I can't let him slip in his treatments, he could—he could die. Don't you get this? It isn't a game!"

Laydi came to her feet just as Andrew rounded the corner behind Renee.

"Sweetheart, what the hell is wrong?"

She couldn't answer, for her heart was in her throat and she tried to keep it from jumping out of her mouth. The fact that Dad's situation worsened, something she hadn't considered. She wasn't prepared for it.

"Oh my," Renee murmured.

The smooth, suave woman stood and turned to Andrew. He tossed a distracted glance at Renee, but moved toward Laydi. Even with the worry on his face, he was so damn handsome. Wearing a skintight black tee, faded jeans, and black boots, Andrew could pull off casual just as much as he could business. He moved like a man comfortable in any clothing.

He took her face in his palms, stepped close, and tilted her head back, his eyes connecting with hers. "Baby, what's wrong?"

"I think I'm having a heart attack," she said, and at his eye flare, went on, "It's all this stuff with my dad. I just never figured I'd have to be the one to pay for this before the pension department got their shit together."

"Like I said, Ms. Michaels," Renee jumped in, speaking in a tone one would to a child. Laydi's spine stiffened. "It was your father's responsibility to get his affairs in order. He did not."

Laydi didn't realize how still Andrew had gone, but opened her mouth to respond only to have Andrew brush a thumb over her lips, effectively shutting her up.

Then he turned toward Renee, but stayed at Laydi's side. "And who are you?"

Renee lifted a dainty palm and presented it to him with an eye flutter. "Renee Conish. Administrator for Pearl Village Pension."

Andrew ignored her hand. Feeling his eyes on her, Laydi looked to his disbelieving face. "Babe. Is this the one?"

"What one?"

The side of his mouth quirked. "The one you were telling me about that stole what's his name?"

A hot ball of shame formed in her stomach, and she swallowed heavily. "His name was Tommy Conish, and yes. This is her." God, how humiliating. She tried to pull away, but he tightened his grip on her shoulders, looked to Renee, then back at her. "No contest, babe."

She brought her brows down in confusion.

He dipped his head, but stated clearly and loudly, "Between you and her. No contest. You win every time."

Renee gasped, and Laydi's shame turned into something a whole lot warmer, and much more beautiful. Andrew focused on Renee. "Trust me when I say I understand the law, Ms. Conish. And I'm pretty fucking good at reading contracts. So you have one of two options here."

"I really don't like your tone, Mr—"

"One, you can take those forms Laydi just gave you and fast-track it as she's so kindly requested, and do this in a manner that means her father's care wouldn't be interrupted. You do this, and you'll look like a hero to all involved. It'd be good press, too. Or, two, you can continue to sit on your ass and worry about your nails. I'll make sure to dig deep." He rocked forward. "And yes, Ms. Conish, I mean deep"—he squeezed Laydi's shoulders—"and I'll make sure that everyone, on from the Chief, to the town counsel and whoever I can get ahold of will know just exactly what you've done here today. Furthermore," he went on with his voice rising as Renee opened her mouth, "let me just make this extremely clear to you. Either way, Benjamin Michael's bills will be paid, whether it's through the department that he's served for years, or through myself. His treatment won't be stopped, but there's two ways you'll come out of this. It just depends on you on which way you want it to end. You understand?"

Oh wow. Ohwowohwowohwow. Laydi clenched her hands to her sides in order to resist kissing Andrew.

She hit replay on his words while silence sank heavily into the room, and frowned.

"Wait, Andrew," she called, and he looked down at her.

"Yeah, babe?"

"You can't...I can't allow you to pay for Dad's bills. That's too much."

"You can," he stated.

She shook her head. "No, really, do you know how much that will cost? I can't do it. I won't let you."

Andrew sighed and shifted her until she faced him. He dropped his arms and wound them around her waist. "Lay, baby, it's just money."

"A lot of it."

"Let me finish. I don't have many worries, but I do have a lot of money. You're important to me. Your dad is important to you. And so, by association, it's important that I take care of him, even if that includes making sure I pay for his bills until Mrs. Conish gets her head out of her ass."

Another gasp, but this time they both ignored it.

"I've promised to support you, baby, and I'll do anything to get that done and make you happy. Even if it means giving them every last penny. Do you understand what I'm saying to you?"

Laydi's heart melted. Sure, sappy as shit, but that's the only thing she could describe as happening inside her. Warmth flowed from the center of her chest outward.

"Laydi," he called and gave her a small squeeze. "Do you hear what I'm saying?"

She nodded, put her head to his chest, and whispered only for his ears, "Thank you."

He wrapped a palm around the back of her neck and squeezed. "Ms. Conish, I think we're done here. You know what to do."

"What," Renee stammered. "What's going on? Who are you?"

"Who I am is none of your business," Andrew snapped, his entire body tight. "What's going on is you're deliberately trying to fuck with someone just because you have history, and a bad one. Get your head out of your ass and get the paperwork processed. Then maybe, just maybe, I won't bring a suit against you and your entire department. You don't want to test me on this."

"Is that a threat?"

"We're done here, Ms. Conish. I'd appreciate if you would close the door on your way out."

"Perhaps we can start over, Mr..."

At this coaxing tone, Laydi went stiff, and a low growl erupted from Andrew's chest.

"Mr. Cox. And for your information, you got her name wrong earlier. It's Mrs. Laydi Cox, and if you'd pardon my language, you're really starting to piss me off. Now, I'll state this slowly so you can try to catch it this time, but you...need...to...leave. You have some papers to process, and I have a wife to tend to. I'd appreciate if you'd close the door, for I'd like to fuck my wife before your Botox injections are needed again. You feel me?"

Laydi gasped against Andrew's chest and tried to pull back, but his grip kept her right where she was.

"Well, I never," Renee said haughtily.

"Exactly, you'll never. Good day, Mrs. Cornish."

Heels clicked before the front door slammed. The grip on Laydi's neck disappeared, but went to her waist.

"Andrew!" she snapped.

He grinned down at her. "Right here, baby."

God, she liked him calling her *baby*, but still. "Was that necessary?"

He cracked his neck, and pulled her closer, as if she wasn't already close. "Look, I'm not going to apologize for telling her exactly like it is. I know women, have been around types like her, and I really didn't like the shit she was pulling. We're going to get through this, you and me, and we're going to get through it as a team. I don't know how many times I have to repeat that, and, baby, I'm just saying it now, I won't stop until you get it through your pretty little head. I'm here for the long run, and if anyone fucks with you, they're going to have to go through me first. That woman was fucking with you, I decided it went on long enough, then she thought she could try and pull shit on both of us, so I laid it out." He shrugged. "It's done. She wants to take it to the next step and continue this game, I'll be ready for her."

Well, that was all nice and everything. But this all seemed way too fast. "Did you really have to tell her you were going to…do me?"

"Do you?" he asked, laughing.

She glared.

"Baby," he said, leaning closer, laughter in his voice. "I didn't tell her I was going to 'do you,' I told her I was going to fuck you. And yeah, I really had to."

"It's going to be all over town in an hour!"

He grinned. "Good. Less chance I'll have to warn others off."

She blinked. "Warn others off?"

He pulled back and gave her a look as if she'd lost her mind. With everything that had gone on the past few days, she most likely had. "Seriously?"

"What does that even *mean*, Andrew?"

He pulled her into his chest just as his phone rang in his back pocket. "I'm thinking it'll be much more fun to show you." He flipped open his phone. "Yeah?"

Oh, she had to admit, the vibration of his voice while she was against him felt very…nice.

"You're here?" Andrew asked whoever was on the phone. "Yeah." His face got tight. "I've got Dick sitting on him at the hospital. What did you find?" A muscle popped in his jaw as several minutes went by.

She tried to pull away, but he wasn't having any of it. Instead of fighting a battle she'd lose, she wrapped her arms around his waist and settled in.

"I don't like the sound of that." Pause. "Yeah, well, how would you feel if someone was asking around about your wife?" His eyes flashed. "I do not give one iota of a fuck that you're not married, Derek."

Uh oh.

His grip tightened. She sucked in a breath.

"Find him," he growled into the phone and then tossed it on the table. His eyes stared over her head at nothing, but having so much activity behind them, she didn't want to interrupt. Obviously, the case had escalated, and, from what she knew of Andrew, he was trying to get a grip on his control, or the lack thereof, currently spinning with this new turn. Derek was in town, that much she figured out. Andrew had put some guy named Dick—and don't get her started on how cliché that name was for a PI—and someone else was asking about her. The world around her seemed to be crumbling, with Dad, losing her job, being thrust into marriage… But this entire time, Andrew had been working to make sure nothing on the security slip fell back on her.

She hated she'd withheld her memories of their wedding night, because yes, she remembered every detail. Sure, she hadn't at first. Now, yes, it was all there like a movie, one she was intimately familiar with.

He'd done everything he could to protect both of them, hadn't he? While he fired her, his reasoning made sense. She hadn't talked to him, hadn't told him she'd been working for both partners at once. And he'd asked. Lord knew he had asked so much she'd come to wince when he'd call.

Instead of making the whole dismissal an impersonal ordeal, he'd taken her away from the office, seen to treat her as the friend she'd thought they'd grown to be. He'd protected her from the backlash of clients, from her mistakes, and from herself.

At the same time, he'd given her everything she'd wanted. Him. His body. His mind. His world. He had welcomed her into his arms and his bed—well, a hotel bed. And yet, he had hope for them. Had hope for her.

Could this work? Would she dare?

She touched his cheek, and the action brought his gaze to hers.

"Truth or dare?"

A muscle in his cheek jumped beneath her fingers. "I'm done with games. There's way too much going on, and you want to play?"

She held her wince.

Sure, it looked that way on the outside, but on the inside, she melted at his earlier words, at him treating Dad as if he'd known him for years, for taking her back with this trace on her laptop, and for talking Renee down a notch.

She cupped his cheek and stroked her thumb across his plump lips. "Truth or dare?" she whispered again.

He blew air out. "Fuck," he bit off. "I'm almost scared to choose dare, thinking you'll send me away. I wish you'd get it through your head that I am here for the long run. So fuck it, Laydi, this is it. No more after this, so make it count. Truth."

She smiled. It was small, but she couldn't help it. "Do you want this?" That was it. A simple question, yet the answer said so much.

He reared his head back and stared at her. "Have you been listening at all?"

"I have." She fought a smile and the urge to giggle ridiculously.

"Then, what…" Instead of finishing his answer, he studied her face, looked down at her body and how it'd softened against him. His eyes flared. He dipped his head and kissed her. It wasn't just a mouth-to-mouth kiss, he gave it all. His entire body kissed her. His strong arm wrapped around her waist, hips wedged their way against hers, and one hand tangled in her hair, forcing her to angle her head so he could thrust his tongue deeper. He took over.

Gave.

Demanded.

Conquered.

Teeth nipped at her lips and his tongue left nothing inside her mouth unexplored. Angry and hot, brutal and sweet. Everything that was Andrew Cox.

He backed her to the wall and trapped her. A strong thigh wedged right where she wanted it, holding her in place. Against the wall, unable to move a muscle, and completely at his mercy, was enough to snap her out of the funk she'd been in since she'd woken in Vegas.

Want.

That was what ran through her. She wanted him and was caught in his grip like a fly in a spider's web.

She couldn't think of anywhere else she'd rather be.

Chapter Six

Girl Code Rule #38: Wing-women are considered a necessary accessory.

Damn her. Damn the sweet little minx in his arms, the one who made Andrew feel like he could climb to the top of Mount Saint Helen in one day, and yet at the same time make him want to crawl into a dark hole and hide. She undid him completely.

He'd been running at the mouth with a profession of feelings left and right. Yet he hadn't received anything in return. Just the thought that after all of this, and after getting a taste of Laydi's sweetness, that she could still reject him, caused his stomach to turn inward with bile. He didn't think he'd be able to look at another woman after having her in his arms.

All of the emotions bubbling inside his chest exploded outward in the kiss. He wanted—*no, needed*—her. With a very real threat barreling down on her, with it being so close, with the thought she'd give up on him, he wanted to make sure he got one last chance in her arms to show her what she'd discard. He sought to imprint himself on her soul, and make it where she felt him between her thighs forever.

He pulled back from the kiss. She glanced up beneath thick lashes seeming a mile long. Her eyes danced with gold and green, giving him the urge to go mining. He wanted to dive into riches, swim in a sea of jewels.

Fuck. Dive into riches? Swim in a sea of jewels? She turned him into a damn poet—and a horrible one at that.

Even as he dropped his head again and her surprised gasp brushed against his face, he knew this was crazy. He didn't think, just acted on instinct. Something wild needed to happen, and goddamnit, he was too tired to think, too involved in this woman. Not slowing his intent, he removed the last few inches separating them and slammed his mouth over hers again.

It may have been meant to challenge, to force her to recognize their connection, but hot damn, the second their lips made contact, his entire world shifted. To describe it like that may be corny as shit, but there was no other way to explain the mind-blowing sensation of everything falling into place with one kiss.

She stiffened under his ministrations, and before he could pull away, she kissed him back. She gave it her all.

Oh, hell yes.

Her tongue.

It hesitantly swept inside, and he hummed an approval. When she wrapped the velvet goodness around his, he almost lost his mind. In all his thirty-four years, he'd never had as wicked a made-up image as the reality happening in his arms. Seeing as most of his fantasies involved crude and perverted acts of sexual positions, the usual skipping past the kissing part had been a huge mistake.

Of gigantic proportions.

Each piece of her body fit to his with the same perfection one would find with the missing part of a thousand-piece jigsaw puzzle.

Her hands cupped the sides of his face. He tilted his head and went to push the kiss deeper when she pulled back, held him in place. He stopped and stared.

Wide eyes more brown with the hue of gold surrounding them blinked. Their faces separated by inches, bodies so close air couldn't get through. Breaths tickled over skin as they stared at one another. The beads of her nipples pressed through her shirt and poked his chest. It wasn't much better than his reaction against her hip. He pulsed with a crazy need. The bulge doing its version of the Mexican jumping bean, trying its best to get her attention.

He set his mouth next to her ear. "My mouth is watering," he whispered, his lips brushing against her cheek. "For some reason, all I'm craving is something fruity, and you, Beautiful, smell distinctly of strawberries."

He uncurled his frame and stepped back. She faced him and had to tilt her head back in order to stare into his. Smoldering eyes blazed back at him, a dark lust very evident.

He had her caught.

She almost hummed with a precarious vigor, and the leash he sensed she used to stay in check, strained. It fought against what he wanted her to offer. Giving control of her life, her body, all of it her choice.

Her chance.

She grabbed his ears, and pulled him down for another kiss.

He groaned against her lips, and urged her down the hall and toward her room. Her mouth parted, and he sunk like the Titanic, dipping his tongue deep and tangling it around her wet, velvet flesh. Something deep inside swirled, twisted, and burst free. She tossed her leg over his hip. He lifted her with both his hands on her ass, and pressed her closer.

* * * *

Nope, Laydi wasn't about to talk about anything other than how much she wanted this man, how much the ache between her legs called for him. How much she wanted to lose herself in him for a few hours.

Her world shifted and spun as he picked her up, walked into her room, and tossed her on the bed, settling immediately on top of her. In the time the adjustment took his mouth off hers, he growled before returning to kiss the bejesus out of her.

Her shirt disappeared and she barely had a chance to notice before his hot mouth covered her nipple. Laydi cried out. Heat licked at her breast, and pleasure up her spine. Her body swirled with emotions. She wanted this, him, so damn bad. But her heart clamored, threatened to burst from her chest along with the bubbled-up scream. She tangled her fingers in his hair and held him, then tried to pull him away, unable to make up her mind. It felt so damn good.

Something shifted in the air, a darkness set free. This rough-around-the-edges man, dangerous in a good way, and for the time being, as crazy as it sounded, all hers.

She didn't want sweet.

She didn't care for gentle.

Right now, all she wanted…was him.

She wanted him inside of her, thrusting, filling her with his hard length until she exploded as the friction became unbearable.

A quick rake of her nails down his back had him hissing against her neck. She slicked her hands over his body, reveled in the shift of muscles beneath her palms, and gasped in delight.

He chuckled and pulled at her jeans. She unsnapped the top button of his and they both worked frantically to remove their pants, bodies wiggling, eyes eating each inch of flesh revealed. Her pants caught around her ankles and she growled in frustration before kicking off the offending material.

Turning back to Andrew, she reached for him. He wedged his body between her legs again. "Please tell me you have a condom. I need you inside me." She tunneled her fingers through his hair and pulled him against her chest. Heated skin plastered to her breasts, and she groaned, unable to hold back. Warm, silky friction—like heaven and hell all at once.

He moved his mouth to her shoulder, directly over her tattoo, then went back and traced it again with his tongue. She wiggled beneath him, feeling the emptiness between her legs like a real thing. "Andrew."

"Tell me about your tattoos." He slid a slow, languorous path down the stem to her breast. She held her breath, waiting and hoping he'd move lower and take her nipple in his mouth, but he looked up. Something about him with his mouth on her, her breast heaving from how much he turned her on, and his eyes right there...*hot*.

"Tell me."

"Seriously? Now? There's too many. We'll be here all night."

He grinned, obviously liking that idea.

"I like art," she said simply.

"Well," he drawled, "obviously. And I've seen your arms enough to understand most of them." He trailed his fingers up the length of her arms and back down again. She shivered. One hand dropped and covered the tattoo on her thigh. "Why a cheetah?"

His eyes, while blazing, were also serious. She had no qualms about her body and the art she decorated it with. And he was right, each meant something to her. She'd chosen each one for a specific reason. She palmed his head and lifted her breast in offering. He smiled, and brushed his lips against the pebbled peak.

"Laydi," he warned again.

"The cheetah, known as an intelligent and silent hunter. I got it after I passed my Private Investigators license. Cheetahs are also known as focused animals, and once I discovered how much I loved investigations, I had to get one. It stands for the focus one needs in order to see a case through. Some of them can be quite tedious."

"Baby," he said softly, and wrapped his mouth around her nipple, sucked.

She arched her back and held tight to the back of his head. She didn't know where the softness had come from, after they'd started so urgently, but she was coming to realize Andrew could give great either hard or soft. His hand moved to her left calf.

"And this?" he asked, popping the nipple from his mouth. His lips trailed across her chest, going toward the neglected breast.

"My first tattoo. Sort of like a rite of passage. I was eighteen and had been asking for a tat for years from Dad, but he'd always told me I had to wait until my eighteenth birthday. So, the night I turned eighteen, he packed me in his cruiser and took me down to see a guy he knows. He told me I could get anything, and that's what I chose. It doesn't stand for much other than being a rite of passage tribal tattoo." She said all this breathlessly and lifting her chest toward Andrew, pushing on his head to bring him down. Once finished, he grinned and wrapped his lips around her ignored nipple. She gasped and tossed her head back, closing her eyes.

His hand shifted to her right ankle, and her eyes burned. Out of all the ink she had, this tattoo was the most special. He lifted his head, but she told him before he could ask. "It means persistence. There were four of us who grew up together, four lonely friends who found each other when we needed one another the most. Mine is a Zibu Angelic symbol for persistence."

He stared at her as if he knew there was more. Of course he would. "I didn't have the greatest childhood," she continued, and shook her head when he frowned. "It's done now, and I've moved on. But there were several lessons I had to learn early on. Things no child should have to, about trials and tribulations. About not giving up. Keeping promises. Fighting for more. Each of my sisters have one that stands for something they believe in, all different, but that's how we remember our bond."

"Honey." He brushed his lips back to the stem of the rose.

She tensed.

"The rose, Lay. Why a blue rose?"

She moved beneath him, this time for a different reason than being turned on. Oh, God, he'd think she was an idiot!

"Ummm," she muttered.

His brows drew down. "Laydi."

She took a deep breath, closed her eyes, and just let it out. "The blue is the same color as your eyes, Andrew. Oddly enough, blue roses also signify the unattainable, a fantasy. I thought it fitting, seeing as you'd never be mine."

The air in the room went wired, and Laydi braced for his laughter, for him to pull away, anything. He was still above her for so long she peeked open her eyes and found his attention on her rose. He glanced at her and back at the rose as his thumb traced down the stem.

"You've been mine all along, haven't you?" he asked with a distracted murmur, his attention on her tattoo.

"Andrew," she whispered.

Instead of answering or asking another question, it was suddenly go, go, go, for he dropped and captured her mouth in a rough, hard, wet kiss.

She didn't know how it happened, but somehow, he managed to thrust a hand between them, push down his boxers, and then…he was there. Deliciously hard, gloriously jutting with an angry purple head, and on board with her plan. They both watched as guided his erection to her entrance. Then—*oh my God*—he pushed, hot and throbbing against her core. Tormenting. He teased and wetted the length between her folds until he glided without effort.

With a quick yank of her hips, he brought her beneath him more, and pressed forward. His mouth tugged on her nipple and she tossed her head back at the feeling of him taking over. He pushed so damn slow, unhurried, and slid inch-by-inch inside. She bit her lip.

He's huge! The invasion almost seemed too much.

He paused and growled against her chest. She understood the feeling. She wanted him seated to the hilt. With a pop, he released her breast and returned to capture her mouth. His hands squeezed feverishly at her thighs, communicating a gathering storm. She felt it, too. Urgency. She leaned back, broke the kiss, and kept his gaze as she tilted her hips, spread her legs wider, and pushed her heels against his ass. His hand wrapped around her neck, a possessive touch against her collarbone, and his eyes flared as his gaze jumped from her face to where he worked his way inside her body.

Hot. Thick. Wonderful. Bare.

"Andrew," she warned, out of breath, "condom."

He paused and held her gaze, his entire frame shaking with barely contain control. "You're my wife." That's it. His only explanation.

She took a deep breath, closed her eyes, and relaxed her inner muscles.

He must have felt it, for in the next moment he powered forward—*finally!*—and was blessedly seated. They both cried out. He stretched her, filled her so full she doubted she would ever be the same. Every nerve vibrated, every touch heightened.

His head fell to her chest. He lay there, breathing heavy and exaggerated. She wiggled her hips to relieve some of the pressure. Release hovered so damn close, she wanted it so bad. She needed just the slightest touch to send her over the edge.

He stilled her hips and pushed out a heavy breath. "Easy, Lay, Christ, I'm trying to slow it down here."

"There's no reason to go slow. I want you," she stressed, "now."

"Laydi," he warned.

"Please!"

All she had left to do was hang on for the ride, for the tide rushed and he moved. He surged back and forth, his rhythm never faltering. The pressure spun out of control. She rose higher, soaring above the roof like an eagle freed for the first time. Her body, nothing but sensation, pulsing with liquid pleasure as she exploded. The warm tingling started in her womb and worked its way out, pulsating through her limbs and taking over.

"Sweet Jesus," he growled, and jerked. His face pressed to her neck and hot air gushed out of him in a rush—his low, tormented groan filling the air.

* * * *

Unable to see straight, stand, or think, Andrew lay still, soaking up each different impression. Perspiration coated between their chests, and their breathing sputtered erratically.

He lifted his head and pulled out of her, struggled to catch his breath, and fell to his side. Tossing an arm over his eyes, he reached over with the other, tugged her close, and asked, "I have a question for you now."

He didn't want to push things between them, but damn if he didn't feel settled. She hadn't given him much to go on with what she wanted to happen.

"Yeah?" she answered, her face glowing with post-orgasmic bliss.

He fought a grin. A soft, rose color filled her cheeks, and her hair fell in soft tendrils around her head. Her pleasure-dazed eyes stared at him, and lips swollen from his kisses curved.

She was so damn beautiful.

"If I hadn't chosen truth, what would you have asked me to do with the dare?"

A slow grin spread, like the sun rising over a mountain, so sure and brightening his life with each passing second.

"I would have dared you to kiss me."

Hot damn. He grinned.

Chapter Seven

Girl Code Rule #40: It isn't called, "Playing Hard to Get." It's "Make Him Work for it."

The next day, after calls to the hospital to get an update on Dad, Laydi learned he was doing well and would be available for discharge in a few hours. His insurance was also working properly. A surprise, but indeed all set. She sat at her table with her laptop. She wanted to check the tracer. Seeing as whoever had sent the malware to her computer was obviously monitoring her now, instead of the other way around—not much more damage could be done.

Behind her, Andrew spoke with Derek, going over business stuff and updates from surveillance and their own brand of tracking from the night before. Laydi booted up her computer and waited, all the while taking in the low, rumbling tones of Andrew, each sending a caress over her skin that brought thoughts of how they spent their afternoon and night.

Having sex with him was much better than any fantasy she could ever imagine. His touch much more potent than anything she could have dreamed.

And the feel of falling asleep in his arms a treasure she didn't know how to wrap her mind around.

She hadn't been thinking of anything else last night, only of what she wanted to give—and receive—from Andrew. His history of going through woman after woman, her troubles here in Ohio, all of it swept away by a wave of erotic intentions. This morning had been much of the same, Andrew waking her, his head between her thighs, taking his time with his tongue and hands until she thought she'd break apart. And when she'd almost risen over that peak, he covered her body with his own and made slow, sweet love to her. His eyes had held hers, his hips steady, and she'd been surrounded by nothing but him until she swept over the edge with an orgasm that brought tears to her eyes.

Reality crashed down in the shower like a piece of glass. Those realities were very much the problem in why she didn't have faith that Andrew and she would work together.

The Windows home icon popping up had her blinking at the screen for a second. She immediately went to work, checking if her virus program could identify any Trojan horses or lingering strangers behind the usual processing system. Not wanting to rely only on her anti-virus, she went into DOS and painstakingly double-checked everything, looking for anything that seemed out of sort.

Minutes later, she found the reverse-tracker, but even though it was in her system, apparently it only had a door into her processor when her tracking program activated. Any attempts to delete the program or open it would cause the Trojan horse to become operational again. So as long as she didn't access it or try to delete it, she should be fine.

Maybe.

Laydi bit her lip and decided to set that aside until Scott showed, for surely he'd be able to give her some sort of direction. She couldn't just get a new laptop, nor could she stop working altogether. This computer had years of her hard work on it, and, until she figured out a safe way to transfer information, she was stuck in a pattern of "The Waiting Game."

Opening her email instead, she shifted through and responded to different ones, made sure to send her latest case reports to Andrew and Derek, and froze as another email popped up from her contact in the Cayman Islands. She had originally reached out to the banker to try to see about tracing the money that had left through the advisor in New York.

It had been a long shot, especially with the strict privacy laws on the Island, but she'd known this banker for years and had met him long ago when she'd first started out as a PI.

Quickly opening it, she felt Andrew's presence at her back, but ignored him as she read.

Laydi,

I hope you plan to visit us soon. I still remember the last time we hung out, and I have to say, if there's anyone to party or get ink with, it is you. Our home is open to you and yours anytime.

In reference to your request, please forgive me for taking so long to respond. I ran into some trouble as I traced the wires, and surprisingly enough the final destination of these funds was hidden through so many accounts, it took me days to find it, and what I found deeply concerns me. Please tell me you will treat this information confidentially, and handle it with extreme care. I do not know what dealings you have with this individual, but I do hope to see you in the future, and despite knowing the trouble this will cause, I'm still giving you a name.

Tayseer al-Libi

Be careful, Laydi.

"Holy shit," Andrew muttered, reading over her shoulder. If not for the harshness of his statement and the concern on his face, she would have set him in his place for reading her emails. As it was, his expression sent a shiver down her spine.

"Andrew?"

"Who is this from?"

"What's wrong?"

"Damn it, Laydi, who is this email from?"

The hairs on her neck stood. "A guy I know who works for Cayman Island Bank. I had traced the money leaving our banker in New York to this bank, knew him, and reached out."

Andrew tore his eyes from her email. "Please tell me this isn't the case I think it is."

She twisted toward him. "Of course it is. I'm not working another banker case right now."

He dropped his head, but stood straight. One hand reached around to rub the back of his neck as he stared at his feet, in a pose of masculine contemplation.

"What's wrong?" she asked, feeling the first real tremors of fear. Between his expression and his pose, she didn't think what he had to say would be good.

He lifted his head and pinned her with his gaze. His eyebrows scrunched, and his expression could only be described as barely contained fury. "What's wrong? Well…" He pursed his lips and shook his head. "It seems we just positively identified a link to a terrorist organization, our US financial system, and the CI fucking A.

"Tayseer al-Libi," he said with a quick tortured glance at her computer screen, "isn't a man I like to see anywhere near you, much less connected to you through an investigation. Damn it, if I had known there was even a chance of this, I would have never agreed with Derek to take this case. Fuck." He did a quick swipe at his hair. "How did this happen?"

Laydi stood and bit her lip, not knowing what to do, but also not liking him upset. "What do you mean connected?"

Pain filled his eyes. "Tayseer al-Libi is on America's Top Most Wanted Terrorists. A few months ago, we were approached by some very black op members who don't even report to anyone within the US Government with their suspicions that someone at the CIA was feeding intel to al-Libi. Anytime anyone got close to finally catching this guy, he went up in smoke. Chatter in the networks was traced, and in one of those searches, there was a dotted link to an analyst at the CIA."

Laydi leaned against the table and nodded. The ugly tension in her stomach churned with nausea.

"Not knowing what was going on, and not knowing just who could be involved, an old contact of mine reached out to see if Derek and I would look into it. They handed everything over to us: the history, reconnaissance, search missions gone wrong, all of it. Then they also gave us another file and asked us to look into this banker out of New York who had more dotted links to the suspected analyst. And obviously, you know what you and Derek found with the embezzlement."

"Wait." She lifted a hand. "I thought the company owner had reported that."

Andrew crossed his arms over his chest and gave a nod. "He did. But that was after Derek's initial findings. There was money moving through this banker's account, and we knew where it was coming from, but didn't know if it was legit and authorized. A conversation with him proved it wasn't."

Laydi wrapped her arms around her stomach, and fisted her hands. "Okay. So how is this linked to the CIA guy?"

"Well, the trace on your system has been linked to him, and now he's missing. He hasn't shown for work, and his supervisors are scrambling to figure out what's going on. But there's more."

More? *Jesus.* "What's more?"

"Apparently, some stuff was found on his computer at work that leads the CIA to believe there might be an imminent threat against a Special Forces Team moving in on al-Libi."

"Okay, well, pull them back. Surely they can do that."

Andrew shook his head, and Laydi's stomach dropped. "The team is already black, which means no communication. They were dropped in conveniently right after their commanding officer was briefed."

"What does that mean?" she pushed out on a breathless whisper.

Andrew grimaced and reached for her, taking her within his arms. "Sweetheart, it could mean anything. I'm not—we're not—privy to why they're there. It could mean al-Libi has a heads up that they're looking for him, or even that the team moving in has been set up. Unfortunately, it's unlikely we'll know anything unless it's leaked to the media, which I doubt."

Despite being in his arms, the hairs on the back of Laydi's neck stood at attention. Something didn't add up, as if this nightmare was far from over. It caused nausea to swirl in her belly like an old record on a turntable, and her head to pound.

"Andrew—" she started, but was cut off by a deafening boom rocking through her living room windows.

Andrew pushed her to the floor and covered her with his large frame. Another blast went off at the front door and sunlight spilled into the room from two different angles. She couldn't get a look as Andrew pinning her down didn't give her much leeway to move.

"Fuck," he hissed in her ear. "God, no."

She gripped his shirt. Heavy booted feet entered her house. A loud gunshot echoed through the room and his body jerked. He grunted in her ear and his entire weight relaxed onto her. She wheezed, unable to take in a full breath. He was abruptly removed and rolled to the side. What happened? Someone roughly jerked her up by her hair. Pain erupted from her scalp, her hair pulled from the root. She cried out.

"Quiet!" a deep voice boomed.

She was turned, her back to her assailant's front. A bloom of red spread across Andrew's shoulder, and a large purple mark to the back of his head.

"Andrew!" she screamed, before something pricked her neck.

All went black.

Chapter Eight

"Oh-em-gee, will you sit down already!" Laydi snapped. Her heart thudded in her chest, both from a mixture of fear and concern for Andrew, but with also a healthy dose of really pissed off.

She'd had enough.

With everything tossed at her in the past week, she was done. One problem after another shoved at her, and despite the precariousness of the situation, she was finished with it all.

The guy who hadn't given his name, or any indication of who he was, kept pacing in front of her. Wearing a black A-line tank top, black cargo pants, and muscles as big as two of her thighs, he looked like a big, bad-ass man that she, *no, really* didn't want to know better.

She'd been heaved out of a non-descript black car, thrown over his shoulder—which she did not appreciate—and brought into some shady motel. She hadn't had the time to figure out where she was as the world had been spinning *right round, baby, right round* on the way in. But one look at the 70s style bedspread, the cracked lone table next to the front window, and the air conditioner leaking water to the ugly brown carpet, told her the room didn't scream "classy resort" or "four star hotel."

Since he'd failed to use some manners and introduce himself, she'd resorted to sarcastically calling him Tough Guy, which, from his glare, he didn't take as a compliment.

Well, good. She hadn't meant it as one.

Of course, he didn't appreciate much of what she'd been saying, if his increasing jerky movements were anything to go by. All he'd done when they arrived was toss her on top of the disgusting bed, cuff her to the slates on the headboard, and ordered her to be quiet. He'd picked up the phone and called someone named Cherif. He'd made several calls over the past however long it'd been since they arrived. And with each missed call, his messages had grown more demanding and agitated.

Seeing as her hands were cuffed to the bed with no way to free them, her cell in her back pocket felt as if it were burning a hole.

Even if she could get free, the cell reception in Ohio was so spotty she'd likely not be able to use it.

With a scowl in her direction, Tough Guy rounded the bed and backhanded her. Pain blossomed across her cheek, and pulsed in time with her heartbeat. Her eyes watered, and she blinked hard to try to clear her fuzzy focus. He grabbed her chin roughly, pushed down to part her lips, and shoved a cloth inside, gagging her.

She glared at him, meeting his bottomless dark eyes. "That'll do it," he muttered and went back to his phone.

She watched him, but Andrew's face flashed in her vision. The last image of him—on the floor, bleeding from his shoulder, and a bright welt bubbling on his head.

For all she knew—and she guessed with the darkening shadows dancing on the wall, it had been hours—and unless someone had gone to her house, he'd bleed out.

Jesus. Despair crashed over her with a heavy wave. She had no one. Her father was at the hospital, and while he'd be concerned she didn't show to pick him up, she didn't know if he would reach Andrew in time, should he have called someone else to pick him up.

"What do you mean, he's gone?" Tough Guy wailed, and Laydi opened her eyes to find him scrubbing a hand through his hair. The even-more-bad news in this situation was she'd seen his face. She knew what that meant. Kidnappers didn't do that unless they had an end game in sight.

One that meant she wouldn't be breathing by the time this was over.

"Fuck, Samual, what am I supposed to do now? I have her with me."

She lifted a brow. His question and even more increasing panic didn't bode well.

"He's down, I made sure of it. Shot him myself." Tough Guy conducted an about-face and paced to the other side of the room.

Laydi sucked in a sharp breath through her nose at the image of Andrew again. Her eyes stung, but she'd be damned if she would cry or lose her mind. She needed to try to get out of this, somehow, some way.

Andrew counted on her, and she needed to focus on that.

Escape so she could get to Andrew and help him.

"I'm right outside of Pearl. Fuck! What am I supposed to do?" Tough Guy repeated.

Laydi wanted to answer with, "Um, release me, maybe?" but with the gag, well...obviously, it wouldn't work. Not that she expected he would actually agree, but *hey*, it *was* worth trying.

"Don't you dare leave me on this, Samual! No!" he roared and sent his phone across the room. It crashed to the wall and broke in to two pieces before hitting the floor. She snapped her attention to Tough Guy. Wild, hunted, trapped. His eyes were wide and on her, but there was no reason behind his black gaze. His chest heaved with quick breaths and his hands clenched by his sides.

He blinked once and reached behind to his waistband, coming out with a gnarly silver gun.

Jesus! She scrambled to push away from him, kicking her feet on the bed, bringing herself closer to her bound hands. She curled into a ball, her feet beneath her, and pleaded with him using her eyes and shaking her head. She tried to talk behind the gag, but nothing formed.

He lifted his gun, aimed it at her. "You should have never taken the job," he said.

Two deafening booms echoed through the room.

She braced for the pain of a bullet, curling as small as she could against the headboard, squeezing her eyes closed. A second later, a louder sound wrenched through the air, but no pain came. Instead, shuffling, followed by a grunt. Then nothing but the wind blowing and heavy breathing.

She opened her eyes and widened them at the sight of two large males— Derek and Scott—dressed head-to-toe in black, chests heaving, eyes glittering toward the ground at the foot of the bed.

The same area where Tough Guy had been standing seconds before.

Her heartbeat clamored for attention in her throat, and despite her relief at seeing her colleagues, she couldn't gain enough control of her facilities to speak. Her mouth opened, but nothing came out. Her eyes stung, but no tears came. It was as if time had frozen in a tiny, shady motel room.

Derek, apparently having recovered first, turned his head toward her as Scott bent to the ground. Derek's almond-shaped brown eyes raked a thorough path over her, and for some reason, his mouth went tight and his lips thinned.

She'd always found it extremely unfortunate that she worked for two of the most handsome men she'd ever known.

Where Andrew had the lighter boy next-door good looks, Derek was the complete opposite. Dark hair a few weeks past needing a cut, curled at his shoulders and messy as if he'd been on a motorcycle, or crawled out of bed where he'd had a woman who'd done nothing but shove her fingers through it for hours.

He had a hard, square jaw, always with a five o'clock shadow. And then there were his full, sensual lips. To go along with those dark looks was an even darker danger hovering beneath the surface of his skin. Depending on the person, his aura usually screamed either for one to run, away, or to the closest bed to do wicked, naughty things with.

"Are you hurt?" he asked, his low voice barely controlled with a shaky fury.

She still couldn't speak, not that she tried, but more because the pulse in her throat screamed for release, and well, she *was* gagged.

Damn if she'd break down now.

She shook her head.

A muscle popped in his cheek, and he glanced at Scott before returning to her. He progressed slowly around the bed, and she had a moment's wonder at why he seemed to be acting as if he had to move a certain way.

The Derek she had known for years had absolute control over his body and never twitched a muscle unless there was a specific intent behind the action. The Derek now had careful control over everything—holding her gaze as if he watched for any hint of a reaction. Her eyes widened as he lifted his hands even slower, palms toward her, and spoke, his voice soothing, calm, and careful.

"I'm just going to remove whatever has you tied to the bed, Laydi. Then take the gag out. That's it. Do you understand?"

She knitted her brows. Why did he act like this? Normally, Derek was the fun guy, goofy, always cutting inappropriate jokes at the best of times. Cop humor, some called it. For they never really saw the best in people. It was usually the worst.

She took a deep breath through her nose and tried to push down on the tightness in her throat. It didn't work, so she nodded at Derek instead.

Shuffling at the end of the bed drew her attention to Scott, who came out of a crouch with Tough Guy slung over his shoulder. He bounced the dead weight, took a better grip around the guy's hind legs, and moved out of the room without a glance in her direction.

The bed shifted, and Laydi drew her attention to the door, searching. Derek pulled the gag out of her mouth, and she grimaced at the stale taste left. Warm fingers gently brought her forward and wrapped around her wrists. She kept looking at the open door where Scott had disappeared, hoping to see Andrew, and bit her lip.

A cold, turbulent storm developed in her chest—he wouldn't be coming.

Even though she knew this, had seen it, and worried over it for as long as she'd been here, the thought that he wasn't coming hadn't popped into her mind until now.

She tamped down on her emotions, and fought like hell to get control. Her hands were released from behind. She sucked in a sharp breath. Pins and needles shot through her arms. Derek settled his weight next to her, brought her hands up, and rubbed her wrists vigorously, yet with a mellow touch.

"Laydi," he began, his voice hesitant. He opened his mouth, shut it, and breathed out a sigh through his nose. "I need to know, did he…touch…you? Do you need to go to the hospital?"

She frowned again, and all at once, it hit her. From Derek's question, barely contained fury, and treatment of her, he thought something had transpired. Rape. The worst thing that could happen to a woman held captive by a man.

That thought, one she needed to clear up quick, got her vocal cords working. She shook her head. "No," she croaked out, and cleared her throat. "He didn't touch me like that. Just pushed me around, backhanded me, and pissed me off." She smiled at him in an attempt to soothe his concern. "I'll be okay, but Andrew—"

"He's okay," Derek cut in with what sounded like a relieved breath.

"He was shot."

Derek nodded and released her hands. "Yes, and thankfully you've got some nosey," he said with a big smile to take out the bite to his words, "friends. Juliette and Selena found him, called an ambulance, and are sitting with him at the hospital as we speak. He's lucky in the sense that the bullet passed right through his shoulder, but he does have a mild concussion. And I hate to be the one to tell you this, but none of this has improved his mood. I had to enlist in Dick and a nurse to cuff him to the hospital bed in order to prevent him from coming with me."

Relief hit her so strong she bowed back from the force.

Movement from the door drew her attention. Scott stood there, his profile to the side, talking in low tones to someone she couldn't see. Another individual clad in all-black moved behind him, but with the darkening sky and the distance, she couldn't make out anyone else.

"How did you know where I was?" She turned back to Derek, only to find his eyes had been on the door, too. He pivoted back to her.

"Your cell. All of our PIs have a tracking device in them, and while it took a bit to get a lock on your location, Scott gave us a pinpoint. We didn't know which room you were in, but luckily, Scott can be very persuasive with his questioning." He flashed a quick grin, then sobered. "I need you to do me a favor."

Her brows knitted. "Okay…"

He stared in her eyes for a moment and thinned his lips again, before nodding. "I'm taking you to the hospital. I want you to be checked out despite your assurances. But before we do that, I need you to keep your head down and your ears shut."

She scoffed, not understanding his request. "Excuse me?"

He glanced over his shoulder again and leaned closer. "I can't explain this now, but there are some individuals here that you…" He hesitated for words, and decided on, "can't know about. Not yet. Do you understand?"

She studied his expression, hated like hell she didn't know what was going on, but rather than wait any longer, she nodded. There was time for quibbling, and despite her nosy nature, that time wasn't now.

The important thing was she was okay, Andrew was okay.

And an urge inside her refused to wait much longer to see for her own eyes that Derek's assurances were the truth.

He shot her a relieved look and rose from the bed, holding out his hand to help her up. Once she got her legs under her, he wrapped an arm around her shoulders, reminded her to keep her head down, and led her out of the room.

Epilogue

Girl Code Rule #33: A girl can never have too many accessories

Four weeks later...

Laydi pushed her foot off the ground, shoving her body backward, and let go. The tire caught in a downward swing as she lifted a hand to wave at Juls, Josephine, Selena, and their men driving away in separate cars. She grinned as Josephine leaned out of the passenger side of the car blowing kisses.

The sun slowly sank in the sky, and despite the heat of the afternoon, a gentle breeze kicked up, cooling her sweaty skin.

The barbeque had been a blast and the cause for celebration one Laydi felt deep inside her heart: Dad's tumor had shrunk forty percent since he'd started treatment.

They were about halfway through and the doctors considered this as good news. Once he finished in a few months, they'd complete another scan to check for any "hot spots." If all turned out well, he'd undergo surgery to remove the remaining tumor, and would be classified in remission.

Good news—the best—and it gave her hope she'd have a bit more time with one of the men in her life who meant so much.

The front screen door shut with a soft clang. Andrew came down the steps toward her.

"Is he doing okay?"

He nodded as he reached her and leaned against the trunk of the tree.

"He was just a bit wiped. Seeing as we kept him outside all afternoon, I think it was more a result of the heat than anything else. You shouldn't worry, baby. Your pops is going to be fine."

She bit her lip, and gratitude swelled in her chest. Andrew—a man she'd always thought unattainable. One who she'd seen go from woman to woman, treating each with respect and care, but never settling down. Those relationships hadn't lasted any longer than a couple of weeks. Now, if she counted correctly, she had been married to him for over five, and things were still as hot as that first day in Vegas.

Sure, they'd had a lot to deal with since, between her computer being infected with a tracing malware, Andrew being shot, her kidnapping, and the tracking of a rogue CIA analyst—one who was still, to Andrew's increasing frustration, "in the wind."

But he had stayed by her side through it all, included her in conversations about the progress of a multi-agency investigation, and made her feel like a partner in everything, rather than some dimwit employee.

Turned out the black-clothed men who helped Derek and Scott rescue her were part of some super-secret non-government agency. Knowing he was in over his head, Derek had called in a favor that had a big payback value and didn't make him happy at all.

She didn't know the whole story, but Andrew had told her it'd be worth it to sit back and watch what happened. He said this with a huge grin and laughter in his voice.

While, again, her nosy nature didn't want to agree, she'd hadn't had the time to protest before Andrew wiped her mind blank with a scorching kiss.

The only bad news was the team that had been sent in to get al-Libi had been set up. While they detained and recovered one of America's Most Wanted Terrorists, they hadn't done so without casualties, and with more than one major injury. As she understood, there was even a military working dog struggling to heal. Andrew kept an eye on things, but she could tell the whole thing frustrated him, too.

Worse, al-Libi had managed to escape from the military camp holding him. So now, after everything, they were back at square one.

All Andrew had said when he learned of the escape was to have patience. In the end, al-Libi would be caught, and they'd be there to make sure he stayed down.

"Walk with me, Beautiful." Andrew held out his hand.

Laydi slid her palm into his, slipped out of the tire swing, and followed as he led the way up a hill next to her house. Once they reached the top, she stared out over the pasture, seeing the woods her sisters and she had played in numerous times, knowing hidden within the thick treetops would be a magical pond that helped hold four lonely girls together. That they had all come as far as they did caused the warmth in her chest to expand.

She'd never been a big believer in happily ever after's, but seeing not one, but three actually happen, made everything worthwhile.

Andrew interlaced their fingers and tugged her to his side, not looking at her, but being with her in every sense of the word. She hoped there could be a fourth happily ever after—hers.

She took in his profile, the strong, chiseled cut of his jaw. His full, soft lips that had discovered every inch of her body. His long throat, and wide shoulders, big enough to hold her against a wall while he had his wicked way, or to rest her shoulder on when she felt distraught over her father. A man who'd surprised her with his tender ways. A man who delighted her with his inventive treats in bed. He always sought her opinions in matters that concerned him, and even though they didn't agree on everything, he never dismissed her opinion. And while his over-protectiveness was a bit much at times, they worked through that, too.

All in all, Andrew had become part of her circle, one of her best friends, and he had no hesitation in showing her she was equally important to him.

She turned back to the landscape, content to be just here with him.

"So," he murmured and pulled their interlocked hands to his mouth, where he nipped at her knuckles once, then brushed a soothing kiss over the skin. "I've been thinking."

Despite all of it…

Dammit, tightness formed in her throat. She didn't say anything and didn't turn toward him, but she knew he knew he had her full attention. Could *feel* his gaze on her like a possessive touch.

A few silent moments passed before he turned toward her and went down on a knee, adjusting his hand to where he held hers. Only once he settled did she look at him in surprise.

"What is this?"

"Our relationship didn't start traditional," he started. "Nor was our friendship formed in a normal fashion. However, that's not us. You and I, Laydi, will never be a common couple."

She smirked and cocked her hip. "You're so sure? Never?"

He smiled, and damn, it was a beautiful sight.

"Never," he vowed and went serious again. "It's never going to be nine-to-five, Monday through Friday, missionary position on Wednesday, and you on top Thursday for us, baby." He gave her hand a gentle squeeze. "And that's my point. We're not traditional, and the way we came together shouldn't matter when I have every faith that we'll last a lifetime."

She drew in a sharp breath at his words, her eyes stinging.

"Laydi, if I didn't fully get it before, I do now. The past few weeks have shown me it's easy to be your husband. It's even easier to be your friend. There's no other woman out there I'd rather build a family with and grow old. And if you don't get it by now, I'm so in love with you it's not even funny."

Her vision went blurry with tears, and she gave a short laugh. "Why are you on the ground? Get up and kiss me, you big 'ole sap."

He flashed a grin. "Not just yet." He took a deep breath and let it out. "I didn't do this right the first time, but Laydi Marie Michaels, I'd marry you all over again. And so I'm asking you now, on your family's land, after getting consent from your father and girlfriends, after pouring my heart out to you, will you do the honor of making me the happiest man in the world and marry me again?"

"Yes," she answered without hesitation.

And so he did as she asked earlier.

He rose quickly, took her in his arms, and kissed her.

* * * *

Ben

His little girl never had it easy, with losing her mother at such a young age and being raised by some of the gruffest men on the force. But as he stood at the front window and watched Andrew take his sweet Laydi in his arms, he thought no matter what, his girl would be loved for the rest of her life.

And that made everything all right.

~The End~

~About the authors~

Jessica Jayne, Lea Bronsen, Cait Jarrod, and D.C. Stone are the **Writers in Crime**.

Find them on http://writersincrime.weebly.com/

Jessica Jayne is a born and raised small town Ohio girl, who moved to the Sunshine State after graduating from college. She graduated with a bachelor's degree in English because she could not imagine doing anything else but reading and writing. In the journey of life, she obtained her law degree (and bar license) and also became a wife and a mother of three children. So, life is always an adventure.

She loves to read and write... obviously! She's a huge sports fan, especially college football and The Ohio State Buckeyes! Go Steelers! Go Rays! Go Lightning! She LOVES to travel... LOVES, LOVES, LOVES to travel. She loves to drink coffee in the morning and tea at night! She loves a good glass of wine, especially if it comes from a bottle made by the FOOLS wine club... yep, she's a founding member of that crazy group! She loves hanging out with her family and friends! Music makes her happy. She's a mix between country girl and city chic. She's a sucker for a cowboy hat!

Find her on www.jessicajayne.com

Also by Jessica Jayne:
More than Friends
In Flames
Board Approved
Board Stiff
Alpha's Claim
Board Indiscretion

Lea Bronsen has always had a vivid imagination and written since an early age. Now juggling life as a mother of three, full-time worker, and thriving author, she struggles to find any reading time—but when she opens a book, she wants it fast, hot, and edgy! Striving to give her own stories the same intensity, she currently divides her writing time between psychological thriller, romantic suspense, and erotic contemporary romance.

Find her on www.leabronsen.com

Also by Lea Bronsen:
Wild Hearted
My Biggest Fan
The Perfect Shoot
High-Risk Fever

From writing 'every girl's dream heroes' to 'strong, down-to-earth heroines,' **Cait Jarrod** twists 'cliff hanging plots' and 'clever, unpredictable sub-plots'. She loves diving into a good book as much as she loves writing one. Mother of three gorgeous daughters, she's married to her best friend, hangs out with a great group of women—the WWC, and loves a good glass of wine.

Find her on www.caitjarrod.com

Also by Cait Jarrod:
Kidnapped Hearts
Rekindled
Entangled Love
Mystic Hearts
Breaking All Barriers

D.C. Stone has over sixteen years of investigative experience, including working as a criminal investigator in the United States military and a private investigator. Currently, she works as an internal affairs investigator by day and a romantic suspense author by night. She has her Master's degree in Criminal Justice and is dubbed, "The Investigative Whisperer." Commonly called upon to act as an expert witness, she also trains with local, state, and federal law enforcement officers. She provides numerous workshops that help authors gain insight into "digging" into a character's mind to better understand motives, create suspense, and help maintain conflict.

When she isn't trying to solve a new puzzle in the world of fraud, she is engulfed with coffee, her laptop, and all those crazy characters in her head. She is a member of the Romance Writers of America, Hudson Valley Romance Writers, Rom Vets, RWA Kiss of Death, and the Liberty State Fiction Writers. She served as the 2014 Vice President and Conference Chair for NJRW.

Find her on www.authordcstone.com

Also by D.C. Stone:
High Scandal
Feral Craving
Armed and Desired
What Could Have
Intimate Danger
Intimate Fear

Made in the USA
Middletown, DE
25 July 2015